W9-ASZ-695
DISCARDED BY THE
GLEN COVE PUBLIC LIBRARY

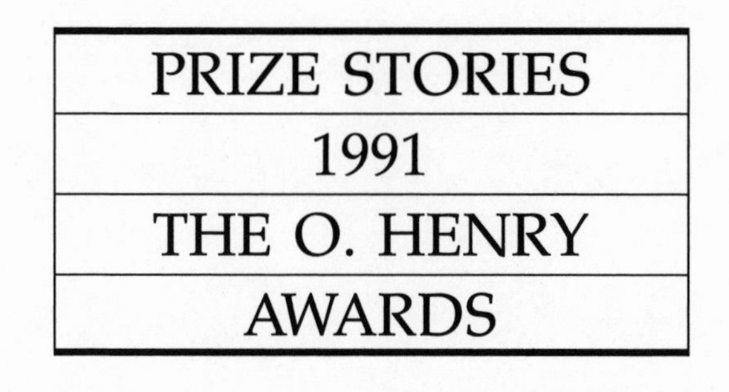
PRIZE STORIES
1991
THE O. HENRY
AWARDS

PRIZE STORIES 1·9·9·1 THE O. HENRY AWARDS

Edited and with an introduction by

William Abrahams

DOUBLEDAY

NEW YORK LONDON TORONTO SYDNEY AUCKLAND

PUBLISHED BY DOUBLEDAY
a division of Bantam Doubleday Dell Publishing Group, Inc.
666 Fifth Avenue, New York, New York 10103

DOUBLEDAY and the portrayal of an anchor with a dolphin
are trademarks of Doubleday,
a division of Bantam Doubleday Dell Publishing Group, Inc.

Book Design by Patrice Fodero

Library of Congress Cataloging-in-Publication Data
Prize stories. 1947–
New York, etc. Doubleday
v. 22 cm.
Annual.
The O. Henry awards.
None published 1952–53.
Continues: O. Henry memorial award prize stories.
ISSN 0079-5453 = Prize stories
1. Short stories, American—Collected works.
PZ1.011 813'.01'08—dc19 21-9372
MARC-S
Library of Congress [8804r83]rev4

ISBN 0-385-41512-5
ISBN 0-385-41513-3 (pbk.)

April 1991
1 3 5 7 9 10 8 6 4 2
First Edition

CONTENTS

PUBLISHER'S NOTE

This volume is the seventy-first in the O. Henry Memorial Award series, and the twenty-fifth to be edited by William Abrahams.

* * *

In 1918, the Society of Arts and Sciences met to vote upon a monument to the master of the short story: O. Henry. They decided that this memorial should be in the form of two prizes for the best short stories published by American authors in American magazines during the year 1919. From this beginning, the memorial developed into an annual anthology of outstanding short stories by American authors, published, with the exception of the years 1952 and 1953, by Doubleday.

Blanche Colton Williams, one of the founders of the awards, was editor from 1919 to 1932; Harry Hansen from 1933 to 1940; Herschel Brickell from 1941 to 1951. The annual collection did not appear in 1952 and 1953, when the continuity of the series was interrupted by the death of Herschel Brickell. Paul Engle was editor from 1954 to 1959, with Hanson Martin coeditor in the years 1954 to 1960; Mary Stegner in 1960; Richard Poirier from 1961 to 1966, with assistance from and coeditorship with William

Abrahams from 1964 to 1966. William Abrahams became editor of the series in 1967.

In 1970, Doubleday published under Mr. Abrahams's editorship *Fifty Years of the American Short Story,* and in 1981, *Prize Stories of the Seventies.* Both are collections of stories selected from this series.

The stories chosen for this volume were published in the period from the summer of 1989 to the summer of 1990. A list of the magazines consulted appears at the back of the book, as does a list of all the authors whose stories have appeared in the collection since 1967. The choice of stories and the selection of prizewinners are exclusively the responsibility of the editor. Biographical material is based on information provided by the contributors and obtained from standard works of reference.

INTRODUCTION

Prize Stories 1967: The O. Henry Awards was the first collection in this annual series for which I chose the stories. That year there were sixteen selections; among the authors were Joyce Carol Oates, who was awarded First Prize, and John Updike. We have now arrived at the twenty-fifth, *Prize Stories 1991.* This year there are twenty stories, and among the authors are John Updike, awarded First Prize, and Joyce Carol Oates, proving by their presence that continuity in the art is not only possible, but also admirable. Indeed, this year's collection seems to me to be outstandingly good. That I have said approximately this in each of the twenty-five volumes thus far suggests an undiminished enthusiasm for the art of the story, in all its possibilities. And that is the case. But the task of choosing has been complicated by the fact that the number of stories in the final siftings has almost always been large enough to make for some difficult choices—and there are omissions that I regret. Still, choices have been made—474 stories in the series from 1967 to 1991.

The public historical events, concerns and preoccupations of those years have at most a kind of shadow life in the story, and it is a misunderstanding of the art of the story to expect otherwise. Private life, the private individual experience, becomes the subject of a story, and the form is congenial to that, unlike the novel which can accommodate a richly detailed background of public history and experience against which the private lives of its characters are revealed. The short story insists upon selection; and although sometimes of considerable length, the story is not and should not be confused with a miniature novel.

Accordingly, we must not expect of the stories written during a quarter of a century that, taken all altogether, they would yield a history of their time (our time, too), although they might well prove to be a part of it. Two of the stories in this present volume, John Updike's "A Sandstone Farmhouse" and Joyce Carol Oates's "The Swimmers"—alike in their mastery but otherwise so very different—beautifully illustrate the point. "A Sandstone Farmhouse" is essentially the story of the loving, difficult relationship of a son and his mother over some fifty years. The passage of those years is artfully, glancingly suggested, and there are allusions to the world in which public events occur and impinge upon Joey and his mother. But public history is never allowed to express itself, or dominate the chronicle being told to us. The result is a kind of single-mindedness, a depth and intimacy of feeling. Seeming to tell us all, the narrator *excludes* all that he would count as unessential—which makes what he actually tells us all the more moving, more humane, and painful, and credible.

If Updike's narrator excludes a good deal of what he knows, Oates's wants to *include* all that she can—all that she knows—about Clyde Farrell, her uncle, and the woman Joan Lunt with whom he falls in love. But there is a mystery at the heart of this story, which must remain so: the narrator, as it were in spite of herself, can't solve it for us. The story takes place at the end of the 1950s and in the 1960s, a time that Oates has re-created vividly in her novels. But in this lyric and enigmatic tale the effect is deliberately timeless, leading to a conclusion hinted at in an early description of Joan Lunt swimming in the pool at the "Y": ". . . emerging from the water, head and shoulders and flashing arms the woman didn't miss a beat, just continued as if she hadn't been confronted with any limit, any boundary. It was just water, and her in it, water that might go on forever, and her in it, swimming sealed off and invulnerable."

* * *

Traditionally, a twenty-fifth anniversary is held to have a special significance; at the least it justifies a note of celebration. What I want to celebrate are the three hundred and seven authors whose stories I have chosen over these past twenty-five years. In the alphabetical list that follows, the date given with each name represents a first inclusion in the 1967–1991 series. (Many, I should add, were already O. Henry prizewinners before 1967.)

Lee K. Abbott, Jr. (1984)
Felicia Ackerman (1990)
Alice Adams (1971)
Renata Adler (1974)
Woody Allen (1978)
Max Apple (1978)
Ann Arensberg (1975)
Linda Arking (1975)
Thomas Fox Averill (1991)
Sheila Ballantyne (1977)
Russell Banks (1975)
John Barth (1969)
Donald Barthelme (1967)
Rick Bass (1989)
John Batki (1972)
Jonathan Baumbach (1979)
Richard Bausch (1987)
Charles Baxter (1991)
Ann Bayer (1975)
Ann Beattie (1980)
Saul Bellow (1980)
Elizabeth Benedict (1983)
Gina Berriault (1987)
John Berryman (1976)
Leigh Buchanan Bienen (1983)
George Blake (1970)
James P. Blaylock (1990)
Robert Boswell (1987)
Kay Boyle (1981)
T. Coraghessan Boyle (1989)
Eldon Branda (1968)
Claudia Smith Brinson (1990)
Harold Brodkey (1975)
Henry Bromell (1973)
E. M. Broner (1968)
Ben Brooks (1982)
T. Alan Broughton (1991)
Brock Brower (1968)
Margery Finn Brown (1972)
Rosellen Brown (1972)
Perdita Buchan (1970)
James Buechler (1967)
Jerry Bumpus (1976)
Frederick Busch (1974)
Peter Cameron (1985)
Anthony Caputi (1979)

Guy A. Cardwell (1971)
David Carkeet (1982)
Raymond Carver (1973)
John Casey (1989)
Helen Chasin (1980)
John Cheever (1973)
John J. Clayton (1974)
Mary Clearman (1972)
Eldridge Cleaver (1971)
Tom Cole (1970)
Laurie Colwin (1977)
Eunice Luccock Corfman (1969)
John William Corrington (1976)
Richard Currey (1988)
Guy Davenport (1974)
Philip F. Deaver (1988)
Charles Dickinson (1984)
Anthony DiFranco (1986)
Millicent Dillon (1980)
Thomas M. Disch (1975)
Stephen Dixon (1977)
E. L. Doctorow (1975)
Harriet Doerr (1989)
H. E. F. Donohue (1970)
Andre Dubus (1980)
Robert Dunn (1980)
Stuart Dybek (1985)
William Eastlake (1970)
Charles Edward Eaton (1972)
Janice Eidus (1990)
Deborah Eisenberg (1986)
Susan Engberg (1969)
Louise Erdrich (1985)
Irvin Faust (1983)
Andrew Fetler (1977)
Ernest J. Finney (1967)
Bruce Fleming (1990)
Sandra Hollin Flowers (1981)
Starkey Flythe, Jr. (1972)
Jesse Hill Ford (1967)
H. E. Francis (1976)
F. K. Franklin (1968)
Blair Fuller (1974)
John Gardner (1974)
Merrill Joan Gerber (1986)
T. Gertler (1980)
Kenneth Gewertz (1982)
Brendan Gill (1972)
Jane Brown Gillette (1990)
Gail Godwin (1980)
Herbert Gold (1972)
Lester Goldberg (1979)
Miriam Goldman (1967)
Ivy Goodman (1981)
Mary Gordon (1983)
Elaine Gottlieb (1972)
William Goyen (1976)
Gwen Gration (1968)
Joanne Greenberg (1990)
Philip L. Greene (1971)
Patricia Browning Griffith (1970)
David Grinstead (1970)
Nancy Hale (1968)
James Baker Hall (1968)
Martha Lacy Hall (1991)
Anne Halley (1976)
Nancy Hallinan (1980)
R. C. Hamilton (1985)
Marilyn Harris (1968)
Barbara Grizzuti Harrison (1989)

Evelyn Harter (1971)
Shirley Hazzard (1977)
Florence M. Hecht (1971)
Julie Hecht (1979)
Mary Hedin (1977)
Steve Heller (1979)
Mark Helprin (1976)
Robert Hemenway (1970)
Robert Henson (1974)
Ellen Herman (1989)
Richard Hill (1974)
Edward Hoagland (1971)
Rolaine Hochstein (1974)
T. E. Holt (1982)
Lewis Horne (1987)
Helen Hudson (1976)
Robert Inman (1971)
John Irving (1981)
Josephine Jacobsen (1967)
David Jauss (1983)
Devon Jersild (1990)
Curt Johnson (1973)
Diane Johnson (1973)
Greg Johnson (1986)
Joyce Johnson (1987)
Nora Johnson (1982)
Wayne Johnson (1991)
Willis Johnson (1984)
Ward Just (1985)
Donald Justice (1984)
David Michael Kaplan (1990)
Shlomo Katz (1968)
Susan Kenney (1982)
Calvin Kentfield (1968)
Perri Klass (1983)
Norma Klein (1968)
Conrad Knickerbocker (1967)
Claude Koch (1985)
Sheila Kohler (1988)
Joyce R. Kornblatt (1986)
William Kotzwinkle (1975)
Marilyn Krysl (1980)
M. R. Kurtz (1967)
Salvatore La Puma (1988)
Charles R. Larson (1971)
Banning K. Lary (1989)
Peter LaSalle (1988)
Norman Lavers (1987)
Peter Leach (1974)
Patricia Lear (1991)
Anne Leaton (1979)
David Leavitt (1984)
Ella Leffland (1977)
Ursula K. Le Guinn (1991)
Diane Levenberg (1991)
Curt Leviant (1978)
John L'Heureux (1980)
Gordon Lish (1984)
Leo E. Litwak (1969)
Lynda Lloyd (1983)
James Lott (1987)
Robie Macauley (1967)
Ben Maddow (1969)
Bernard Malamud (1969)
John Malone (1973)
Michael Malone (1982)
Bobbie Ann Mason (1986)
Jack Matthews (1972)
Peter Matthiessen (1990)
William Maxwell (1975)

Jane Mayhall (1973)
Julian Mazor (1971)
J. D. McClatchy (1972)
Susannah McCorkle (1975)
Emily Arnold McCully (1977)
Joseph McElroy (1982)
Dennis McFarland (1991)
Reginald McKnight (1990)
James Alan McPherson (1970)
Peter Meinke (1983)
Daniel Menaker (1984)
Leonard Michaels (1969)
Stephen Minot (1971)
Susan Minot (1983)
Thomas W. Molyneux (1979)
Wright Morris (1983)
H. L. Mountzoures (1969)
Marvin Mudrick (1967)
Jay Neugeboren (1968)
Gloria Norris (1983)
Helen Norris (1984)
Marian Novick (1981)
Joyce Carol Oates (1967)
Tim O'Brien (1976)
Diane Oliver (1967)
Carolyn Osborn (1990)
Cynthia Ozick (1975)
Nancy Huddleston Packer (1969)
Grace Paley (1969)
Thomas Parker (1971)
Edith Pearlman (1978)
Mary Peterson (1979)
Catherine Petroski (1989)
Fred Pfeil (1979)
Jayne Anne Phillips (1980)
Jim Pitzen (1987)
Richard Plant (1988)
David Plante (1983)
Reynolds Price (1971)
Melissa Brown Pritchard (1984)
Judith Rascoe (1972)
Ilene Raymond (1985)
Barbara Reid (1981)
Randall Reid (1973)
Norval Rindfleisch (1970)
Mary Robison (1987)
Daniel Asa Rose (1980)
Jean Ross (1989)
Annette T. Rottenberg (1981)
Michael Rubin (1969)
Joanna Russ (1977)
Ira Sadoff (1976)
James Salter (1970)
John Sayles (1976)
Susan Fromberg Schaeffer (1978)
Jessie Schell (1975)
James Schevill (1978)
Mark Schorer (1978)
Julie Schumacher (1990)
Lynne Sharon Schwartz (1979)
Steven Schwartz (1983)
Lore Segal (1990)
David Shaber (1973)
Evelyn Shefner (1969)
Eve Shelnutt (1975)
Frances Sherwood (1989)
Anita Shreve (1976)
Marilyn Sides (1990)
Shirley Sikes (1973)
Charles Simmons (1977)

Jane Smiley (1982)
Lee Smith (1979)
Elizabeth Spencer (1983)
David Stacton (1968)
Jean Stafford (1980)
Sharon Sheehe Stark (1991)
Max Steele (1969)
Meredith Steinbach (1990)
Thomas Sterling (1969)
Daniel Stern (1987)
Steve Stern (1981)
Jonathan Strong (1967)
Ronald Sukenick (1991)
Walter Sullivan (1980)
Hollis Summers (1977)
Linda Svendsen (1983)
Marly Swick (1991)
James Tabor (1981)
Shirley Ann Taggart (1980)
Elizabeth Tallent (1984)
Barry Targan (1980)
Eleanor Ross Taylor (1971)
Peter Taylor (1969)
Robert Taylor, Jr. (1987)
Paul Theroux (1977)
Annabel Thomas (1979)
Florence Trefethen (1982)
Anne Tyler (1969)
Paul Tyner (1968)
John Updike (1967)
Henry Van Dyke (1979)
William F. Van Wert (1983)
Stephanie Vaughn (1980)
Alice Walker (1981)
Charlotte Zoë Walker (1991)
David Foster Wallace (1989)
Warren Wallace (1987)
Sylvia A. Watanabe (1991)
Gordon Weaver (1979)
Eudora Welty (1968)
W. D. Wetherall (1981)
Kate Wheeler (1982)
Allen Wheelis (1967)
Gloria Whelan (1983)
Nancy Willard (1970)
Joy Williams (1988)
Jeanne Wilmot (1986)
Eric Wilson (1985)
Tobias Wolff (1981)
Richard Yates (1967)
Patricia Zelver (1972)

A final note of thanks. For invaluable assistance with the present volume I wish to acknowledge Heidi von Schreiner and Arabella Meyer in New York, and in California, John M. Dean.

—William Abrahams

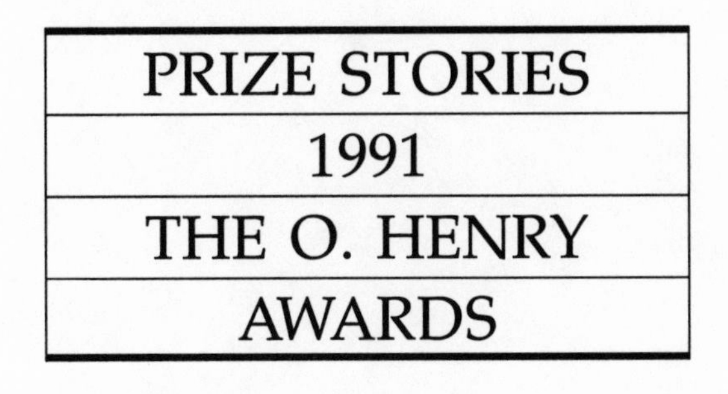
PRIZE STORIES
1991
THE O. HENRY
AWARDS

John Updike

A SANDSTONE FARMHOUSE

Joey's first glimpse of the house was cloudy in his memory, like an old photo mottled by mildew. During the Second World War, his family owned no car, and renting one, for their infrequent excursions out of the compact brick city where his father worked, embarrassed the twelve-year-old boy to the point that he didn't see clearly through the windows, or was not conscious of much beyond his internal struggle not to be carsick. He fought the swaying, jiggling motion, which was mixed with the warm confluent smells of rubber floor mat and petroleum combustion, and the patient pale veiny look of his father's hand on the gearshift knob. Farm country, miles of it, poured past. Depressing, monotonous fields moved up and down beneath their hazy burden of crops. A winding asphalt highway climbed a hill, passed a lumpy stone church, then settled into a flat stretch where they slowed to turn left down a dirt washboard road that shook the car sickeningly. Not a building in sight. No sign of civilization but telephone poles carrying a single wire. Another turn, right this time, down an even smaller dirt road, and they stopped, and in the sudden flood of fresh air as Joey opened the car door, the green of the grass rose waxy and bright to greet his giddiness, his nausea. In his cloudy memory, they went up to the house and there were people in it, farm people, wearing cotton and thick muddy shoes, shyly trying to get out of their way, like animals. There was a front porch, he remembered that much. With a bannister upheld by boards jigsawed into an ornamental shape, and a secret space underneath, of weeds and pebbly dirt. A space where chickens could scratch, and dogs could lie and pant during hot weather, the kind of space that is friendly and inviting to a boy of the age he was just outgrowing.

By the time they had bought the house with its surrounding eighty acres and moved in, he was thirteen, and the front porch had vanished, leaving a space between the front of the house and the cement walk where they eventually planted crocuses and tulips and erected a grape arbor. Joey as an adult could not remember how or when it had happened, their tearing down the rotten old porch. Pieces of it remained in the barn—segments of bannister with the ornamental balusters cut of inch-thick pine. Once he even took a baluster home with him, back to New York City, as some kind of memento, or sample of folk art. The pattern held a circle in the center, a circle with a hole, between two shapes jigsawed into the wood, one like an arrow and one like a fish. Different-colored flakes fell dryly from it, brittle layers of old-time lead paint. The object, not quite of art, rested sideways on the black marble mantel of his apartment for a while, then found its way to the back of a closet, with broken squash rackets and college textbooks and table lamps that might someday be made to glow again. Like his mother, he had trouble throwing anything away.

If he and his father and grandfather had torn the porch down themselves, he would have remembered so heroic a labor, as he did the smashing of the lath-and-plaster partition that separated the two small parlors downstairs, making one big living room, or the tearing out of the big stone kitchen fireplace and its chimney, right up into the attic. Joey remembered swinging the great stones out the attic window, he and his grandfather pushing, trying not to pinch their fingers, while his father, his face white with the effort, held the rope of a makeshift pulley rigged over a rafter. Once clear of the sill, the heavy stones fell with a ghostly slowness, seen from above, and accumulated into a kind of mountain it became Joey's summer job to clear away. He learned a valuable lesson, that first summer on the farm, while he turned fourteen: even if you manage to wrestle only one stone into the wheelbarrow and sweatily, staggeringly trundle it down to the swampy area this side of the springhouse, eventually the entire mountain will be taken away. On the same principle, an invisible giant, removing only one day at a time, will eventually dispose of an entire life.

When, over forty years later, his mother died, and the at last uninhabited house yielded up its long-buried treasures, he came upon a photograph of her at the age of ten, posing in front of the porch. Someone in pencil, in a flowing handwriting not his mother's—hers was tiny, and cramped, and backslanted—had marked on the back, "Taken August 1914. Enlarged August 1917." Someone had loved this snapshot enough to have it enlarged and mounted on thick gray cardboard: who?

His mother, wearing a low-waisted dress, dark stockings, and black shoes with big, thick heels, her hair done up in a long braid that hangs over one shoulder, is holding the collar of a young medium-sized dog, part collie. Both the child and the dog are looking straight into the camera with similar half smiles and wide-spaced, trusting eyes. They are standing on a cement walk that is still there, uncracked; behind them the porch balusters repeat their simple artful pattern and a small rosebush blooms. The long-dead dog, the recently dead human female look identically happy. Joey would hardly have recognized his mother but for the thick abundance of her hair—a chestless cheerful little girl in old woman's shoes. Beyond the edge of the barn to her right, ghostly in the enlargement, are fences and trees of which no trace remains and, just barely visible, an entire building that has vanished—a tobacco shed, perhaps. The lawn is edged around the walk, and the fences look trim. This was the private paradise, then, to which she attempted to return, buying back the old sandstone farmhouse that her parents, feeling full enough of tobacco profits to retire, had sold while she was innocently off at normal school. Precocious, she had been skipped, and was sent off at the age of twelve, and hated it, hated it all, including the hour-long trolley ride to Kutztown. The swaying, the ozone, the drunk men who sat down beside her made her sick.

* * *

She loved the old house; she loved the *idea* of it. For most of her life, except for the twenty years of exile in her young womanhood, when she went to normal school, then to college, and married a man she met there, and travelled with him until the Depression cost him his travelling job, and bore him a son, in the heart of the Depression, while they were all living with her parents in the brick city house—except for these twenty years, she happily inhabited an idea. The sandstone house was built, her fond research discovered, in 1812. In that era, teams of masons and stonelayers roamed the countryside, erecting these Pennsylvania farmhouses on principles of an elegant simplicity. Their ground plan was square, set square to the compass. The south face basked in the maximum of sunshine; the east windows framed the sunrise, and the west the sunset. The cornerstones were cut at a slightly acute angle, to emphasize the edge. The stout scaffolding was rooted in holes in the thirty-inch walls as they rose, and these holes were plugged with stones four inches square as the masonry was pointed, and the scaffolding dismantled, from the top down. In the mortar, lime from the lime kiln was mixed with sand from creek beds, to match the stones. Though the size of the stones raised and fitted into place was prodigious, the real feats of leverage occurred in the quarrying. Sandstone exposed in an outcropping was rendered useless by weather, but underneath the earth the sound stone slept, to be painstakingly split by star drills and wedges and "feathers" of steel, and then hauled out by teams of horses, on wagons or sleds. Sometimes the wagons shattered under the load of a single great stone. But this vast hauling and lifting continued, a tidal movement like that of the glaciers which here and there had deposited huge moraines, acres frightening in their sheer stoniness, in the middle of the forests—heaped-up depths of boulders in which no tree could take root, barren geological deposits fascinating and bewildering to nineteenth-century minds, so eager to see God's hand everywhere.

For sensitive, asthmatic Joey, removed from a brick semi-detached city house where he had felt snug, where he could hear through his bedroom walls the neighbors stirring as he awoke, and the milk being delivered on the porch, and the trolley cars clanging at the corner a block away, the silent thickness of stones just behind the old plaster and wallpaper, and the rough hearths and fireplaces visible within the country house, seemed to harbor nature's damp and cold. A sullen held breath dwelled in the walls. The summer's heat brought swarms of wasps, millipedes, carpenter ants, and silverfish out from the crannies. That first winter in the house, before an oil furnace was installed in the basement, a kerosene-burning stove in the living room provided the only heat. Joey remembered the stove clearly; it was painted chocolate brown, and stood on little bent legs on an asbestos sheet papered with imitation wood grain. He spent days huddled in blankets next to this stove, on a grease-spotted sofa that had been brought close. With his constant cold, he missed days of school, and hated to, for it was warm at school, and there was running water, and flush toilets. And girls in long pleated skirts and fuzzy sweaters and bobby socks, who belonged to the modern era, to civilization. He clung to civilization by reading; huddled in the brown stove's aura of coal oil, he read anything—P. G. Wodehouse, Ellery Queen, John Dickson Carr, Thorne Smith—that savored of cities and took him out of this damp, cold little stone house.

His mother remembered that first winter with rueful pleasure, as a set of tribulations blithely overcome. "It was really very hard, I suppose, on everybody—you were *so* sick, and your father had to struggle so to get to work in that old Chevrolet that was all we could afford, and for my parents it was a terrible defeat, to come back to the farm when they had gotten away; they would hide together in the corner just like children—but I was so happy to be here I hardly noticed. The movers had broken the large pane of glass in the front door, and for some reason that whole first winter we never managed to replace it; we lived with a sheet of cardboard wedged over the hole. It's incredible that we survived." And she would laugh gaily, remembering. "We tried to light fires in the living-room fireplace but all the wood the Schellenbargers had left us in the basement was moldy elm, and that fireplace never did draw well, even when the swifts' nests weren't plugging it up. Smoke leaks out into the room, I've never understood why. If you look up the flue with a flashlight, the stonework has a twist."

Joey seemed to remember, though, waking upstairs and putting his feet onto the bare wood floor and grabbing his school clothes and hurrying in his pajamas down the narrow stairs—the treads worn in two troughs by generations of footsteps, the nailheads protruding and shiny and dangerous—to dress in front of the fireplace, where logs were crackling. The freezing upstairs air would lick at his skin like flame, like the endless conversations between his mother and her parents, incessant flowing exchanges that would ripple into quarrel and chuckle back again into calm while he focussed, when he was home, into the pages of his book. His grandfather had a beautiful, patient, elocutionary voice; his grandmother spoke little, in guttural responses. His mother, unlike most adults, hadn't parted from her parents, and clung to them with old tales and grievances, like someone adding up the same set of figures day after day and always expecting a different answer. As Joey huddled by the stove, heated conversations were in his ears as the smell of coal oil was in his nostrils, but always, those five years (only five!) that he lived in the sandstone house with four adults, his attention was aimed elsewhere—on schoolwork, on the future. He tried to ignore what was around him. The house, even when plumbing and central heating and a telephone were installed, and new wallpaper made the repainted rooms pretty, embarrassed him.

* * *

He was never more embarrassed than in that summer before they moved in, before they owned even the erratic old Chevrolet. Several times, his mother made him travel with her by bus out to the farm they already owned. She had a vision of a windbreak of pines rimming the big field, along the road, and she and Joey carried seedlings in boxes, and shovels, and pruners, and a watering can—all this humiliating apparatus dragged onto a city bus by a red-faced middle-aged woman and a skinny boy with ears that stuck out and dungarees that were too short. His mother wore a checked shirt like a man's and a straw sun hat and a pair of light-blue overalls with a bib; she looked like a farmer in a Hollywood musical comedy. There was no space inside the bus for the shovels; the driver had to store them in the luggage compartment and then stop and get out in the middle of nowhere to hand the tools over. It was a relief when the bus, headed south toward Washington, D.C., disappeared around a bend in the highway.

Joey and his mother walked down the dirt washboard road in the heat, carrying their equipment. He had never been so humiliated, so ridiculous, and vowed never to be again. He couldn't blame his mother, he still needed her too much, so he blamed the place—its hazy, buggy fields, its clouds of blowing pollen that made him sneeze and his eyes water, its little sandstone house like a cube of brown sugar melting in the heat, in a little dip of hillside beneath an overgrown, half-dead apple orchard. All through noon and into the afternoon they cleared little spaces at the edge of the field, where the Schellenbargers' last crop of field corn was pushing up in limp green rows, and cut away burdock and poison ivy and honeysuckle, and dug holes, and set in each hole a little six-inch puff of pine tree, and sprinkled water over the socket of sandy red earth. Moving a few paces farther on to plant the next tree, Joey could no longer see the last one amid the weeds and wild grass. The work seemed hopeless. Yet when the afternoon breeze came up, he felt a purity of silence—perhaps one car an hour passed, the people staring at this woman and boy in clothes neither country nor city—that didn't exist in his beloved street of semi-detached houses. And there was a kind of heroism to his periodic trudge, with the empty sprinkling can, the half mile along the edge of the cornfields to the empty house, with its rusty iron pump on the back porch, and then the long haul back, the sloshing can as heavy as a stone.

He felt heroic to himself. Space for heroism existed out here. He was determined to impress his mother—to win her back, since here on this farm he for the first time encountered something she apparently loved as much as she loved him.

At last, the weeds threw feathery long shadows upon one another and the tiny pines were all planted in the hopeless roadside jungle and it was time to walk back up the dusty washboard road to wait for the bus from Washington to round the corner. Having gone and come so far, the bus could be as much as an hour late, and their eyes would sting, staring down the gray highway for it, and his stomach would sink at the thought that they had missed it and were stranded. But not even this possibility daunted him, for he had forged a mood of defiant collusion in which he was numbed to humiliation and played a role both stoic and comic, co-starring with his heavy mother in her straw sun hat and his lanky, sharp-faced sidekicks, the clippers and the shovel. Years later, he could even laugh with her about it, those awkward hot trips to plant a line of trees most of which never thrived, choked by thistles and bindweed or severed by a too zealous mower. Yet a few of the pines, perhaps six or seven, did live to tower along the road bank—shaggy-headed apparitions taller than a ship's mast, swaying in the wind. By this time, the dirt road was macadamized and hummed with traffic, and the bus route to Washington had long ago been abandoned as unprofitable.

* * *

Five years after the September when they had moved, Joey went to college and, essentially, never returned. He married in his senior year, and after graduation moved to New York City. Another of his mother's visions, along with that of the farm as paradise, was of him as a poet; he fulfilled this heroic task as best he could, by going to work for an ad agency and devoting himself to the search for the arresting phrase and image, on the edge of the indecent, that incites people to buy—that gives them permission, from the mythic world above, to buy. The business was like poetry in that you needed only a few lucky hits, and he had his share, and couldn't complain. He never again had to get on a bus with a shovel.

The numbers attached to the years and decades slowly changed, and with them the numbers in his bank account and on his apartment building. His first marriage took place in three different apartments, his turbulent second in four, his short-lived third in only one, and now he wondered if women had not quite been his thing all along. He had always felt most at ease, come to think of it, in the company of men, especially those who reminded him of his father. But it was the AIDS-conscious eighties by then, and his hair had passed through gray into virtual white, and he found the personalities of young men an effective barrier to thinking about their bodies, and he was content to share his life with his books, his CDs (compact disks, certificates of deposit), his modest little art collection mixed of watery commercialism and icy minimalism. On the other side of the white walls of his apartment he could hear the mumble and thump of his neighbors, and he liked that. He was home.

Three hours away, his widowed mother lived alone in the sandstone house. Joey had been the first to depart, and then a few years later his grandfather died, suddenly, with a stroke like a thunderclap, and then, after a bedridden year, his grandmother. This created an extra room upstairs, so Joey and his first wife and young children, when they came to visit in the sixties, no longer had to camp out downstairs, on cots and the sofa spotted by the peanut-butter crackers he used to eat when sick and consigned to reading the days away. The upstairs had two real bedrooms, to which the doors could be closed, and a kind of hallway beside the head of the stairs where he had slept for five years, listening to the four adults rustle and snore and creak while girls and prayers and the beginnings of poems all ran together in his brain. His grandfather, on his way downstairs in the early morning, would ruffle the hair on the sleeping boy's head, and the gathering sounds of family breakfast, as Joey's grandmother and parents followed, would rise under him with the smell of toast, a doughy warmth of life rising beneath the cold bare floorboards.

There was a fourth room, a small room in the northwest corner, where his mother had once been born, in a long agony of labor—a rural calvary, as Joey imagined it, with flickering lamps and steaming kettles and ministering cousins arriving by horse and buggy—that shaped her relations with her own mother into, it seemed, a ferocious apology, a futile undying adhesion in an attempt to make amends. She nursed her mother in the old woman's long paralyzed agony of dying, but not always patiently, or tenderly, and when the ordeal at last was over she was left with additional cause for self-blame, more sorry images. "I spent my whole life," she concluded, "trying to please my mother, and never did."

Joey would ask, irritated by these pat surges of self-dramatization, "Did she ever say so?"

"No, but you knew her. She never said anything."

"Unlike *my* mother," he said, with an ironic pretense of gallantry.

She heard the irony. "Yes, I inherited Pop's gift of gab," she said. "It's been a curse, really. If you talk enough, you don't feel you have to *do* anything."

This fourth room had become the bathroom, with a tub but no shower, a basin but no cabinet. Toothpaste, sun lotion, hand creams, razors, dental floss, slivers of soap thriftily stuck together all accumulated on the deep sill overlooking the blackening shingles of the back-porch roof. After his father died, in the early seventies, the house gradually lost the power to purge itself of accumulation. Their occupancy, which had begun with removal of the porch and the chimney stones, now silted the attic and cellar and windowsills full with souvenirs of his mother's lengthening residence. On the theory that it would save the wild birds from being eaten, she had fed a stray cat that came to the back porch; this cat then became several, and the several became as many as forty. The kitchen became choked with stacked cases of cat food, and a site in the woods, at the end of a path overgrown with raspberry canes, became a mountain of empty cat-food cans. Tin Mountain, Joey's children called it. Magazines and junk mail and church pamphlets sat around on tables and chairs waiting to be bundled and taken to the barn, to wait there for the Boy Scouts' next paper drive. Photographs of Joey and his children, Christmas cards and valentines from relations and neighbors piled up on available spaces like a kind of moss. Even the table where his mother ate had room eventually for only one plate and cup and saucer, her own. The house was clogging up, Joey felt, much as her heart—coronary angiography had revealed—was plugging with arteriosclerosis, and her weakly pumped lungs were filling with water.

His arrivals, as the years went on, seemed to accumulate. He would park his car by the barn and pick his way across the line of stepping stones that in the decades since they were laid (even Granny, stiff and bent over, helping with the crowbar) had been silted over by the sandy soil and its crabgrass. On the back porch there would be a puddle of cats and kittens mewing to be fed. Entering the back door with his suitcase was like stepping into a quicksand smelling of cat food and damp cardboard. His mother saved, in separate sections of the floor, the plastic bags the supermarket bagged her groceries in, and slippery stacks of mail-order catalogues, and a bucketful of maddeningly snarled baling twine, to make bundles for the barn with. He recognized in this accumulation a superstition he had to fight within himself—the belief that everything has value. The birds in the trees, the sunflower at the edge of the orchard, the clumsily pasted-up valentine received years ago from a distant grandchild—all have a worth that might, at any moment, be called into account. It was a way of saying that one's own life was infinitely precious.

There would be a peck of a kiss at the door, and he would carry the suitcase upstairs, past the whirling, nipping mongrel bitch, who was thrilled to have a man in the house. The guest room had been his parents' old room. When she became a widow, his mother had moved into her parents' old room, closer to the room in which she had been born. The move was part, Joey felt, of an obscure religious system that had nothing to do with Christianity. He remembered how, in a surprising rite of that system, his parents, the day after his grandmother died, took her stained, urine-soaked mattress outdoors and burned it, down near the stones he had dumped, darkening the sky all morning with the smoke.

Here, in this guest room, at night, without a wife to distract and comfort him, he would begin to fight for his breath. The bed sagged so that his back hurt. The pillow felt heavy and dense. The sandstone hearth of the never-used fireplace in the room would emit an outdoor dampness. Birds and bats and mice would stir in the porous walls, and his mother's motions would make her bed beyond the thin wall creak. Was she awake, or asleep? He could relax deeply only in the early morning, when the dog would wake her, scrabbling on the bare boards with her claws, and the two of them would slowly, noisily head downstairs, and the can opener would rhythmically begin to chew through the first installment of cat-food cans.

The guest room for some reason had no curtains; in the dead of the night the moon burned on the wide sills as if calling to him, calling him back to a phase his whole adult life had been an effort to obliterate. The asthma, the effect of inner tightening and complication, wasn't so bad, usually, the first two nights; he might manage five or six hours of sleep each if he could then get away, back to cozy, salubrious New York. But on long holiday weekends he would struggle through the whole third night with the accumulated house dust and pollen in his lungs, and the damp hard pillow, and the obdurate moonlight, so accusatory in its white silence.

He was aware of his mother and himself, lying each in bed, as survivors of the larger party that had once occupied this house. It was as if, on a snowy pass, they had killed and eaten the others, and now one of the two remaining must perish next. She, too, in her eighties, had breathing problems, and slept with her head up on two pillows. One night she woke him, with the soft words, "Joey. I'm not doing so well. Put on your daddy's old overcoat and come downstairs with me."

He was awake, his head clear as moonlight, in an instant. "Shall we call the hospital?"

"No, I just need to sit up. You know which overcoat, it hangs at the foot of the stairs."

It had hung there for years, one of those curious comforting rags his father would acquire in thrift shops or outlet stores. Joey had often seen it on him, in the last year of the old man's life, when his legs turned white and phlebitic and his nose turned blue with poor circulation and his eyes sank deeper and deeper into his head and his deafness worsened. But to the end his father had held his head high, and took a lively interest in the world. Once a social-science teacher, he continued to read fat history books, and wrote Joey, in one of his rare letters, in his patient, legible schoolteacher's hand, that being deaf made it easier for him to concentrate.

Joey wondered why his mother was being so insistent about the coat, but obediently put it on. It had a fuzziness unusual in dark overcoats, and was big for him, since his father had been bigger than he. She was right; once it was on, over his pajamas, he became a child again, and calm, and trusting. They went downstairs and turned up the thermostat and sat in the dark living room together, he on the sofa and she in her television-watching chair, and he watched her struggle for breath, in little sudden shuddering gasps like the desperate heaves of a bird caught in the chimney.

"Do you hurt?" he asked.

She had little breath for speaking, and shook her head no, and her head underwent again the convulsion, as if trying to keep above water. "It's like," she gasped, "a squeezing."

"Sure you wouldn't like to drive to the hospital?"

A vigorous headshake again. "What can they do, but torture you?"

So he sat there, in his father's overcoat, fighting sleepiness, wondering if his mother would die before his eyes. The dog, agitated at first by this predawn rising, wheezed and resettled on the floor. The moonlight weakened on the sills across the room, with their potted geraniums and violets and a night-blooming cereus that had been allowed to grow grotesquely long, so that its stem filled the window. His mother's shudders lessened, and eventually she told him to go upstairs, she would sit here a while longer. In her old age she had become almost grafted onto this chair of hers. On a previous visit, she had shocked him by refusing, when the evening run of television comedies that she faithfully watched was over, to come upstairs at all; morning found her still sitting there, in her clothes. This irritated him, along with her television watching. "Why do you watch all these idiots?" he once asked her. "They seem realer to you than I am."

She did not deny it. "Well," she had answered, "they're always here."

Now, her crisis past, he accepted her dismissal gratefully and yet reluctantly. He went upstairs feeling that this hour had been the most purely companionable he had ever spent with her in this house. To Joey in his father's fuzzy, overlarge coat, as he silently watched his mother struggle and the dog stir and doze and the night-blooming cereus cast its gawky shadow in the deep window recess beyond the tasselled bridge lamp and the upright piano, it had been like one of those scenes we witness in childhood, from under the table or over the edge of the crib, understanding nothing except that large forces are moving around us—that there is a heavy dynamism from which we are, as children, sheltered.

* * *

When she had her next attack of breathlessness, he was not there, and she called the neighbors, and they called the township ambulance, which came at five in the morning. For all her talk of "torture," she seemed to settle gratefully into the hospital's ministrations. "They said I was quite blue, the oxygen in my blood was down to nothing." Rather gaily, she described the emergency-room doctors thrusting some violent sucking instrument down her throat and into her lungs.

Her bathrobe was turquoise with a maroon hem; she ordered her clothes from catalogues now and was attracted to decisive colors. With her white hair all about her on the pillow, and the baby-blue tubes of oxygen making a mustache, and the identification bracelet looped on her wrist, she looked festive and hectic and feminized. All day, young men in antiseptic garb came and tended to her, cutting her toenails, interrogating her bowels. Her bowels, to Joey's embarrassment, had become a topic of supreme fascination to her. Her insides in general were brought uncomfortably close to the surface by the wearing away of her body. His father's method of coping with what seemed to Joey her unaccountable whims, including moving them all to the farm, had been to say, "She's a femme. Your mother's a real femme. What can you do?" He would shrug, and sometimes add, "I should have put her on the burleycue stage."

This had seemed one of the man's lofty, pained jokes; but now her femininity, which Joey's father and succession of wives had shielded him from, was upon him. In her slightly dishevelled, revealing gowns, in her gracefully accepted helplessness and fragility, in this atmosphere of frank bodily event, his mother had her sex on her mind. She told him, remembering the first years of her marriage in Pittsburgh, "There was this young doctor, Dr. Langhorne over on Sixth Street, who when I went to him with these pains on my chest I couldn't understand, told me to take off my clothes. Well, I trusted him, and did, and he looked me over for the longest time, and then told me, 'You're not obese.' That was all he said."

His own birth, her conviction that she couldn't do such a normal thing as conceive and bear a child, recurred in her self-accounting; old Dr. Berthoff, who kept brusquely calming her fears, who treated her as a normal woman and not as the monstrous product of her own mother's agony, emerged as a kind of erotic hero, and Joey suddenly saw that his own self, which he had imagined she cherished for qualities all his own, was lovable to her above all as a piece of her body, as a living proof of her womanhood.

And she recalled, of those straitened Depression days when he was an infant, how she left him in the care of his grandparents and went off on the trolley car to work in the drapes department of the department store downtown. She had lost a tooth, a bicuspid, and the upper partial plate containing its replacement was uncomfortable, and one day she didn't wear it to work and was chastised by the department manager, Mr. Wirtheimer, for not wearing it. The image of her missing tooth, this tidy black hole leaping up within her young woman's smile, seemed erotic, too, along with the thought of his then-slender mother's charm as a saleswoman. "On my good days," she said, "I could sell anything. But then the people would bring it all back for exchange on Monday. As if I had bewitched them. Mr. Wirtheimer said there was such a thing as being *too* good."

But not all her days were good days, she told Joey. She took her periods too hard, they knocked her flat for thirty-six, forty-eight hours; and this brought the conversation back to her body, her body arching over his life like a firmament, and he would leave the hospital building and find relief in the reality of the city, Alton, with its close-packed suburbs, which he loved as his mother loved her farm, because it had formed his first impressions, when the wax was soft. He ate at aluminum diners, shopped at hardware stores for parts and tools the sandstone farmhouse in its long decrepitude needed, and bought a new vacuum cleaner, since his mother's old Hoover had hardly been used for years. He even got himself a haircut in a front-parlor barbershop—the kind of shop, with a radio playing and a baby crying in rooms out of sight, and a spiral pole out front, that he thought had disappeared, because such shops had disappeared in New York. A small child of his, years ago, had knocked the porcelain lid off the toilet water tank and it had shattered. Now, between visits to his mother, he went about the city with the cardboard box of fragments, dusty and cobweb-ridden after years in the attic, to plumbing-supply houses, where overweight, hard-smoking, not quite sardonic men would return from digging in their cavernous storerooms and give him, free, old spare lids that did not, it would turn out, quite fit. He kept trying. Alton had lost factories and population since he was a boy, and appeared in smaller letters on the maps of Pennsylvania, but it was still a place where things were made and handled, where brute matter got its honest due, and he recognized as still alive in himself the city's blue-collar faith in hardware and industry and repair, a humble faith that had survived all his heady traffic in imagery.

Life was a series of plumbing problems. After a week, the hospital had cleared out his mother's lungs, and now the cardiologists wanted to operate on the malfunctioning heart that had let the pulmonary edema occur. The angiography had revealed coronary arteries stenosed almost shut. "Oh, Joey—I could go any day," she blurted to him after the test results had been described to her. She showed him with a forefinger and thumb how small the lumen had become. "Worse than they thought." She was sitting on the bed with her hair wild and one shoulder bared by a loose tie in the hospital johnny, and her facial expression was girlish, womanhood's acquired composure all dissolved. Their intermittently shared life was being lifted into new octaves, and they seemed in these moments of hospital conference simply a man and a woman, both with more white hairs than dark, taking counsel because no one else who mattered was left. They were it.

To his relief, she did not want the open-heart operation, sparing him the trouble, the expense, the tests, the trips to Philadelphia. He tried to suppress his relief and to argue for the coronary bypass that was recommended. She said, making a wryly twisted mouth just as her father used to when discussing the county's politicians, "Of course, *they* recommend it. It's what they have to sell. They're in business, just like their fathers, only peddling different things. They pass me around, one to another; I've yet to see a Christian."

In the frankness that her closeness to death allowed, as her composed womanhood melted, an anti-Semitism was one of the things that emerged, shockingly. She could not see the doctors as saviors and allies but only as opportunists and exploiters. She even developed with one solemn young cardiologist a banter that cast her as a Palestinian: "You've taken me away from my village," she said. Joey was dismayed; his third wife, the briefest one, had been Jewish, and she and his mother had seemed especially friendly, and as he imagined now his mother's suppressed feelings in those years it was like seeing silverfish tumble out of old books. On her less lucid days, she seemed to think that the doctors and their allies ("One big fella, looked just like Danny Thomas, came and cut my toenails; now how much do you think *that's* going to add to the bill?") were scheming to do her out of her house and its priceless eighty acres—that she was territory they wanted to seize and develop. Each day she spent in the hospital, the little sandstone house pulled at her harder. "Get me home," she begged Joey.

"And then what?"

"Then we'll take what comes." Her eyes widened, watching

his, and her mouth as it clamped shut over "what comes" was very like a child's, stubborn in its fright. For, however close their consultation and their agreements, both were aware that she was the star and he merely the prompter: though his turn would come, the spotlight burned upon her.

* * *

When, six months later, she died—instantly, it seemed to the coroner—in the kitchen, just under the room where she had been born, the neighbors, who were patient Mennonites and Lutherans, took a day to find her and another twelve hours to find him in at his apartment telephone number. It was midnight when he let himself into the house. The door keys had been lost long ago, in that distant, fabulous era after they had moved. When his mother would be away for more than a day, she would lock the doors from the inside and go out through the cellar bulkhead. Her neighbors knew this and had left the house that way after her body was removed. Joey had brought no flashlight; after parking the car by the barn, he walked to the slanted cellar doors by moonlight, and within the dark cellar was guided by memory. A Lally column here, a pyramid of paint cans there. His father and he had laid this cement floor one frantic long day when three cubic yards of ready-mix concrete were delivered in a giant gob by a truck. He would have been fifteen or so, his father in his late forties. The cellar floor of these old farmhouses was typically dirt, the red clay of the region packed more or less hard, except when the foundation walls wept in the spring and it turned to mud. His father had talked with construction men, and set out boards to frame the platform for the furnace, and dug a clay pipe into the dirt for drainage, and stretched strings here and there to determine the level and pitch, but none of these preparations encompassed the alarming dimensions of the slowly hardening concrete when it arrived early that Saturday morning. With rakes and shovels and boards and trowels they pushed and tugged the sluggish stuff level, into the far corners, around the furnace and the mouth of the drainage pipe. His father's face went white with effort, as it had when struggling with the chimney stones several years before, and the ordeal went on and on, by the light of a few bare bulbs, this panicky race with time and matter, as the concrete grew stiffer and stiffer, and in drying pushed its water toward the surface, and exuded its sonorous underground smell, its inexorable stony scent. The floor had come out surprisingly well, out of that day's sweaty panic—smooth and gray and delicately sloped so that hardly a puddle lingered after a flooding. It sometimes seemed, in the mottled perspectives of hindsight, that there had been a third man in the cellar with them, something of a professional, for it seemed unlikely that he and his father, a history teacher and a would-be poet, could have made such a satisfactory cellar floor. But if there had been such a man, Joey had mentally erased him, jealous of this arduous day at his father's side fending off disaster, doing a man's job. He was just becoming a man, and his father was wearying of being one; this was the last project so ambitious that he tackled around the house.

In the blackness, Joey's city shoes slithered on the smooth cement, and then thumped on the echoing wooden cellar stairs; he pushed the door open into the moon-striped kitchen, and a warm whimpering hairy body hurtled up against him, and he thought that his mother had not died after all. But it was the dog, who took his hand in her mouth and unstoppably whimpered and whined as if telling him a long story, the story of her hours alone in the house with her mistress, with the body, with her hunger and bafflement.

Things work out. One of his former wives, who had remarried into the Connecticut suburbs, agreed to take the dog. The cats a man from the county Humane Society came and trapped and carried away to be gassed, a few each day. Joey stacked the magazines and catalogues and Christmas cards and tied them with baling twine from the bucket and carried them to the barn to be trucked to a landfill. The Boy Scouts no longer collected paper and bottles; nothing was precious anymore. As his family assembled, Joey impressed them with his efficiency, portioning out the furniture and heirlooms among his children, his ex-wives, the local auctioneer, the junkman.

For himself he kept little but odd small items that reached back into his boyhood in the brick house they moved to the farm from —a brass tiger that sat on the piano there, when he still took piano lessons, and a curved leather-backed brush he remembered his grandfather using on his black hightop shoes before setting off to the Lutheran church. He kept some of his father's college notebooks, preserved in the attic, penned in a more rounded version of his legible schoolteacherish hand. A set of Shakespeare, with limp red covers, of which the silverfish had nibbled some pages into lace. His mother's sun hats—these were hard to throw away, though none of the assembled females wanted them. His daughters sorted through the clothes for him. He couldn't bear to touch and sort the dresses hanging in the closet, dozens of garments pressed together in an anthology of past fashions, all the way back to a fox-trimmed spring coat whose collar he remembered close to his face, its tingling black-tipped red-brown hairs. In the toolhouse, where his father had left a pathetic legacy of rusty screws and nails neatly arranged in jars, and oily tools, half of them broken, mounted on pegboard, there were also antique implements worn like prehistoric artifacts: an ancient oblong pink whetstone pointed at either end and soapily warped by all its use, and an old-fashioned square hoe worn into a lopsided metal oval, its edges had struck so many stones. Such wear couldn't have occurred in the merely forty years they were here, but must have been the work of generations; these tools had travelled back and forth across the county, surviving many moves, to end in his impatient hands. They seemed sacred—runes no one else could decipher. He was the last of his line to have ever hoed a row of carrots or sharpened a scythe.

Relatives and neighbors spoke to him with a curious soft gravity, as if he were fragile in grief. He knew he and his mother were regarded as having been unusually, perhaps unnaturally close;

when in fact between themselves the fear was that they were not close enough. Why grieve? She was old, in pain, worn-out. She was too frail in her last half year to walk to the mailbox or lift a case of cat food or pull a clump of burdock: it was time; dying is the last favor we do the world, the last tax we pay. He cried only once, during the funeral, quite unexpectedly, having taken his seat at the head of his raggedly extended family, suddenly free, for the moment, of arrangements and decisions, and seeing an arm's reach away the gleaming cherry-wood casket he had picked out in the undertaker's satiny showroom three days before. The lustrous well-joined wood, soon to be buried; the sumptuous waste of it; and the image of his mother as he first remembered her, a young slim woman dressed in a navy-blue suit, with white at her throat, to go off to her job at the downtown department store, hurrying to catch the trolley car. She had once reminisced, "Oh, how you'd run, and if you just missed it, there wouldn't be another for twenty minutes, and you wanted to cry." She had laughed, remembering.

His tears came and kept coming, in a kind of triumph, a breakthrough, a torrent of empathy and pity for that lost young woman running past the row houses, under the horse-chestnut trees, running to catch the trolley, the world of the thirties shabby and solid around her, the porches, the blue midsummer hydrangeas, this tiny well-dressed figure in her diminishing pocket of time, her future unknown, her death, her farm, far from her mind. This was the mother, apparently, he had loved, the young woman living with him and others in a brick semi-detached house, a part of the world, youthfully finding her way. During the war she worked in a parachute factory, wearing a bandanna on her head like the other women, plump like them by this time, merging with them and their chatter one lunch break when he, somehow, had bicycled to the side entrance to see her. She was not like them, the tough other women, he knew, but for the moment had blended with them, did a job alongside them, and this too renewed his tears, his naïve pride in her then, when he was ten or eleven. She had tried to be a person, she had lived. There was something amazing, something immortal to him in the image of her running. He remembered, from their first years on the farm, a crisis with the roof; it was being reshingled by a team of Amishmen and they had left it partially open to the weather on the night of a thunderstorm. Crashes, flashes. Joey's parents and grandparents were all awake, and he, boy though he still was, was expected now to wake and help too; they rushed up and down the attic stairs with buckets, to save the plaster of the walls and ceilings below. There was a tarpaulin in the barn that might help; he found himself outdoors, in the downpour, and he had retained an image of his mother running across the lawn in a flash of lightning that caught the white of her legs. She would not have been much over forty, and was still athletic; perhaps his father was included in this unsteady glimpse; there was a hilarity to it all, a violent-health. Working his way, after her death, through all the accumulated souvenirs of her life, Joey was fascinated by the college yearbooks that preserved her girlish image above a line or two of verse:

> She's blest with temper, whose unclouded ray
> Can make tomorrow cheerful as today.

Group photographs showed his mother as part of the hockey team, the hiking club. With a magnifying glass he studied her unsmiling, competitive face, with her hair in two balls at her ears and a headband over her bangs. Her face seemed slightly larger than the other girls', a childlike oval broadest at the brow, its defenses relatively unevolved. As he sat there beside the cherry casket crying, his former wives and adult children stealing nervous peeks at him, the young woman ran for the trolley car, her breath catching, her panting mixed with a sighing laughter at herself, and the image was as potent, as fertile, as a classic advertisement, which endlessly taps something deep and needy within us. The image of her running down the street, away from him, trailed like a comet's tail the maternal enactments of those misty years when he was a child—crayoning with him on the living-room floor, sewing him Halloween costumes in the shape of Disney creatures, having him lift what she called the "skirts" of the bushes in the lawn while she pushed the old reel mower under them—but from her point of view; he seemed to feel from within his mother's head the situation, herself and this small son, this defenseless gurgling hatched creature, and the tentative motions of her mind and instincts as she, as new to mothering as he was to being a child, explored the terrain between them. In the attic he had found a padded baby-blue scrapbook, conscientiously maintained, containing his first words, the date of his first crawl, and his hospital birth certificate imprinted with his inky day-old feet. The baths. The cod-liver oil. Trying to do the right thing, the normal thing, running toward her farm, her death. In his vision of her running she was bright and quick and small, like an animal in a trap. This was the mother he had loved, the mother before they moved, before she betrayed him with the farm and its sandstone house.

* * *

Ruthlessly, vengefully, weekend by weekend, he cleaned the place out—disconnecting the phone, giving the auctioneer the run of the attic, seeing the refrigerator and stove hauled off for a few dollars each, by a truck that got stuck in the muddy winter lawn. With his new vacuum cleaner Joey attacked the emptying rooms, sucking up the allergen-laden dust from the cracks between the floorboards, sweeping the walls and ceilings clean of their veils of cobwebs upon cobwebs. How satisfying this was, one room after another that he would not have to do again. Joey discovered that his mother had been far from alone in the house; while the cats mewed and milled outside on the porch, a tribe of mice, year after year, ancestors and descendants, had been fed sunflower seeds, whose accumulated stored husks burst forth by the bucketful from behind where the stained-pine corner cupboard had stood, and the back of the dish-towel drawer of the kitchen sink. He set traps for the mice. He set out d-Con, and the next weekend tossed their small stiff bodies, held gingerly by the tail, down into the swamp, where the rocks were, and the ashes of his grandmother's mattress.

The old house had curious small cabinets built into the stone thickness, and they disgorged packets of his father's index cards, riddled with anxious, harried reminder notes to himself, and pads of old high-school permission slips, and small boxes of dull pencils and hardened erasers, and playing cards from the remote days when he and his parents played three-handed pinochle at the dining table. At first, he could scarcely hold the cards, sixteen fanned in one little hand, and would stifle tears when his meld was poor and he lost. Once at the farm, they never played cards again. There were animals of petrified Play-Doh made by Joey's children, and useless pretty vases and bowls sent distractedly as seasonal gifts, and plush-bound old-fashioned albums, with little mildewed mirrors on the covers, of stiffly posed ancestors he could not identify. His mother had offered, over the years, to teach him their names and relation to him, but he had not been interested, and now she was not there to ask, and his ancestors floated free and nameless like angels.

There were things she had offered to tell him he had not wanted to hear. "What didn't you like about him?" he had once asked her—a bit impatiently, wearying of her voice—about his father.

Sitting in her television-watching chair, her weight and strength so wasted that only her mouth and mind could move, she had been telling him about her youthful romantic life. She had gone to a one-room country school—when she was dead, he came upon a photograph of the student body and its corpulent mustachioed instructor, his mother's broad little face squinting toward the camera under a ponderous crown of wound braids. Among the other children there had been a dark-haired, dark-eyed boy she had fancied, and who had fancied her. But her parents had disapproved of the boy's "people," and of several other dark-eyed substitutes that over the years she had offered them. But no, not until Joey's blondish, pale-eyed father did she bring home a suitor they could endorse. "They liked him, and he liked them. I'll say this for your father, not every man could have lived with his in-laws that cheerfully all those years. He really admired my mother, that style of little woman. He loved energetic little women. He thought they could make money for him. It's true, Mother was a money-maker. She was the one who got up in the dark to drive the cart into Alton to market. The tobacco they retired on had been her project. But admiring Mother was no reason to marry me. I was *big.* It was a mistake, and we both knew it. We knew it the first day of our honeymoon." Joey had often heard his mother's views on little women, how they have the best of it, and take the men from the big women like herself, big women who have tortured their little mothers in the birthing. Behind these formulations there was something—about sex, he believed—that he didn't want, as a boy or a man, to hear. *A real femme.* Even as a very small child he had been aware of a weight of anger his mother carried; he had quickly evolved—first word, first crawl—an adroitness at staying out of her way when she was heavy with it, and a wish to amuse her, to keep her light. But now as they were nearing the end, and her flesh was dissolving, and her inner self rising to the surface, he had become more daring, less catering, even challenging. Her own blue eyes, that had never needed a cataract operation, widened at his question as if she were seeing ghosts over his shoulder. "Oh, Joey," she said, "don't ask. It was un*speak*able."

He had to smile at the old-fashioned concept. "Unspeakable? Daddy?"

A bit of flush had crept into her colorless creased cheeks. She was getting angry, once again. She kept staring, not so much at him as at the space in his vicinity. She knew from watching television what the talk shows permitted people to say these days. "Well, maybe you're old enough. Maybe I *should* speak it."

"Oh, no, no thanks, that's all right," he said, jumping up from his chair and heading into the kitchen, much as his father used to in the middle of a marital exchange. *Poor Daddy,* was his thought. Let the dead alone. Now she too was dead, and there were many things Joey would never know. Though he grew used to the sandstone house without her in it, he still found it strange, back in his Manhattan apartment, that she never called on Saturday mornings the way she used to, with her playful, self-mocking account of her week. The dead can't even telephone. The phone's silence more than any other conveyed the peace of the dead, their absolute and, as it were, hostile withdrawal.

* * *

The real-estate appraiser, an old high-school classmate, stood in his gray suit in the cobwebbed cellar, next to the rickety furnace, among the paint cans and rusty hot-air ducts, and said to Joey, "Seventeen years here alone. It took a lot of guts." Yes, she had been brave, he could now afford to see, all those years alone, alone but for the animals she fed, and the ghosts on television. Over the telephone, even when reporting an insomniac night of breathlessness and terror, she had tried to keep it light for his sake, and mocked herself, mocking her very will, at the age of eighty-five, to live. "It's strange, but I really don't intend to die. Though a lot of people would like me to."

"Really? Who?"

"The real-estate developers. The neighbors. They think it's time for this old lady to move over and make some room."

"Do they really?" He was grateful she had not included him among the many who wished her dead.

"Really," she mocked. "But I have a responsibility here. The place still needs me."

"We all need you," Joey said, sighing, giving up. The fate of the place was another unspeakable matter. She wanted the place to go on and on, as it was in her idea of it.

He had scanned her in vain for some sign of sunset resignation.

She had choked down her pills and vitamins to the end, and her fear of life's sensations ceasing had seemed as pure as a child's. The last time he had visited, on a cool fall day, she came outdoors to supervise his planting, in two arcs by a curve of the cement walk, two dozen tulip bulbs she had ordered from a catalogue. At first he had arranged the bulbs point down, and then realized that the point was what would grow upward, toward the sun. His mother had stood there on her unsteady feet, in her gaudy bathrobe, looking down; the sight of the fat cream-white bulbs nested in the turned red earth startled a kind of grunt out of her. "Oh, how dear they look," she said. To Joey she added, "How nicely you do things."

In all of her leavings that came to light he was most touched by her accounts—her tax forms and used checkbooks, meticulously kept, even though her tiny backward-slanting hand had become spasmodic and shaky. (Could that big pencilled handwriting on the back of the enlarged photograph have been hers after all, at the age of thirteen?) She had kept, on a large pad of green paper, spreadsheets of her monthly expenses, ruled off by hand at the beginning of each month. The last entries had been made the day before the morning of her death. This financial and mathematical niceness of hers was something quite unpredictable, like a musical passion in a banker. Among the stored sheets of figures were several drawn up before they moved, with lists of expenses side by side, taxes, heating, utilities, upkeep—absurdly small amounts they now seemed, from that frozen wartime world. By her calculations, their reduced costs in the little sandstone house, and the projected rentals of their eighty acres to the neighboring farmers, would save them five hundred dollars—a third of her husband's salary. It had never really occurred to Joey that their move here had had a practical side. When he came to sheets showing how the money for his college education could be squeezed out among their other expenses, he couldn't bear to keep reading.

Gradually, through the stark months of a winter that was, according to the forecasters, unseasonably cold, and then unseasonably warm, he reduced the house to its essence, removing every trace, even a rusty pencil sharpener screwed to a windowsill, of his life and the four lives that had ended. Here on this patch of now uncarpeted wood his grandfather had fallen, having convulsively leaped from the bed where, a year later, his widow would breathe her last. Here, in the bedroom adjacent, his father had sat up with such pains in his chest that he told his wife to call the ambulance. He had died in the ambulance. Here in this same space Joey had lain sleepless, wondering how to tell his mother of his next divorce. Here on the other side of the wall he would lie after a date, his head still whirling with cigarette smoke and the perfume-counter smell of the girl. Here on the worn linoleum his mother had died, at the base of a wall she had had the Amish carpenters make of old chestnut boards, boards left in the barn from the era before the blight, to cover the rough stones exposed when the big kitchen chimney had been removed. The rooms had a soft beauty, empty. The uncovered floorboards drank the sunlight. Joey looked through the curtainless windows, seeing what his mother had seen—the sloping old orchard to the north, the barn and road and fields to the east, the lilac bushes and bird feeder and meadow to the south, the woods and the tall blue spruce to the west.

On his final cleanup visit, Joey found something devil-like—a small dark stiff shape, in size between a mouse and a rat, its legs attached by webs—floating in the bathroom toilet. A flying squirrel. It had come down from the attic and drowned, sick and thirsty from the d-Con. Joey remembered watching at twilight, that summer he moved the stones, a pair of flying squirrels sail, as if sliding swiftly on a wire, from the attic window over to the blue spruce. The house had stood empty before his family had moved in the previous fall, and this pair had moved in ahead of them.

He had bought a padlock for the cellar bulkhead, and closed the house with a key, having installed new locks. The house was ready for sale in the spring. But in the meantime, as he lay awake in his apartment three hours away, its emptiness called to him. It needed him. Suppose a fire, or local vandals, jealous of the price the place would fetch . . . Housing developments were all around, and even Philadelphians were moving into the area. His mother had made a shrewd investment, buying back paradise.

Those weekends alone in the house, sorting, cleaning, staying away from the motel until moonlight had replaced sunlight on the floors, he had discovered himself talking aloud, as if in response to a friendly presence just behind the dry old wallpaper, in the thick sandstone walls. His own uncluttered rooms, suspended above Manhattan's steady roar, with an ornamental piece of porch bannister hidden at the back of a closet, felt as if they were flying somewhere. He felt guilty, anxious, displaced. He had always wanted to be where the action was, and what action there was, it turned out, had been back there.

Joyce Carol Oates

THE SWIMMERS

There are stories that go unaccountably wrong and become impermeable to the imagination. They lodge in the memory like an old wound never entirely healed. This story of my father's younger brother Clyde Farrell, my uncle, and a woman named Joan Lunt, with whom he fell in love, years ago, in 1959, is one of those stories.

Some of it I was a part of, aged 13. But much of it I have to imagine.

* * *

It must have been a pale, wintry, unflattering light he first saw her in, swimming laps in the early morning in the local Y.M.C.A. pool, but that initial sight of Joan Lunt—not her face, which was obscured from him, but the movement of her strong, supple, creamy-pale body through the water, and the sureness of her strokes—never faded from Clyde Farrell's mind.

He'd been told of her; in fact, he'd come to the pool that morning to observe her, but still you didn't expect to see such serious swimming, 7:45 A.M. of a weekday, in the antiquated white-tiled

"Y" pool, light slanting down from the wired glass skylight overhead, a sharp medicinal smell of chlorine and disinfectant pinching your nostrils. There were a few other swimmers in the pool, ordinary swimmers, one of them an acquaintance of Clyde's who waved at him, called out his name when Clyde appeared in his swim trunks on the deck, climbed up onto the diving board, then paused to watch Joan Lunt swimming toward the far end of the pool . . . just stood watching her, not rudely but with a frank, childlike interest, smiling with the spontaneous pleasure of seeing another person doing something well, with so little waste motion. Joan Lunt in her yellow bathing suit with the crossed straps in back and her white rubber cap that gleamed and sparked in the miniature waves: an attractive woman in her mid-30s, though she looked younger, with an air of total absorption in the task at hand, swimming to the limit of her capacity, maintaining a pace and a rhythm Clyde Farrell would have been challenged to maintain himself, and Clyde was a good swimmer, known locally as a very good swimmer, a winner, years before, when he was in his teens, of county and state competitions. Joan Lunt wasn't aware of him standing on the diving board watching her, or so it appeared. Just swimming, counting laps. How many she'd done already he couldn't imagine. He saw that she knew to cup the water when she stroked back, not to let it thread through her fingers like most people do; she knew as if by instinct how to take advantage of the element she was in, propelling herself forward like an otter or a seal, power in her shoulder muscles and upper arms, and the swift scissors kick of her legs, feet flashing white through the chemical-turquoise glitter of the water. When Joan Lunt reached the end of the pool, she ducked immediately down into the water in a well-practiced maneuver, turned, used the tiled side to kick off from, in a single graceful motion that took her a considerable distance, and Clyde Farrell's heart contracted when, emerging from the water, head and shoulders and flashing arms, the woman didn't miss a beat, just continued as if she hadn't been confronted with any limit or impediment, any boundary. It was just water, and her in it, water that might go on forever, and her in it, swimming, sealed off and invulnerable.

Clyde Farrell dived into the pool, and swam vigorously, keeping to his own lane, energetic and single-minded, too, and when, after some minutes, he glanced around for the woman in the yellow bathing suit, the woman I'd told him of meeting, Joan Lunt, he saw, to his disappointment, that she was gone.

His vanity was wounded. He thought, She never once looked at me.

* * *

My father and my uncle Clyde were farm boys who left the farm as soon as they were of age: joined the U.S. Navy out of high school, went away, came back and lived and worked in town, my father in a small sign shop and Clyde in a succession of jobs. He drove a truck for a gravel company, he was a foreman in a local tool factory, he managed a sporting-goods store; he owned property at Wolf's Head Lake, 20 miles to the north, and spoke with vague enthusiasm of developing it someday. He wasn't a practical man and he never saved money. He liked to gamble at cards and horses. In the Navy, he'd learned to box and for a while after being discharged, he considered a professional career as a welterweight, but that meant signing contracts, traveling around the country, taking orders from other men. Not Clyde Farrell's temperament.

He was good-looking, not tall, about 5'9", compact and quick on his feet, a natural athlete, with well-defined shoulder and arm muscles, strong, sinewy legs. His hair was the color of damp sand, his eyes a warm liquid brown, all iris. There was a gap between his two front teeth that gave him a childlike look and was misleading.

No one ever expected Clyde Farrell to get married, or even to fall seriously in love. That capacity in him seemed missing, somehow: a small but self-proclaimed absence, like the gap between his teeth.

But Clyde was powerfully attracted to women, and after watching Joan Lunt swim that morning, he drifted by later in the day to Kress's, Yewville's largest department store, where he knew she'd recently started to work. Kress's was a store of some distinction, the merchandise was of high quality, the counters made of solid, burnished oak; the overhead lighting was muted and flattering to women customers. Behind the counter displaying gloves and leather handbags, Joan Lunt struck the eye as an ordinarily pretty woman, composed, intelligent, feminine, brunette, with a brunette's waxy-pale skin, carefully made up, even glamourous, but not a woman Clyde Farrell would have noticed, much. He was 32 years old, in many ways much younger. This woman was too mature for him, wasn't she? Probably married or divorced, very likely with children. Clyde thought, In her clothes, she's just another one of them.

So Clyde walked out of Kress's, a store he didn't like anyway, and wasn't going to think about Joan Lunt, but one morning a few days later, there he was, unaccountably, back at the Y.M.C.A., 7:30 A.M. of a weekday in March 1959, and there, too, was Joan Lunt in her satiny-yellow bathing suit and gleaming white cap. Swimming laps, arm over strong, slender arm, stroke following stroke, oblivious of Clyde Farrell and of her surroundings, so Clyde was forced to see how her presence in the old, tacky, harshly chlorinated pool made of the place something extraordinary that lifted his heart.

That morning, Clyde swam in the pool for only about ten minutes, then left and hastily showered and dressed and was waiting for Joan Lunt out in the lobby. Clyde wasn't a shy man, but he could give that impression when it suited him. When Joan Lunt appeared, he stepped forward and smiled and introduced himself, saying, "Miss Lunt? I guess you know my niece Sylvie? She told me about meeting you." Joan Lunt hesitated, then shook hands with Clyde and said in that way of hers that suggested she was giving information meant to be clear and unequivocal, "My first name is Joan." She didn't smile but seemed prepared to smile.

Joan Lunt was a good-looking woman with shrewd dark eyes, straight dark eyebrows, an expertly reddened mouth. There was an inch-long white scar at the left corner of her mouth like a sliver of glass. Her thick, shoulder-length dark-brown hair was carefully waved, but the ends were damp; although her face was pale, it appeared heated, invigorated by exercise.

Joan Lunt and Clyde Farrell were nearly of a height, and comfortable together.

Leaving the Y.M.C.A., descending the old granite steps to Main Street that were worn smooth in the centers, nearly hollow with decades of feet, Clyde said to Joan, "You're a beautiful swimmer —I couldn't help admiring you in there," and Joan Lunt laughed and said, "And so are you—I was admiring you, too," and Clyde said, surprised, "Really? You saw me?" and Joan Lunt said, "Both times."

It was Friday. They arranged to meet for drinks that afternoon, and spent the next two days together.

* * *

In Yewville, no one knew who Joan Lunt was except as she presented herself: a woman in her mid-30s, solitary, very private, seemingly unattached, with no relatives or friends in the area. No one knew where exactly she'd come from, or why; why here of all places, Yewville, New York, a small city of fewer than 30,000 people, built on the banks of the Eden River, in the southwestern foothills of the Chautauqua Mountains. She had arrived in early February, in a dented rust-red 1956 Chevrolet with New York State license plates, the rear of the car piled with suitcases, cartons, clothes. She spent two nights in Yewville's single good hotel, The Mohawk, then moved into a tiny furnished apartment on Chambers Street. She spent several days interviewing for jobs downtown, all of which you might call jobs for women specifically, and was hired at Kress's, and started work promptly on the first Monday morning following her arrival. If it was sheerly good luck, the job at Kress's, the most prestigious store in town, Joan

Lunt seemed to take it in stride, the way a person would who felt she deserved as much. Or better.

The other saleswomen at Kress's, other tenants in the Chambers Street building, men who approached her—no one could get to know her. It was impossible to get beyond the woman's quick, just slightly edgy smile, her resolute cheeriness, her purposefully vague manner. Asked where she was from, she would say, "Nowhere you'd know." Asked was she married, did she have a family, she would say, "Oh, I'm an independent woman, I'm well over eighteen." She'd laugh to suggest that this was a joke, of a kind, the thin scar beside her mouth white with anger.

It was observed that her fingers were entirely ringless.

But the nails were perfectly manicured, polished an enamel-hard red.

It was observed that, for a solitary woman, Joan Lunt had curious habits.

For instance, swimming. Very few women swam in the Y.M.C.A. pool in those days. Sometimes Joan Lunt swam in the early morning, and sometimes, Saturdays, in the late morning; she swam only once in the afternoon, after work, but the pool was disagreeably crowded, and too many people approached her. A well-intentioned woman asked, "Who taught you to swim like *that?*" and Joan Lunt said quietly, "I taught myself." She didn't smile and the conversation was not continued.

It was observed that, for a woman in her presumed circumstances, Joan Lunt was remarkably arrogant.

It seemed curious, too, that she went to the Methodist church Sunday mornings, sitting in a pew at the very rear, holding an opened hymnbook in her hand but not singing with the congregation; and that she slipped away afterward without speaking to anyone. Each time, she left a neatly folded dollar bill in the collection basket.

She wasn't explicitly unfriendly, but she wasn't friendly. At church, the minister and his wife tried to speak with her, tried to make her feel welcome, *did* make her feel welcome, but nothing came of it, she'd hurry off in her car, disappear. In time, people began to murmur that there was something strange about that woman, something not right, yes, maybe even something wrong; for instance, wasn't she behaving suspiciously? Like a runaway wife, for instance? A bad mother? A sinner fleeing Christ?

Another of Joan Lunt's curious habits was to drink, alone, in the early evening, in the Yewville Bar & Grill, or the White Owl Tavern, or the restaurant-bar adjoining the Greyhound Bus Station. If possible, she sat in a booth at the very rear of these taverns where she could observe the front entrances without being seen herself. For an hour or more she'd drink bourbon and water, slowly, very slowly, with an elaborate slowness, her face perfectly composed but her eyes alert. In the Yewville Bar & Grill, there was an enormous sectioned mirror stretching the length of the taproom, and in this mirror, muted by arabesques of frosted glass, Joan Lunt was reflected as beautiful and mysterious. Now and then, men approached her to ask if she were alone. Did she want company? How's about another drink? But she responded coolly to them and never invited anyone to join her. Had my uncle Clyde approached her in such a fashion, she would very likely have been cool to him, too, but my uncle Clyde wasn't the kind of man to set himself up for any sort of public rejection.

One evening in March, before Joan Lunt met up with Clyde Farrell, patrons at the Yewville Bar & Grill, one of them my father, reported with amusement hearing an exchange between Joan Lunt and a local farmer who, mildly drunk, offered to sit with her and buy her a drink, which ended with Joan Lunt's saying, in a loud, sharp voice, "You don't want trouble, mister. Believe me, you don't."

Rumors spread, delicious and censorious, that Joan Lunt was a man-hater. That she carried a razor in her purse. Or an ice pick. Or a lady's-sized revolver.

* * *

It was at the Y.M.C.A. pool that I became acquainted with Joan Lunt, on Saturday mornings. She saw that I was alone, that I was a good swimmer, might have mistaken me for younger than I was (I was 13), and befriended me, casually and cheerfully, the way an adult woman might befriend a young girl to whom she isn't related. Her remarks were often exclamations, called across the slapping little waves of the turquoise-tinted water, "*Isn't* it heavenly!"—meaning the pool, the prospect of swimming, the icy rain pelting the skylight overhead while we, in our bathing suits, were snug and safe below.

Another time, in the changing room, she said almost rapturously, "There's nothing like swimming, is there? Your mind just *dissolves.*"

She asked my name, and when I told her, she stared at me and said, "*Sylvie*—I had a close friend once named Sylvie, a long time ago. I loved that name, and I loved *her.*"

I was embarrassed, but pleased. It astonished me that an adult woman, a woman my mother's age, might be so certain of her feelings and so direct in expressing them to a stranger. I fantasized that Joan Lunt came from a part of the world where people knew what they thought and announced their thoughts importantly to others. This struck me with the force of a radically new idea.

I watched Joan Lunt covertly, and I didn't even envy her in the pool—she was so far beyond me. Her face that seemed to me strong and rare and beautiful and her body that was a fully developed woman's body—prominent breasts, shapely hips, long firm legs—all beyond me. I saw how the swiftness and skill with which Joan Lunt swam made other swimmers, especially the adults, appear slow by contrast; clumsy, ill-coordinated, without style.

One day, Joan Lunt was waiting for me in the lobby, hair damp at the ends, face carefully made up, her lipstick seemingly brighter than usual. "Sylvie," she said, smiling, "let's walk out together."

So we walked outside into the snow-glaring, windy sunshine, and she said, "Are you going in this direction? Good, let's walk together." She addressed me as if I were much younger than I was, and her manner was nervous, quick, alert. As we walked up Main Street, she asked questions of me of a kind she'd never asked before, about my family, about my "interests," about school, not listening to the answers and offering no information about herself. At the corner of Chambers and Main, she asked eagerly if I would like to come back to her apartment to visit for a few minutes, and although out of shyness I wanted to say "No, thank you," I said "Yes" instead, because it was clear that Joan Lunt was frightened about something, and I didn't want to leave her.

Her apartment building was shabby and weather-worn, as modest a place as even the poorest of my relatives lived in, but it had about it a sort of makeshift glamour, up the street from the White Owl Tavern and the Shamrock Diner, where motorcyclists hung out, close by the railroad yards on the river. I felt excited and pleased to enter the building and to climb with Joan Lunt—who was chatting briskly all the while—to the fourth floor. On each floor, Joan would pause, breathless, glancing around, listening, and I wanted to ask if someone might be following her, waiting for her. But, of course, I didn't say a thing. When she unlocked the door to her apartment, stepped inside and whispered, "Come in, Sylvie," I seemed to understand that no one else had ever been invited in.

The apartment was really just one room with a tiny kitchen alcove, a tiny bathroom, a doorless closet and a curtainless window with stained, injured-looking Venetian blinds. Joan Lunt said with an apologetic little laugh, "Those blinds—I tried to wash them, but the dirt turned to a sort of paste." I was standing at the window peering down into a weedy back yard of tilting clotheslines and wind-blown trash, curious to see what the view was from Joan Lunt's window, and she came over and drew the blinds, saying, "The sunshine is too bright, it hurts my eyes."

She hung up our coats and asked if I would like some coffee or fresh-squeezed orange juice. "It's my half day off from Kress's," she said. "I don't have to be there until one." It was shortly after 11 o'clock.

We sat at a worn dinette table, and Joan Lunt chatted animatedly and plied me with questions, as I drank orange juice in a tall glass, and she drank black coffee, and an alarm clock on the window sill ticked the minutes briskly by. Few rooms in which I've lived even for considerable periods of time are as vividly imprinted in my memory as that room of Joan Lunt's, with its spare, battered-looking furniture (including a sofa bed and a chest of drawers), its wanly wallpapered walls bare of any hangings, even a mirror, and its badly faded shag rug laid upon painted floor boards. There was a mixture of smells—talcum powder, perfume, cooking odors, insect spray, general mustiness. Two opened suitcases were on the floor beside the sofa bed, apparently unpacked, containing underwear, toiletries, neatly folded sweaters and blouses, several pairs of shoes. A single dress hung in the closet, and a shiny black raincoat, and our two coats Joan had hung on wire hangers. I stared at the suitcases thinking how strange, she'd been living here for weeks but hadn't had time yet to unpack.

So this was where the mysterious Joan Lunt lived! The woman of whom people in Yewville spoke with such suspicion and disapproval! She was far more interesting to me, and in a way more real, than I was to myself; shortly, the story of the lovers Clyde Farrell and Joan Lunt, as I imagined it, would be infinitely more interesting, and infinitely more real, than any story with Sylvie Farrell at its core. (I was a fiercely introspective child, in some ways perhaps a strange child, and the solace of my life would be to grow, not away from but ever more deeply and fruitfully into my strangeness, the way a child with an idiosyncratic, homely face often grows into that face and emerges, in adulthood, as "striking," "distinctive," sometimes even "beautiful.") It turned out that Joan liked poetry, and so we talked about poetry, and about love, and Joan asked me in that searching way of hers if I were "happy in my life," if I were "loved and prized" by my family, and I said, "Yes—I guess so," though these were not issues I had ever considered before, and would not have known to consider if she hadn't asked. For some reason, my eyes filled with tears.

Joan said, "The crucial thing, Sylvie, is to have precious memories." She spoke almost vehemently, laying her hand on mine. "That's even more important than Jesus Christ in your heart, do you know why? Because Jesus Christ can fade out of your heart, but precious memories never do."

We talked like that. Like I'd never talked with anyone before.

I was nervy enough to ask Joan how she'd gotten the little scar beside her mouth, and she touched it, quickly, and said, "In a way I'm not proud of, Sylvie." I sat staring, stupid. The scar wasn't disfiguring in my eyes but enhancing. "A man hit me once," Joan said. "Don't ever let a man hit you, Sylvie."

Weakly, I said, "No, I won't."

No man in our family had ever struck any woman that I knew of, but it happened sometimes in families we knew. I recalled how a ninth-grade girl had come to school that winter with a blackened eye, and she'd seemed proud of it, in a way, and everyone had stared—and the boys just drifted to her, staring. Like they couldn't wait to get their hands on her themselves. And she knew precisely what they were thinking.

I told Joan Lunt that I wished I lived in a place like hers, by myself, and she said, laughing, "No you don't, Sylvie, you're too young." I asked where she was from and she shrugged, "Oh—nowhere," and I persisted, "But is it north of here, or south? Is it the country? Or a city?" and she said, running her fingers nervously through her hair, fingering the damp ends, "My only home is *here, now,* in this room, and, sweetie, that's more than enough for me to think about."

It was time to leave. The danger had passed, or Joan had passed out of thinking there was danger.

She walked with me to the stairs, smiling, cheerful, and

squeezed my hand when we said goodbye. She called down after me, "See you next Saturday at the pool, maybe—" but it would be weeks before I saw Joan Lunt again. She was to meet my uncle Clyde the following week and her life in Yewville that seemed to me so orderly and lonely and wonderful would be altered forever.

* * *

Clyde had a bachelor's place (that was how the women in our family spoke of it) to which he brought his women friends. It was a row house made of brick and cheap stucco, on the west side of town, near the old, now defunct tanning factories on the river. With the money he made working for a small Yewville construction company, and his occasional gambling wins, Clyde could have afforded to live in a better place, but he hadn't much mind for his surroundings and spent most of his spare time out. He brought Joan Lunt home with him because, for all the slapdash clutter of his house, it was more private than her apartment on Chambers Street, and they wanted privacy, badly.

The first time they were alone together, Clyde laid his hands on Joan's shoulders and kissed her, and she held herself steady, rising to the kiss, putting pressure against the mouth of this man who was virtually a stranger to her so that it was like an exchange, a handshake, between equals. Then, stepping back from the kiss, they both laughed—they were breathless, like people caught short, taken by surprise. Joan Lunt said faintly, "I—I do things sometimes without meaning them," and Clyde said, "Good. So do I."

* * *

Through the spring, they were often seen together in Yewville; and when, weekends, they weren't seen, it was supposed they were at Clyde's cabin at Wolf's Head Lake (where he was teaching Joan Lunt to fish) or at the Scholharie Downs race track (where Clyde gambled on the standardbreds). They were an attractive, eye-catching couple. They were frequent patrons of local bars and restaurants, and they turned up regularly at parties given by friends of Clyde's, and at all-night poker parties in the upstairs, rear, of the Iroquois Hotel—Joan Lunt didn't play cards, but she took an interest in Clyde's playing, and, as Clyde told my father, admiringly, she never criticized a move of his, never chided or teased or second-guessed him. "But the woman has me figured out completely," Clyde said. "Almost from the first, when she saw the way I was winning, and the way I kept on, she said, 'Clyde, you're the kind of gambler who won't quit, because, when he's losing, he has to get back to winning, and when he's winning, he has to give his friends a chance to catch up.' "

In May, Clyde brought Joan to a Sunday gathering at our house, a large, noisy affair, and we saw how when Clyde and Joan were separated, in different rooms, they'd drift back together until they were touching, literally touching, without seeming to know what they did, still less that they were being observed. So that was what love was! Always a quickness of a kind was passing between them, a glance, a hand squeeze, a light pinch, a caress, Clyde's lazy fingers on Joan's neck beneath her hair, Joan's arm slipped around Clyde's waist, fingers hooked through his belt loop. I wasn't jealous, but I watched them covertly. My heart yearned for them, though I didn't know what I wanted of them, or for them.

At 13, I was more of a child still than an adolescent girl: thin, long-limbed, eyes too large and naked-seeming for my face and an imagination that rarely flew off into unknown territory but turned, and turned, and turned, upon what was close at hand and known, but not altogether known. Imagination, says Aristotle, begins in desire: But what *is* desire? I could not, nor did I want to, possess my uncle Clyde and Joan Lunt. I wasn't jealous of them, I loved them both. I wanted them to *be.* For this, too, was a radically new idea to me, that a man and a woman might be nearly strangers to each other, yet lovers; lovers, yet nearly strangers; and the love passing between them, charged like electricity, might be visible, without their knowing. Could they know how I dreamt of them!

After Clyde and Joan left our house, my mother complained irritably that she couldn't get to know Joan Lunt. "She's sweet-seeming, and friendly enough, but you know her mind isn't there for you," my mother said. "She's just plain *not there.*"

My father said, "As long as the woman's there for Clyde."

He didn't like anyone speaking critically of his younger brother apart from himself.

* * *

But sometimes, in fact, Joan Lunt wasn't there for Clyde: He wouldn't speak of it, but she'd disappear in her car for a day or two or three, without explaining very satisfactorily where she'd gone, or why. Clyde could see by her manner that wherever Joan had gone had, perhaps, not been a choice of hers, and that her disappearances, or flights, left her tired and depressed; but still he was annoyed, he felt betrayed. Clyde Farrell wasn't the kind of man to disguise his feelings. Once, on a Friday afternoon in June before a weekend they'd planned at Wolf's Head Lake, Clyde returned to the construction office at 5:30 P.M. to be handed a message hastily telephoned in by Joan Lunt an hour before: CAN'T MAKE IT THIS WEEKEND. SORRY. LOVE, JOAN. Clyde believed himself humiliated in front of others, vowed he'd never forgive Joan Lunt and that very night, drunk and mean-spirited, he took up again with a former girlfriend . . . and so it went.

But in time they made up, as naturally they would, and Clyde said, "I'm thinking maybe we should get married, to stop this sort of thing," and Joan, surprised, said, "Oh, that isn't necessary, darling—I mean, for you to offer that."

Clyde believed, as others did, that Joan Lunt was having difficulties with a former man friend or husband, but Joan refused to speak of it; just acknowledged that, yes, there was a man, yes, of course he was an *ex* in her life, but she resented so much as speaking of him; she refused to allow him re-entry into her life.

Clyde asked, "What's his name?" and Joan shook her head, mutely, just no; no, she would not say, would not utter that name. Clyde asked, "Is he threatening you? Now? Has he ever shown up in Yewville?" and Joan, as agitated as he'd ever seen her, said, "He does what he does, and I do what I do. And I don't talk about it."

* * *

But later that summer, at Wolf's Head Lake, in Clyde's bed in Clyde's hand-hewn log cabin on the bluff above the lake, overlooking wooded land that was Clyde Farrell's property for a mile in either direction, Joan Lunt wept bitterly, weakened in the aftermath of love, and said, "If I tell you, Clyde, it will make you feel too bound to me. It will seem to be begging a favor of a kind, and I'm not begging."

Clyde said, "I know you're not."

"I don't beg favors from anyone."

"I know you don't."

"I went through a long spell in my life when I did beg favors, because I believed that was how women made their way, and I was hurt because of it, but not more hurt than I deserved. I'm older now. I know better. The meek don't inherit the earth and they surely don't deserve to."

Clyde laughed sadly and said, "Nobody's likely to take you for meek, Joan honey."

* * *

Making love, they were like two swimmers deep in each other, plunging hard. Wherever they were when they made love, it wasn't the place they found themselves in when they returned, and whatever the time, it wasn't the same time.

* * *

The trouble came in September: A cousin of mine, another niece of Clyde's, was married, and the wedding party was held in the

Nautauga Inn, on Lake Nautauga, about ten miles east of Yewville. Clyde knew the inn's owner, and it happened that he and Joan Lunt, handsomely dressed, were in the large public cocktail lounge adjacent to the banquet room reserved for our party, talking with the owner-bartender, when Clyde saw an expression on Joan's face of a kind he'd never seen on her face before—fear, and more than fear, a sudden sick terror—and he turned to see a stranger approaching them, not slowly, exactly, but with a restrained sort of haste: a man of about 40, unshaven, in a blue seersucker sports jacket now badly rumpled, tieless, a muscled but soft-looking man with a blunt, rough, ruined-handsome face, complexion like an emery board, and this man's eyes were too bleached a color for his skin, unless there was a strange light rising in them. And this same light rose in Clyde Farrell's eyes, in that instant.

Joan Lunt was whispering, "Oh, no—*no,*" pulling at Clyde's arm to turn him away, but naturally, Clyde Farrell wasn't going to step away from a confrontation, and the stranger, who would turn out to be named Robert Waxman, Rob Waxman, Joan Lunt's former husband, divorced from her 15 months before, co-owner of a failing meat-supplying company in Kingston, advanced upon Clyde and Joan smiling as if he knew them both, saying loudly, in a slurred but vibrating voice, "Hello, hello, hello!" and when Joan tried to escape, Waxman leapt after her, cursing, and Clyde naturally intervened, and suddenly, the two men were scuffling, and voices were raised, and before anyone could separate them, there was the astonishing sight of Waxman, with his gravelly face and hot eyes, crouched, holding a pistol in his hand, striking Clyde clumsily about the head and shoulders with the butt and crying, enraged, "Didn't ask to be born! Goddamn you! I didn't ask to be born!" And "I'm no different from you! Any of you! *You!* In my heart!" There were screams as Waxman fired the pistol point-blank at Clyde, a popping sound like a firecracker, and Waxman stepped back to get a better aim—he'd hit his man in the fleshy part of a shoulder—and Clyde Farrell, desperate, infuriated, scrambled forward in his wedding-party finery, baboon style, not on his hands and knees but on his hands and feet, bent double, face contorted, teeth bared, and managed to throw himself on Waxman, who outweighed him by perhaps 40 pounds, and the men fell heavily to the floor, and there was Clyde Farrell straddling his man, striking him blow after blow in the face, even with his weakened left hand, until Waxman's nose was broken and his nostrils streamed blood, and his mouth, too, was broken and bloody, and someone risked being struck by Clyde's wild fists and pulled him away.

And there on the floor of the breezy screened-in barroom of the Nautauga Inn lay a man, unconscious, breathing erratically, bleeding from his face, whom no one except Joan Lunt knew was Joan Lunt's former husband; and there, panting, hot-eyed, stood Clyde Farrell over him, bleeding, too, from a shoulder wound he was to claim he'd never felt.

* * *

Said Joan Lunt repeatedly, "Clyde, I'm sorry. I'm so sorry."

Said Joan Lunt carefully, "I just don't know if I can keep on seeing you. Or keep on living here in Yewville."

And my uncle Clyde was trying hard, trying very hard, to understand.

"You don't love me, then?" he asked several times.

He was baffled, he wasn't angry. It was the following week and by this time he wasn't angry, nor was he proud of what he'd done, though everyone was speaking of it, and would speak of it, in awe, for years. He wasn't proud because, in fact, he couldn't remember clearly what he'd done, what sort of lightning-swift action he'd performed; no conscious decision had been made that he could recall. Just the light dancing up in a stranger's eyes, and its immediate reflection in his own.

Now Joan Lunt was saying this strange, unexpected thing, this thing he couldn't comprehend. Wiping her eyes, and, yes, her voice was shaky, but he recognized the steely stubbornness in it, the resolute will. She said, "I do love you. I've told you. But I can't live like that any longer."

"You're still in love with *him*."

"Of course I'm not in love with him. But I can't live like that any longer."

"Like what? What I did? I'm not *like* that."

"I'm thirty-six years old. I can't take it any longer."

"Joan, I was only protecting you."

"Men fighting each other, men trying to kill each other—I can't take it any longer."

"I was only protecting you. He might have killed you."

"I know. I know you were protecting me. I know you'd do it again if you had to."

Clyde said, suddenly furious, "You're damned right I would. If that son of a bitch ever—"

Waxman was out on bail and returned to Kingston. Like Clyde Farrell, he'd been treated in the emergency room at Yewville General Hospital; then he'd been taken to the county sheriff's headquarters and booked on charges of assault with a deadly weapon and reckless endangerment of life. In time, Waxman would be sentenced to a year's probation: He had no prior record except for traffic violations; he was to impress the judge with his air of sincere remorse and repentance. Clyde Farrell, after giving testimony and hearing the sentencing, would never see the man again.

Joan Lunt was saying, "I know I should thank you, Clyde. But I can't."

Clyde splashed more bourbon into Joan's glass and into his own. They were sitting at Joan's dinette table beside a window whose grimy and cracked Venetian blinds were tightly closed. Clyde smiled and said, "Never mind thanking me, honey: Just let's forget it."

Joan said softly, "Yes, but I can't forget it."

"It's just something you're saying. Telling yourself. Maybe you'd better stop."

"I want to thank you, Clyde, and I can't. You risked your life for me. I know that. And I can't thank you."

So they discussed it, like this. For hours. For much of a night. Sharing a bottle of bourbon Clyde had brought over. And eventually, they made love, in Joan Lunt's narrow sofa bed that smelled of talcum powder, perfume and the ingrained dust of years, and their lovemaking was tentative and cautious but as sweet as ever, and driving back to his place early in the morning, at dawn, Clyde thought surely things were changed; yes, he was convinced that things were changed. Hadn't he Joan's promise that she would think it all over, not make any decision, they'd see each other that evening and talk it over then? She'd kissed his lips in goodbye, and walked him to the stairs, and watched him descend to the street.

But Clyde never saw Joan Lunt again.

* * *

That evening, she was gone, moved out of the apartment, like that, no warning, not even a telephone call, and she'd left only a brief letter behind with CLYDE FARRELL written on the envelope. Which Clyde never showed to anyone and probably, in fact, ripped up immediately.

It was believed that Clyde spent some time, days, then weeks, into the early winter of that year, looking for Joan Lunt; but no one, not even my father, knew exactly what he did, where he drove, whom he questioned, the depth of his desperation or his yearning or his rage, for Clyde wasn't, of course, the kind of man to speak of such things.

Joan Lunt's young friend Sylvie never saw her again, either, nor heard of her. And this hurt me, too, more than I might have anticipated.

And over the years, once I left Yewville to go to college in another state, then to begin my own adult life, I saw less and less of my uncle Clyde. He never married; for a few years, he continued the life he'd been leading before meeting Joan Lunt—a typical "bachelor" life, of its place and time; then he began to spend more and more time at Wolf's Head Lake, developing his property, building small wood-frame summer cottages and renting them out to vacationers, and acting as caretaker for them, an increasingly solitary life no one would have predicted for Clyde Farrell.

He stopped gambling, too, abruptly. His luck had turned, he said.

I saw my uncle Clyde only at family occasions, primarily weddings and funerals. The last time we spoke together in a way that might be called forthright was in 1971, at my grandmother's funeral: I looked up and saw through a haze of tears a man of youthful middle age moving in my general direction, Clyde, who seemed shorter than I recalled, not stocky but compact, with a look of furious compression, in a dark suit that fitted him tightly about the shoulders. His hair had turned not silver but an eerie metallic blond, with faint tarnished streaks, and it was combed down flat and damp on his head, a look here, too, of furious constraint. Clyde's face was familiar to me as my own, yet altered: The skin had a grainy texture, roughened from years of outdoor living, like dried earth, and the creases and dents in it resembled animal tracks; his eyes were narrow, damp, restless; the eyelids looked swollen. He was walking with a slight limp that he tried, in his vanity, to disguise; I learned later that he'd had knee surgery. And the gunshot wound to his left shoulder he'd insisted at the time had not given him much, or any, pain gave him pain now, an arthritic sort of pain, agonizing in cold weather. I stared at my uncle thinking, *Oh, why? Why?* I didn't know if I were seeing the man Joan Lunt had fled from or the man her flight had made.

But Clyde sighted me and hurried over to embrace me, his favorite niece, still. If he associated me with Joan Lunt—and I had the idea he did—he'd forgiven me long ago.

Death gives to life, to the survivors' shared life, that is, an insubstantial quality. It's like an image of absolute clarity reflected in water—then disturbed, shattered into ripples, revealed as mere surface. Its clarity, even its beauty, can resume, but you can't any longer trust in its reality.

So my uncle Clyde and I regarded each other, stricken in that instant with grief. But, being a man, *he* didn't cry.

We drifted off to one side, away from the other mourners, and I saw it was all right between us, it was all right to ask, so I asked if he had ever heard from Joan Lunt after that day. Had he ever heard of her? He said, "I never go where I'm not welcome, honey," as if this were the answer to my question. Then added, seeing my look of distress, "I stopped thinking of her years ago. We don't need each other the way we think we do when we're younger."

I couldn't bear to look at my uncle. *Oh, why? Why?* Somehow, I must have believed all along that there was a story, a story unknown to me, that had worked itself out without my knowing, like a stream tunneling its way underground. I would not have minded not knowing this story could I only know that it *was.*

Clyde said, roughly, "*You* didn't hear from her, did you? The two of you were so close."

He wants me to lie, I thought. But I said only, sadly, "No, I never hear from her. And we weren't close."

Said Clyde, "Sure you were."

The last I saw of Clyde that day, it was after dark and he and my father were having a disagreement just outside the back door of our house. My father insisted that Clyde, who'd been drinking, wasn't in condition to drive his pickup truck back to the lake, and Clyde was insisting he was, and my father said, "Maybe yes, Clyde, and maybe no," but he didn't want to take a chance, why didn't *he* drive Clyde home, and Clyde pointed out truculently that, if my father drove him home, how in hell would he get back here except by taking Clyde's only means of transportation? So the brothers discussed their predicament, as dark came on.

Sharon Sheehe Stark

OVERLAND

Twenty odd miles out of Terre Haute and too many miles to count any more from Vermont. They are stroking through endless tides of high-summer, heartland green, the windows flickering greenly; a green dream. Everything about the bus seems deep and dim and subaqueous, the day drawing imperceptibly the dust of night, night always opening a chary eye on new terrain, people floating off forever into tiny, Christmas-tree towns. On this cross-country run you are never there, only on your way, always moving. A dream you wake from only to drift off into the same dream. "When are we going to be there?" Pet asks Marnie. "When are we going to be there?" Marnie asks Pet. In full awareness of the scheduled arrival time, again and again, they say it. *When are we going to be there?* A dream.

The human faces change faster than the face of the land. Fellow passengers are no more real or reliable than actors in a foreign film that you might have to watch a long time before giving up your stiff posture, your perplexed, uneasy detachment. Did New England smiles ever show so much gum? Are gums everywhere that pale or that purple and could you realistically expect a

Brice, Ohio, mouth to ladle words in the same sequence as your own? Every English syllable astonishes you. And you cannot count on their gestures to correspond in any way to standard equivalents. Maybe a shrug means "go pound sand." And what if they grimace to show pleasure and it means nothing at all when someone they love dies?

Several faces stay put; by now Pet and Marnie have identified the other thru-people. Front-seat opposite, a man named Loomis clutching a large zippered case from which he routinely extracts a handful of paper strips that never fail to tickle him. Once when he'd opened the case Pet got up to go to the bathroom just for the chance to look over his shoulder. The case was stuffed with clippings, cartoons and joke columns from newspapers and magazines. Loomis was travelling with a stock of laughs fat enough to keep him in stitches all the way to the coast.

Directly across the way a Pennsylvania farmer who occasionally acknowledges them with a curt nod. He spoke to them but once, in a thick gluey dialect. "The daughter moved to Anaheim in '65," he said. Then leaning closer, he whispered, "Out there folks run bare-nekkid in the streets." He held their eyes with a look that dared them not be aghast. He shook his head and went back to his maps. He marks time by keeping meticulous track of space. With a ball point pen he paves over the highway lines as distance is covered. And when they pull into a depot, he exes it off his schedule, looking very business-like and satisfied.

Behind him, two spinsterish sisters chatter ceaselessly but only with each other. The one with a high bright voice has managed to enlighten everybody as to their demure purposes. Stationers from Maine, they are on a quest for a certain tiny wildflower called Elspeth's Tears that grows only above the treeline in the San Bernardino Mountains.

Thru people. Bitter enders. They *do* grow on you, taking concrete shape from continuous exposure. And the steady grit and grind of land travel has a way of rubbing strangeness away, polishing each face to a common dogged greyness, and the time comes when they rest as snugly in the subconscious as those neighbors you never have over but whose comings and goings have fluttered at your windows for years.

And Vi. Oh, she is real and binding and inescapable as Mrs. O'Dwyer, the parish fanatic back in Shelburne. What with all the round sounds, the ceaseless engines, her hair the color of old string, she seems to be unwinding from a large yellow spool. At the moment she is casting her voice toward the bus driver. Pet and Marnie pick up only the Clark or Betty or Ronnie they've come to know mean Gable and Bacall and Coleman. Then she half-inclines a sharpening profile toward them. "You girls don't remember the Matchless Minn Sisters?" They shake their heads less vigorously than when she asked the other times; with mixed suspicion and dismay she replicates their gesture. She has quick kaleidoscopic eyes, fine grained skin though she is far from young. She resettles her legs across the front seat, her back against the window and continues addressing the dry little driver who has abided her attentions with brittle courtesy through a million acres of corn.

In the peeling pink diner, over BLT's and warmish milk, Marnie says to Pet: "Anyhow, did you hear what Vi called us—you *girls?*" Trying only to press the pride out of her voice, she has managed instead to sound coy. "And that's the third time."

Pet refuses to smile. "We could easily pass for sisters, Ma." She levels her dark, serious gaze, giving the words the weight of a minor but distinguished truth.

Blushing, her mother reaches unconsciously for the confirming cloth of her Springsteen shirt, the patched travelling jeans. Her hair—several shades darker than Pet's—in a thick braid down her back; no makeup. Since her husband's death, she has lost weight and that flat, finished look.

The hard fact of Marnie's youth strikes Pet for the very first time. When she was born her mother would have been fifteen, which is Pet's age now. The connection rocks her momentarily; then she presses on to the irresistible point: "Why can't we be sisters? Who'd it hurt? This trip isn't, well, isn't like regular life anyhow." Her eyes mellow with persuasion, go soft sand-brown in her pale upstater's face.

"Oh, I know what you mean!" Marnie says breathlessly, her face strangely luminous. She leans forward across the table. "Throwaway days," she says, furtive and whispery.

"What?"

"I mean don't the days seem, like sheets you just tear off a roll. Paper towels. Disposable days."

"Of course," says Pet. "That's just what I'm trying to tell you. We can do anything we want. Who the heck cares?" And couldn't they, by a slight shift of image, get lost among strangers, anonymous even to themselves, and the dogs of sorrow would prowl the aisles in duped confusion. Oh they'd give grieving the slip, they would.

The farmer eats alone at the counter. They'd overheard his inquiries before ordering. "Any garlic in these eats? I hate garlic. Don't yiz have no head cheese, no souse?" He always asks these questions and he always settles for the same thing, known components, Campbell soup and a stack of white bread, with applebutter if they have it.

And then their attention is drawn to the booth across the aisle where Vi is busy running her customary suppertime scam. "You dare hand me a check for this—gristle! This larrrd!" She points to something grey and miniscule on the white plate.

"But you ate the whole thing!" the waitress wails.

"Is Trailways going to wait on me till you duffers learn to cook? Not hardly. Gotta eat when you can, gotta survive, dontcha know?" And off she goes, huge black patent tote swinging, calabash hips indignant in floral stretch pants; out she goes huffing into the hot huffy Illinois eventide.

As usual, having eaten abstemiously and fast, the stationers have gone trundling off in search of local flora, and the bus driver, eyeing his watch, clucking like an uncle, has to go out casing the vacant lots. He comes back in a mutter, the ladies in tow. They clutch limp, unpretty bouquets to their bosoms, the cornflowers already beginning to close and pale to the lavender-grey of coming dusk.

* * *

Without being sure what, Pet watches for something; and there is, in her mother, a sudden new tension and spring, a certain struggling flippancy. Swinging into the bus, she flops down in the aisle seat, forcing Pet to clamber awkwardly over her teasing knees; they laugh, as if this is some kind of leg trap they always set for one another.

Fifteen minutes out of the parking lot, Pet opens the month-old PEOPLE she'd found in the pink diner. Slouching, they jam matching flat-top knees into Vi's seat and talk derisively, deliciously about this international beauty, that soap star, until Marnie remembers she never could read on the bus.

"Barfing section in the back," Pet teases, adding, "Marnie" as a kind of test. "Can't take you anywhere, Margaret Mary."

But Marnie is looking out past her to where the winey sunset is making mountain mirages on the flat, vast plains: Marnie is far away. Pet's father had been a tender man though not much for "gainful" work. He made tiny dovetailed boxes and an alarming number of maple end tables: the way he'd rub his cheek against the polished wood, the time they came from Sears to repossess his lathe. His dark moods, his delusions of better days ahead. He dreamed of taking them to live in New Mexico, though they had no car.

Or maybe it's California in her mother's eyes, *their* California: the tiny fenced yard of Uncle Jack, the art classes "down the road," a landscape free of woodpiles, soft blossomy air—a world painstakingly concocted from all the usual sources and from the gentle coaxings of Jack himself. ("There's lots of work, we'll make room. Pettie, put a bug in my sister's ear.") For months they'd offered each other these good visions (and a fortune to be made on game shows) but each retained, cherished, in a way, the gritty New England pessimism they'd acquired on top of their reckless French Canadian verve: it was the habit of hardship and the icy winds off Lake Champlain; it was a kind of mystical leave they had to have before they could go. Each laid by a private store of hazards: smog, traffic and the Santa Ana winds. West Coast weirdos. And all the time they were making plans, media prophesies of California doom frightened them and thereby mollified their qualms.

Now the inevitable endless layover. To Pet and Marnie St. Louis will forever be the smell of candy wrappers and urine, the indiscriminate sleep of old men. When they pull out of the depot, there is a new driver, young, rangy, impudent. Vi works on him a long time, poking here, probing there; but he is apparently not interested in the weather, the price of Dentu-Cream or the triumphs of the Matchless Minns. Instead he speaks laconically into a hand set, the voice of middle America scratching back at him.

"Name, please," Vi demands in official tones, flipping back her notebook cover, pen at the ready.

"Claycomb," he says, his shoulders rocking time to some private rhythm.

"Clay?"

"Comb," he says, "as in hair. C-O-M-B."

Twisting around to Pet and Marnie, she says, announcingly, "Think he knows he can get in biiiiiiig trouble using them things on the job?"

"What things?" Marnie asks.

Her voice squeaks with impatience, "Why, Cee bees."

Marnie thinks to smile. "*I'll* never tell."

Vi snorts and turns silent and then, having no other audience for the time being, relents: "You girls on vacation?"

"Well . . .", Marnie begins.

Pet quickly says, "Yes, we are."

"Where to?"

Marnie says, "Escondido" and Pet knows she can be trusted now not to say that they are moving west and everything they own rides below, in the belly of the bus. It seems to Pet an irreparable oddity: People moved their things in vans, themselves in cars or planes. Buses didn't dump you off on the far side of the continent and just leave you there.

"Where *you* headed?" Politeness, a bright stain on Marnie's voice.

"Why, Hollywood," she says: *You have to ask?* "I'm always promising this one or that one . . ."

Pet shoulders in closer, her eyes eager. "Who is it this trip, Vi—Barbie Streisand?"

"Ooh, no. She's real snotty, dontcha know? No, this is more a consultation kind of thing."

Pet twangs "Wowww!", elbow-taps her mother's ribs.

"Writers, producers—ya know."

"Wow," Pet hears her mother say. *Wow:* tenuous as a breath. The farmer inks another centimeter off the trip.

* * *

The dark, the monotony, the rolling rhythm make a dusky potion. By half past nightfall, almost always, most of the bus is asleep. Now up and down the aisle several glowing points, like the tips of lit cigarettes, cast narrow conical beams for reading or dispelling dread.

"Damn it, Marn, he should have left us better."

"Well, you know how André was. And maybe it was my fault too. I never made it my business, I mean money matters, bills . . ." She drew her lips thin and tight. "You're right, dammit, he should have!" In the small light their eyes meet and fill with wonder that they should talk so, that here is a parenthetical place outside of grief and guilt and the terrible shared vision of the young man grown bony as a crone, trembling fingers trying to wrest from the plump bunch a single Concord grape. They lower their voices and Pet steals timid drags from Marnie's cigarette, then braver, more bitter ones. Here where no eye pries or cries for them, they whisper and laugh together, make unmemorable mischief, exactly like the best kind of sisters.

Later, when the farmer has removed himself to the quieter middle of the bus, Pet wastes no time usurping the vacancy. Thus, for their second night on the road they occupy separate seats, no mean achievement when the bones ache for space. Pet falls asleep in comfort, opposite her mother, and awakens hours later to the steep quiet, the clean pressing knife blade of pure speed as the bus makes up time on some deserted stretch. She becomes slowly aware of strange doings in the front of the bus, a shadowy *pas de deux.* Vi with her notebook and pen, the driver hunched protectively over his wheel, body splayed a bit to the right. Now Vi settles back, eyes closed; *his* eyes hold hard to Vi's likeness in the rear-view mirror. She slows her breath, starts to snore; he begins to relax himself: Surprise! Vi springs up, catching him off guard. Claycomb lurches forward, hiding, Pet guesses, the speedometer. Vi is left holding her pen like a dart. Marnie wakes; in silence they watch the pantomime play again and again to the same stalemate. They watch, their smiles tricky in the thin dark; their witness secret and insubstantial; and as soon as Vi sets aside her pad, gives it up, they drop into the slurry of communal sleep.

"You know what I used to hate?" Pet says this to Marnie as the bus sits stalled in the cool white Missouri morning just north of Joplin. She says this in the manner of someone discussing bygone days, a closed case.

"What's that?" Having mastered the simple ploy of pretending to be asleep when new passengers board, they continue to hold last night's seats.

"When you used to peel off those little scabs of orange rind for your tea and make me eat the mangy-looking orange before it went bad."

"Well now, that's real tough, isn't it?"

"And creamed hard-boiled eggs for dinner."

"Poor little orphan girl!"

"And when you'd grab my arms and shake the daylights out of me."

"I never hit you."

"I know, I know—but you used to dig your nails into my wrist. Cripes, you'd leave those little half-moon claw marks. Once you even broke the skin."

Marnie turns abruptly away, rubs her coarsened knuckles, the leathery palms. Chain saw, splitting axe. Garden mud makes deep grooves. She chews on a hangnail. "Oh I'm sorry, heartily sorry! Wanna hear what *I* used to hate?"

"No." Pet shoves over near her window, Marnie against hers. They draw their knees up and occasionally glance slyly across the aisle until their eyes, sparking like struck flints, set their sulks flaring into self-conscious smiles. They pelt one another with gum wrappers and the little throw-pillows Marnie had wisely rescued from the tag sale at the last minute. Five hours later—after wrong parts, puzzled mechanics, an aggressive quiet broken only by the laughing man and Vi's grumpy insistence that "Claycomb musta burnt the engine out"—they are back on the road.

They run together now through crumbling parking lots, down highways a piece to set their footprints in the never-before-never-again dust. Occasionally Pet feels her mother break pace with a single skip, like a grace note or a missed heartbeat. A caught-back sob.

Guessing how Vi will get out of paying for meals becomes a game. In Silver Creek she finds a shirt button in her mashed potatoes; they watch her fish the same button out of a bowl of chili in Henryetta, Oklahoma. In the bus they play-push, argue over the window. They buy one can of beer and with the ebullient pluck of novice scofflaws, pass it back and forth in a paper bag. When people ask, Pet says meet my nutty sister, Margaret Mary. She is out from under, hooray, and freer still the widow who has not been a child since long before the year she stopped growing.

* * *

Every day by late afternoon the bus bloats with light, thick and yellow as chicken fat. Over-worked air conditioners start to falter; the air becomes dense and dangerous. Having managed all this time to avoid sharing her space, Vi is better off than most. Nonetheless she mops her brow and holds forth testily from the front seat. "Circulitis" she tells all claimants, pointing to her legs as if they were resting patients under her professional care.

The new driver is something of a gift to Vi: large, expansive, a compulsive tipster, the kind who would know where to get the best deal on chicken wire. They converse aggressively, each waiting with taut forbearance for the others "breath." She boasts and pries, he enlightens. Of the two, Pet soon understands that Vi is the more clever, having deftly steered him onto private grounds: his income, his wife's "bust." He goes on to digestive upsets and preventive medicine: "Get rid of your aluminum cookware," he says.

"Yeah?"

"Cancerate yer innards sure."

"I'll be darned."

Into this rugged patter comes a third: the farmer shuffles up and sits down on the double step just behind the driver. Pet and Marnie catch only the hard edges of certain words, the bus driver's robust replies. The men laugh easily, the way men laugh on park benches or front stoops, notes full of corny jokes and gentled philosophies.

Vi takes out her compact, dabs viciously at her chin and her nose, snaps it shut: fair warning. Fretfully, she plucks at her hair and reaching down, tugs on the man's shirt as if she would pinch him right off the step. When he squints up at her, she points to the sign over the mirror: *NO TALKING TO OPERATOR WHILE VEHICLE IS IN MOTION.*

He draws air through his teeth. "Uh-oh," he says, rising slowly to his feet. "Well, make good out," he tells the driver. He slaps his hand over his mouth; in mud-colored work boots, he clomps back to his seat.

"Ya hate to be mean," Vi explains to them, "but the law's the law." Then she swivels forward again. She tells the driver about Bogie in the quaint bistro; he comes back with roughage, Serutan and "your leafy greens."

Night comes again; surely it should frame some aspect, mark some completion of the trip but aside from the slippage of light through endless declensions, nothing changes, life grinds on, continues perversely against the simple human hunger for a clean distinction between beginning and end. Oklahoma or maybe Texas now; the landscape has been toughening up for some time. Long past, the whispery cornfields, the homely Missouri hills; just before dark there was yellow dust and a barrenness that clogged the throat.

The back of the bus rocks with shenanigans. The soldiers got on way back at Fort Leonard Wood. A skinny old woman, drunk and full of sass, has somehow strayed into their midst. Just to get her scolding they call her Old Beulah, Mother Thunderbird, and once one of them pulls on the door handle and won't let her out of the toilet; she claws and squawks and scratches. All the little lights click on and the spinsters crane back, their faces lit with wan delight, like the faces of entertained invalids.

At the next stop Pet looks out at the bedraggled bunch waiting in the rain to board. "Damn!" she says, growing ever more at ease with her franker style. "So much for deluxe accommodations." She slips across the aisle into the seat with Marnie, doubling up against the onslaught.

Everybody finds a place but one slender girl in velvet sandals and a peasant dress. She stands shyly up front waiting for Vi to make room. When it appears such is not likely, the bus driver says, "Sorry, ma'am, you'll have to share."

Vi points to the leg. "Doctor said to keep it raised."

"You got two tickets, lady?"

"Of course not, but . . ."

"You'll have to let the little girlie sit down."

Vi goes "Tssssk," glances quickly back as if to nudge the sleeping forces for good and right. "Tssssk." She waits, fingers drumming on her thigh.

Pet leaps to her feet. Sensing Marnie stiffen, she reaches an arm back, to warn her off while she lights into Vi. "Lady," she says, "you don't own this bus. What's the kid supposed to do, sleep in the aisle?"

The forces for good and right have been minutely roused: they stare dumbly at the small spectacle up front, all but Loomis, who solemnly shakes his case, shuffling tomorrow's chuckles. Vi's eyes are hopping hens from one face to the other. "My, but isn't she the scrappy one," she says generally. Then she turns sternly to Pet. "If you must know, young lady, I happen to be an official *spotter,* for the bus company."

"Get serious! Why would Trailways hire some old looney takes up *two* seats . . ." Pet is hardly prepared for the shrinking, the pale porcelain breakable face aging before her eyes, and she is not expecting the sudden knot around her wrist, the digging in of something like scratchy old buzzard claws. Then Marnie's harsh whisper: "Sit down, Perpetua. Now!" Uh-oh, the mother is back. Relief easing her the way stillness slackens a kite, Pet slips quietly back into her seat. Vi heaves a mighty sigh before shoving over to let the newcomer sit down.

* * *

It is three, maybe four, and somewhere out there Texas is sluicing away beneath them. Crowded feed lots, refineries, miles of tufting badlands. At one point they'd overheard the new girl say yes, of course, she'd heard of the Minn Sisters. She spoke little and attended Vi's gibber with a lovely tidal rhythm, inclining her head and slowly withdrawing, swaying close, pulling back, nodding, laughing, touching long white fingers to the older woman's sleeve. And now she sleeps with her head on Vi's shoulder. Vi is plainly awake but does not move, does not jostle the fragile tie.

Pet is tinny with insomnia; despite the Texas heat pressing in, she feels chilled. It has been a while since the new driver boarded. His voice hangs in the air with the cloying menace of bug fogger: "Yew are now in the Yewnited States of Texas. We main what we say. Get caught with hooch ah hay-of ta toss ya offa cheer. Ah'm required by law to turn ya in for smokin the bad stuff. Ya'll hayve a nice trip, hear?"

The door to the john opens and shuts, the distant watery sough of livestock. Marnie opens her mouth to say something. She is hesitant, shaky. Pet is terrified she will mention *him.*

"When I was growing up," she begins, "I only ever had one nice—*good* thing. It was a little black plastic box called a Viewmaster. I won it at nine, for knowing my Catechism cover to cover."

Pet smiles, but uneasily.

"It came with just three slides. The banquet room of some English castle. Snow White looking awful sweet in a circle of little men." She drew a tattered breath. "What you had to do was hold the little box up to light, you see, and suddenly, there they were, these wonderful visions, realer even than your mama's kitchen. Close but far away, I don't know, I'm not saying this right."

"You said three. What was the third one?"

"It was . . . ," she says. "It was . . ." Pet leans in, to hear better, but also out of some need to put herself protectively between Marnie's thin voice and the bullyish hulk of the slow-tongued driver.

"It was a Christmas scene," Marnie says. "Madonna and child surrounded like Snow White, but with beautiful angels. Dozens of them, large and small in pink satin robes. Their wings were way too big for them."

"Angels, Ma?"

"I kept reaching up into the light. I thought I could touch them. Those wings would be so soft, like hoot owl feathers."

"Hmmmmmm," says Pet. She cannot imagine her mother at nine. She does not want to.

"Somebody took it," Marnie says. When she turns to Pet her eyes are shiny, wide with fighting tears. "I took my Viewmaster to school, to show it off. Somebody stole it out of the cloakroom."

Pet draws back from her mother's endangered face. "God, ma, that was so long ago. It was just a toy."

Marnie's mouth begins to work and her throat moves as if gulping something furry and live.

"Please don't." Pet clamps her hand across Marnie's mouth. Stop! Don't let the dogs of sorrow out. Rouse just one and all the losses of a lifetime will stir and moan and leap out of your soul. "Shhhhh, Ma, we'll be there soon."

"Where?" her mother asks, cheeks gleaming wet, eyes bewildered in the chittery glow of some blinking Texas town.

Where? Where is *there?* Pet sits dumb, tongue-tied, caught without an answer to a first-grade question. She tries to summon her uncle's house, but all she can picture is some wobbly tropical hut waiting to wrap them in alien leaves, in the shocked light of impossible seasons. Her eyes sting with impotence and confusion. So far from home. Where is home? Only these miles of swimming dark, the strangers. Snow White. Snow.

Soon there will be snow where her father lies, and temperate winds will perplex their hearts and shame their faces. And someday Vermont itself will settle like an old grave in her chest. And she will be sun-streaked and muscular, given to living, too busy to mourn. Mourn now, Perpetua, now.

Already the future rushes under the bus's wheels, feeding itself like rough cloth. Pet and Marnie press close, fold together as might any clever collapsible travelling thing. The new girl shifts against Vi's shoulder and the daughter rocks the mother to sleep in her arms. How strange, thinks Pet, how unstable are the arrangements of things. Circles open and circles close, losses gather, and already the future is dust under their wheels. Pet has never felt more alive, or more alone.

She closes her eyes lightly, as one does when there's little wish for sleep. Everything slips from her but the sleek slide of night. Her own heartsounds, the slower pulse of breath, burly engine throb and thrumming rubber, countless rhythms pumping together, the spinning seamlessness of the trip. If they continued west they would reach the east and pressing on, the west. And around and around. Without trying, she has arrived at a place that is nowhere and everywhere, and where nothing, *nothing* is missing. If only she dare, she might lay her cheek against the night and listen, all the lives that ever lived brushing soft as wings in the silent bus.

She dares only wakefulness. Opening her eyes, she looks around. What she sees, she sees with the raw clarity of the absolutely new. Marnie's braid has come undone. The farmer snoring under a duckbill cap. The *real* sisters rest primly clutching their weeds. Loomis's laugh bag doubles as his pillow. How brave and blameless the soldiers look in sleep. The fragile curve of the young girl's neck.

And a man called André, sanding, sanding, nose to the grain, sawdust furring his knuckles, red dust on his brow. *Oh, Papa, when are we going to be there?*

No matter that he keeps to himself, holds to his craft. Pet knows what she knows. Home is where they came from and home is where they are going and *there* is now, and maybe they are already there.

Her watching is deep as sleep; she could as well be dreaming. Tomorrow she will speak nothing of circles or angels or time. Tomorrow she will forget how they gathered, living and dead, the delicate web of breath connecting them. Tomorrow she will check the farmer's map. She will want sweet rolls and cold milk and room for her growing legs. Tomorrow is smoke at the window. She watches the window with a quiet, vibrant expectancy. She thinks of Marnie nudging her Viewmaster into better light. Night shreds and drifts off to wherever night goes. What's left is light. The soft shock of New Mexico, terra cotta mesa lands, polished tables as far as the eye can see.

T. Alan Broughton

ASHES

When Damon White finished his second cup of coffee, he decided to go directly to his cabin rather than sit on the clubhouse porch and read his newspaper. He left the dining room without pausing to chat with any of the other members. Even though he had arrived two days earlier he had not relaxed, and in casual conversations he often found himself inattentive.

At the far end of the porch Harold Corvallis had set up his easel and was painting once again the graceful outlines of Noonmark. Damon paused with one hand on the railing of the steps. He felt his father's presence vividly. The colonel was always present to Damon in a blurred manner, especially here where they had spent so much time and had been thrown so close together in those final years of ill and querulous dependency. Damon had spent Augusts in the small cabin on the club grounds, pushing his father's wheelchair on its fixed rounds of porch or lobby, meals in the main dining room, walks along various pathways past tennis courts or bowling greens. Once when Damon's father asked Corvallis how he could bear to paint the same heap of rocks and trees so often, Harold had replied *You wouldn't think it was wrong if I were Japanese.* The colonel had snapped *The hell I wouldn't. We wouldn't have a Jap in this club.* Damon's father had served in the second world war, and he never forgave Japan. But he had not been a colonel at any time. Friends from his college days had started calling him that long before he ever donned a uniform. Since his earliest days Augustus Hoar White had been assertive and demanding.

In his apartment in New York, Damon had decided that this should be his last summer at the club. The decision had seemed simple and necessary, but now that he was in his cabin again, back in the all-too-familiar surroundings, he was not certain he was emotionally ready to give the place up.

Such forms of ambivalence had always made his life difficult. *My son,* his father had announced to the companion whom he had paid to accompany Damon one summer after his release from Payne-Whitney, *has always been weak when defending himself against his own feelings. The worst enemy,* and the colonel had stared hard at the small bottle of Damon's pills, *is always the enemy within.*

Colonel White's forte had been tennis: he possessed a devastating overhead smash that always raised a dust of lime on the line farthest away from his opponent, unless he chose to aim for the kneecaps. Damon had taken his childhood tennis lessons seriously, tried out for the team at Exeter, and from time to time stood on the opposite side of a net from the colonel. But the farther he advanced into adolescence, the more such contests were tainted with attempted parricide. Once he understood that, he blocked the sin with double faults and backhands soaring far beyond the baseline. *My boy,* Colonel White said once to the junior singles champion at the end of the last August tournament Damon ever entered at the club, *has more talent than you, son. That's in his genes. But he never had the killer instinct.*

Even walking through warm patches of sunlight to the cabin, Damon shuddered at the phrase, the way his father could make it sound like the last punch to the face of a defenseless Benny Paret. Was his lack derived from his mother's genes? He would never know for certain because she had disappeared before much more could be recorded in Damon's mind than gentle thin-fingered hands and many long necklaces with variegated beads that he loved to tangle his own hands in. When he was six, she died, leaving a vacancy that not even the most well-intentioned of his father's companions could begin to fill, and certainly not those other women who read or sang or scrubbed him into shape to face the evening meal. That was followed by brief after-dinner conversations with a father who used his hands so diligently at a place called the office that they could only make the most terse gestures at home—removing the stopper of a decanter, snipping the end of a cigar, ruffling the hair on the top of Damon's head before he was tucked in bed by Minnie or Evita or Peg, a gesture he felt in the roots beneath the scalp until sleep distanced him by one more night from the first six years of his life. If only he could once again hear his mother's voice, specific words, but his frozen memory was obdurate.

The maid had already tidied his bedroom, and what few books he had disarranged on the table the previous evening were neatly lined up. Damon stood in the living room, a rusticated square of stone and oak and doorways branching off to bedrooms with cedar closets. By family rights the place was his in August. Damon's mother had been here too, introducing his memory to the resinous odors of old blankets, the chirping of tree frogs, the crickets' rasp.

He always showered after breakfast, and now he took off his clothes and folded them carefully. Habits. Rituals. When they were muddled, the mind too could become confused. Through the open window of his bedroom, he could hear the high pulsing calls of the Morrison children taking turns swinging each other violently in the hammock. Damon sighed. He knew their play always ended in shouts and tears.

But he could not free himself from the memory of that summer after Payne-Whitney. *He's perfectly all right now,* the colonel had said to the young man across the luncheon table, a stranger to them both who had been recommended by the minister downtown to help keep an eye on Damon. *The problem never amounted to much anyway, did it, old boy?*

His father had tried not to believe in Damon's breakdown, but subsequently had relented enough to lapse into less stern expressions in his son's presence like "old boy" or once even "buddy" followed by a rough clasp on Damon's shoulder. Damon knew how extremely difficult such gestures were for the man to wrest from the grip of his ultimate belief that mental illness was merely submitting to frail tendencies any man should sternly subdue.

It's really the pills we worry about now, eh, Damon? Tell him about the pills.

Damon turned to the young man's face, letting it remain blurred. He found it embarrassing that his father's voice carried to nearby tables.

I take pills.

They waited. The young man stared at a triangular sandwich denuded of crusts and nestled in garnishing parsley. The colonel's fingers drummed impatiently on the tabletop.

For his nerves, you see. And they make him a bit groggy. Forgetful. Found him wandering up Noonmark yesterday. But on the trail at least. Do you play tennis or golf, Mr. Anthony?

No sir.

Just as well. They tell me competition's not the thing for Damon right now. Well, it's up to you fellows. But I'd suggest fishing. Damon always liked that. Try the river. Do you like to fish, Mr. Anthony?

Yes sir.

I suppose most of you fellows use worms. Can't use 'em in our stretch of the river, though.

I tie flies, sir.

Hell, Damon. Hear that? A real fisherman. Why don't you see who can get us the biggest brookie for dinner?

Damon focused now on the young man's face, and for a moment he stared back. What Damon saw was pity, not merely purchased but genuine, that softening gaze a person turns on a cripple. But he was so used to seeing that expression in the past months, as well as being talked about by others in his presence as if he were not there, that he merely reached up to make certain his bow tie had not twisted off line.

They began fishing below the dam at the Lower Lake, a place Damon had loved since childhood because he could stand on the high log bridge below it and look at eye level along the surface of the lake's water. Today it was a calm sheet, bearing only minute glints of ripples, and the steeply wooded and rocky mountain-sides seemed to be squeezing in slowly, extruding the water toward him and the frail white birches along the nearby banks. He became, in mid-bridge, the focus of the whole landscape, even of the sun directly above the cleft. Here as a child he had believed that one day if he touched the water it would turn to gold and all the evil persons would drop into stones hunched against the molten swirl.

I caught one. The voice piped against the uneven slap of water falling over the log dam onto the boards below and the pools where fat stocked trout nudged each other lazily to gulp at an ambundance of drowning insects. Mr. Anthony was holding up a fish, finger hooked through a gill. *Come on. There's plenty.*

On the bank Damon assembled his rod, gazed at the box of flies, and chose one he knew was inappropriate for the season. By the time he had successfully crossed the slithery stones his companion had caught another and was stuffing it in his canvas creel.

Jesus. I've always wanted to fish this river. Legally, I mean.

Damon spoke as little as possible because when he did, his tongue moved with swollen numbness. After the first few weeks in Payne-Whitney when he had known and remembered nothing but a succession of days and nights in which the dead were alive and eager to talk, the living were sleepwalkers, beds grew straps to keep him there, and the sheets sometimes flapped ineffectually around him like the broken wings of a gull, Damon had become an expert practitioner of minimal discourse. This was a reversal for a man who had spent the previous eight years gabbing away each week on the radio as Uncle Ralph, the kindly, garrulous host of the children's program *Please Pretend.* The nod, the slight slant of head to right or left with eyes open or closed, the pursed lips of doubt, the bit lip and raised eyebrow were all he would share with Doctor Salvador for many a session of questions and dumb-show responses.

Would you mind, Damon said, choosing and laying down his monosyllables as if they had the ability of marbles to roll away, *if I go first down the stream to fish?*

Suit yourself.

Until he was out of sight Damon paused to cast from time to time, making certain his fly landed on the bare backs of rocks. He did not blame the young man for his greed, in fact blessed it since that permitted his escape. Around the first bend he took down his rod, clambered up the bank to the trail and began walking slowly downstream, through the quiet beaver meadows where he startled a solitary deer, past the falls where he paused on rocks close to the base to let spray scatter over his face and arms, walking on until the path left the brook which cut more deeply into the gorge. On a high slanting rock where the ancient hemlock and spruce clung to stone and shallow soil, he sat and stared down at white water and its distant thundering. When a white-throated sparrow began repeating its clear-toned intervals, he was certain he had never heard anything more perfect, and he wept.

Well, the colonel said when the largest trout was served up for dinner that night in a delicate sauce of butter and parsley, its white flesh tinged toward pink, *I knew Mr. Anthony had to be a good fisherman, but I didn't expect him to skunk you, old boy,* and then he laughed through a red face to show how his words were intended only as a joke.

Damon stepped out of the shower and burrowed his face in the white towel with the club monogram. His father, even in the city and ever since Damon could recall, had been in the habit of holding himself unflinchingly erect, on parade, beneath a cascade of absolutely cold water. Once as a child Damon had said admiringly, *I don't see how you can stand it.* The colonel had barked a laugh of pleasure, and henceforth Damon was permitted to watch his father take the shower. The colonel's stern profile refused to grimace or mutter. The man did not curtail even one motion of soaping and rinsing. When he was seven Damon had tried it, held still with gritted teeth and nails cutting into his palms, until, pale and mottled with bluish patches, he had curled into his bed, admitting he would never be able to emulate his father.

A sharp cry. Silence. Then shrieks. Nate Morrison stood focusing his howls into the interior of the Morrisons' cabin. His brother Rory sat, legs crossed, a stick grasped upright—a small chieftain scowling at a cowardly subject who had ducked an assigned lashing. Mimi Morrison arrived in her bathrobe, ample figure blurred by the screen, rings on her fingers glinting in the light. Recriminations began, and Damon turned away. This could go on all morning.

Damon loved children, but with a love that contained a component of fear. A whole morning could be shattered again and again by these raucous outbreaks unless Rory and Nathan were trussed up and dragged to the lake. Buckling his belt, pausing to hear the voices becoming subdued, Damon could imagine walking out into the no-man's land between his cabin and theirs, beckoning to the boys, sitting with them under the white pine to tell them stories. Or they would join him on a walk in search of lady's slipper or toads or maybe a red fox with kits. This was a living version of *Please Pretend,* an Uncle Ralph unleashed from his microphone and script.

But the voice coming over the radio had always been more effectual than his presence. He had been permitted once to stand behind a curtain in a large room filled with children listening to a recording of one of his programs. He was accustomed to the way the voice did not sound like his own, but he had not realized what power it had over his listeners. The bodies still squirmed and talked and giggled through the theme and plug for some glutinous morning cereal, then Uncle Ralph chuckled, said, *Well, hello there boys and girls,* and the children grew still, leaned to the loudspeakers, were silent except for the hypnotized few who called out, *Hello, Uncle Ralph.* The voice began a tale. *Once upon a time, boys and girls, in a country very, very far away, there lived an old man who had two children, a girl and a boy.* A page or two later he shifted his Ralph voice and spoke for all the others—the harsh stepmother, the beguiling but evil wandering tinker, the frog who could speak.

When he was fired, Damon took the memory of that occasion with him more than any other moment during his career, although he never confronted his employers with it. For them the simple fact was that Damon White, no matter how good the voice was, could not translate to television.

What? the colonel had said, at first outraged at the network. *Fired?* But that lapsed eventually into a conversation at dinner two nights later and only a few days before Damon's breakdown. *Hell, son. We both know you don't have to work for a living, but what will you do with your life if you can't even hold onto a job telling fairy stories to kids?* Damon had said, *Nothing.* His father appeared almost frightened when Damon began laughing and repeated the same word again and again in hilarious shouts.

The listeners were the children he loved—rapt faces, minds concentrated—perhaps because he identified himself with them then, sinking into some image he carried in himself of his own attentive being, leaning into memory, into stories that were the patterns of everything he did not and never would quite know. He longed to take Nate and Rory by the hand and lead them off through some door in the hillside where all three of them could sit and listen and understand over and over again.

But he had also watched until the end of the recording when the children's bodies began to twist and turn again. He walked away from the curtain utterly depressed. What had the storytelling been for? Again they were pinching and scratching, surreptitiously kicking. The harmony was achieved only on the surface. The shattered interior was so deep that Damon could never reach it. His chest tightened; he dreamed at night of ominous motions in the other rooms of houses too large for him to secure by completely inhabiting. Even now Nate and Rory hunched together over something on the ground between them, hands on their knees, heads turned down. Why could that picture empty him toward dread, turn them into stone figures of a sculpted group, the rest of whom, hidden by the slope, were doing something fierce and utterly forbidden?

He managed to spend most of the day by himself, walking along the river or reading in his cabin. But at dinner he saw Dede Raynes across the room, sitting with the Plimptons. She smiled and waved. He had known her sister Phyllis, and last winter Phyllis Raynes had died. No longer Raynes, actually—Phyllis Birge, since many years ago she had married, then divorced, a local man. She had died locally also, and most of her adult life was an unusual swerve away from the people he knew, as if the summer landscape they had all come to love in childhood had suddenly reached out and claimed one of them for its own, and in doing so had put a barrier between her and the rest of their set as sturdy as the steep ridges of the mountains. For the rest of his dinner Damon tried to avoid looking at Dede, but a loud persistent tinkle of glass drew his attention to her. She was standing and hitting her wine glass with a spoon.

"Your attention please, could I . . . thank you."

Not as slim as she used to be, always chunkier in figure than the sylphlike Phyllis anyway, but still she was attractive with her neatly coiled black hair and the skin that always seemed slightly tanned. She held a small piece of paper that she glanced at from time to time.

"I know many of you were acquainted with my sister Phyllis, and I want to take this opportunity on behalf of the family to thank you for your lovely letters we received following her death. Many of you expressed a desire to share our grief and regretted that you could not attend her funeral service. I'm happy to tell you that there will be a service at the Congregational Church this Thursday, and I hope any of you who wish to join us will do so at three o'clock. Since this is not in the nature of a formal religious ceremony, which, as you know, was held here last winter, we would like to bring her to mind by sharing some music and memories, and I have also asked Dr. Blanton to say a few words. I will be singing, and I'm sure I can talk our old friend Damon White into accompanying me. Also perhaps he'll play a tune by Chopin that Phyllis always liked?" A slight turn to him, silence, with everyone waiting, but Damon was staring at her, dumbstruck. "Well, I'm asking any of you who have some memories to please come and share them with us. Very informal, as I said. Thursday, three o'clock," and then into the hubbub of renewed conversation she shouted, "Thank you."

She did not sit down but dodged through the other tables until she came to his.

"I tried to call this morning, Damon. You will be a sweetie, won't you?"

"I can't, Dede."

Her hand was on his shoulder. "Of course you will. What would the occasion be without you? And what would they think if you didn't?"

"I tell you, Dede, I don't play Chopin anymore. I never did very well."

"Try, Damon. For Phyllis."

To his dismay the hand shifted across his shoulder to flutter on his neck, brush his ear, and withdraw, leaving a trail of some scent as it passed his face.

"There's so much more about this than you know or than I can explain now. They had a service here last winter. The daughters, their father, some of the village people. Mummy and Dad and I weren't even invited. Please. At least let me pick you up tomorrow. I'd have a drink and talk now but I'm due at the Baileys' already. Stupid little party for Doris and Bill Armitage. I'll bring my music. We can try out the Schubert, and talk. I know what I'm doing is right. For her."

The annoyance at the end was incomprehensible, surely meant

to pass beyond him to some other target. He could not stop looking into those steady eyes whose pupils were so startlingly black against a shimmering blue.

She shook a finger at him. "Remember. Dede is relentless." The eyes, the face swooped at him, lips plucking once at his, the quick peck of a bright-plumed but predatory bird. "Tomorrow. Eleven. Ta-ta."

He did not watch more than her first few paces because those hips swung against the revealing silk of her skirt as if to taunt him.

Damon tucked his hands behind his back and strode out, looking neither right nor left until he was well past all the other guests and onto the path to the cabin. There he sat on the steps in the dim light from living-room windows, his head cupped in his hands. It was not Dede he thought of, but her sister . . .

Phyllis sat with him by the brook, late August, where one slim maple on the opposite bank had flushed into deep scarlet well before the proper season. Damon told her the dry month and cold nights had confused the tree into thinking it was fall. He moved on to express to her the nature of confusion, of yearning, and he was lyrical and elliptical and totally uncertain of what he should do next. Although he was twenty-four and she only nineteen, he feared she had more experience. He had never made love to a woman, had hardly ever held one close until that summer.

Finally she interrupted breathlessly, not letting him talk any more about trees or seasons. *It doesn't matter whether we're certain we love each other. I want you.*

She took him by the hand, and they walked to a ferned glade in the woods. Damon tumbled into a state of shocked separation from his body when he saw her unbuttoning her shirt, knew that he was doing the same to his own, and that they were stretching out beside each other on the ground. Beyond the blurred side of her face and a whorled ear, the wing of a butterfly was crushed into the matted leaves—yellow with a small orange and black circle like an unblinking eye.

When he saw her in subsequent years, at the club or downtown after her marriage to Birge, they talked only of weather, her daughters, the recent fire at the general store, how time passed. She seemed to have no idea of the intensity with which that afternoon was fixed in his mind. *Mummy,* one of her children had shrilled at his knees once, *why has he got such a funny name?*

I never would have named you Damon, the old man muttered, that strong-featured head now looking powerless in the nest of pillows, the white hair disheveled. *Her idea. What kind of name is that, I said? Not a man's name. Foreign sounding. In her family, she said. Names are important. Sorry for you at school. They called you sissy. What did she expect?*

Damon leaned over the book in his lap. He had been reading to his father and wished to continue.

Never could argue with her and win. Ah, Christ, Damon. She should not have died. I needed her.

And me? he wanted to call out but instead said *The Battle of Corregidor. Chapter Three. In the fall of . . .*

I don't want to die.

The face turned to him. Damon tried not to look but a glance defeated him. The eyes would not let him go. Never had his father spoken like this. The face opened out into an expression of helpless terror, mouth spread downward and trembling, voice issuing from a mask.

I tell you I dream at night. It comes down over me. Black and heavy and I can't move. No one listens to me. You must. Don't leave me. I will not die.

The book slipped. The heavy volume of history struck the edge of the bed, then Damon's foot, and made a hollow beat on the floor as if the house were a drum set sturdily on the earth, signaling. The man was weeping, his face still stiffly immobile. Damon too could not move. They stared at each other, waiting for an answering signal, but only his father's shuddering intake of breath sounded in the room.

When the coffin was lowered, ropes straining, past the dense and cleanly sliced sides of clay soil until only its massive black top with bronze fittings showed, Damon was reminded again of the jerk of his shoulders forward to catch the book slipping away, pulled down between them, and everything about that afternoon of the burial pressed downward with crushing weight. The body in its coffin was not turning to dust but condensing, the unbreathing earth above it was pressed by a shaft of solid air. His father did not die. He folded under.

Damon rose and went into the cabin. He turned out all the lights, undressed, paused by the door to what had always been his father's room, then rolled himself in the blanket and slept. There were no dreams that he remembered except that when he woke he believed for a moment that the day before had been a dream and that soon the voice of the colonel would call gruffly through the flimsy paneling just as he had the day after that one evening of weakness. For the months of tenacious living left to him he returned to his unbending self. His last words, stuttered against the pressure of a stroke that left him nearly speechless for the final weeks, had been *G—get out. I wa—want to do this alone.*

While Dede drove, Damon listened, staring forward at the road because someone ought to, and from time to time he almost grabbed the wheel himself to correct her tendency to drift into the opposite lane as she talked to him.

"I want her ashes," Dede said, "that's all. That's not asking much. I don't care if they come or not, the little bitches, but I want her presence, what's left of it—not just our memories. Don't you see?"

"But why haven't they buried them, scattered them, done something?"

"*Why* is not a question I lavish on that side of the family, Damon dear. Why did Phyllis even marry that hulk Gus Birge rather than just having the twins and letting him lumber off into the woods again? Why, once she divorced him, didn't she just pick up and take the girls and go back to Connecticut instead of settling into this godforsaken place? Mummy and Dad kept begging her to move into an apartment near home. It would have been easy enough."

"Too easy?"

"She wasn't just stubborn. She was perverse."

Dede turned the car onto the driveway, stopped to shift into low gear, and began a slow ascent, avoiding the worst of the exposed rocks and eroded channels. The road ended abruptly in a cluster of stunted spruce and birch, a bungalow that did not pretend to be more than a serviceable place to sleep and eat. At the farther end the yard dropped to a sweeping view of valleys and ridges. She yanked on the brake, cut off the engine, and breathed deeply.

The girls had come out of the house and were waiting for them. They walked slowly across the lawn as Dede's voice warbled in her best mezzo-soprano, "Here he is, girls, just as I promised. Damon, these are Phyllis's daughters. Leona and Danda. Mr. Damon White."

They were not identical twins, for which Damon was grateful. Leona was smaller, built more like her aunt but even more sturdily, and after tugging Damon's hand she stuffed both of hers into back pockets and perched forward on the top step. The face tended to withhold any expression, as if wary. Her sister Danda, however, was tall and willowy like Phyllis, and if her face had been a little less narrow, the nose less aquiline, she might have been her mother's twin. He looked at her so long that she glanced away to Leona, a shy swerve of eyes, and his reaction to her beauty was almost resentment. It seemed unfair that she should have taken her mother's best features and heightened them with some other lines and colorations, the contributions of Gus Birge.

"We've heard of you." Leona kept the voice toneless, not revealing whether what they had heard was good or bad.

"We've even *heard* you." The slightest hitch of a speech impediment made some of Danda's vowels sound swallowed.

"Where, I wonder?"

The girls gave way as he advanced up the steps, preceding him onto the porch. Beyond its edge was a sheer plummet to the glinting brook below. He gripped the rail hard.

"On the radio," Leona was saying just behind his shoulder. "They had you on the Nostalgia Hour last week. Danda thought you did the princess best. But if I'd been a kid, your witch would have kept me up all night."

"It must be weird," Danda murmured over his other shoulder. "Hearing yourself like that. Would you listen if they did all the programs again?"

"No."

"I wouldn't either. I hate my voice when I hear it. And I want everything to be new," she said.

The bitterness of his own laugh surprised him. "Lots of luck."

He turned around slowly, hesitating to put the drop behind him. He could feel it in the tightening of his thighs, the slight lean forward to pull away from it. The girls were both dressed casually in jeans and open-necked men's shirts, their feet bare, but Leona's flesh pushed and spread against her clothes, and Danda's body seemed self-contained in the slim, curved outlines of denim and cotton. Still dizzied, he could not forgive her mother for standing naked by the bank of an August brook, their love-making done, her shocked laughter as she plunged into the water coming back to him for months afterwards.

"You make it sound impossible," she said.

"Nothing is very new after we've lived for a while."

". . . 'Scuse," Dede murmured. "I'll just go to the bathroom a sec," and she disappeared through the glass doors into the dim living room where Damon could vaguely make out sofa and chairs, a stone fireplace and sharp square of light from the side door to the driveway.

"Mother," Danda continued, "said nothing ever seemed exactly the same to her and that was one of the reasons she did not want to die. Even the pain, she said, was different."

Both the girls stared at him unblinking, as if the statement of Phyllis's death was made to judge his reactions.

"I'm sorry about your mother. That must have been difficult for you."

"It was." Leona jerked her head toward the living room behind her. "And they didn't help. Our aunt, the grandparents. Where were they when she needed them, when she married Dad and had us and moved here?"

"We don't want to go into that, though." Danda leaned one hip onto the wooden table behind her, crossed her arms. "We don't mean to seem unreasonable, but we won't lend Aunt Dede the ashes because we don't agree with this whole second service for the summer people, and Dad doesn't either."

"It's a form of prejudice, don't you think?" Leona's tone, in spite of the words, was becoming less truculent. "I mean, if you wanted a service for her, you would have been welcome to come last winter. We didn't turn anyone away. And this kind of splitting of things into summer people and winter people is exactly what she had to take a lot of crap from all her life, you know? We won't be part of that, or let her seem to be either."

A breeze rose straight up along the cliff to the porch bearing the tang of sun-baked rock from the brook far below.

"But all this isn't your fault." Danda moved now to sit fully on the table, her bare feet off the deck. "Aunt Dede gets a bee in her bonnet and she can't be stopped. It makes Dad furious, but I told him just to let her have her service. We won't be there, and that's enough. And I know you're doing this because you care about her, so I don't want you to think we're angry at you for it. We asked Aunt Dede if we could meet you. She always liked you."

"How do you know?" He tried to keep the voice toneless.

Leona shrugged. "Nothing special. I remember one of those times we saw you on the street downtown. We started laughing because we thought you looked funny. I mean it was mid-August and here was this guy in a plaid jacket and bow tie and saddle shoes and all. We'd only seen that in old movies."

"Leona."

"He asked, didn't he? Anyway, she said we shouldn't make fun of you. She said you were just eccentric and you were a nice guy who'd gone through some tough things. She said you'd always been good friends."

As if the long drop behind him were pulling his blood away, he felt slowly drained, light-headed. He stared at Danda who was frowning, those thin delicate features perplexed. He turned suddenly, put both hands on the railing, and leaned out toward the sweep. He knew the mountains as well as his own name—Hedgehog, Wolf Jaws, Armstrong, Gothics, Saddleback, Basin, a thin peel of Haystack's ridges, then Marcy's perfect cone.

"Well, mountains don't change, do they?" he said loudly to the uprush of breeze that died before he finished speaking. "Tell me their names."

They were standing close behind him, one on each side, and he yearned to pull them closer against him. He could not change himself sufficiently to make such a gesture, but their shoulders brushed him, and he was grateful for that.

"If you start furthest left," and Leona stuck a finger decisively into the landscape, "that's Hedgehog."

Chanting together in their different voices, they named the peaks, and to slow the progress at one point, Damon said, "Which, the one with the sharp top or the rounded one?" and then, even more mercifully, Danda moved, stood directly behind him, breathing against his neck, along his cheek, and with both hands on his face from behind, she directed his gaze, moving one hand slowly forward past his eyes. He aimed along the fine hairs of the forearm, along the finger until it ended in bright warm air, the blurred shape of a mountain. He ached, not to hold her body or the body she had been delivered from, but to hold everything they could see for only a moment before letting it go forever.

"I see," he murmured, utterly emptied by her motions as she pulled away from him. "I see."

"I hate to break this up. But I'm going to have to go to the florist's in Lake Placid."

Dede stood by the stairs with her keys dangling.

"Won't you come back sometime, Mr. White?" Danda was saying. "You should meet Dad."

"I'd like to. Thank you."

Damon waved a hand, they both lifted theirs, and then he was groping for his seat belt as Dede backed out the drive, putting a screen of trees quickly between them and the figures posed as if for a snapshot. Dede did not say anything and Damon was glad to let her concentrate on driving. She began humming softly, something she was much better at than full-voiced destruction of Schubert. As the car turned off the highway onto the drive to the club, she began chanting in a high childlike voice.

"Ring around the roses, a pocket full of posies, ashes, ashes, we all fall down."

She laughed and repeated the verse. Damon found the tone and her nervous playfulness irritating.

"I learned it as *A-tishoo! A-tishoo! We all fall down."*

"Of course you did, Damon dear. That's the English version. Much more correct. You've always been very correct."

She stopped below his cabin and turned off the engine.

"You loved Phyllis, didn't you? Old flame. That sort of thing. But I've always wondered. Did you ever make love? She never would tell me that summer."

With his face turned to the side window he listened to the engine ticking as it cooled.

"I'm sorry your mission failed," he said politely.

He looked with longing at the cabin door. He could shut it and sit inside and think. Even if he had to leave suddenly that evening, he would find a way of avoiding the service tomorrow. He was glad Dede did not have the ashes, although the idea of the daughters clinging to them in their home seemed wrong as well—or dangerous for them in ways he could not yet understand.

"Not at all. The ashes are mine, and this is where you come in again, my dear."

He smiled back deliberately at her smile. "I think you underestimate their determination."

"I think you underestimate mine."

"I never have."

"Good. Come along."

He clambered out and came around the back where she was opening the trunk. She stooped in, lifted an urn, thrust it into his hands that clutched involuntarily because if he had not, she would have let it drop.

"I'll have to ask you to keep this until tomorrow. I'm afraid that once they know the urn is gone, they'll be pestering me."

The smooth bulge pressing against his chest made him want to cry out sharply. She slammed the trunk lid and backed away.

"You stole it."

"See you tomorrow."

"Take it back."

Her door slammed.

"Wait," he yelled.

The car flung loose gravel against his leg, her fingers were waggling, and she swerved just in time to miss the pines. A door slapped on the neighboring cabin. Ames Morrison stared toward him from the shadow of his porch and nodded wordlessly. Damon strode into his cabin trying not to run, dropped the urn on a couch and wiped both hands up and down against his chest, unable to stop staring at the squat object tilting back against the armrest.

The urn filled the whole room with an expanding pressure. His hands had begun to shake at his sides, and he clasped them to make his fingers stop jerking. He thought he was afraid of it and that he would rush forward, seize it, run to his own car, and drive back to the twins. But then he realized he was not trembling with fear, but with excitement. The ashes were his.

Certainly he would leave before the service. He did not doubt Dede's determination, and also did not doubt his weakness if she netted him again. In arranging inescapable situations, she was obviously most creative. No, distance was the only way. But he did not find that dissatisfying. Distance from all of this world was what he needed. The more he gazed around him, the more the room was drained of familiarity or attraction. The couch with its bamboo arms and legs deserved to be part of a decaying hotel's lobby. Everything he knew of the objects and the patina of their history were being absorbed by the urn on the mantel. Small as it was, it could contain a lifetime.

That evening, having decided to forego dinner since he was too happy with his solitude, Damon sat on the porch or in the living room and was pleased by the way the cabin and landscape, in exchange for his pledge of leaving, were giving up secrets to him that he had forgotten. The metal candle stand on the wall with the face of a dragon had been his friend and defender in his childhood fantasies. The volume of Colvin's topographical survey squashed into a dark corner of the bookcase was a book he had read avidly when he was ten, since it turned the surrounding countryside into a place as fiercely unknown as Africa. When a breeze blew, a hole appeared between the upper limbs of the pine grove, displaying the peak of Noonmark as if in an oval brooch. He thought of packing, but decided there was no hurry. He knew at various times that this was merely euphoria, but accepted that. He regretted he had no peanuts left for the tame chipmunk that scampered timorously to his feet on the porch.

The evening was calm and clear. He watched the Morrisons climb into their station wagon, all of them dressed in their finest. When he stood, a faint dizziness reminded him that he had not eaten since breakfast. He pulled his chair toward the last square of sunlight and sat so that it fell onto his lap and down his legs like a quilt patterned with clustered bursts of pine needles. Nothing mattered but this utter calm, not securely his yet, but recoverable—perhaps, he even dared to think, his for longer periods and with greater intensity. He could not destroy it even when he allowed himself to look over the lawn toward the vacant tennis courts, the gray and green expanse of the clubhouse, thinking that he would never see all this again.

The light faded into dusk; the dusk lapsed into night and

blinking of fireflies above the lush dewy grass by the courts. He went back into the cabin but did not turn on the lights. As he stretched out on the couch, he held onto one fixed point of reference—that somehow to give the urn back would be bad for all of them. If he could burn the cabin down in a quick stroke of fire, he would.

They are yours, Damon, his mother's voice was saying, but it was muffled because between him and her face was the clear globe of a fishbowl filled with water, wavering green plants, five bright goldfish that flashed in their new home. Not just her face, his father's too, were side by side, staring through water and fish and plants.

Mine?

Yours, she said again.

Feed them, his father's mouth was saying underwater. *Go on.*

Damon lifted the little can above the water and dusted some food onto the surface. It floated a moment, then soaked through the surface and began drifting down. The fish darted in and out through the particles, blotting specks with their quick mouths. He focused through the bowl onto his parents, but their eyes were on the fish, not him, their faces intent. They were not breathing. Two fleeting faces. Quavering. Drowning.

What? her voice kept saying when he ran around to her and hid his face against her belly. *What's wrong?*

Damon rose quietly and stood in the dark room. In all those years he had not been able to hear his mother's voice, but now memory had thrown it up to him as if not even a door stood between them. He groped to the bureau, found his flashlight, and flicked it on. He lifted the urn and walked out the back door. He took the road into the reserve, aware of how loudly his footsteps sounded in the silent woods. He remembered how the giant woke when his lyre cried out in alarm, how he roared in anger and Jack tumbled down the vine.

It was three miles up the road and through the woods to the dam. He held the urn tucked under one arm, flashlight in the other hand. A deer crossing the road froze, eyes bright, then it leapt away, crashing up the slope. A startled bird fluttered with a single cry from its ground nest when he turned onto the trail. The air was chill, the sky fiercely starred. To keep his own fear of the dark in check he began talking.

"Once upon a time there was a poor widow who lived in a lonely cottage . . . ," and when he spoke for them he tried to make Rose-Red sound like Leona, and Danda was Snow-White, but in some speeches he had to pause and start again to get it right. The dwarf gave him no trouble at all and never had. The evil characters were always easiest to do. He stopped reciting when the sound of the river neared. Soon the woods thinned away and he could see the wide cleft of the lake, the line of wooden bridge. The water splashed unevenly over the dam.

He walked carefully across the broad stones to the largest pool. His light shone down through clear water, fish darted away from it, but in the deepest part two long, wide trout hung still, moving only their fins. Their backs were nearly black.

Damon knelt on the wide rock, turned off the light, and placed it beside his leg. He waited for his eyes to become accustomed to the night. At first he saw only the brightest stars, vague contours of peaks, the block of watery blackness that was the dam. Then the sky began to reveal its layers, the mountains cut clear lines in sharp descent to the lake, trees nearby took shape, and even the rocks rose out of pools of reflected stars.

His father's face drew nearer, from above, unshaven and grieving. Hands seized him under the arms and lifted him, and now his own face brushed against harsh stubble, but it did not hurt him because he needed to feel those arms around him, and the disheveled face seemed far more soft than when it was shaved to a marble hardness. In his ear the choked voice said: *She's gone, boy, gone. It's just you and me now.*

He pried at the lid, paused, then dipped his hand in, and sowed ash onto the water. But most of it was too fine to grasp and so he held out the urn and turned it over. The ash and pieces of bone scattered the reflected stars into smaller fragments. The water heaved slightly, then swirled although the fish did not break the surface. Briefly a sinuous turmoil made disordered waves around the pool.

He looked down at the palm that had held her ashes. They had been so weightless, nearly air. There was nothing to say, but he wanted to listen, not to the voices that memory might give to him, but to the water and quick passing of wind that altered the waves falling over the dam and shook leaves with a rush. He listened and did not close his eyes, and kept listening until a faint light began to blur the stars on the edge of the eastern ridge. He hid the urn under the lip of the bank. The first high water would take it away.

The batteries died before he reached his cabin, but by then the light was strong enough for him to see tan windings of the dirt road. He would call the sisters before he left, perhaps visit them. They would still be sleeping now. He imagined them lying together in a large bed, not grown women but the children their mother might lean over in the middle of the night. Leona's face would be pressed into a pillow, Danda would have clasped her sister's arm to her face, lying back peacefully, mouth slightly open. He and Phyllis stood looking down.

He would tell them what he had done. Above all he would tell them how for a moment before they woke he was certain they were two sisters asleep in the dark woods. He had come to wake them from their dangerous enchantment.

Charles Baxter

SAUL AND PATSY ARE PREGNANT

A smell of spilled gasoline: when Saul opened his eyes, he was still strapped in behind his lap-and-shoulder belt, but the car he sat in was upside down and in a field of some sort. The Chevy's headlights illuminated a sky of dirt, and, in the distance, a tree growing downward from that same sky. Perhaps he had awakened out of sleep into another dream. "Patsy?" he said, turning with difficulty toward his wife, strapped in on the passenger side, her hair hanging down from her scalp, but, from Saul's perspective, standing up. She was still sleeping; she was always a sound sleeper; she could sleep upside down and was doing so now. The car's radio was playing Ray Charles' "Unchain My Heart," and Saul said, "You know, I've always liked that song." His voice was thick from beer and cigarettes, and he knew from the smell of the beer that this was no dream because he had never been able to imagine concrete details like that. No: he had fallen asleep at the wheel, driven off the road, and rolled the car. Here he was now. A thought passed through him, in an unpleasant slow-motion way,

"Saul and Patsy Are Pregnant" appeared originally in *The Iowa Review* and is reprinted from *A Relative Stranger,* stories by Charles Baxter, with permission of the author and the publisher, W.W. Norton & Company, Inc.

that the car was tilted and that the ignition was still on; he switched it off and felt intelligent for three seconds, until the lap belt began to hurt him and he felt stupid again. No ignition, no Ray Charles. His mind, often anxiety prone, was moving slowly down a dark narrow alleyway cluttered with alcohol, fatigue, and the first onset of shock. Probably the car would blow up, and the only satisfaction his mother would receive from this accident would come years from now, when she would tell people, when they were all through reminiscing about Saul, "I *told* him not to drink. I told him about drinking and driving. But he never listened to me. Never."

"Patsy." He reached out and gave her a little shake.

"What?"

"Wake up. I rolled the car. Patsy, we've got to get out of here."

"Why?"

"Because we have to. Patsy, we're not at home. We're in the car. And we're upside down. Come on, honey, wake up. Please. This is serious."

"I am awake." She blinked, twisted her head, then looked calm. Her opal earring glittered in the light of the dashboard. The earring made Saul think of stability and a possible future life, if only he would normalize himself. Patsy smiled. Saul thought that this smile had something to do with guardian angels who, judging from the evidence, flew invisibly around her head, beaming down benevolence. "Well," she said, turning to look at him carefully, "are you all right?"

"Yes, yes. I'm not hurt at all."

"Good. Well. Neither am I." She reached up for the ceiling. "This isn't fun. Did *you* do this, Saul?"

"Yes, I did. How do we get out of here?"

"Let's see," she said, speaking calmly, in her usual tone. "What I think you do is, you release your seat belt, stick your arms straight up, then lower yourself slowly so you don't break your neck. Then you crawl out the window, the higher one. That would be yours."

"Okay." He held his arm up, then unfastened the clasp and felt himself dropping onto the car's ceiling. He pulled himself toward the side window. When he was outside, he leaned over, back in, and extended his hand to Patsy to help her out.

As she was emerging through the window, she was smiling. "Haven't you ever rolled a car before, Saul? I have. Or one of my boyfriends did, years ago." She was breathing rapidly. She dragged herself out, dusted her jeans, and strolled a few feet beyond the car's tire tracks in the mud, as if nothing much had happened. "Beautiful night," she said. "Look at those stars."

"Jeez, Patsy," Saul said, jumping down close to where she stood, "this is no time for being cosmic." Then he gazed up. She was right: the sky was pillowed with stars. She took his hand.

"Are you really okay?" she asked. "My God, feel that. You're shaking like a leaf. You must be in shock." She wrapped her arms around him and held him for half a minute. "There," she said, "now that's better."

"We could have died," Saul said, his mouth dry.

"But we didn't."

"We *could* have."

"All right. Yes. I know. You can die in your sleep. You can die watching television." She watched him in the dark. "I wish I had been driving. It's so warm, a spring night, I think I would have been singing along to the radio. 'Unchain My Heart'—I would have been singing along to Ray Charles and we'd be home by now." She leaned over. "Smell the soil? It's loamy. You know, Saul, you should turn the car's headlights off."

"Patsy, the car is *wrecked!* Look at it."

"Don't be silly." She studied the car with equanimity, one hand raised to her face, the other hand cradling her elbow. Patsy's equanimity was otherworldly and constant. Her psychic economy, combined with her beauty and persistent unexplainable interest in Saul, was the cause of his love for her; he loved her desperately and addictively. He had loved her this way before they were married, and it was still the same now. "Saul, that car is fine. We might be driving it tomorrow. The roof will have a dent, that's all. The car turned over slowly and softly. It's hardly hurt. What we have to do now is get to a house and call someone to help us. We could walk across this field, or we could just take the road back to Mad Dog's." Mad Dog was the host of the party they had come from. He was a high school gym teacher whose real name was Howard Bettermine. He looked, in fact, like a dog, but not a mad dog, as he thought, but a healthy and sober golden retriever.

"Patsy, I can't think. My brain has seized up."

"Well," she said, taking his hand, "I happen to like these stars, and that looks like a nice field, and I'd rather stay away from highway fourteen this time of night, what with the drunks on the road, and all." She gave him a tug on his sleeve, and he almost fell. "There you are," she said. "Come on."

* * *

As Saul walked across the field, hearing the slurp of his shoes in the spring mud, he saw the red blinking light of a radio tower in the distance, the only remotely friendly sight anywhere beneath the horizon. The fact that he was here at all was a sign, he thought, that his life was disordered, abandoned to chaos among Midwesterners, connoisseurs of violence and piety. He smelled manure, and somewhere behind him he thought he heard the predatory wing of a bat or an owl.

Sick of cities, Saul had come to the Midwest two years before from Baltimore as a high school history teacher, believing that he was a missionary of some new kind, bringing education and the higher enlightenments to rural, benighted adolescents, but somehow the conversion had gone the other way, and now he was acting like them: getting drunk, falling asleep, rolling his car. It was the sort of accident Christians had. He felt obscurely that he had given up personal complexity and become simple. He was like those girls who worked in the drug store arranging greeting cards. They were so straightforward that two seconds before they did anything, like give change, you could see every gesture coming. He was becoming like that. As a personality, Saul had once prided himself on being interesting, almost byzantine, a challenge to any therapist. But he had lately joined the school bowling league and couldn't seem to concentrate on Schopenhauer on those days when, at odds and ashamed of himself, he took the battered Signet Classic down from the shelf and glowered at the incomprehensible lines he had highlighted with yellow magic marker in college. When he did understand, the philosopher no longer seemed profound, but merely a disappointed idealist with a bad prose style.

"Saul?"

"What?"

"I've been talking to you. Didn't you hear me?"

"Guess not. I was lost in thought." He stumbled against a bush. He couldn't see much, and he reached out for Patsy's hand. "I was thinking about girls in drugstores and Schopenhauer and the reasons why we ever came to this place."

"Oh. That. If you had been listening to me, you wouldn't have stumbled into that bush. That's what I was warning you about."

"Thanks. Where are we?"

"We're going down into this little gully, and when we get up on the other side, we'll be right near that farmhouse. What's the matter?"

He turned around and saw, across the field, the headlights of his car shining on the upturned dirt; he saw the Chevy's four tires facing the air; and he thought of his new jovial recklessness and of how he had almost killed himself and his wife. He said nothing because he was beginning to feel soul-sick, a state of spiritual dizziness. He was possessed by disequilibrium; he felt the urge to giggle, and was horrified by himself. He had a sudden marionette feeling.

"Saul! You're drifting off again. What is it this time?"

"Puppets."

"Puppets?"

"Yeah. You know: the way they don't have a center of gravity. They way they look. . . ."

"Watch out for that stump."

He saw it in time to avoid it. "Patsy, how do you live in the world? This is a serious question."

"Stop it, Saul. You've been to a party. You're tired. Don't get metaphysical. It's two in the morning. You live in the world by knocking on the door of that farmhouse, that's what you do. You ring the doorbell."

They walked up past a shed whose flaking red door was hanging open, and they crossed the pitted driveway onto a small front yard with an evenly mowed lawn. A tire swing, pendulating slowly, hung down from a tree branch. Saul couldn't see much of the house in the dark, but as they crossed the driveway, kicking a few stones, they heard the bark of a dog from inside the house, a low bark from a big dog: a farm dog.

"Anti-Semites," Saul said.

"Just ring the bell."

After a moment, the porch light went on, yellow, probably a bug light, Saul thought; and then under the oddly colored glare a very young woman appeared, pale blond hair and skin, very pretty, but under the effect of the bulb, looking a bit jaundiced. With her fists she was rubbing her eyes with sleepiness. She wore a bathrobe decorated with huge blue flowers. Saul and Patsy explained themselves and their predicament—Saul was sure he had seen this young woman before—and she invited them in to use the phone. When they entered, the dog—old, with a gray muzzle—growled from under a living room table but did not bother to get up. After Patsy and the woman, whose name was Anne, began talking, it developed that they had met before in the insurance office where Patsy worked as a secretary. They leaned toward each other. Their voices quickly rose in the transfiguration of friendliness as they disappeared into the kitchen. They seemed suddenly chipper and cheery to Saul, as if a new party had started. He had the impression that women enjoyed being friendly, whereas for men it was an effort; at least it was an effort for *him.* He heard Patsy dialing a number on a rotary phone, laughing and whispering as she did so.

He was left alone in the living room. Having nothing else to do, he looked around: high ceilings and elaborate wainscoting, lamps, table, rug, dog, calendar, the usual crucifix on the wall above the TV. There was something about the room that bothered him, and it took a moment before he knew what it was. It felt like a museum of earlier American feelings. Not a single ironic sentence had ever been spoken here. Everything in the room was sincere, everything except himself. In the midst of all this Midwestern earnestness, he was the one thing wrong. What was he doing here? What was he doing anywhere? He was accustomed to asking himself such questions.

"Mr. Bernstein?"

Saul turned around and saw the man of the house, who at first glance still seemed to be a boy, standing at the bottom of the stairs. He had his arms crossed, and he wore a sleepy but alert look on his face. He had on boxer shorts and a tee-shirt, and Saul recognized, underneath the brown hair and the beard, a student from last year, Emory . . . something. Emory McPhee. That was it. A good-looking, solid kid. He had married this woman, Anne, last year, both of them barely eighteen years old, and moved out here. That was it. That was who they were. Saul had heard that Emory had become a housepainter.

"Emory," Saul said. The boy was stocky—he had played varsity football starting in his sophomore year—and he looked at Saul now with pleased curiosity. "Emory, my wife and I have had an accident, over there, on the other side of your field."

"What kind of accident, Mr. Bernstein?"

"We drove off the road." Saul waited, his hands in his pockets. Then he said the rest of it. "The car turned over on us."

"Wow," Emory said. "You're lucky you weren't hurt. That's amazing. Good thing it wasn't worse."

"Well, yes, but the car was going slow." Saul always sounded stupid to himself late at night. The boy's bland blue-eyed gaze stayed on him now, not moving, genial but inquisitorial, and Saul thought of all the people who had hated school, never liked even a minute of it, and had had a low-level suspicion toward teachers for the rest of their lives. They voted down millages. They didn't even like to buy pencils.

"How did you go off the road?"

"I fell asleep, Emory. We'd been to a party and I fell asleep at the wheel. Never happened to me before."

"Wow," Emory said again, but slowly this time, with no real surprise in his voice. He shrugged his shoulders, then bent down as if he were doing calisthenics. Saul knew that his own breath smelled of beer, so there was no point in going into that. "Do you want a cup of coffee? I'd offer you a beer, but we don't have it."

Saul tried to smile, an effort. "I don't think so, Emory, not tonight." He looked down at the floor, at his socks—he had taken off his muddy shoes—and saw an ashtray filled with cigarette butts. "But I would like a cigarette, if you could spare one."

"Sure." The boy reached down and offered the pack in Saul's direction. "Didn't know you smoked. Didn't know you had any vices at all."

They exchanged a look. "I'm like everybody else," Saul said. "Sometimes the right thing just gets loose from me and I don't do it." He picked up a book of matches. He would have to watch his sentences: that one hadn't made any sense. On the outside of the matchbook was an advertisement.

SECRETS
OF THE
UNIVERSE
*** see inside ***

Saul put the matchbook into his pocket, after lighting up.

"Were you drunk?" the boy said suddenly.

"No, I don't think so."

"Teachers shouldn't drink," Emory said. "That's my belief."

"Well, maybe not."

Saul inhaled from the cigarette, and Emory came closer toward him and sat down on the floor. He gave off the smell of turpentine; he had flecks of white paint in his hair. He rubbed at his beard again. "Do you remember me from school?"

Saul leaned back. He tried to think. "Sure, of course I do. You sat in the back and you played with a ballpoint pen. You used to sketch the other kids in the class. Once when we were doing the First World War, you said it didn't make any sense no matter how much you read about it. I remember your report on the League of Nations. You stared out the window a lot. You sat near Anne in my class and you passed notes to her."

"I didn't think you'd remember that much." Emory whistled toward the dog, who thumped his tail and waddled over toward Emory's lap. "I wasn't very good. I thought it was a waste of time, no offense. I wanted to get married, that's all. I wanted to get married to Anne, and I wanted to be outside, not cooped up, doing something, making a living, earning money. The thing is, I'm different now." He stood up, as if he were about to demonstrate how different he had become or had thought of something important to say.

"How are you different?"

"I'm real happy," Emory said, looking toward the kitchen. "I bet you don't believe that. I bet you think: here's this kid and his wife, out here, ignorant as a couple of plain pigs, and how could they be happy? But it's weird. You can't tell about anything." He was looking away from Saul. "Schools tell you that people like me aren't supposed to be happy or . . . what's that word you used in class all the time? 'Fulfilled'? We're not supposed to be that. But we're doing okay. But then I'm not trying to tell you anything."

"I know, Emory. I know that." Saul raised his hand to his scalp and touched his bald spot.

"Hell," Emory said, apparently building up steam, "you could work all your life to be as happy as Anne and me, and you might not do it. People . . . they try to be happy. They work at it. But it doesn't always take." He laughed. "I shouldn't be talking to you this way, Mr. Bernstein, and I wouldn't be, except it's the middle of the night, and I'm saying stuff. You know, I respected you. But now here you are, smelling of beer, and I remember the grades you gave me, all those D's, like you thought I'd never do anything in life except fail. But you can't hurt me now because I'm not in school anymore. So I apologize. See, I apologize for messing up in school and I forgive you for flunking me out."

Emory held out his hand, and Saul stood up and took it, thinking that he might be making a mistake.

"You shouldn't flunk people out of school," Emory said, "if you're going to get drunk and roll cars."

Saul held on to Emory's hand and tried to grip hard and diligently in return. "I didn't get drunk, Emory. I fell asleep. And you didn't flunk out. You dropped out."

Emory released his hand. "Well, I don't care," he said. "I was sleeping when you came to our door. I don't go to parties anymore because I have to get up and work. I sleep because I'm married and working. I can't see anything outside that."

Saul suddenly wanted Patsy back in this room, so that they could go. Who the hell did this boy think he was, anyway?

"Well, none of this is anything," Emory said at last. "I don't blame you for anything at all. Maybe you did me a favor. I had to do something in my life, so I got my mom and dad to buy us this farm, which we're paying them back for every month, every dollar and cent, even though we aren't farming it. But we might. I'm reading up on horticulture." He pronounced the word carefully and proudly. "You want to sleep on the floor, you can, or in the sofa there. And there's a spare bed upstairs, you want it."

"Sorry about the bother," Saul said.

"No trouble."

"I appreciate this."

"Forget it." Emory patted the dog.

"But thanks."

"Sure."

The two men looked at each other for a moment, and Saul had one of his momentary envy-shocks: he looked at this man, this boy—he couldn't decide which he was—his hair standing up, and he thought: whatever else he is, this kid is real. Emory was living in the real; Saul felt himself floating up out of the unreal and rapidly sinking back into it, the lagoon of self-consciousness and irony.

In a kind of desperation, Saul looked up at the wall, where someone had hung a picture of a horse with a woman beside it, drawn in pencil, and framed in a cheap dime-store frame. The woman was probably Anne. She looked approximately like her. "Nice picture."

"I drew it."

"You have real talent, Emory," Saul said, insincerely examining the details. "You could be an artist."

"I *am* an artist," Emory said, staring at his old teacher. He picked at a scab on his calf. He turned his back to Saul. "I could draw from when I was a kid." A baby's cry came from upstairs. Emory looked at the ceiling, then exhaled.

"What kind of horse is that?" Saul asked, in what he vowed silently would be his final effort at politeness this evening. "Is that any kind of horse in particular?"

Emory was going back up the stairs. Then he faced Saul. "Every horse is some horse in particular, Mr. Bernstein. There aren't any horses in general. You can sleep there on the sofa if you want to. Good night."

"Good night."

Whatever happened to the God of the Old Testament, Saul wondered, looking at Emory's house, the God that had chosen Israel above the other nations? Why had He allowed this scene to take place and why had He allowed Emory McPhee, this dropout, to make him feel like a putz? The Red Sea had not parted for Saul in a long time; he felt he had about as much clout with God as, perhaps, a sparrow did. The whole evening was a joke at Saul's expense. He heard God laughing, a sound like surf on rocks.

When Patsy and Anne came out of the kitchen, announcing that an all-night towing service was on its way and would probably have the car turned over and running in about half an hour, Saul smiled as if everything would be as fine as they claimed. Anne and Patsy were laughing. The flowers on Anne's bathrobe were laughing. God was, even now, laughing and enjoying the joke. Feeling like a zombie, and not laughing himself, but wearing the smile of the classically undead, Saul hooked his hand into Patsy's and went back outside. Some nights, he knew, had a way of not ending. This was one.

"How was Emory?" Patsy asked.

"Emory? Oh, Emory was fine," Saul told her.

* * *

On the days following, Saul began to be obsessed with happiness, an unhealthy obsession, but he couldn't get rid of it. His feelings had always been the city of dreadful night. He was ball-and-chained to his emotions. On some days the obsession weighed him down so heavily that he could not get out of bed to go to work without groaning and reaching for his hair, as if to drag himself up bodily for the working day.

Prior to his accident and his meeting with Emory McPhee, Saul had managed to forget about happiness, a state that had once bothered him for its general inaccessibility. He loved Patsy; that he knew. Now he believed that compared to others he was actually and truly unhappy, especially since his mind insisted on thinking about the problem, pouring over it, ragging him on and on. It was like the discontent of adolescence, the discontent with situations, but this was larger, the discontent with being itself, a psychic itch with nowhere to scratch. This was like Schopenhauer arriving at the door with a big suitcase, settling down for a long stay in the brain.

Patsy wasn't ordinary for many reasons but also because she

loved Saul. Nevertheless, she was happy. Early in the summer he stole glances at her as she turned the pansies over in their pots, tamping them out, and planting them in the flowerbeds near the front walk. Blue sky, aggressive sun. She was barefoot, because she liked to go barefoot in the summer—her tomboy side—and she was squatting down in her shorts, wearing one of Saul's old flannel shirts flecked with dirt, and the sleeves rolled up to the elbows. Her brown hair fell backward down her shoulders. From the front window he watched her and studied her hands, those slender fingers doing their work. Helplessly, his eyes took in the clothed outlines of his wife. He was hers. That was that. She liked being a woman. She liked it in a way that, Saul now knew, he himself did not like being a man. There was the guilt, for one thing, for the manly hobbies of war and the thoroughgoing destruction of the earth. Patriarchy, carnage, rape, pleasurable bloodletting and bloodsport: Saul would admit a gender responsibility for all these, if anyone asked him, though no one ever did.

Patsy wiped her forehead with the back of her hand, saw Saul, and waved at him, turning her head slightly, tilting it, as she did whenever she caught sight of him. She smiled, a smile he had gladly given his life away for, a look of radiant intelligence. She was into the real, too; she didn't ponder it, she just planted flowers, if that was what she wanted to do. Beyond her was the driveway, and their Chevrolet with its bashed-in roof.

Saul turned from the window—it was Saturday morning—and tried to think for a moment of what he wanted to do. Taking a Detroit Tigers cap off the front hall hat rack, he went outside and with great care put it, from behind and unannounced, on Patsy's head. "Save you from sunburn," he said, when she turned around and looked at him. "Save you from heatstroke."

"I want a motorcycle," Patsy said. "I've been thinking about it. We don't need another car, but I want a motorcycle. I always have. Women *can* ride motorcycles, Saul, don't deny it. Oh. And another thing." She dropped one hand into the dirt and balanced herself on it. "This morning I was trying to think of where the

Cayuse Indians lived, and I couldn't remember, and we don't have an encyclopedia to check. We need that." She put her hand over her eyes, to shade them. "Saul, why are you looking like that? Are you in a state?"

"No, I'm not in a state."

"A motorcycle would do wonders for *both* of us, Saul. A small one, not one of those hogs. Do you like my petunias? Should I have some purple over there? Maybe this is too much red and white. What would you think of some dianthus right there?" She pointed with her trowel. "Or maybe some sweet william?"

"Sure, sure." He didn't know what either variety looked like. Flowers seemed so irrelevant to everything. He looked down at her bare feet.

"Where *did* the Cayuse Indians live, Saul?"

"Oregon, I think."

"What do you think about a motorcycle? For little trips into town."

"Sounds okay. They aren't exactly safe, you know. People get killed on motorcycles."

"Those people aren't careful. I'll be careful. I'll wear a helmet. I just want to do it. Imagine a girl—me—on one of those machines. Makes you feel good, doesn't it? A motorcycle girl in Michigan. The car's silly for small trips. Besides, I want to visit my friends in town."

It was true: Patsy already had many friends around Five Oaks. She belonged here, but she always seemed to belong anywhere. Now she stood up, dropping her trowel, and put her feet on Saul's shoes and leaned herself into him. The visor of her cap bumped into his forehead. But she embraced him for only a moment. "Want to help, Saul? Give me a hand putting the rest of these flowers in? And what do you say to some dianthus over there?"

"Not right now, Patsy. I don't think so."

"What's the matter?"

"I don't know."

"You *are* in a state."

"I guess I might be."

"What is it this time? Our recent brush with death? The McPhees?"

"What about the McPhees?" he asked. She had probably guessed.

"Well, they were so cute, the two of them. So sweet. And so young, too. And I know you, Saul, and I know what you thought. You thought: what have these two got that I don't have?"

She had guessed. She usually did. He stepped backward. "Yes," he said, "you're right. What *do* they have? And why don't I have it? I'm happy with *you,* but I—"

"—You can't be like them because you can't, Saul. You fret. That's your hobby. It's how you stay occupied. You've heard about spots? About how a person can't change them? Well, I *like* your spots. I like how you're a professional worrier. And you always know about things like the Cayuse Indians. I'm not like that. And I don't want to be married to somebody like me. I'd put myself to sleep. But you're perfect. You're an early warning system. You bark and growl at life. You're my dog. You do see that, don't you?"

"Yes." He nodded.

After he had kissed her, and returned to the house, he took the matchbook he had pocketed at the McPhees' up to his study. At his desk, with a pair of scissors, he cut off the flap of the matches, filled in his name and address, and wrote a check for six dollars to the Wisdom Foundation, located at post office box number in Cincinnati, Ohio. Just to make sure, he enclosed a letter.

Dear Sirs,

Enclosed please find a check for six dollars for your SECRETS OF THE UNIVERSE. Also included is my name and address, written on the back of this book of matches. You will also find them typed at the bottom of this letter. Thank you. I look forward, very much, to reading the secrets.

Sincerely,
Saul Bernstein

He examined the letter, wondering if the last sentence might not be too ironic, too . . . something. But he decided to leave it there. He took the letter, carefully stamped—he put commemorative stamps on all his important mail—out to the mailbox, and lifted the little red flag.

He thought: I am no longer a serious person. My Grandfather read the Torah, my father read Spinoza and Heine and books on immunology, and here I am, writing off for this.

* * *

On his trips into town, Saul began to take the long route, past the McPhees' house, slowing down when he was close to their yard. Each time that he found himself within a mile of their farm, he felt his stomach knotting up in anxiety and sick curiosity. He felt himself twisting the coils of something like envy, but not envy, not exactly. Driving past, at evening, he occasionally saw them out in the yard, Emory mowing or clipping, their baby strapped to his back, Anne up on a ladder doing something to the windows, or out in the garden like Patsy, planting. They could have been anybody, except that, for Saul, they gave off a disturbing aura of unreflective happiness.

The road was far enough away from their house and the flaking shed so that they wouldn't see him; his car was just another car. But on a particular Friday, in early June, after work, he drove past their property and saw Emory in the front yard, in the gold twilight, pushing his wife, who was sitting in the swing. Emory, the ex-football player, had on his face (through Saul's binoculars) a solemnly contented expression. The baby was in a stroller close by. His wife was in a white tee-shirt and jeans, and Emory himself was wearing jeans but no shirt. She was probably proud of her breasts and he was probably proud of his shoulders. Anne held on to the ropes of the swing. Her hair flew up as she rose, and Saul, who took this all in in a few seconds, could hear her cries of delight from his car. Taking his surreptitious glances, he almost drove off the road again. Of course they were children, he knew that, and that wasn't it. They gave off a terrible glow. They had the blank glow of angels.

They lived smack in the middle of reality and never gave it a minute's thought. They'd never felt like actors. They'd never been sick with irony. The long tunnel of their thoughts had never swallowed them. They'd never had restless sleepless nights, the urgent wordless unexplainable wrestling matches with the shadowy bands of soul-thieves.

God damn it, Saul thought. Everybody gets to be happy except me. Saul heard Anne's cries. The sun was sweating all over his forehead. He felt faint, and Jewish, as usual. He turned on the radio. It happened to be tuned to a religious station and some choir was singing "When Jesus Wept."

* * *

"It's your play, Saul."

"I know, I know."

"What's the matter? You got some bad letters?"

"The worst. The worst letters I've ever had."

"You always say that. You whine and complain. You're such a whiner, Saul, you even whine in bed. You were complaining that time just before you spelled out 'axiom' over that triple word score and got all those points last winter. You do this act when we play Scrabble and then you always beat me." Patsy was sitting cross-legged in her chair, as she liked to do, with a root beer bottle positioned against her instep, as she arranged and rearranged the letters on her slate.

Saul examined the board. The only word he could think of spelling out was "paint," but the word made him think of Emory McPhee. The hand of fate again, playing tricks on him. Glancing down at the words on the board, he thought he saw that same hand at work, spelling out some invisible story. Saul always treated Scrabble boards as if they were fortunetelling equipment, with the order creating a narrative. Patsy had started with "moon," and he had added "beam" onto it. When she hung a "mild" from the moonbeam, he spiced it up with "lust," but she had replied to his interest in sex with "murky," hanging the word from that same moonbeam. "Mild" and "murky" came close to how he felt. His mother, Delia, had said so on the phone yesterday. "Saul, darling," she said, "you're sounding rather *dark* and *mysterious* lately. What's gotten into you?" He had not told her about the accident. She would have been alarmed and would have stayed alarmed for several months. She was a fierce mother, always had been. "I'm okay, Ma," he had said. "I'm just working some things through."

"You're leaving Five Oaks?" she asked hopefully.

"No, Ma," he had said. "This town suits me."

"All that mud, Saulie," she had said, dubious as always about the soil. "All those farms," she added vaguely. "You didn't have a *seder* this year, did you?"

"No, Ma. I told you we didn't."

"You didn't open the door for Elijah? When you were a little boy you loved to do that. When it came time in the service, you always ran for the front door and held it open and you—"

"—Saul," Patsy said. "Wake up." She shook him. "You're woolgathering."

"Just thinking about my mother," he said. He looked up at Patsy. "What are all those deer doing on our Scrabble board?" he asked. "Give me a swig of your root beer."

She handed it to him. He appreciated the golden color of the fine hairs on her arm in the lamplight. "I think I saw some, as a matter of fact," she said. "I thought I saw, what would you call it, a herd of deer, far in back, beyond our property line, a few nights ago. If you ever go back up to the roof, honey, give a look around. You might see them."

"Right, right." He couldn't put all five of his letters for "paint" on the Scrabble board. He removed the 't.' Pain. He held the four letters for pain in his hand, and he added them to the final 't' in "lust."

"Funny how 'pain' and 'lust' give you 'paint,' " Patsy said. "Sort of makes me think of the McPhees and the heady smell of turpentine."

They glanced at each other, and he tried to smile. A fly was buzzing around the bulb in the lamp. He was thinking of Patsy's new blue motorcycle out back, shiny and powerful and dangerous to ride. The salesman had said it could go from zero to fifty in less than six seconds. The hand of fate was ready to give him a good slapping around. It had announced itself. Saul felt a groan coming on. He looked at Patsy with helpless love.

"Oh, Saul," she said. She clambered into his lap. "You always get this way during these games. You always do." He saw her smiling in the reflection of his love for her. "You're so cute," she said, then kissed him a long time.

* * *

At ten minutes past three o'clock, he rose out of bed, half to get a glass of water and half to look out the back window. When he did, he saw them: just about where Patsy said they would be, far in the distance, beyond their property line, a herd of deer, silently passing. He ran downstairs in his underwear and went out through the unlocked back door as quietly as he could. He stood in the yard in the June night, the crickets sounding, the moon dimly outlined behind a thin cloud in the shape of a scimitar. In this gauzy light, the deer, about eight of them, distant animal forms, walked across his neighbor's field into a stand of woods. He found himself transfixed with the mystery and beauty of it. Hunting animals suddenly made no sense to him. He went back to bed. "I saw the deer," he said. He didn't know if Patsy was asleep. During the summer she wore Saul's tee-shirts to bed, and that was all; her arms were crossed on her chest like a Crusader. "I saw the deer," he said again, and, awake or asleep, she nodded. Two days later, the letter containing the secrets of the universe came from the Wisdom Foundation in Cincinnati. Saul sat down on the front stoop and tore the letter open. It was six pages long and had been printed out by a computer, with Saul's name inserted here and there.

Dear **Mr. Bernstein,**

Nothing is settled. Everything is still possible. Your thoughts are both yours and someone else's. Sometimes we say hellow to the world and then goodbye, but that is not the end and we say hello again. God is love, **Mr. Bernstein** , denying it only makes us unhappy. Riches are mere appearances. **Our thoughts are more real than hammers and nails.** We can make others believe us, **Mr. Bernstein** , if the truth is in us. Buddha and Jesus the Christ and Mohammed agreed about just about everything. Causing pain to others only prolongs our own pain. A free and open heart is the best thing. Live simply. Don't pretend to know something you don't have a clue about. You may feel as if you are headed toward some terrible fate, **Mr. Bernstein** , but that may not come to pass. You can avoid it. **Throw your bad thoughts into the mental wastebasket.** There is a right way and a wrong way to dispose of bad thoughts. Everything about the universe worth knowing is known. What is not known about the universe is not worth knowing. Follow these steps. Remember that trees will always be with us, mice will always be with us, mosquitoes will always be with us. Therefore, avoid mental cleanliness. Never start a sentence with the words, "What if everybody. . . ."

It went on for several more pages. Saul liked the letter. It sounded like his other grandfather, Isaac, the pious atheist, an exuberant man much given to laughter at appropriate and inappropriate moments, who offered advice as he passed out candy bars and halvah to his grandchildren. This letter, from the Wisdom Foundation, was signed by someone named Giovanni d'Amato.

Saul looked up. For a moment the terrifying banality of the landscape seemed to dissolve into geometrical patterns of color and light. Taken by surprise, he felt the habitual weight on his heart lifting, as if by pulleys, or, better yet, birds of the spirit sent by direct mail from Giovanni d'Amato. He decided to test this happiness and got into the dented car.

He drove toward the McPhees'. The dust on the dirt road whirled up behind him. He thought he would be able to stand their middle-American happiness. Besides, Emory was probably working. No: it was Saturday. They would both be home. He would just drive by and that would be that. So what if they were happy, these dropouts from school? He was happy, too. He would test his temporary happiness against theirs.

The trees rushed past the car in a kind of chaotic blur.

He pressed down on the accelerator. A solitary cloud—wandering and thick with moisture—straying overhead but not blocking the sun, let down a minute's worth of vagrant rainbowed shower on Saul's car. The water droplets, growing larger, actually bounced on the car's hood. He turned on the wipers, causing the dust to streak in perfect protractor curves. The rain made Saul's car smell like a nursery of newborn vegetation. He felt the car drive over something. He hoped it wasn't an animal, one of those anonymous rodents like mice and chipmunks that squealed and died and disappeared.

Ahead and to the left was the McPhees'.

As usual, it looked like something out of an American genre painting, the kind of second-rate canvas hidden in the back of most museums near the elevators. Happiness lives in such houses, where people like Saul had never been permitted. In the bright standing sunshine its midwestern gothic acute angles pointed up straight toward heaven, a place where there had been a land rush for centuries and all the stakes had been claimed. Standing there in the bright theatrical sun—the rain had gone off on its way—the house seemed to know something, to be an answer ending with an exclamation point.

Saul crept past the front driveway. His window was open, and, except for the engine, there was no sound: no dog barking. And no sign, either, of Anne or Emory or their baby, at least out here. Nothing on the front porch, nothing in the yard. He *could* stop and say hello. That was permitted. He could thank them for their help two weeks ago. He hadn't done that. Emory's pickup was in the driveway, so they were at home; happy people don't go much of anywhere anyway, Saul thought, backing his car up and parking halfway in on the driveway.

When he reached the backyard, Saul saw a flash of white, on legs, bounding at the far distances of the McPhees' field into the woods. From this distance it looked like nothing he knew, a trick of the eye. Turning, he saw Anne McPhee sitting in a lawn chair, reading the morning paper, a glass of lemonade nearby, their baby in the crib in the shade of the house, and Emory, some distance away, in a hammock, reading the sports section. Both of them held up their newspapers so that their view of him was blocked.

Quietly he crossed their back lawn, then stood in the middle, between them. Emory turned the pages of his paper, then put it down and closed his eyes. Anne went on reading. Saul stood quietly. Only the baby saw him. Saul reached down and picked out of the lawn a sprig of grass. Anne McPhee coughed. The baby was rattling one of its crib toys.

He waited for a minute, then walked back to his car. Anne and Emory had not seen him, and he felt like a prowler, a spy from God. He felt literally now what he had once felt metaphorically: that he was invisible.

When he was almost home, he remembered, or thought he remembered, that Anne McPhee had been sunning herself and had not been wearing a blouse or a bra. Or was he now imagining this? He couldn't be sure.

* * *

Patsy nudged him in the middle of the night. "I know what it is," she said.

"What?"

"What's bothering you."

He waited. "What? What is it?"

"You're like men. You're a man and you're like them. You want to be everything. You want to have endless endless potential. But then you grow up. And you're one thing. Your body is, anyway. It's trapped in *this* life. You have to say goodbye to the dreams of everything."

"Dreams of everything."

"Yes." She rolled over and made designs on his chest with her fingers. "Don't pretend that you don't understand. You want to be an astronaut and a Don Juan and Elvis and Einstein."

"No. I want to be Magic Johnson."

"Whatever. But you want to be all those people. You want to be a whole roomful of people, Saul. That's kid stuff." She let her head drop so that her hair brushed against him.

"What about you?"

"Me? I don't want to be anything else," she said sleepily, beginning to rub his back. "I don't have to be a great person. I just want to do a little of this and a little of that."

"What's wrong with ambitions?" he asked. "You could be great at something."

Her hand moved into his hair, tickling him. "Being great is too tiring, Saul, and it's boring. Look at the great ambition people. They're wrecking the earth, aren't they. They're leaving it in bits and scraps." She concentrated on him in the dark. "Saul," she said.

"Your diaphragm's not in."

"I know."

"But."

"So?"

"Well, what if?"

"What if? You'd be a father, that's what if." She had turned him so that she was right up against him, her breasts pressing him, challenging him.

"No," he said. He drew back. "Not yet. Let me figure this out on my own. There'd be no future."

"For the baby?"

"No. For me." He waited, trying to figure out how to say this. "I'd have to be one person forever. Does that make sense?"

"From you, it does." She pulled herself slightly away from him. They rearranged themselves.

* * *

The following Saturday he drove into Five Oaks for a haircut. When his hair was so long that it made the back of his neck itch, he went to Harold, the barber, and had it trimmed back. Harold was a pale, slightly bland-looking Lutheran, a terrible barber with a nice disposition who was in the same bowling league with Saul and who sometimes practiced basketball at the same times that Saul did. Many of the men in Five Oaks looked slightly peculiar and asymmetrical, thanks to Harold. The last time Saul had come in, Harold had been deep in a conversation with a woman who was accusing him of things; Saul couldn't tell exactly what Harold was being accused of, but it sounded like a lovers' quarrel, and Saul liked that. Anyone else's troubles diminished his.

By coincidence, the same woman as before was back again in the barbershop with her son, whose hair Harold was cutting when Saul rang the bell over the door when he entered. To pass the time and achieve a moment's invisibility, he picked up a newspaper from the next chair over and read the morning's headlines.

SHOTS FIRED AT HOLBEIN REACTOR
Iranian Terrorists Suspected

Shielded by his paper, Saul heard the woman whispering directions to Harold, and Harold's faint, exasperated, "Louise, I can do this." Saul pretended to read the article; the shots, as it turned out, had been harmless. Even though there had been no damage, some sort of investigation was going on. Saul thought Iranians could do better than this.

There was more whispering, which Saul tried not to hear. After the woman had paid for her son's haircut and left, Saul sat himself down in Harold's chair.

"Hey, Saul," Harold said, covering him with the white cloth. "You always come in when she does. How do you do that?"

"Beats me. Her name Louise?"

"That's right. The usual trim, Saul?"

"The usual. Harold, this time try to keep it the same length on both sides, okay?"

"I try, Saul. It's just that your hair's so curly."

"Right, right." Saul saw his reflection in the mirror and closed his eyes. He felt like asking Harold, the Lutheran, a moral question. "Harold," he said, "do you ever wonder where your thoughts come from? I mean, do we own our thoughts, or do they come from somewhere else, or what? For example, you can't always control your thoughts or your impulses, can you? So, whose thoughts are those, anyway, the ones you can't control? And another thing. Are you happy? Be honest."

The scissors stopped clipping. "Gosh, Saul, are you okay? What drugs have you been taking lately?"

"No drugs. Just tell me: are your thoughts always yours? That's what I need to know."

The barber looked into the mirror opposite them. Saul saw Harold's plain features. "All right," Harold said. "I'll answer your question." Then, with what Saul took to be great sadness, the barber said, "I don't have many thoughts. And when I do, they're all mine."

"Okay," Saul said. "I'm sorry. I was just asking." He tried to slump down in his chair, but the barber said, "Sit up straight, Saul." Saul did.

* * *

Days later, Saul is asleep. He knows this. He knows he is asleep next to Patsy. He knows it is night, that cradle of dreams, but the earth's mad companion, the moon, is shining stainless steel beams across the bed, and Saul is dreaming of being in a car that cannot stop rolling over, an endless flip of metal, and this time Patsy is not belted in, and something horrible must be happening to her, judging from the blur of her head. She is being hurt terribly thanks to the way he has driven the car, the mad way, the un-American way, and now she is walking across a bridge made of moonlight, and she falls. The door, Saul's door, is being kept open for Elijah, but Elijah does not come in. How will we recognize him? Saul's mind is not in Saul's head; it is above him, above his yarmulke, above his prayer shawl, his tallith. Patsy is hurt, she lies in a ditch. Deer and doubt mix with the murky roar of mild lust on the Scrabble board. And here, behind the barber chair, is Giovanni d'Amato, sage of Cincinnati, saying, "You shouldn't flunk people out of school if you're going to get drunk and roll cars." Saul, the child, is speaking to Saul the grown-up: "You'll never figure it out," and when Saul the adult asks, "What?" the child says, "Adulthood. Any of it." And then he says, "Saul, you're pregnant."

* * *

Saul woke and looked over at Patsy, still sleeping. He groaned audibly with relief that she hadn't been hurt. What an annoying dream. He had never even owned a tallith. After putting on his shirt, jeans, and boots, he went downstairs, and, taking the keys off the kitchen table, stepped outside.

The motorcycle felt quiet and powerful underneath him as he accelerated down Whitefeather Road. He had driven a motorcycle briefly in college—until a small embarrassing accident—and the process all came back to him now. This one, Patsy's new machine, painted pink and blue, 250 cc's, was easy to shift, and the machine gave him the impression that he was floating, or better yet, was flowing down the archways of dark stunted Michigan trees. His eyes watered, and bugs hit him in the face as he speeded up. He felt the rear wheel slip on the dirt. He didn't know what he was doing out here and he didn't care.

He turned left onto highway fourteen, and then County Road H, also dirt, and he downshifted, feeling the tight, close gears meshing, and he let the clutch out, slowing him down. On the road the cycle's headlight was like a cone, leading him forward, away from himself, toward something more inviting and dangerous. In the grip of spiritual longing, a person goes anywhere, travelling over the speed limit. The night was warm, but none of the summer stars was visible. Behind the clouds the stars were even now rushing away in the infinity of expanding space. Saul felt like an astral body himself. He too would rush away into emptiness. In the green light of the speedometer he saw that he was doing a respectable fifty. Up ahead the wintry white eyes of a possum glanced toward him before the animal scurried into the high grass near the road. Saul wanted to be lost but knew he could not be. He knew exactly where he was: fields, forest, fields. He knew each one, and he knew whom they belonged to, he had been here that long.

And of course he knew where he was going: he was headed toward the McPhees', that house of happiness, that castle of light, where everyone, man woman and child, would be sleeping soundly, the sleep of the happy and just and thoughtless. Saul felt blank, gripped by obsession, simultaneously vacant and full of shame.

He looked at his watch. It was past midnight. Their house would be dark.

But it was not. On the road beyond their driveway, Saul slowed down and then shut off the engine, holding on tightly to the handlebars as he stared, like the prowler he was, toward the second floor windows, from which sounds emerged. From where he was spying, Saul could see Anne sitting in a rocking chair by the window with their baby. The baby was crying, screaming; Saul could hear it from the road. And, in the background, back and forth, Saul could see Emory McPhee pacing, the all-night walk of the helpless father. An infant with colic, a rocking mother, a pacing father, screams of infant misery, and now the two of them, Anne and Emory, beginning to shout at each other over what to do.

Saul turned his motorcycle around, pushed it down the road, then started the engine. He felt better. He could have gone to their front door and welcomed them as the official greeter of ordinary disharmony. I was always just as real as they were, Saul thought. I always was.

On the left the broken fences bordering the farmland quavered up and down and seemed to start bouncing, visually, as he accelerated. The lines on the telephone poles jumped nervously as he passed them until they had the rapid and nervous movements of pens on graph paper marking an erratic heartbeat. Rain—he hadn't known it was going to rain, no one had told him—began falling, getting into his eyes and falling with cold precision on the backs of his hands. He felt the cloth of his shirt getting soaked and sticking to his shoulders. The rain was persistent and serious. He felt the tires of Patsy's motorcycle slipping on the mud, nudging the rear end of the bike off, slightly, thoughtfully, toward the left side. Then the road joined up with the highway, where the traction improved, but the rain was falling more heavily now, soaking him so he could hardly see. He came to a bridge, slowed the bike, and huddled in its shelter for a moment, until the rain seemed to let up, and he set out again. Accelerate, clutch, shift. He wanted to get home to Patsy. He wanted to dry his hair and get into bed next to her. He couldn't think of anything else he wanted.

A few hundred feet from his own driveway, he looked through the rain, only a drizzle now, and he saw, looking back at him, their eyes lit by his headlamp, the deer he had seen before, closer now, crossing his yard. They stood there, on his property. But this time, there was another, a last deer, one he hadn't seen before, behind the others, slightly smaller, as if reduced somehow. It was an albino. In the darkness and rain it moved in a haze of whiteness. Seeing it, Saul thought: Oh my God, I'm about to die. The deer had stopped, momentarily frozen in the light. The albino's eyes—it was a doe—were pink, and its fur was as white as linen. The animal flicked its tail, nervously hypnotized. Its terrible pink eyes, blank as stars at the center, stared at him. Saul turned off the engine and the headlight. Now, in the dark, two brown deer bounded toward the west, but the albino stood still, staring in Saul's direction, a purposeful stare. He gripped the handlebars so hard that his forearms began to knot into a cramp. The animal was a sign of some kind, he was sure—only a fool would think otherwise—and he felt a moment of dread pass through his body as the deer now turned her eyes away from his and began to walk off into the night. He saw her disappear behind a maple tree in his backyard, but he couldn't follow her beyond that. He was trembling now. Shivering spasms began at his wet shoulders and passed down his chest toward his legs. The dread he had felt before was turning rapidly into pure spiritual fright, alternating waves of chill and heat rushing up and down his body. He remembered to get off the road. He pushed the motorcycle into the garage, kicking down its stand, and by the time he had crossed the yard and had reached the back door, he felt that he knew one thing, which was that he would not despise his own life. He had been told not to. The rain picked up again and sprayed into him as the wind carried it. In his mind's eye he saw the deer looking back at him. He had been judged, and the judgment was that he, Saul, was only and always himself, now and onward into infinity. His boots were wet. They stank of wet leather. Outside the back door, on the lawn, he took the boots off, then his wet shirt and his jeans. It occurred to him to stand there naked. With no clothes on he stood in the rain and the dark, and he fell to his knees. He wasn't praying. He didn't know what he was doing. Something was filling him up. It felt like the spirit, but the spirit of what, he didn't know. He lay down on the grass. One sob tore through him, and then it was over.

He felt like getting up and running out into the field in back of the house, but he knew he couldn't break through his self-consciousness enough to do that. In the rain, which no longer felt cold, he sensed that he was entering a condition that had nothing to do with happiness because it was so far beyond it. All he was sure about was that he was empty before and now was filled, filled with both fullness and emptiness. These emotions didn't quite make sense, but he didn't care. The emptiness was sweet; he could live with it. He hurried into the house and dried off his hair in the dark downstairs bathroom. Quickly he toweled himself down and then rushed up the stairs. There was a secret, after all. In fact there were probably a lot of secrets, but there was one he now knew.

He entered their bedroom. Rain fingernailed against the window glass. Patsy lay in bed in almost complete darkness, wearing one of Saul's tee-shirts. Her arms were up above her head. He could see that she was watching him.

"Where were you?"

"I went for a ride on your motorcycle. I couldn't sleep."

"Saul, it's raining. Why are you naked?"

"It's raining now. Not when I started."

"Why are you standing there? You don't have any clothes on."

"I saw something. I can't tell you. I think I'm not supposed to tell you what I saw. It was an animal. It was a private animal. Patsy, I took off my clothes and lay down on the lawn in the rain, and it didn't feel weird, it felt like just what I should do."

"Saul, what is this about?"

"I'm not sure."

"Try. Try to say."

"I think I'm pregnant."

"What does that mean?"

"I think it means that whoever I am, I'm not alone with myself."

"I don't understand that."

"I know."

"Come to bed, Saul. Get in under the sheet."

He climbed in and put his leg over hers.

"I can't quite get used to you," she said. "You're quite a mess of metaphors, Saul, you know that."

"Yes."

"A man being pregnant." She put her hand familiarly on his thigh. "I wonder what that means."

"It's a feeling, Patsy. It's a secret. Men have secrets, too."

"I never said they didn't. They love secrets. They have lodges and secret societies and stuff—the Fraternal Order of Moose."

"Can we make love now, right this minute? Because I love you. I love you like crazy."

"I love you, too, Saul. What if you make *me* pregnant? It could happen. What if I get knocked up? Is it all right now?"

"Yeah. What's the problem?"

"What will we say, for example?"

"We'll say, 'Saul and Patsy are pregnant.' "

"Oh sure we will."

"Okay, we won't say it." He had thrown the sheet back and was kissing the backs of her knees.

"Are you crying? Your face is wet."

"Yes."

"But you're being so jokey."

"That's how I handle it."

"Why are you crying?"

"Because. . . ." He wanted to get this right. "Because there are signs and wonders. What can I tell you? It's all a feeling. In the morning, I'll deny I said this."

She was kissing him now, but she stopped, as if thinking about his recent sentences. "You *want* to make me pregnant, too, don't you?"

"Yes."

"So you're not alone in this."

"That's right."

"One more little ambassador from the present to the future. That's what you want."

"Sort of." He moved up and took her fingers one by one into his mouth and bit them tenderly. Patsy had started to hum. She was humming "Unchain My Heart." Then she opened her mouth and sang quietly, "Unchain my heart, and set me free."

"I'll try, Patsy."

"Yes." They often talked while they made love. A moment later, she said, "This won't solve anything. There'll be tears. People—babies—you know how they cry."

"Yes." And even now Saul felt as though he heard someone wailing softly in the next room. Still he continued. Then he had a thought. "Patsy," he said, "the window. We should stand by the window."

"Why?"

"To try it." He disentangled himself from her, stood, and brought her over to the window. He opened it so that droplets of rain blew in over them. "Now," he said. There was a bit of lightning, and he lifted her to him. She held on, her arms clasped behind his neck. He felt as though a thousand eyes, but not human eyes, were looking in on them with tender indifference. They were and were not interested. They would and would not care. They would and would not love them. Finally they would turn away, as they tended to turn away from all human things, in time. Saul felt Patsy begin to tremble, a slight shivering along her back, a rising in tension before release. More rain came in, warm June rain on his arm. He felt Patsy's mouth on his curls, the ones recently cut by Harold; she was panting, and so was he, and for a split-second, he understood it all. He understood everything, the secret of the universe. After an instant, he lost it. Having lost the secret, forgotten it, he felt the usual onset of the ordinary, of everything else, with Patsy around him, the two of them in their own familiar rhythms. He would not admit to anyone that he had known the secret of the universe for a split-second. That part of his life was hidden away and would always be: the part that makes a person draw in the breath quickly, in surprise, and stare at the curtains in the morning, upon awakening.

Ursula K. Le Guin

HAND, CUP, SHELL

The last house on Searoad stood in the field behind the dunes. Its windows looked north to Briton Head, south to Wreck Rock, east to the marshes, and, from the second story, across the dunes and the breakers, west to China. The house was empty more than it was full, but it was never silent.

The family arrived and dispersed. Having come to be together over the weekend, they fled one another without hesitation, one to the garden, one to the kitchen, one to the bookshelf, two north up the beach, one south to the rocks.

Thriving on salt and sand and storms, the rose bushes behind the house climbed all over the paling fence and shot up long autumn sprays, dishevelled and magnificent. Roses may do best if you don't do anything for them at all except keep the swordfern and ivy from strangling them; bronze Peace grows wild as well as any wild rose. But the ivy, now. Loathsome stuff. Poisonous berries. Crawling out from hiding everywhere, stuffed full of horrors, spiders, centipedes, millipedes, billipedes, snakes, rats, broken glass, rusty knives, dog turds, dolls' eyes. I must cut the ivy right back to the fence, Rita thought, pulling up a long stem that led her back into the leafy mass to a parent vine as thick as a garden hose. I must come here oftener, and keep the ivy off the spruce trees. Look at that, it'll have the tree dead in another year. She tugged. The cable of ivy gave no more than a steel hawser would. She went back up the porch steps, calling, "Are there any pruning shears, do you think?"

"Hanging on the wall there, aren't they?" Mag called back from the kitchen. "Anyway they ought to be." There ought to be flour in the canister, too, but it was empty. Either she had used it up in August and forgotten, or Phil and the boys had made pancakes when they were over last month. So where was the list pad to write *flour* on for when she walked up to Hambleton's? Nowhere to be found. She would have to buy a little pad to write *pad* on. She found a ballpoint pen in the things drawer. It was green and translucent, imprinted with the words HANK'S COAST HARDWARE AND AUTO SUPPLIES. She wrote *flour, bans, oj., cereal, yog, list pad,* on a paper towel, wiping blobs of excess green ink off the penpoint with a corner of the towel. Everything is circular, or anyhow spiral. It was no time at all, certainly not twelve months, since last October in this kitchen, and she was absolutely standing in her tracks. It wasn't *déjà vu* but *déjà vécu,* and all the Octobers before it, and still all the same this was now, and therefore different feet were standing in her tracks. A half size larger than last year, for one thing. Would they go on breaking down and spreading out forever, until she ended up wearing men's size 12 logging boots? Mother's feet hadn't done that. She'd always worn 7N, still wore 7N, always would wear 7N, but then she always wore the same kind of shoes, too, trim inch-heel pumps or penny loafers, never experimenting with Germanic clogs, Japanese athletics, or the latest toe-killer fad. It came of having had to dress a certain way of course as the Dean's wife, but also of being Daddy's girl, smalltown princess, not experimenting just knowing. "I'm going on down to Hambleton's, do you want anything?" Mag called out the kitchen door through the back-porch screen to her mother fighting ivy in the garden.

"I don't think so. Are you going to walk?"

"Yes."

They were right: it took a certain effort to say *yes* just flatly, to refrain from qualifying it, softening it, *Yes I think so, Yes I guess so, Yes I thought I would* . . . Unqualified *yes* had a gruff sound to it, full of testosterone. If Rita had said *no* instead of *I don't think so,* it would have sounded rude or distressed, and she probably would have responded in some way to find out what was wrong, why her mother wasn't speaking in the mother tongue. "Going to Hambleton's," she said to Phil, who was kneeling at the bookcase in the dark little hall, and went out. She went down the four wooden steps of the front porch and through the front gate, latched the gate behind her, and turned right on Searoad to walk into town. These familiar movements gave her great pleasure. She walked on the dune side of the road, and between dunes saw the ocean, the breakers that took all speech away. She walked in silence, seeing glimpses between dune grass of the beach where her children had gone.

Gret had gone as far as the beach went. It ended in a tumble of rusty brown basalt under Wreck Point, but she knew the ways up through the rocks to the slopes and ledges of the Point, places where nobody came. Sitting there on the windbitten grass looking out over the waves bashing on Wreck Rock and the reef Dad called Rickrack and out to the horizon, you could keep going farther still. At least you ought to be able to, but there wasn't any way to be alone any more. There was a beer can in the grass, a tag of orange plastic ribbon tied to a stake up near the summit, a Coast Guard helicopter yammering and prying over the sea up to Briton Head and back south again. Nobody wanted anybody to be alone, ever. You had to do away with that, unmake it, all the junk, trash, crap, trivia, David, the midterms, Gran, what people thought, other people. You had to go away from them. All the way away. It used to be easy to do that, easy to go and hard to come back, but now it was harder and harder to go, and she never could go all the way. To sit up here and stare at the ocean and be thinking about stupid David, and what's that stake for, and why did Gran look at my fingernails that way, what's wrong with me? Am I going to be this way the rest of my life? Not even seeing the ocean? Seeing stupid beer cans? She stood, raging, backed up, aimed, and kicked the beer can in a low, fast arc off the cliff into the sea unseen below. She turned and scrambled up to the summit, braced her knees in soggy bracken, and wrenched the orange-ribboned stake out of the ground. She hurled it southward and saw it fall into bracken and salal scrub and be swallowed. She stood up, rubbing her hands where the raw wood had scraped the skin. The wind felt cold on her teeth. She had been baring them, an angry ape. The sea lay gray at eye level, taking her immediately now into its horizontality. Nothing cluttered. As she sucked the heel of her thumb and got her front teeth warm, she thought, My soul is ten thousand miles wide and extremely invisibly deep. It is the same size as the sea, it is bigger than the sea, it *holds* the sea, and you cannot, you cannot cram it into beer cans and fingernails and stake it out in lots and own it. It will drown you all and never even notice.

But how old I am, thought the grandmother, to come to the beach and not look at the sea! How horrible! Straight out into the back yard, as if all that mattered was grubbing ivy. As if the sea belonged to the children. To assert her right to the ocean, she carried ivy cuttings to the trash bin beside the house and after cramming them into the bin stood and looked at the dunes, across which it was. It wasn't going to go away, as Amory would have said. But she went on out the garden gate, crossed sandy-rutted Searoad, and in ten more steps saw the Pacific open out between the grass-crowned dunes. There you are, you old gray monster. You aren't going to go away, but I am. Her brown loafers, a bit loose on her bony feet, were already full of sand. Did she want to go on down, onto the beach? It was always so windy. As she hesitated, looking about, she saw a head bobbing along between the crests of dune grass. Mag coming back with the groceries. Slow black bobbing head like the old mule coming up the rise to the sagebrush ranch when? old Bill the mule—Mag the mule, trudging obstinate silent. She went down to the road and stood first on one foot then the other emptying sand out of her shoes, then walked to meet her daughter. "How are things at Hambleton's?"

"Peart," Mag said. "Right peart. When is whatsername coming?"

"By noon, I think she said." Rita sighed. "I got up at five. I think I'm going to go in and have a little lie-down before she comes. I hope she won't stay hours."

"Who is she, again?"

"Oh . . . damn . . ."

"I mean what's she doing."

Rita gave up the vain search for the lost name. "She's some sort of assistant, research assistant I suppose, to whatsisname at the University, you know, doing the book about Amory. I expect somebody suggested to him that maybe it would look odd if he did a whole biography without talking to the widow, but of course it's really only Amory's ideas that interest him, I believe he's very theoretical the way they are now. Probably bored stiff at the idea of actual *people.* So he's sending the young lady into the hencoop."

"So that you don't sue him."

"Oh you don't think so."

"Certainly. Co-optation. And you'll get thanked for your invaluable assistance, in the acknowledgments, just before he thanks his wife and his typist."

"What was that terrible thing you told me about Mrs. Tolstoy?"

"Copied *War and Peace* for him six times by hand. But you know, it would beat copying most books six times by hand."

"Shepard."

"What?"

"Her. The girl. Something Shepard."

"Whose invaluable assistance Professor Whozis gratefully, no, she's only a grad student, isn't she. Lucky if she gets mentioned at all. What a safety net they have, don't they? All the women the knots in the net."

But that cut a bit close to the bones of Amory Inman, and his widow did not answer his daughter as she helped her put away the flour, cornflakes, yoghurt, cookies, bananas, grapes, lettuce, avocado, tomatoes, and vinegar Mag had bought (she had forgotten to buy a list pad). "Well, I'm off, shout when she comes," Rita said, and made her way past her son-in-law, who was sitting on the hall floor by the bookcase, to the stairs.

The upstairs of the house was simple, rational, and white: the stairs-landing and a bathroom down the middle, a bedroom in each corner. Mag and Phil SW, Gran NW, Gret NE, boys SE. The old folks got the sunset, the kids got dawn. Rita was the first to listen and hear the sea in the house. She looked out over the dunes and saw the tide coming in and the wind combing the manes of the white horses. She lay down and looked with pleasure at the narrow, white-painted boards of the ceiling in the sea-light like no other light. She did not want to go to sleep but her eyes were tired and she had not brought a book upstairs. She heard the girl's voice, below, the girls' voices, piercing soft, the sound of the sea.

"Where's Gran?"

"Upstairs."

"This woman's come."

Mag brought the dishtowel on which she was drying her hands into the front room, a signal flag: I work in the kitchen and have nothing to do with interviews. Gret had left the girl standing out on the front deck. "Won't you come in?"

"Susan Shepard."

"Mag Rilow. That's Greta. Gret, go up and tell Gran, OK? "

"It's so lovely here! What a beautiful place!"

"Maybe you'd like to sit out on the deck to talk? It's so mild. Would you like some coffee? Beer, anything?"

"Oh, yes—coffee—"

"Tea?"

"That would be wonderful."

"Herbal?" Everybody there at the University in the Klamath Time Warp drank herbal tea. Sure enough, chamomile-peppermint would be wonderful. Mag got her sitting in the wicker chair on the deck and came back in past Phil, who was still on the floor in the hall by the bookcase, reading. "Take it into the *light,*" she said, and he said, "Yeah, I will," smiling, and turned a page. Gret, coming down the stairs, said, "She'll be down in a minute."

"Go talk to the girl. She's at the U."

"What in?"

"I don't know. Find out."

Gret snarled and turned away. Edging past her father in the narrow hall, she said, "Why don't you get some *light?*" He smiled, turned a page, and said, "Yeah, I will." She strode out onto the deck and said, "My mother says you're at the U," at the same time as the woman said, "You're at the U, aren't you?"

Gret nodded.

"I'm in Ed. I'm Professor Nabe's research assistant for his book. It's really exciting to be interviewing your grandmother."

"It seems fairly weird to me," Gret said.

"The University?"

"No."

There was a little silence filled by the sound of the sea.

"Are you a freshman?"

"Freshwoman." She edged towards the steps.

"Will you major in Education, do you think?"

"Oh, God, no."

"I suppose having such a distinguished grandfather, people always just expect. Your mother's an educator, too, isn't she?"

"She teaches," Gret said. She had got as far as the steps and now went down them, because they were the shortest way to get away, though she had been coming into the house to go to her room when Sue Student drove up and she got caught.

Gran appeared in the open doorway, looking wary and rather bleary, but using her politically correct smile and voice: "Hello! I'm Rita Inman." While Sue Student was jumping up and being really excited, Gret got back up the steps, past Gran, and into the house.

Daddy was still sitting on the floor in the dark hall by the bookcase, reading. She unplugged the gooseneck lamp from the end table by the living-room couch, set it on the bookcase in the hall, and found the outlet was too far for the cord to reach. She brought the lamp as close to him as she could, setting it on the floor about three feet from him, and then plugged in the plug. The light glared across the pages of his book. "Oh, hey, great," he said, smiling, and turned a page. She went on upstairs to her room. Walls and ceiling were white, the bedspreads on the two narrow beds were blue. A picture of blue mountains she had painted in ninth-grade art class was pinned to the closet door, and she reconfirmed with a long look at it that it was beautiful. It was the only good picture she had ever painted, and she marveled at it, the gift that had given itself to her, undeserved, no strings attached. She opened the backpack she had dumped on one bed, got out a geology textbook and a hi-liter, lay down on the other bed, and began to reread for the midterm examination. At the end of a section on subduction, she turned her head to look at the picture of blue mountains again, and thought, "I wonder, what would it be like?"—or those are the words she might have used to express the feelings of curiosity, pleasure, and awe, which accompanied the images in her mind of small figures scattered among great lava cliffs on the field trip in September, of journeys, of levels stretching to the horizon, high deserts under which lay fossils folded like tissuepaper; of moraines; of long veins of ore and crystals in the darkness underground. Intent and careful, she turned the page and started the next section.

Sue Shepard fussed with her little computer thing. Her face

was plump, pink, round-eyed, and Rita had to make the interpretation "intellectual" consciously. It would not arise of itself from the pink face, the high voice, the girlish manner, as it would from the pink face, high voice, and boyish manner of a male counterpart. She knew that she still so identified mind and masculinity that only women who imitated men were immediately recognizable to her as intellectuals, even after all these years, even after Mag. Also, Sue Shepard might be disguising her intellect, as Mag didn't. And the jargon of her subject was a pretty good disguise in itself. But she was keen, it was a keen mind, and perhaps Professor Whozis didn't like to be reminded of it, so young, so bright, so close behind. Probably he liked flutter and butter, as Amory used to call it, in his graduate-student women. But fluttery buttery little Sue had already set aside a whole sheaf of the professor's questions as timewasting, and was asking, intently and apparently on her own hook, about Rita's girlhood.

"Well, when I was born we lived on a ranch out from Prineville, in the high country. The sagebrush, you know. But I don't remember much that's useful. I think Father must have been keeping books for the ranch. It was a big operation—huge—all the way to the John Day River, I think. When I was nine, he took over managing a mill in Ultimate, in the Coast Range. A lumber mill. Nothing left of all that now. There isn't even a gravel road in to Ultimate any more. Half the state's like that, you know, it's very strange. Easterners come and think it's this wild pristine wilderness and actually it's all Indian graveyards underfoot and old homesteads and second growth and towns nobody even remembers were there. It's just that the trees and the weeds grow back so fast. Like ivy. Where are you from?"

"Seattle," said Sue Shepard, friendly, but not to be misled as to who was interviewing whom.

"Well, I'm glad. I seem to have more and more trouble talking with Easterners."

Sue Shepard laughed, probably not understanding, not having

met enough Easterners, and pursued: "So you went to school in Ultimate?"

"Yes, until high school. Then I came to live with Aunt Josie in Portland and went to old Lincoln High. The nearest high school to Ultimate was thirty miles on logging roads, and anyhow it wasn't good enough for Father. He was afraid I'd grow up to be a roughneck, or marry one . . ." Sue Shepard clicketed on her little machine, and Rita thought, but what did Mother think? Did she want to send me away at age thirteen to live in the city with her sister-in-law? The question opened on a blank area that she gazed into, fascinated. I know what Father wanted, but why don't I know what she wanted? Did she cry? No, of course not. Did I? I don't think so. I can't even remember talking about it with Mother. We made my clothes, that summer. That's when she taught me how to cut out a pattern. And then we came up to Portland the first time, and stayed at the old Multnomah Hotel, and we bought shoes for me for school—and the oyster silk ones for dressing up, the little undercut heel and one strap, I wish they still made them. I was already wearing Mother's size. And we ate lunch in that restaurant, the cut-glass water goblets, the two of us, where was Father? But I never even wondered what she thought, I never knew. I never know what Mag really thinks, either. They don't say. Rocks. Look at Mag's mouth, just like Mother's, like a seam in a rock. Why did Mag go into teaching, talk, talk, talk all day, when she really hates talking? Although she never was quite as gruff as Gret is, but that's because Amory wouldn't have stood for it. But why didn't Mother and I say anything to each other? She was so stoical. Rock. And then I was happy in Portland, and there she was in Ultimate . . . "Oh, yes, I loved it," she answered Sue Shepard. "The twenties were a nice time to be a teen-ager, we really were very spoiled, not like now, poor things. It's terribly hard to be thirteen or fourteen now, isn't it? We went to dancing school, they've got AIDS, and the atomic bomb. My granddaughter's twice as old as I was at eighteen. In some ways. She's amazingly young for her age in others. It's so complicated. After all, think of Juliet! It's never *really* simple, is it? But I think I had a very nice, innocent time in high school, and right on into college. Until the crash. The mill closed in '32, my second year. But actually we went right on having a good time. But it was terribly depressing for my parents and my brothers. The mill shut right down, and they all came up to Portland looking for work, everybody did. And then I left school after my junior year, because I'd got a summer job bookkeeping in the University accounting office, and they wanted me to stay on, and so I did, since everybody else in the family was out of work, except Mother finally got a job in a bakery, nights. It was terrible for men, the Depression, you know. It killed my father. He looked and looked for work and couldn't find anything, and there I was, doing what he was qualified to do, only of course at a very low level, and terrible pay—sixty dollars a month, can you imagine?"

"A week?"

"No, a month. But still, I was making it. And men of his generation were brought up to be depended on, which is a wonderful thing, but then they weren't allowed ever *not* to be depended on, or even to admit that they could be dependent on anybody, which is terribly unrealistic, I think, a real whatdyoucallit. Doubletime?"

"Double bind," said young Sue, sharp as tacks, clicketing almost inaudibly away on her little lap computer, while the tape-recorder tape went silently round and round, recording Rita's every maunder and meander. Rita sighed. "I'm sure that's why he died so young," she said. "He was only fifty."

But Mother hadn't died young, though her husband had, and her elder son had drifted off to Texas to be swallowed alive so far as his mother was concerned by a jealous wife, and her younger son had poured whisky onto diabetes and died at thirty-one. Men did seem to be so fragile. But what had kept Margaret Jamison Holz going? Her independence? But she had been brought up to be dependent, hadn't she? Anyhow nobody could keep going long on mere independence, when they tried to they ended up pushing shopping carts full of stuff and sleeping in doorways. Mother hadn't done that, she had sat here on the deck looking out at the dunes, a small, tough, old woman. No retirement pension of course and a tiny little dribble of insurance money, and she did let Amory pay the rent on her two-room apartment in Portland, but she was independent to the end, visiting them only once or twice a year at the University, and then always for a full month here, in summer. Gret's room now had been Mother's room then. How strange it was, how it changed! But recently she had wakened in the deep night or when it was just beginning to get light and had lain there in bed thinking, not with fear but with a kind of frightened, lively thrill, "It is so strange, all of it is so *strange!*"

"When were you able to go back to college?" Sue Shepard asked, and she answered, "In '35," resolving to stick to the point and stop babbling.

"And then you met Dr. Inman when you took his class."

"No. I never took a class in Education."

"Oh," Sue Shepard said, blank.

"I met him in the accounting office. I was still clerking there half-time, paying my way. And he came in because he hadn't been paid his salary for three months. People used to be just as good at mistakes like that as computers are now. It took days and days to find out how they'd managed to lose him from the faculty payroll. Did he tell somebody that I'd taken his class and that's how we met?" Sue Shepard wasn't going to admit it; she was discreet. "How funny. It was one of the other women he went out with, and he got his memories crossed. Students were always falling in love with him. He was *extremely* attractive—I used to think Charles Boyer without the French accent—" They both laughed.

Mag heard them laughing on the front deck as she came through the hall, edging around her husband. A gooseneck lamp standing on the floor near him glared in his eyes, but he was holding his book so that its pages were in shadow.

"Phil."

"Mm."

"Get up and go read in the living room."

He smiled, reading. "Found this . . ."

"The interviewer's here. She'll be staying for lunch. You're in the way. You've been in the way for two hours. You're in the dark. There's daylight six feet away. Get up and go read in the living room."

"People . . ."

"Nobody's there! People come through *here.* Are you—" The wave of hatred and compassion set free by her words carried her on past him, though she had checked the words. In silence, she turned the corner and climbed the stairs. She went into the southwest bedroom and looked for a decent shirt in the crowded closet; the cotton sweater she had worn from Portland was too warm for this mild coastal weather. The search led her into a rummage-out of summer clothes. She sorted, rehung, folded her clothes, then Phil's. From the depths she pulled out paint-stiff, knee-frayed bluejeans, a madras shirt with four buttons gone that had been stuffed into the closet unwashed. Even here at the beach house, her father's clothes had always been clean, smelled clean, smelled of virtue, *virtù.* With a violent swing she threw the madras shirt at the wastebasket. It draped itself half in half out, a short sleeve sticking up pitifully. Not waving but drowning . . . But to go on drowning for twenty-five years?

The window was ajar, and she could hear the sea and her mother's voice down on the front deck answering questions about her husband the eminent educator, the clean-bodied man: how had he written his books? When had he broken with John Dewey's theories? Where had the UNICEF work taken him? Now, little apple-cheeked handmaiden of success, ask me about my husband the eminent odd-job man: how did he quit halfway through graduate school, when had he broken with the drywalling contractor, where had his graveyard shift at the Copy Shop taken him? Phil the Failure, he called himself, with the charming honesty that concealed a hideous smugness that probably but not certainly concealed despair. What was certain was that nobody else in the world knew the depth of Phil's contempt for them, his absolute lack of admiration or sympathy for anything anybody did or was. If that indifference was originally a defense, it had consumed what it had once defended. He was invulnerable, by now. And people were so careful not to hurt him. Finding that she was Dr. Rilow and he was an unemployed drywaller, they assumed it was hard for him; and then when they found that it wasn't, they admired him for being so secure, so unmacho, taking it so easily, handling it so well. Indeed he handled it well, cherished it, his dear failure, his great success at doing exactly what he wanted to do and nothing else. No wonder he was so sweet, so serene, so unstrained. No wonder she had blown up, teaching *Bleak House* last week, at the mooncalf student who couldn't see what was supposed to be wrong with Harold Skimpole. "Don't you see that his behavior is totally irresponsible?" she had demanded in righteous wrath, and the mooncalf had replied, with aplomb, "I don't see why *everybody* is supposed to be responsible." It was a kind of Taoist koan, actually. For Taoist wives. It was hard to be married to a man who lived in a perpetual condition of *wu wei* and not to end up totally *wei;* you had to be very careful or you ended up washing the ten thousand shirts.

But then of course Mother had looked after Father's shirts.

The jeans weren't even good for rags, even if they would sell in the Soviet Union for a hundred dollars; she threw them after the shirt, and knocked the wastebasket over. Faintly ashamed, she retrieved them and the shirt and stuffed them into a plastic bag that had been squirreled away in a cranny of the closet. An advantage of Phil's indifference was that he would never come downstairs demanding to know where his wonderful old jeans and madras shirt were. He never got attached to clothes, and wore whatever was provided. "Distrust all occasions that require new clothes." What a prig Thoreau was. Ten to one he meant weddings but hadn't had the guts to say so, let alone get married. Actually Phil liked new clothes, liked to get them for Christmas and birthdays, accepted all presents, cherished none. "Phil is a saint, Mag," his mother had said to her shortly before they were married, and she had agreed, laughing, thinking the exaggeration quite forgivable; but it had not been a burble of mother love. It had been a warning.

She knew that her father had hoped that the marriage wouldn't last. He had never quite said so. By now the matter of her marriage, between her and her mother, was buried miles deep. Between her and her daughter it was an unaskable question. Everybody protecting everybody. It was stupid. It kept her and Gret from saying much to each other. And it wasn't really the right question, the one that needed asking, anyhow. They were married. But there was a question. No one had asked it and she did not know what it was. Possibly if she found out, her life would change. The headless torso of Apollo would speak: *Du musst dein Leben ändern.* Meanwhile, did she particularly want her life to change? "I will never desert Mr. Micawber," she said under her breath, reaching into yet another cranny of the closet and discovering there yet another plastic bag, which when opened disclosed rust-colored knitted wool: a sweater, which she stared at dumbly till she recognized it as one she had bought on sale for Gret for Christmas several years ago and had utterly forgotten ever since. "Gret! Look here!" she cried, crossing the hall, knocking, opening the door of her daughter's room. "Merry Christmas!"

After explanations, Gret pulled the sweater on. Her dark, thin face emerged from the beautiful color with a serious expression. She looked at the sweater seriously in the mirror. She was very hard to please, preferred to buy her own clothes, and wore the ones she liked till they fell apart. She kept them moderately clean. "Are the sleeves kind of short, a little?" she asked, in the mother tongue.

"Kind of. Probably why it was on sale. It was incredibly cheap, I remember, at the Sheep Tree. Years ago. I liked the color."

"It's neat," Gret said, still judging. She pushed up the sleeves. "Thanks," she said. Her face was a little flushed. She smiled and glanced around at the book lying open on the bed. Something was unsaid, almost said. She did not know how to say it and Mag did not know how to allow her to say it; they both had trouble with their native language. Awkward, intrusive, the mother retreated, saying, "Lunch about one-thirty."

"Need help?"

"Not really. Picnic on the deck. With the interviewer."

"When's she leaving?"

"Before dinner, I hope. It's a good color on you." She went out, closing off the door behind her, as she had been taught to do.

Gret took off the orange sweater. It was too hot for the mild day, and she wasn't sure she liked it yet. It would take a while. It would have to sit around a while till she got used to it, and then she would know. She thought she liked it; it felt like she'd worn it before. She put it into a drawer so her mother wouldn't get hurt. Last year when her mother had come into her room at home and stared around, Gret had suddenly realised that the stare wasn't one of disapproval but of pain. Disorder, dirt, disrespect for objects, caused her pain, like being shoved or hit. It must be hard for her, living, in general. Knowing that, Gret tried to put stuff away; but it didn't make much difference. She was mostly at college now, and Mother went on nagging and ordering and enduring, and Daddy and the boys didn't let it worry them. Just like some God damn sitcom. Everything about families and people was exactly like some God damn sitcom. Waiting for David to call, just like a soap opera. Everything the same as it was for everybody else, the same things happening over and over and over, all petty and trivial and stupid, and you couldn't ever get free. It clung to you, held on, pinioned you. Like the dream she used to have of the room with wallpaper that caught and stuck to you, the Velcro dream. She reopened the textbook and read about the nature of gabbro, the origins of slate.

The boys came back from the beach just in time for lunch. They always did. Still. Just as when your milk spurts and the baby in the next room cries at the exact same moment. Their clomping in to go to the bathroom finally got Phil off the hall floor. He carried out platters to the table on the front porch and talked with whatsername the interviewer, who got quite pink and pleased. Phil looked so thin and short and hairy and vague and middle-aged that they never expected it till whammy! right between the eyes. Wooed and won. Go it, Phil. She looked like an intelligent girl, actually, over-serious, and Phil wouldn't hurt her. Wouldn't hurt a fly, would old Phil. St. Philip, bestower of sexual favors. She smiled at them and said, "Come and get it!"

Sue Student was being nice to Daddy, talking with him about forest fires or something. Daddy had his little company smile and was being nice to Sue Student. She didn't sound too stupid, actually. She was a vegetarian. "So is Gret," Gran said. "What is it about the U these days? They used to live on raw elk." Why did she always have to disapprove of everything Gret did? She never said stuff like that about the boys. They were scarfing up salami. Mother watched them all loading their plates and making their sandwiches with that brooding hawk expression. Filling her niche. That was the trouble with biology, it was the sitcom. All niches. Mother Provides. Better the dark slate levels, the basalt plains. Anything could happen, there.

She was worn out. She went for the wine bottle; food later. She must get by herself for a while, that bit of a nap in the morning hadn't helped. Such a long, long morning, with the drive over from Portland. And talking about old times was a most terrible thing to do. All the lost things, lost chances, all the dead people. The town with no road to it any more. She had had to say ten times, "He's dead now," "No, she's dead." What a strange thing to say, after all! You couldn't *be* dead. You couldn't *be* anything but alive. If you weren't alive, you weren't—you had been. You shouldn't have to say "He's dead now," as if it was just some other way of being, but "He isn't now," or, "He was." Keep the past in the past tense. And the present in the present, where it belongs. Because you didn't live on in others, as people said. You changed them, yes. She was entirely different because Amory had lived. But he didn't live on in her, in her memory, or in his books, or anywhere. He had gone. He was gone. Maybe "passed away" wasn't such a whatdyoucallit, after all. At least it was in the passed tense, the past tense, not the present. He had come to her and she had come to him and they had made each other's life what it had been, and then he had gone. Passed away. It wasn't a euphemism, that's what it wasn't. Her mother . . . There was a pause in her thoughts. She drank the wine. Her mother was different, how? She came back to the rock. Of course she was dead, but it did not seem that she had passed away, the way he had. She went back to the table, refilled her glass with the red wine, laid salami, cheese, and green onions on brown bread.

She was beautiful now. In the tight, short, ugly fashions of the sixties, when Mag had first looked at her from any distance and with any judgment, she had looked too big, and for a while after Amory's death and when she had the bone marrow thing she had been gaunt, but now she was extraordinary: the line of the cheek, the long, soft lips, the long-lidded eyes with their fine wrinkle-pleating. What had she said about raw elk? The interviewer hadn't heard and wouldn't understand if she had heard, wouldn't know that she had just been told what Mrs. Amory Inman thought of the institution of which her husband had been the luminary, what indeed she thought, in her increasing aloofness, her oldwomanhood, of most human institutions. Poor little whatsername, trapped in the works and dark machinations of that toughest survivor of the Middle Ages, the university, ground in the mills of assistantships, grants, competitions, examinations, dissertations, all set up to separate the men from the boys and both from the rest of the world, she wouldn't have time for years yet to look up, to look out, to learn that there were such bare, airy places as the place where Rita Inman lived.

"Yes, it is nice, isn't it? We bought it in '55, when things over here were still pretty cheap. We haven't even asked you indoors, how terrible! After lunch you must look round the house. I think I'm going to have a little lie-down, after lunch. Or perhaps you'd like to go down on the beach then—the children will take you walking as far as you'd like, if you like. Mag, Sue says she needs an hour or two more with me. She hasn't asked all . . ." a pause, "the professor's questions yet. I'm afraid I kept wandering off the subject." How sternly beautiful Mag was, her rockseam mouth, her dark-waterfall hair going silver. Managing everything as usual, seeing to everything, the good lunch. No, definitely her mother was not dead in the same way Father was dead, or Amory, or Clyde, or Polly, or Jim and Jean; there was something different there. She really must get by herself and think about it.

"Geology." The word came out. Spoken. Mother's ears went up like a cat's, eyebrows flickering, eyes and mouth impassive. Daddy acted like he'd known her decision all along, maybe he had, he couldn't have. Sue Student had to keep asking who was in the Geo department and what you did with geology. She only knew a couple of the professors' names and felt stupid not knowing more. She said, "Oh, you get hired by oil companies, mining companies, all kinds of landrape companies. Find uranium under Indian reservations." Oh, shut up. Sue Student meant well. Everybody meant well. It spoiled everything. Softened everything. "The grizzled old prospector limps in from twenty years alone in the desert, swearing at her mule," Daddy said, and she laughed, it was funny, Daddy was funny, but she was for a moment, a flash, afraid of him. He was so quick. He knew that this was something important, and did he mean well? He loved her, he liked her, he was like her, but when she wasn't like him did he like it? Mother was saying how geology had been all cut and dried when she was in college and how it was all changed now by these new theories. "Plate tectonics isn't exactly new," oh, shut up, shut up. Mother meant well. Sue Student and Mother talked about academic careers in science and got interested comparing, colleaguing. Sue was at the U but she was younger and only a grad student; Mother was only at a community college but she was older and had a Ph.D. from Berkeley. And Daddy was out of it. And Gran half asleep, and Tom and Sam cleaning up the platters. She said, "It's funny. I was thinking. All of us, the family, I mean, nobody will ever know any of us ever existed. Except for Granddaddy. He's the only real one."

Sue gazed mildly. Daddy nodded in approval. Mother stared, the hawk at bay. Gran said in a curious, distant tone, "Oh I don't think so at all." Tom was throwing bread to a seagull, but Sam, finishing the salami, said, in his mother's voice, "Fame is the spur!" At that, the hawk blinked, and stooped to the prey: "Whatever do you mean, Gret? Reality is being a dean of the School of Education?"

"He was important. He has a biography. None of us will."

"Thank goodness," Gran said, getting up. "I do hope you don't mind, if I have just a bit of a lie-down now I'll be much brighter later, I hope."

Everybody moved.

"Boys. You do the dishes. Tom!"

He came. They obeyed. She felt a tremendous, a ridiculous surge, as warm and irresistible as tears or milk, of pride—in them, in herself. They were lovely. Lovely boys. Grumbling, coltish, oafish, gangling, redhanded, they unloaded the table with efficiency and speed, Sam insulting Tom steadily in his half-broken voice, Tom replying on two sweet notes at intervals like a thrush, "Ass-sole . . . Ass-sole . . ."

"Who's for a walk on the beach?"

She was, the interviewer was, Phil was, Gret surprisingly was.

They crossed Searoad and went single file between the dunes. Down on the beach she looked back to see the front windows and the roof above the dune grass, always remembering the pure delight of seeing it so the first time, the first time ever. To Gret and the boys the beach house was coeval with existence, but to her it was connected with joy. When she was a child they had stayed in other people's beach houses, places in Gearhart and Neskowin, summerhouses of deans and provosts and the rich people who clung to University administrators under the impression that they were intellectuals; or else, as Mag got older, she and her mother had been taken along with Dean Inman to one of his ever more exotic conferences, to Botswana, Brasilia, Bangkok, until she had rebelled at last. "But they are interesting *places,*" her mother had said, deprecating, "you really don't enjoy going?" And she had howled, "I'm sick of feeling like a white giraffe, why can't I ever stay home where people are the same *size?*" And at some indefinite but not long interval after that, they had driven over, to look at this house. "What do you think?" her father had asked, standing in the small living room, a smiling sixty-year-old public man, kindly rhetorical. There was no need to ask. They had all three been mad for it from the moment they saw it at the end of the long sand road between the marshes and the sea. "My room, OK?" Mag had said, coming out of the southwest bedroom. She and Phil had had their honeymoon summer there.

She looked across the sand at him. He was walking at the very edge of the water, moving crabwise east when a wave came washing farther in, following the outwash back west, absorbed as a child, slight, stooped, elusive. She veered her way to intersect with his. "Phildog," she said.

"Magdog."

"You know, she was right. What made her say it, do you think?"

"Defending me."

How easily he said it. How easy his assumption. It had not occurred to her.

"Could be. And herself? And me? . . . And then geology! Is she just in love with the course, or is she serious?"

"Never anything but."

"It might be a good major for her. Unless it's all labs now. I don't know, it's just a section of Intro Sci at CC. I'll ask Benjie what geologists do these days. I hope still those little hammers. And khaki shorts."

"That Priestley novel in the bookcase," Phil said, and went on to talk about it, and novelists contemporary with Priestley, and she listened attentively as they walked along the hissing fringes of the continent. If Phil had not quit before the prelims, he would have got much farther in his career than she in hers, because men got farther easier then of course, but mainly because he was such a natural; he had the right temperament, the necessary indifference and passion of the scholar. He was drawn to early twentieth-century English fiction with the perfect combination of detachment and fascination, and could have written a fine study of Priestley, Galsworthy, Bennett, that lot, a book worth a good professorship at a good school. Or worth at least a sense of self-respect. But self-respect wasn't a saint's business, was it? Dean Inman had had plenty of self-respect, and plenty of respect, too. Had she been escaping the various manifestations of respect when she fell for Phil? No. She still missed it, in fact, and supplied it when she could. She had fallen for Phil because she was strong, because of the awful need strength has for weakness. If you're not weak how can I be strong? Years it had taken her, years, until now, to learn that strength, like the lovely boys washing the dishes, like Gret saying that terrible thing at lunch, was what strength needed, craved, rested in. Rested and grew weak in, with the true weakness, the fecundity. Without self-defense. Gret had not been defending Phil, or anybody. Phil had to see it that way. But Gret had been speaking out of the true weakness. Dean Inman wouldn't have understood it, but it wouldn't have worried him; he would have seen that Gret respected him, and that to him would have meant that she respected herself. And Rita? She could not remember what Rita had said, when Gret said that about their not being real. Something not disapproving, but remote. Moving away. Rita was moving away. Like the gulls there ahead of them, always moving away as they advanced towards them, curved wings and watchful, indifferent eyes. Airborne, with hollow bones. She looked back down the sands. Gret and the interviewer were walking slowly, talking, far behind, so that she and Phil kept moving away from them, too. A tongue of the tide ran up the sand between them, crosscurrents drawing lines across it, and hissed softly out again. The horizon was a blue murk, but the sunlight was not. "Ha!" Phil said, and picked up a fine white sand dollar. He always saw the invaluable treasures, the dollars of no currency; he went on finding Japanese glass netfloats every winter on this beach, years after the Japanese had given up glass floats for plastic, years after anyone else had found one. Some of the floats he found had limpets growing on them. Bearded with moss and in garments green, they had floated for years on the great waves, tiny unburst bubbles, green, translucent earthlets in foam galaxies, moving away, drawing near. "But how much Maupassant is there in *The Old Wives' Tale,*" she asked, "I mean that kind of summing-up-women thing?" And Phil, pocketing his sea-paid salary, answered, as her father had answered her questions, and she listened to him, and to the sea.

Sue's mother had died of cancer of the womb. Sue had gone home to stay with her before college was out, last spring. It had taken her four months to die, and Sue had to talk about it. Gret had to listen. An honor, an imposition, an initiation. From time to time, barely enduring, she lifted her head to look out across the gray level of the sea, or up at Briton Head towering closer, or ahead at Mother and Daddy going along like slow sandpipers at the foam-fringe, or down at the damp brown sand and her grotty sneakers making footprints. But she bent her head again to Sue, confining herself. She had to tell and she had to listen, to learn all the instruments, the bonds, the knives, the racks and pinions, and how you became part of the torture, complicit with it, and whether in the end the truth, after such efforts to obtain it, would be spoken.

"My father hated the male nurses to touch her," Sue said. "He said it was woman's work, he tried to make them send women nurses in."

She talked about catheters, metastases, transfusions, each word an iron maiden, a toothed vagina. Woman's work. "The oncologist said it would get better when he put her on morphine, when her mind would get confused. But it got worse. It was the worst. The last week was the worst thing I will ever go through." She knew what she was saying, and it was tremendous. To be able to say that meant that you need not be afraid again. But it seemed like you had to lose a good deal for that gain.

Gret's escaping gaze passed her mother and father, who had halted at the foot of Briton Head, and followed the breakers on out to where the sea went level. Somebody had told her in high school that if you jumped from a height like Briton Head, hitting the water would be just like hitting rock.

"I didn't mean to go on telling you all that. I'm sorry. I just haven't got through it yet. I have to keep working through it."

"Sure," Gret said.

"Your grandmother is so—she's a beautiful person. And your whole family. You all just seem so real. I really appreciate being here with you."

She stopped walking, and Gret had to stop too.

"What you said at lunch, about your grandfather being famous."

Gret nodded.

"When I suggested to Professor Nabe about talking to Dean Inman's family, you know, maybe getting some details that weren't just public knowledge, some insights on how his educational theories and his life went together, and his family, and so on—you know what he said? He said, 'But they're all quite unimportant people, aren't they?' "

The two young women walked on side by side.

"That's funny," Gret said, with a grin. She stooped for a black pebble. It was basalt, of course, there was nothing but basalt this whole stretch of the coast, outflow from the great shield volcanoes up the Columbia, or pillow basalts from undersea vents; that's what Mother and Daddy were clambering on now, big, hard pillows from under the sea. The hard sea.

"What did you find?" Sue asked, over-intense about everything, strung out. Gret showed her the dull black pebble, then flipped it at the breakers.

"*Everyone* is important," Sue said. "I learned that this summer."

Was that the truth that the croaking voice had gasped at torture's end? She didn't believe it. Nobody was important. But she couldn't say that. It would sound as cheap, as stupid, as the stupid professor. But the pebble wasn't important, neither was she, neither was Sue. Neither was the sea. Important wasn't the point. Things didn't have rank.

"Want to go on up the Head a ways? There's a sort of path."

Sue consulted her watch. "I don't want to keep your grandmother waiting when she wakes up. I'd better go back. I could listen to her talk forever, she's just amazing." She was going to say, "You're so lucky!" She did.

"Yeah," Gret said. "Some Greek, I think it was some Greek said don't say that to anybody until they're dead." She raised her voice. "Ma! Dad! Yo!" She gestured to them that she and Sue were returning. The small figures on the huge black pillows nodded and waved, and her mother's voice cried something, like a hawk's cry or a gull's, the sea drowning out all consonants, all sense.

Crows cawed and carked over the marshes inland. It was the only sound but the sound of the sea coming in the open window and filling the room and the whole house full as a shell is full of sound that sounds like the sea, but is something else, your blood running in your veins, they said, but how could it be that you could hear that in a shell but never in your own ear or your cupped hand? In a coffee cup there was a sound like it, but less, not coming and going like the sea sound. Caw, cark, caw! Black heavy swoopers, queer. The light like no other on the white ceiling boards. Tongue and groove, tongue in cheek. What had the child said that for, that Amory was the only real one of them? An awful thing to say about reality. The child would have to be very careful, she was so strong. Stronger even than Maggie. Because her father was so weak. Of course that was all backwards, but it was so hard to think the things straight that the words had all backwards. Only she knew that the child would have to be very careful, not to be caught. Cark, ark, caw! the crows cried far over the marshes. What was the sound that kept going on? The wind, it must be the wind across the sagebrush plains. But that was far away. What was it she had wanted to think about when she lay down?

Patricia Lear

POWWOW

The deadeye sun just up and moves over, and this changes things; with the trees in the front yard staying put, not moving, and being no longer in the way, everything is cleared for the sun to slap light across Alma's spun-sugar hair, her blue-tinted hair, where Alma sits dialing the phone. She is calling up the girl, Avery.

And now Avery, she picks up at the kitchen extension in the house where she lives with all the children and all the boarders, and Alma, introducing herself, says to Avery, "I am Alma from the complex," but in a smart voice, not in an old-lady voice with cracks in it and whistling air, but in a smart voice, a voice so smart that Avery thinks this must be another real-estate lady calling, until this crazy thing is said, namely, until Alma says, "Avery? Marian—you know Marian—just hung herself and Popo cannot make a thing of anything."

"Who is Popo?" Avery says, though truthfully in a way mostly looking at her gauzy dog through the kitchen-door screen, the skinny dog bending himself around to get to something on his rear half with his tiny front teeth.

"Popo is your granddaddy, Avery. I am his friend. I am Alma from the complex."

"I never heard anyone call him Popo," Avery says.

"That is the name Marian gave him."

"Who is Marian?" Avery says. "Who is this Marian?"

"The old lady Marian. Your granddaddy's girlfriend Marian. The half-breed lady Marian."

"Is that what happened? She hung herself?" says Avery.

"Avery, I am trying to tell you these things. I am just one of your granddaddy's friends," Alma says, sounding worn out to Avery all of a sudden.

"Popo?" Avery says.

"It's the only name your granddaddy will answer to. And hey, listen," Alma says. "Popo is set back with this thing and all I hear him talking about now is family, hear?"

* * *

No matter. At this point, Avery herself is frankly worn down a notch or two by the flow of life, and not knowing what is what, anyway, she is actually ready to pull up the slack some and come across the state line for a visit, to see the granddaddy she remembers mostly for his bad temper and the ice-cream plant he built up from nothing that seemed to cause the bad temper, and not as much for his Cherokee blood, which was the main thing when she was a kid. She is ready to see him in his retirement condominium, where she has heard there are old ladies and romance. Avery has heard these things in letters, and vaguely of Alma too, and of Marian in these letters, and so, leaving her three children in the good hands of her boarders, some of these boarders even living just behind screens that partition off sections of the huge house, like the screen decorated with a heron standing on one foot in the living room, and another screen painted with flaking Chinese red and age-deepened gold fencing off an alcove on the third floor, Avery packs up some things in a beaten-up leather bag, borrows the big car with air conditioning, and goes to Popo, her granddaddy, with the idea of a powwow lighting on her spirit and rising like a bubble in her heart.

Back at Avery's, there is no man there now on a permanent basis but for the boarders, some of them are men. And Avery is just now coming to an age—to the other side of life, the darker side—where she feels some things are gone and others are not the same, and something in her has the common sense to want and yearn for what is slipping away.

* * *

And now here comes Avery in the big loaded car she has borrowed, her hair sliding around and across her shoulders, driving through the tollbooth, tossing coins at the toll basket, and also now picking up the car phone and calling up Alma, to say to Alma just where she is, she is at the tollbooth ten minutes away, "so start checking whatever it is you need to check, maybe the stove and the coffeepot, because we are rushing and—my fault entirely—we are running late."

Alma twisting the fingers of her gloves, which lie across her lap like little kittens gone limp, with her scared to meet Avery and wanting Avery both (she is not Avery's mother, though she might be, would want to be) her chin lifts up with purpose as she is talking to Avery, and she says, softly now, into the phone, "I am bringing you here for your granddaddy. It's just something I have thought to do for him with what has happened."

Avery nods a wisp of a nod, the breath of a nod, and crawls her hand around inside her purse for some lipstick to slick her lips with. She says, "I hope somebody will just tell me what happened."

* * *

Alma is old and has skin so softened with fine powder film that Avery is aroused to touch it with her finger when she meets Alma in person for the first time at the door of her studio apartment in the sprawling retirement condominium. She settles Alma in the backseat of the car, where Alma is a frilly thing, a dressing-table ornament with lacy cuffs that shiver like aspen leaves at her wrists, and whose first conversation is not about death or hanging or love but about keeping the ice-box cake she has put together in her little kitchenette from turning rancid in the furnace blast of this day. Avery thinks to turn the air-conditioning nozzles so they blow cold air all together at the round-cornered cake that Alma cradles in her lap.

Avery starts up the car, and Alma talks, and in her voice Avery is hearing the real-estate lady again.

"You do not look like the trouble I hear you were, Avery," Alma says. "You are a nice-looking young woman."

"I am fat now," Avery says.

"You do not mean it. I would like to know where any fat is, you cute thing!" Alma says.

"Baby fat from the babies," Avery says, pulling her sleeve tight over her upper arm and holding it up to show it is bigger than it should be.

"We all have that!" Alma says.

"To me, it is a new thing," Avery says, and neither of them says anything for a while, just thinking, as embarrassment rises gently between them, and Alma starts fussing with the cake, rotating the cake to check all sides.

"That poor woman, that Marian. I cannot imagine what went wrong with her," Alma says from some new mood.

"I never knew anyone who killed herself so I cannot imagine being on either side of it," Avery says, putting the car in gear and driving off, swinging around the corner of the retirement condominium, a low pale brick building on golf-course-perfect grass.

Dotted with little staked and roped young trees, humming with a sprinkler system, all this out in the middle of nowhere, where only interstates connect, the two women sight Popo. They watch him emerge through an iridescent heat, hanging on to his chrome walker, a torch of bright gladiolas woven in through the bars. Popo, wearing a dark suit, with floppy legs and mile-wide lapels, and looking to Avery, in his old age with the fat padding gone between him and the world, more the Indian he is than ever.

His gladiolas lurch in a springy, fluid fashion with the walker as Popo makes his way, taking two straight-legged steps, then replacing the walker a bit ahead, and then taking two more steps and moving the walker again, the way life has left him to walk now. Small petals and bits of leaves shake loose, and they fall, leaving a little trail.

Sighting who he guesses is Avery, him being alerted to her coming, Popo shouts at her, "Oh, Avery, Avery, did you know about Marian? She is dead," as if they kept each other up with things, a practice they certainly have not had.

"Ohhh—your flowers," Avery says, standing by the car, and her thumb cannot find the strength to punch in the button to open the door for him, so Popo reaches over her and opens it himself, and then, knees cracking, sits sideways in the seat and becomes absorbed with his walker, first thing pulling out the gladiolas and handing them over to Avery to hold, and then collapsing the walker for her to fit in the trunk.

On seeing him again, and up close, Avery gets the feeling things are beginning to change around in her, causing her emotions to mix up and to run together, her getting a firm handle on not one of them. And the sum total of this hodgepodge is to allow yearning to sneak in and to grab up a bigger fistful of her heart than it already has hold of, and to hang on hard. That he is still a big-shouldered man with skin like clay dirt wrapped over carved cheekbones, and though now old, his skin is lined only in the way the skin on her palms is lined, or the bottoms of her feet, there really are no wrinkles, and that at his shirt collar there is a string tie with a jawbreaker-sized chunk of turquoise for a pull, pale sunlit turquoise, a thing she would want to wear at her shirt collar, and that he combs his hair straight back and smooth are some of the reasons. And that her mama is dead.

"Avery, tell me. How are the children? Is everyone all right?" Popo says. "And how are you back there, Alma?" he says to

Alma, twisting his whole body slightly, but not all the way around, to look at her.

Alma's eyes are like saucers looking at Popo from her vantage perch in the backseat with the cake, and this look is not lost on Avery as she walks back and forth, trance-like, to the trunk of the car with the walker, carrying it over her arms in the manner she might carry long-stemmed roses should that occasion ever occur.

"I do not know what happened," Popo says, his eyes black and wide, turning back to Avery, who is now sliding herself under the steering wheel.

"You can never really know what goes on with another person, really," Alma says from the backseat. Avery looks in the rearview mirror at Alma, seeing her just in the shape of the mirror, just her eyes, which are kind of pretty done up as they are with pale colors, in a way that brings to Avery's mind that odd stone they set in rings sometimes, the star sapphire, with its colors flung out from a washed-out sun in the middle.

Popo, waving his hand just from the elbow, as if there is no wrist, says, "Where did you get this fancy car, sister? You got a phone in here, and I do not know what all."

Avery looks over at her granddaddy, at Popo. He is now punching in the lighter, which will not stay punched in, and fumbling in his breast pocket, spilling papers and getting like all men she has known get—exasperated, fed up with things. He places the cigarette between his lips in a delicate way, the way a jeweler might set a star sapphire, Avery thinks, as she gets the lighter to work right for him; it was only a matter of not punching it so hard.

"Today is a shame, a crying shame," he says, moving his lips around the cigarette.

"Well, it is a terrible thing," Avery says.

"Oh, Avery, I do not know how I will ever get over the things that happen in this life," Popo says, finally lighting up and blowing out a rolling cloud of smoke to go slow, down around in the air-conditioned air.

"See, it is the living, not the dead, that are left with the mess, all the guilt," Alma says from the backseat, leaning her tinted head between the two of them. "And here we are, the living, just as they say."

"Where did Marian get that name for you? The name Popo?" Avery says.

Popo glances at her, then busies himself picking at his clothes and doodling with the cigarette, and messing with the tiny ash and hitting it on the side of the ashtray, and looking out the window spellbound by something out there. Avery squirms under his power, the power to ignore her, and Alma says things from the backseat that do not mean anything or fit in with the conversation, as she cannot hear well what they have been saying now that they are on the expressway and the air conditioning is turned up full.

Kind of surprising her, later, he says, "I like it."

Even later, he says, "Avery? Don't you remember the Popo Bar we used to make at the ice-cream factory? The thing dipped in butterscotch?"

* * *

From way up on the expressway bridge where they are, Avery drives them all past the funeral church, seeing it shimmering white down below, and she can hear, even with the windows rolled up and the air conditioning on, the gravel under the wheels of the cars that are slowly rolling into the small church parking lot, where there is a graveyard in back, stone and cement crosses sticking up here and there, none of them straight up or coming out of the ground at the angle they were put in, or the graves kept up as was somebody's plan.

Now, ramping down a cloverleaf, like on a tilt-a-whirl, all of them flattened up against car doors or hanging on to something, Avery, on automatic pilot, her being a mother, automatically sticks her hand out flat across Popo, and Alma crawls a hand up on his shoulder, until the car has righted itself and all four wheels are bearing equal weight. Next, they dive-bomb straight down on the church, like a chunk of ice coming down a chute, as the church is exactly at the bottom of the straight final part of the cloverleaf ramp and their big car is fast.

While all three have their hands occupied, working on the mysterious unlocking device on their seatbelts, Popo mumbles something at Avery. He says, "You sure were a hellion, sister."

Inside the church, they make their way to the front like a single being, hooked together by arms. They place the gladiolas along with the other flowers on top of Marian's casket, and in the pew the two women work together folding up Popo's walker and laying it down flat where it clanks on the uneven wooden floor under their feet. Then Alma and Avery and Popo rest their shoes on top of it, using it to rest their feet.

There are people seated in the sanctuary, most of them near the front, thinning out toward the back, to maybe one or two here or there. The service begins, and Popo thrusts his chin out goosenecked, and holds it that way until the hymn singing, and when Avery pulls open her purse to look for offering money, a wad of thick Kleenex unfurls itself slightly, like a surprise live thing somebody picked a rock up off of. She separates a Kleenex out and offers it to Popo, who takes it with a hand held downhanded and flat.

After the service, there is a reception across the pasture at a nearby farmhouse, a small frame house with forever aluminum siding with a picnic table and chairs scattered around a patio in back, a little place where people can sit and talk and have something cold to drink. Have something to eat. But just desserts. There is a table of wonderful desserts, all like Alma's ice-box cake, and every bit as good.

Under the afternoon sun that cannot touch them, tucked as they are safely under a broad-leafed tree over by a dried-out fence, is where Avery and Alma and Popo pull together for themselves three metal chairs. This is as far away as they can get from the eerie, glowing bug catcher electrocuting bugs, a thing worse even than the sun. Than anything.

Avery leans her broad back forward, reaching a hand out to Popo's knee, Alma leaning in too, and Avery says, "Popo?" and it takes plain effort to say "Popo," the name is so new. "Do you want to tell me what happened?"

"I did not see anything wrong. Did you, Alma?" Popo says to Alma, who has brought over three iced teas with mint sprigs in frosted plastic tumblers to go with their pieces of cake.

"She was happy," Alma says.

But after thinking, she says, "She dyed her hair black, and when she got that bad flu in the winter and had to stay in bed, the roots grew out, and that got her down."

"Then it started with the lateness," Popo says. "Hey, what about those kids, Avery? You better go and call them."

"What about what lateness?" Avery says.

"Well, Marian—she was always late places, ever since I knew her . . ." Alma says.

"And then it got worse," Popo says.

"How late?" Avery says.

"Well, she could be known—nobody was surprised to see her come even two hours late for bridge club," Alma says.

"What did you do?" Avery says.

"We waited for her. We would sit and talk. Some of us started coming even later, so it didn't matter much. And she was always so nice when she got there. She really was just the nicest person. Wasn't she, Popo? Nice?" Alma says.

"What did you say to her?" Avery says.

"I said nothing to her. What would we say? She was so nice," Alma says.

"Me, I would say, 'Marian, why are you late? We don't want to sit around two hours waiting for you,' " says Avery.

"We wouldn't say that, and you know you wouldn't either, Avery. You are not rude."

"Would you, Avery?" Popo says, scraping up some frosting with the side of his finger. "You probably would. She would, Alma."

"Well, what would that have done? What would that have gotten you? Then there would have been no bridge game at all," Alma says. "Our way, we had two hours to visit with each other, and then bridge with a nice person. Your way, you just rock the boat, don't you see?" Alma says, collecting the plates and wandering off inside the house.

Avery watches her, then looks down at her shoes, then at her stocking, which is bunching slightly at one ankle. She reaches her hand down to get it to go smooth while Popo munches on a mint leaf, taking tiny bites.

He says, "What do you think? Let's take her back and go on and do something ourselves, honey. I am tired of old ladies always around."

* * *

Avery and Popo are in the borrowed car making a white slash on black asphalt, parked as they are on the angle at the Dairy Queen. Popo wants to see what is going on here, as he has heard they have a new machine to mix up the ice-cream formula, and he still has vitality, he still wants to see what everybody is doing in ice cream, even though his company has long been sold.

The Dairy Queen is a white cinder-block building with a little glassed-in front porch with pictures everywhere of Dairy Queen treats in smooth shapes on top of brownies, between cookies, with strawberries, pineapple sauce, chocolate, hot fudge, chocolate dip cones, chocolate-chocolate dip cones, shakes, sodas. Then also, tacos, burritos, fries, burgers, pigs in a blanket, chicken in a basket, and more.

"Let's call those kids. We can, can't we? Just use this car phone," he says, tapping the car phone with a thick-nailed finger.

Avery punches out her home number with the area code and starts talking to her oldest; his name is Benny. She says Popo is with her, that Popo is the Indian she has always told them existed, he is their great-grandfather, and that he wants to talk to all the kids, so go find out who is around. Popo gets on the phone, and when the children pick up, he goes from one to another saying, "Do you know who I am? Have you heard my name?" which is how he opens each conversation, and looking over at Avery, he says, "I do not want to scare them, Avery, thinking they are talking to a strange old man and their mama is out of town. You know."

* * *

Avery feels heavy and slow, sitting on the side of the car where the sun shines through the windows the hardest and the air conditioning cannot make much of a difference.

Later, Popo is still going with the phone. "Now put Eurice back on, Ben," he says. "I just thought of something I want to tell her, something I forgot the first time." He leans his head back on the headrest the way Avery has hers, as he waits for Ben to run and drag Eurice back to the phone.

"What kind of ice-cream bar is your favorite?" is the kind of thing Popo is saying, while sitting next to Avery, speaking into the car phone, and stubbing out one cigarette and right away lighting up another.

Avery's back hurts. She shifts her body around and sits hanging her arms over the steering wheel, narrowing her eyes reading the posters to herself, looking at the pictures that are everywhere on the Dairy Queen walls and windows. "What do you want?" Avery finally says.

"Hold on a minute, Anita, your mama wants to say something. What do I want?" he says to Avery.

"I mean, do you want any Dairy Queen?"

"I don't know. I will decide when I get off the phone. I want to come inside and see the whole works, how they do it, talk to them."

Avery climbs out of the car and wanders around looking at the wildflowers that grow up stalky with small leaves and tiny flowers, at the edge of the cinder parking lot, the cinders smelling like hot tar, at least hot-tar smell is in the air; if not from the cinders, it is some kind of road smell.

Inside the Dairy Queen, on the little glassed-in slab of cement, she waits, slapping flies, now wanting a sweater, watching goosebumps from the freezing air conditioning pop out on her arms, in a bunched-up line with adults and kids dressed in summer shorts and T-shirts, jeans and V-necked halter tops, with almost everyone having layers cut into their hair, that is their style, and the line is so long, Avery so bored, she begins seeing artichokes, their heads looking like a field of artichokes turned upside down, some with leaves that are long, and some just baby leaves, little short spiky things thatched on their heads. She orders a marshmallow sundae and rests her elbow on the countertop to look out the window at Popo, who is still talking into the phone.

Avery, now back wandering around, back next to the Dairy Queen kitchen door, too close to the cooking vent, where there is a fly-dotted chair, a fly airport shaded by the building, a chair which is the only place she can find to go and sit and watch for some sign from Popo for her to come to him from the car.

She hears rock music from a beat box. In the kitchen, there are minimum-wage teenagers dressed in jeans and sneakers, wearing white shirts with white aprons wrapped around their waists, the straps tied in mean little nail-breaking knots. The teenagers are crisscrossing the kitchen, running into each other, pulling dripping baskets of fries out of the fat, flipping hamburgers, chopping lettuce for tacos, and Avery sits and watches them as she spoons her sundae.

One of the girls, her face and neck slick with heat, comes slipping out the door, leaning up against the wall close to Avery, her hands little fists balled in the small of her back. She has one knee bent, her foot up behind her against the cinder-block wall, her heavy hair pulled up from her face and tied with a long cotton scarf, or rag, in the way a Sandinista would wear it, behind her ears, her hair spilling over and away and off her neck. The sleeves of her shirt are rolled tight, her hipbones press out against black jeans that go down narrow to black leather clunky shoes that stream their laces. She glances at Avery and tugs the scarf from her hair to wipe it across her face, the way Avery saw Popo do with the Kleenex she gave him at the funeral.

A boy, maybe nineteen years old, maybe twenty-five, comes out the kitchen door holding cold drinks and hands one to the girl. He heads over to a van parked under a tree back deep in the cinder lot, this girl following along, coltish, stumbling, kicking up cinders with her loose black shoes, and she stands, knees and elbows angled, beside the boy, who puts a long arm around her neck, pulling her over toward him; he puts his cheek up against her cheek, maybe saying something, maybe kissing her neck and cheek, until the girl's body, loose as her knees, causes Avery to watch them, to simply stare. Even in their bodies there is light and bend and movement, and what roundness there is is packed over muscle and bone.

The boy and the girl get in the van and drive out of the Dairy Queen lot, passing in front of Avery, then, oddly, stopping, skidding on cinders; the backup lights light up brightly, and the van backs up. It stops in front of Avery as if they had forgotten her and were coming back to get her, Avery sitting still in the fly chair, to see what will happen.

The girl jumps out, runs around the van, stumbling and catching herself up, reaches into the kitchen door, grabbing up the beat box, what she has forgotten.

Avery sits alone looking at the tangle of things growing around the dumpster, endless chain-link fence, off at the expressway, and she sees something dropped, the rag or scarf that is the girl's lying off by some weeds and crumpled papers, some smashed cups. Going over to where the scarf is lying jagged across the cinders like lightning fallen, Avery stoops to pick it up, and holding it to her face, smelling the very girl in it—it is thick cotton—she stands off behind the Dairy Queen for a time, barely making out Popo, who is sitting in the car. The light is failing now. She drops down on the fly chair and goes to work with the scarf, wrapping it thickly around her wrist, around and around like a bracelet or a cuff, and oddly, if Popo looks up at her while he is talking, he will not know, he will not see in this light Avery smiling at him in a small way, then more broadly. She thinks, she knows, that this powwow is finally over, and the smile is just something that bubbles up in her heart in the most natural of ways.

Just Avery, herself.

Wayne Johnson

HIPPIES, INDIANS, BUFFALO

The letter arrived on a cold, rainy Wednesday, a month to the day after the news that Toby had been killed somewhere south of Khe Sanh. The thin blue envelope was traced with postage markings as if with veins, some of them obscured by handling and water damage, some of them razor sharp: strange lions and elephants and multi-headed people with angular limbs. Martin had come home early from the university to avoid the St. Paul rush-hour traffic, and, digging through the mail in the box outside the house, he came upon the letter as if upon a ghost.

In Toby's facetious way, the letter was addressed *"Center for Deviate Recruitment, Sir Martin D. Sorenson, Esq."*

A shiver ran up Martin's legs, and he took the remainder of the mail, a sheaf of bills and advertisements, into the house with the letter. He set the bills and advertisements on the kitchen table—he was tempted to throw Toby's letter in with the rest—and then went into the living room, lowered himself onto the couch, and switched on the lamp. He turned the letter in his hands, watching the clock on the wall—his mother would be home soon—and finally, heart pounding, he edged his thumbnail up the back and slipped out the thin sheet of paper.

"So, you little son of a bitch," his cousin had written, *"you did open this without telling M & D. Am I right?"*

The doorbell rang, and Martin, his hands clumsy, tried to fold the letter neatly. The doorbell rang again, and Martin squashed the whole mess flat on the coffee table and then shoved it into his pants pocket. At the door Martin's mother backed up against the bell, two overstuffed bags of groceries in her arms. Martin opened the door and his mother nearly toppled over onto him.

"I'll get the rest," he said.

Coming up the drive with his first armload, he watched his mother through the kitchen windows. She took a deep breath and assailed the refrigerator, tossing the frozen things into the left compartment, the others into the right. When he had carried in the last two bags, he stood for a minute watching her. She spun around and smiled.

"So how was your day today?" she said.

* * *

Over dinner Martin's father got into it again. The spaghetti sauce had too much sage in it, and the garlic was—too much. Martin shoved another mouthful in, aiding and abetting his mother.

"I like garlic," he said.

But there *was* too much garlic—and it was garlic salt that Martin's mother had used, so the spaghetti was too salty as well—and Martin was determined just to get it down and get away from the table. He could feel something brewing, something bad.

"Did you hear about the Communists?" Martin's father said.

Martin shrugged his shoulders. He didn't want to talk about it. Martin's father was in private practice, and all this Kennedy talk about socialized medicine set him off. He worked hard—too hard, Martin thought—and more often than not he was irritable and argumentative. Now it appeared that he was going to give yet another of his angry lectures.

"Don't you read the paper?" he said.

"Some," Martin said.

"You've got to keep up with what's going on."

Martin looked up from his plate. His father's forehead glistened dully. His father reached out and gripped Martin's forearm, manfully. Martin didn't like it. Martin's father had never had a father, and he was forever trying to be one, something he wasn't very good at.

"It's Cambodia now," he said.

Martin tried to pull his arm out from under his father's hand. His mother, at the other end of the table, ate slowly, and his sister, across from him, carefully picked at her bread.

"Did you hear?" the doctor said. "They've moved into Cambodia now. This whole thing might escalate into something big."

Martin bent his head over his plate.

He felt his father's eyes boring into him. He felt the weight of it, of the man's money, his anger, his certainty.

"Stop staring at him," his sister, Kristen, said.

* * *

At the sink, the radio on, Martin and Kristen washed dishes. The light in the bedroom upstairs was on, and Martin felt relieved. His father would be reading the paper and his mother would be buried in some inspirational book. *Make Love Your Aim* had been the last one.

"He's just tired," Kristen said.

Martin pulled a fork from the water and cleaned between the tines. He didn't know what to say, and what he had read in Toby's letter bounced around in his head.

"So, you little son of a bitch, you did open this without telling M & D. Am I right?"

"You okay, Marty?"

Martin slipped another plate into the water, scrubbing and then rinsing it. He handed the plate to Kristen. He wanted to say something to her, but that wasn't the way. Everyone was holding everything in and had always held it in. He thought of his mystery grandfather, the alcoholic, and the mystery uncle, who was Martin didn't know what, though he sensed the uncle was the source of some family embarrassment. He thought about the disappointment of what some people had told him would be the best years of his life. How could they get worse? And now this thing. At the dinner table Martin had lied. He *had* heard about the Communists in Cambodia. He had read all he could about it. He had heard talk of a big offensive, possibly a full-force offensive to the east, and lots of troops. He had watched Huntley and Brinkley, and Cronkite, and had seen Toby's snapshots, and had read his letters, over and over. For months Toby had been sending Martin letters, most of them facetious, and Martin couldn't make much sense of them. They were composed of cryptic lyrics from songs he barely knew ("Johnny's in the basement, mixing up the medicine/Twenty years of schooling and they put you on the day shift/Watch out Kid!") and weird exhortations: "Beware of the Stobor!" Martin had saved all the letters in a shoe box under his bed, though none of what was in them had seemed real—the heat and the mud and the death—until they had gotten word about Toby and how he had died.

Martin handed a dish to Kristen. "You want to wash and I'll dry for a while?" he said.

They traded places. Kristen churned away in the water. "Hey," she said, bumping Martin with her elbow.

* * *

In his basement room he sat on his bed, a calculus text open beside him. He leafed through a copy of *Goldfinger.* In the past month he had read all of Fleming's books, even the more obscure of them, except for this one. They were pure escape, right up there with pot, a real slug in the arm. Now he couldn't even make it through the first page for thinking about Toby's letter. He wondered what was in it and why it hadn't come earlier, and when Martin heard his father's heavy tread down the stairs, he tossed *Goldfinger* under the bed and opened his calculus text.

Martin's father smiled bitterly in the doorway. He was holding a glass.

"You're not fooling anyone," he said.

Martin felt his face grow hot.

"The only person you're fooling is yourself," Martin's father said.

Martin scratched at the open book with his pencil, trying to think of some way out, but nothing came to him. He had never found a way to fight this man, and the small victories he had won over him in the past year he saw now as nothing more than self-inflicted injuries. He had failed three classes, had gotten into some small trouble with the police, and had refused to have his hair cut. A counselor had straightened him out on the classes ("You won't get into the better graduate schools if you keep this up"), and the mess with the police—a drunken-driving charge and a night in jail—had convinced him of the consequences of screwing up for real. But the hair stayed. Somehow the hair was what got to his father. It was a simple, tangible thing—he had grown it long, and had made a braid of it, like the Indians up at the lodge, where he worked summers—and, as silly as it seemed, the hair had come to represent something, something even Martin didn't quite understand.

Martin turned to face the window. His father stood in the doorway, shifting the glass of soda around and around in his hands.

"Marty," he finally said, "why don't you tell me what's wrong?"

Martin drew his breath in. He picked at a hole in his jeans. A car rumbled by outside. They hadn't talked for so long that there was no place to start.

* * *

Upstairs, Kristen's door shut, and then the house was silent. Martin waited ten long minutes and then carefully tugged the letter from his pants pocket. He laid it on his calculus book and smoothed out the creases with his palm.

"So, you little son of a bitch, you did open this without telling M & D. Am I right?"

Martin shook his head. He was afraid to read the letter. He held it under the lamp, and the blue scrawl seemed to rise up off the page.

December 3, 1969

Dear Marty,

I'm gonna make this short, and I hope to God you get this, only I don't know. We've been held down under mortar fire the last day and a half and I'm damn near deaf. Yesterday that kid Boehmer (remember him from grade school? The guy with the buck teeth?) got gutshot and was screaming like you wouldn't believe. We were pretty close. He said he'd take this stateside (guess how and where? I'll give you a clue—it's a place where the sun don't shine), only he didn't pull through, after all. But this is it, Marty, you smart and screwed-up little bastard.

Here the longhand ended. The remainder was printed, in large block letters.

Whatever you do, don't let them talk you into coming over here. All we're doing is dying like pigs out in this fucking muck. Don't listen to grandpa, and don't listen to your old man. Just keep telling yourself, it's not something worth dying over.

Don't show this to anyone. You were always an okay guy, Marty. I'd say "pray for me" if I believed in that, but I don't, so I'm saying "wish me luck" instead.

Yours,
Tobe

Martin read the letter again. Then again. He read the letter ten times before he turned his light off, and after what seemed like an endless time lying in the dark, he turned on the light and read it five times more. He finally fell asleep, and in the morning he woke with the light on, the letter still in his hand.

"Marty," his father called down the stairs.

Martin rammed the letter behind the bed. He felt as though he had been caught doing something shameful, and he tried to make his body look sleepy.

He heard that heavy tread on the stairs.

"Marty," Martin's father said. Then, shaking Martin by the shoulder, he said, "Come on up. I made breakfast for you."

* * *

Thanksgiving day, 1970.

The gravy tureen made its way around the table again. Martin's grandfather, Spencer, was corralling his peas against a mound of mashed potatoes. "I'll have some of that," he said, taking the tureen.

Martin watched him pour the gravy. Though Spencer ate with his usual gusto, Martin's cousins, Jane and Lucy and Todd, at the smaller table with Kristen, held back.

Nearly a year had passed since Toby's death, and this Thanksgiving was the last of the firsts—the first Christmas without Toby, the first Easter, and so on. Now that Toby would never come back, these times together were different, an adjustment, and this was the last of them. Martin looked from face to face around the table. They were all carefully talking around anything having to do with what had happened to Toby—his aunt red-eyed, his uncle poking at his plate, his mother smiling nervously, his father and grandfather chewing forcefully.

Martin wiped his mouth with a napkin and excused himself.

In the bathroom he sat on the toilet. He held his hand over his mouth. A bitter laughter bubbled up in him.

"And, Lord, let us remember our Toby today," Spencer had

prayed, "that he did not die in vain but that through such sacrifice our lives are made possible."

Someone knocked on the door.

"Marty, you coming out?" Kristen said.

"Just a minute." Martin flushed the toilet for effect and ran the tap. He opened the door, and Kristen smiled at him.

"Come sit at the other table with me," she said.

Martin's father and uncle were talking politics again.

"At least he wasn't one of those goddamned draft dodgers," Spencer said.

Lucy and Jane and Kristen were talking about orchestras. They talked loudly, filling in the gaps. Todd was listening to the other table, and made no effort to disguise his interest. Martin liked that about Todd, and angled his chair to see better.

"I'm proud of Toby," Spencer said.

Martin's father shook his head. "I'm not saying we like the idea, but we can't just let them go wherever they want. They want world control, after all. You know that"—Martin's father gestured with his fork. "You were in right after I was. Remember how it was in Korea?"

Martin's uncle slowly pushed his chair back from the table. He had an especially long face, and it went through a transformation now, his eyes narrowing as he turned to face Martin's father.

"We'll see what you have to say when Marty gets sent over there," he said.

Martin's mother set a pie on the table.

"Dessert's here," she said.

* * *

The letter from "Uncle Sugar," as Toby had called the armed services, came in December. It came on a Monday, along with snow, one of the first really big snows of the season. Martin opened the letter in the kitchen, with a knife. He was to report for training at Fort Hood, Texas, on May 16.

Martin sat at the table, waiting for the news to sink in.

He tried to imagine himself with thousands of other bald-headed kids, running around in green uniforms, practicing killing people, and then, if worse came to worst, actually going off somewhere and doing it. He'd killed plenty of things—a deer every fall for the past six seasons, ducks, pheasants—and he was a crack shot, a natural with a gun. But up at the lodge, with Bear and Osada and Buck, there was a certain reverence in the killing, thanks given, and a reason. This was senseless and evil and, as Toby had put it, *political.* Martin didn't want to be involved in these political things, and he didn't really see why he had to be. No one was threatening his country. Any idiot could see that. In some ways the point of the war had been lost since that business with Lieutenant Calley. So what was going on?

Martin stood and opened the shutters.

The day was so bright, so *white.* The elm in the front yard was covered with snow. Above the trees snow tumbled down, a boiling curtain of white. A plane cut low across the horizon and disappeared into the clouds. Something in the letter caught Martin's attention, and he held it up in the light.

May 16, that was it.

And then the thought struck him, like a fist in the stomach, that May 16 was also opening day on walleyes, and if not for this mess, he would have taken the train up to Wheeler's Point, where he would have caught the launch over to Big Island.

* * *

In February Martin bought a car from a dealer on Lake Street. He didn't know why he had to have the car, but he knew, somehow, that it would be important. The car was an old Nash, one that looked a bit like a bathtub turned upside down. For months Martin had joked with two of his friends about it.

"The World's Ugliest Car," he had said, pointing it out.

It had a grille like that on the bottom of a refrigerator, and bumper guards that looked like chrome tadpoles.

"We ought to paint LOVE BANDIT on the side for you," his friend Tony said the afternoon Martin bought it.

For months after, when Martin went out to look at the car mornings he'd find new slogans spray-painted on the fenders and hood. This had a sense of rightness about it. In some slow way Martin felt himself turning, but in which direction he wasn't sure. In a way he felt as if he were destroying himself, but he also felt good. He had decided he would give as little of himself as possible to things he didn't believe in, and the war was one of these things. It wasn't his war. It wasn't even his country he would be fighting for—it was some *thing,* and Martin was damn sure it wasn't freedom. So he drove around St. Paul in the Nash, feeling out this new direction, and feeling that things could not possibly be other than they were.

* * *

How things were came to him in bits and pieces, and angered and saddened him. Everywhere he saw people divided against each other, and at home it was no different. Mowing his grandfather's lawn one hot April afternoon, Martin stopped to cool off. He lifted the braid off the back of his neck, draping it over the bench. Spencer shook the newspaper he was reading and set it on his knees.

"You look like a *goddamn hippie,*" he said, his voice filled with disgust. "Or worse yet, a *goddamn Indian.*"

Martin scratched his forehead. He fought an impulse to say what he was feeling, for he was afraid he might say things he could never take back.

"What's happened to you?" Spencer said.

Martin stood. The words caught in his throat.

"Nothing," he said.

He dragged the mower around to the front yard and attacked the hill bordering the street. The mower shuddered through the high grass, snapping over spring deadfall. Martin felt hurt and angry. What had Spence meant? That he was like the Ojibway in the housing project, people who lived as if in a war zone? Is that what he had meant? That he was defeated and pitiful? If that was it, then Spence was *wrong.* For if Martin had learned anything from working with the Ojibway up north, it was that they had not been defeated, *couldn't* be defeated, and that was why they had been destroyed. He remembered something Osada had said.

They had been out in the boat, duck hunting, and a plane had flown low over the lake.

"Boy, what I'd give to have one of those," Martin said.

Osada looked at him, cocked his head to one side and then the other, as if he were measuring him up.

"What would you give?" he said.

Martin felt himself caught, and tried to come up with an answer, one that was not a lie.

"I guess I don't know," he said finally.

Osada laughed to himself and then quieted.

"Listen to me," he had said. "The way against the spirit is the evil way, is the way of destruction."

Lifting the mower into the trunk of the Nash, Martin glanced over the hill into the yard. The bench, newly painted, glistened a bright maroon, the grass as flat as a crew cut around it. Martin opened the driver's door and got in. He sat for a few minutes in the heat, fanning his shirt over his chest. Out of the corner of his eye he could see Spence in the front window. When a big bead of sweat ran down Martin's forehead and dropped onto his hand, he turned the key in the ignition and started the car. This time he wouldn't back down.

* * *

The car was not popular.

When Martin asked Kristen what she thought about the car, she hesitated, a studious look on her face, and said, "I like the steering wheel. . . . It looks like pearls." Martin's mother offered to sew him some seat covers for it. Martin's father's friends parked in the street so as not to put their Lincolns or Cadillacs beside it. Martin's father hated the car.

"I want you to get that hulk out of the driveway," he had said the morning after the first spray-painting had been done.

Now Martin stood beside his father, surveying the damage of this past night's raid. Rivulets of white paint dripped from the letters on the doors.

THE LONE RANGER the letters read, and on the trunk was ZOOKS!

"I want it out of the driveway," Martin's father said. "I mean it."

Martin shoved his hands into his pockets. "I don't think it's so—"

"Oh, come off it. It looks like hell."

Martin could see this was becoming something much bigger than a ruined two-hundred-dollar car, and he tried to ease away. His father caught him by the arm.

"Just what do you think you're trying to do?" Martin's father said.

Martin shrugged.

"I want you to tell me—say it straight—what the hell do you think you're doing with this car?"

Martin tugged at his arm, and his father gripped it tighter. Martin got a boiling sensation in his chest, and then he imagined himself banging his father's head against the car until his head split open, and he felt himself torn with grief.

"Don't worry," Martin said.

"What?"

"I said, don't worry."

"What do you mean, 'Don't—' "

"Goddamn it!" Martin said. "It doesn't make a goddamn bit of difference, because three goddamn weeks from now I'll be in goddamn Texas! You hear that?" he said, jerking his arm free. "Tex-ass!"

* * *

Sunday night the week before Martin was to take the train down to Fort Hood, the house was quiet. Martin's father rummaged around in the basement for his old duffel bag.

"You'll need this," he said, setting the bag at the end of Martin's bed.

Martin had packed most of his belongings away, had cleaned out his closet, and had piled the clothes he was planning to take on the bed. He was amused, in a grim way, about the concern over these small things now. He knew that none of it mattered. In his mind, the army would strip him of everything, and he imagined, with bitter humor, showing up in a Bozo the Clown outfit, complete with the red nose, ruffled neck ring, and oversized shoes.

"Hi! I'm Bozo," he would say. "And you must be Commander Bozo . . ."

Martin's mother brought towels from the dryer.

She laid the towels on the bed and wrung her hands. His mother was a birdlike woman, funny at times, sad at others.

"Here's some towels for you," Martin's father said.

Martin smiled at his mother.

"Thanks," he said.

Kristen leaned against the door jamb.

Martin looked from his sister to his mother to his father.

"I got to get some air," he said.

* * *

Hours later, his feet sore and his legs tired from circling the chain of lakes in town, Martin turned the corner of the service road home and went up the drive. The house was dark, and he was tired, and he didn't see his father standing with his back braced against the car.

"Hey," his father said.

It startled Martin, and he could think of nothing to say. They stood like that, staring up into the low-hanging clouds. The night sounds grew in volume and then faded away, fireflies blinking across the lawn. The fireflies got to Martin. He remembered catching them in a jar, him and his father. They had run across the yard, nabbing them off grass stems, two jars, a contest with no winner, a *fun* game, really.

Thinking about the fireflies, Martin felt like saying he was sorry but knew he couldn't. There was always more to remember.

"A chemical process makes them light up," Martin's father had explained.

Martin had looked into the jars, curious.

"You aren't listening," his father said.

"Yes, I am," he said.

Martin's father stood. "No, you're not," he said.

He took the jar from Martin, and with one heartrending swoop of his arms he tossed both jars up into the air, where they turned end over end until they shattered on the driveway.

"I'm sick and tired of this," his father had said, and Martin had tried not to cry.

And now, here they were again.

Martin could sense that his father was trying to say something. But he just stood there, a big, mute presence in the dark, but dangerous, like a buffalo. Standing like this, against the car in the middle of the night, seemed almost his way of saying he was sorry. Martin slapped a mosquito. Now that he had stopped moving, the bugs were biting.

"Can't stand out here all night," Martin said.

Martin's father rubbed his forearms.

If he were to say he was sorry now, Martin thought, *I would let it all go, this night, right now.*

Martin's father shuffled, ran his hand over his thinning hair. He picked at a scab of paint on the Nash, and as he pulled up on it, a whole strip of paint came away from the rusty metal underneath. Martin looked up into the dark sky. A jet lumbered in from the west, its lights cutting bright holes in the dark.

"What are you going to do with the car?" Martin's father said.

"What?" Martin asked.

"The car—what are you going to do with the car?"

Martin turned to face his father; he had been hoping for something else, but this is what it had come to.

"The car?"

"Yes, the car," his father said.

* * *

Martin slipped out of bed. In the dark he dressed in his jeans and moccasins and denim jacket, shouldered the duffel bag, and without turning to look at the nearly bare room, climbed the stairs to the front door. He was turning the knob when he remembered that he had forgotten something. He set the duffel bag down and went into the bathroom, to the cabinet under the sink. He pulled Toby's last letter and a small blue envelope from behind the sink, and stuffed them in his breast pocket. He hadn't realized before why he had kept his savings out of the bank, but now he knew. The daydreams he had had for months, had dismissed as fantasy, now took on real proportions.

* * *

Out on Highway 35 Martin geared the Nash up, and the old six crooned. Martin hung his arm out the window, singing to himself. He tried not to think about what he was doing, and he turned on the radio. He had gotten the radio a few weeks before, and now he turned it up, pretending to enjoy the music. What the hell, he could do a lot of things, he thought. A highway patrol car drove by and then spun around, lights flashing.

On the side of the road the officer held a flashlight beam in Martin's eyes.

"What are you doing out at this time of night?" the officer said, looking down at Martin's license.

"Going fishing," Martin said.

"Let's see your gear."

Martin got out of the car. He reached for the trunk key in his pocket.

"Hold it," the officer said, the gun out of the holster and ready now.

* * *

Around four Martin cleared the last of the plains. To the north the lights of Duluth held off the dark waters of Lake Superior. A huge trucking complex sat off the highway, a diesel stop, and Martin drove the Nash through the labyrinth of roads to the squat brown restaurant in the middle. He took a booth on the far end, away from the door and the counter, where two heavyset truckers sniggered.

"What do you want?" the waitress said.

"A cup of coffee."

The waitress gave Martin a sour face. Behind her the two truckers laughed.

"You've got to get something to eat with it," the waitress said, holding a menu out. "We can't have people just drinking the hell out of our coffee for nothing."

Martin took the menu.

"What do you have?"

"You can read, can't you?" the waitress said, bracing her hand on her hip.

Martin could see now that the truckers had put her up to it, but she was enjoying it as much as they were. The two truckers nudged each other and laughed. The bigger stood and strode to the back, pushing through a red door. Martin patted his breast pocket.

"Two eggs," he said, "hash browns, biscuits, and lots of coffee."

The waitress went around to the kitchen, and the trucker who was still at the counter caught her arm as she went by.

"Is it a boy or a girl?" he said.

Martin tried to ignore them. He traced the marking in the table top, thinking about driving north now, and the gravity of what he was doing. He hadn't thought about it, he had just done what he thought was right. He had believed Toby, but he hadn't thought about what it would be like *not* to go. All he had thought about was what *going* would mean.

The food came and the waitress slapped down the check.

"Anything else?"

"No," he said, poking at the food with his fork.

The energy that had driven him this far, a wiry, unthinking energy, had gone away, and now he felt sick. He wasn't so sure about anything now, and he felt as though he were poised between two starting points all over again, the Nash outside, waiting, this food on the table in front of him, and the big man out of the toilet and laughing with his friend.

He thought of going out to the Nash and getting his .30-06.

"Like deer hunting, Fat Boy?" he would say.

But beneath the anger was something else, and it got all tangled up trying to come out. Martin belted down the hot coffee, trying not to think about it. What was he doing anyway? Who was he fooling? The big trucker gave out a belly laugh, and Martin stood and went into the men's. On the wall was a large vending machine with pictures of naked women spread-legged across it, their mouths big O's of pleasure. Martin stepped up to a urinal. He could hear them laughing out in the restaurant. He stared into the wall, and something in it came clear. Someone had cut through the wallpaper, in big, jagged strokes, HIPPIES ARE LIVING PROOF THAT INDIANS FUCKED BUFFALO.

It stuck in his head like a hot poker, and then he was striding up past his booth to the car, all of it bursting out of him now. He didn't trust himself to drive this way, and he leaned against the fender, watching the waitress. She went over to the table, and when she saw that Martin hadn't paid his tab, she marched to the front door and out, the truckers behind her.

Martin got into the Nash and started it.

"You son of a bitch!" the waitress yelled, pointing.

The big man took off across the gravel drive and Martin swung the Nash around, headed for the waitress. She blinked twice and then saw he meant murder, her face a brilliant moon of fear, and in that moment Martin saw himself, what he had been running from, and he veered off to the right, and burst up the road onto the highway, and with the blood pounding in his head, and the highway howling under him, he went a long time, the Nash swaying from side to side, barreling along as close to death as it would take him, and not until he passed a road sign and slowed down did he admit to himself that it wasn't an accident, he hadn't taken the wrong entrance onto the highway, and the lights of Duluth were now far away and to the south.

Perri Klass

FOR WOMEN EVERYWHERE

Alison, in her ninth month, finds she can no longer turn over in bed at night without waking up. The hydraulics of shifting her belly are just too complex, and to get from her left side to her right, she has to maneuver herself delicately, tucking her elbow under and using it as a lever, swinging her abdomen over the top. Turning over the other way, belly down, is not possible; if she could, she imagines, she would look like a circus seal balancing on a huge ball.

When her best friend from high school arrives to keep her company and wait for the birth, Alison hopes to be distracted; lately, she thinks of nothing but the advent of labor. When will this baby come out, when will the pains start that will be unmistakably something new, something she has never felt before? Her obstetrician suggested that they might feel like bad menstrual cramps, which Alison has never had. And she is now accustomed to the small tightenings inside her belly that occur every now and then; Braxton-Hicks, she tells her friend Doris who thereafter asks her, if she should happen to clutch her belly, "Another Brixie-Hixie?"

It is very nice to have Doris around. For one thing, unpregnant, Doris is easily as big as Alison in her ninth month. Doris was big in high school and she's bigger now. She buys her clothes in special stores that sell silk and velvet and linen for the fat working woman, and all her lingerie is peach. She smells of a perfume named after a designer, which smells familiar to Alison because of little scented cardboard samples in a million magazines—open this flap to enjoy the magic—opposite honey-toned photos of naked bodies arranged like fruit in a basket. Doris's possessions fit surprisingly well into what she calls the tawdry jungle glamour of Alison's apartment. Among the overgrown plants with Christmas lights strung through them, and the life-size stuffed animals, and the bongo drum collection, Doris reclines in her jumpsuits, taking her ease as if waiting for her palanquin. When Doris and Alison walk down the street together on their way for hamburgers and onion rings, Alison feels like a phalanx. Finally she has the nerve to wear a big straw hat with fuchsia flowers out in public, stealing it off her stuffed giraffe. Hey, Big Mamas, she imagines someone shouting (not that anyone ever does). Together, she and Doris take up their share of the street and of the hamburger restaurant where the waitress now greets them by saying, the usual, right?

Alison is by now pretty well used to the rude and stupid and none-of-their-business things that people say to her. Good old Doris walked into her apartment, put down her two suitcases and her handbag and her camera case and informed Alison, looking narrowly at her ballooned abdomen, "Alison, you are doing this For Women Everywhere." Then she gave a Bronx cheer.

"Right," said Alison, with relief, wondering how Doris knew. The world is full of well-meaning people who feel the need to tell Alison how brave she is, how they admire her. I always wanted a baby, but I don't know whether I would dare, they say; or, this is a really great thing you're doing. Alison's mother sends clippings from *People* magazine, keeping her up to date on Jessica Lange and Sam Shepard, Farrah Fawcett and Ryan O'Neal, Mick Jagger and

Jerry Hall. Even Michael, when he calls up, shyly, to ask whether she really thinks this baby might be his, feels a politically correct need to tell her what a strong woman she is.

"Some people never grow up," is Doris's comment after Michael's next call, and at first Alison thinks she is referring to Michael, which is really unfair. Of the three of them, Michael could be considered the one who most notably has grown up; he has a house and a marriage and two children and all the correct car seats and coffeemakers. "You," says Doris, "here you are at your age and the best you can manage is a friend you went to high school with and a boy you've been sleeping with since high school. Don't you ever think about moving on to a later stage?"

There is some justice there, Alison supposes, but if you are thirty-five and your favorite people are left over from when you were fifteen, then that's the way it is. Michael's marriage, acquired in adulthood, does not make Alison's mouth water. Neither does Doris's legendary liaison with a penthouse-dwelling real estate tycoon. Doris is mildly, or maybe avidly, curious to know who the other possible fathers are, and makes some pointed remarks about people who expect their friends to Tell All, and then hold back on their own juicy details, but Alison is not telling and not willing to be drawn into the same game of Twenty Questions that Michael keeps wanting her to play. Is it anyone I know? Is it anyone you care about? How many possibilities are there, anyway? "I am not," Alison says with pregnant dignity, "the kind to kiss and tell."

Alison is consuming something close to four rolls of Tums a day at this point. Automatically before and after every meal she reaches into her pocket for the cylinder, pops off three little chalky disks and crunches them, feeling the burning go away. Doris tells her this is somewhat disgusting, and Alison informs her, loftily "My obstetrician says I have progesterone-induced incompetence of the lower esophageal sphincter."

"Talk about disgusting," says Doris.

But it is a pleasure to have Doris there to go with her to the obstetrician, a pleasure not to go alone for the umpteenth time. She hands Doris the straw hat and steps on the scales unhesitatingly, watches the nurse move the weight from 150 to 200, then back to 150, then start messing around with the next smaller weight. One-eighty-two, very good. Smugly, Alison steps off the scale; how educational for Doris, she thinks, to realize that when you are pregnant you get on the scale proudly and hear a number like 182, and then a commendation. But Doris is studying a wall chart, a drawing of a full-term baby packed into a mother. Note the scrunched-up intestines, the way the baby's head presses on the bladder, and so on. "Yich," comments Doris, and follows Alison into the examining room, where she is notably unmoved by the amplified fetal heart.

Alison's obstetrician, Dr. Beane, is a good five or six years younger than Alison and Doris, and is such an immaculate and tailored little thing that it is rather hard to imagine her elbow-deep in the blood and gore that Alison imagines in a delivery room. Also, she has such tiny hands; can she really grab a baby and pull? Is that what an obstetrician does? Alison started out dutifully attending the classes, but she dropped out long before they got to the movie; she has never been one to read instruction booklets. Dr. Beane gives Doris the once-over, considerately doesn't ask any questions, and feels around on Alison's belly with those small, surprisingly strong hands. "You're engaged!" she says, as if offering congratulations.

Alison wonders briefly whether this is some terribly tactful way of acknowledging Doris's presence (better than, say, is this your significant other?), but it turns out that engaged means that the baby's head has descended into her pelvis, and the baby is in place, all ready to be born.

"Have you thought about anesthesia?" asks the doctor, and launches into an educational lecture on spinals and epidurals, both of which involve having a needle inserted into Alison's back and pumping drugs into her spinal column.

"Yich," comments Doris.

"I think I'd rather die," says Alison.

"You won't die one way or the other. You'll just have pain. And if the pain is too bad, you can have Demerol, just to take the edge off for awhile."

"In sorrow shall you bring forth children," says Doris, biblically enough.

"Pay no attention to that man behind the curtain," says Alison, not to be outdone.

"Any time now," says Dr. Beane, cheerful and unperturbed.

* * *

Twenty years ago in high school, Doris and Alison and Michael were the three smartest of their year, Doris and Alison were best friends and Michael and Alison eventually fumbled their way into bed. Michael and Doris, however, were the true co-conspirators of the high school, the ones who destroyed every sewing machine in the home economics classroom with a tube of Super Glue and a jar of Vaseline; the ones who reprogrammed the guidance computer so that every senior received a printout recommending Notre Dame as the single most appropriate college; the ones who slipped copies of *Oui* and *Penthouse* into the heavy plastic jackets reserved for *Life* and *Smithsonian* in the library. Alison was more or less a chicken. Doris is now more or less the only person in the whole world who understands how Alison can go on sleeping with Michael every couple of weeks or so, year in and year out, and never want either to escalate or to de-escalate. And when Michael got married, and they didn't miss a beat, Doris was the only one to whom it was perfectly obvious that his relationship with Alison was covered by a grandfather clause. Alison knows that Michael called her up at the time, stricken with the kind of moral qualms with which he occasionally likes to agitate himself, and she knows that Doris told him to shut up and put out, and she is grateful. Michael's marriage is a brilliant success, as far as Alison can see, though she has not actually met his wife. They are both professors, Michael of math, of course, and his wife of something with ceramics in it, which is not art, but high-tech semiconductors. Or something; Alison reserves the right not to be interested and wastes almost no time imagining the marriage, two total weirdo science drones trying to be domestic.

Alison and Doris parade themselves to the hamburger joint for the usual, once again. Alison has medium rare with cheddar and onions, Doris has rare with guacamole on top; both have onion rings. Alison's maternity wardrobe has dwindled; nothing fits and she cannot bring herself to buy anything since the whole process should be over in a week or two. She has one floral drop cloth, contributed by her mother who also sent four pairs of support hose that are still intact in their cellophane. Over her one pair of cotton pants with a very stretched-out elastic waistband, she can put either a bright pink, extra-extra large T-shirt or else a breezy little yellow rayon number, bought at a yard sale, which was meant to be a pajama top for a very large lady. She has been working at home since her seventh month, easy enough since much of her work has always been done at home. She writes the in-house newsletter for a large company that manufactures communications equipment, and they have installed a modem in her living room. She is paid a ridiculous amount for this and has no intention of ever teaching Freshman English again. The only problem, as of the last week or two, is that she cannot sit up at her desk anymore for long periods of time. The inhabitant of her abdomen starts to do calisthenics, and to have a full-size baby doing rhythmic jerks in her belly, it turns out, means she has to lie back on the couch and give it room.

She lies back, pulls up the pink T-shirt, pulls down the cotton pants, and she and Doris stare at her belly, at the road map of stretch marks. "God, it's like some kind of earthquake," says Doris, as the striated skin over Alison's belly button heaves upward. Today Doris, in honor of Alison's apartment, is wearing her leopard-print jumpsuit and blood-red earrings to match her fingernails.

"Are you quite comfortable?" Alison asks her abdomen. The

acute angle of a little elbow juts out clearly, squirms around, then retreats into its crowded bath. Actually, Alison finds herself overwhelmed, reduced to awestruck mush, by the contemplation of her belly, by the thought that tightly curled up in there is a full-grown sardine of a baby. How can this possibly be? A fetus was one thing, for all its hormonal cyclone, the morning sickness and all the rest, but how can she be carrying something around that properly belongs in a baby carriage? And something with such a mind of its own; it seems now to want to put its feet just where Alison believes she keeps her own liver.

When Michael calls, Doris takes it upon herself to talk to him. She describes the action in Alison's belly, which she refers to as heavy weather in the Himalayan foothills. Alison, still lying on the couch, can hear the firm tones in which Doris discourages Michael's surreptitious questions. She's fine, we're fine, don't be ridiculous. You'll never know. You'll take care of your own children, Alison will take care of hers and everyone will be just fine. Alison thinks of Doris in the tenth grade, when she wore only black and made frequent references to her dabbles in the occult sciences. Her room, in her parents' pleasant Tudor-style, two-car-garage house, had been converted into a sanctuary of Satan. Doris had removed the light bulb from the ceiling fixture and put two white, skull-shaped candles on either side of an altar on which the girls' high school gym teacher was regularly tortured in effigy before being sacrificed. Doris's mother had minded the writing on the walls more than anything else. But, after all, once the walls were written on they would have to be repainted anyway, so why not write on them some more? So Doris and Alison and Michael decorated them freely with song lyrics that seemed particularly meaningful at the time. Also, poems. The Who, William Blake, Hermann Hesse and Leonard Cohen figured prominently in the graffiti; Doris and Alison and Michael were all smart, but hardly exceptional. Anyway, lying on the couch, Alison remembers Doris in her high priestess phase: massive in black, making oracular pronouncements, suggesting death or disfigurement for those she disliked, promising the favored that they would prosper.

"Lots of Brixie-Hixies, huh?" says Doris, finding Alison leaning against the wall in the kitchen, holding her belly.

"I don't know, this might be more than that."

"No false alarms now, you don't want to go getting me all excited for nothing."

"Let's time them," says Alison.

Twenty minutes apart. Fifteen minutes apart. Starting to hurt a little. Lasting thirty to forty seconds. Doris notes them down systematically in Magic Marker on Alison's one clean dish towel, contributed, needless to say, by her mother. She suggests to Alison that these numbers will make a humdrum dish towel a priceless precious memento. Alison tries to remember whether they said anything about breathing back in those first couple of childbirth classes.

"All right," says Doris, coming to the bottom hem of the dish towel. "Get that cunning little bag you have all packed and waiting and let's get moving."

"You really think it's time?"

"Do you want to wait for Sherman to take Atlanta? Get into the pony cart and let's go."

* * *

At the hospital, the nurse puts Alison into two little gowns, one with the opening in the front, the other in the back. Strangely enough, all the way over in the car, even as she experimented with panting, with taking big deep breaths, with moaning and groaning, Alison expected them to look at her blankly, to send her home, to wonder aloud why she was wasting their time. Instead, along comes this nurse, Madeline, a black woman even larger than Doris. The three of us, Alison thinks, would make quite a singing group. The nurse puts an IV into Alison's left hand and hooks belts around her waist to connect her to a fetal-heart monitor. Doris finds the monitor quite interesting and, when the nurse leaves the room, experiments with the volume control, turning up the gallop-a-trot of the baby's heartbeat as loud as it will go.

"Noisy baby you have there," she remarks. "I thought this was supposed to hurt. Does it hurt yet?"

"Are you looking forward to watching me writhe in pain?"

"Just remember, you will be writhing for women everywhere."

Alison is immeasurably glad to have Doris there. Does this mean, she finds two seconds to wonder in between contractions, that she is in fact going to want someone there from now on, that she is going to find herself alone with this baby and feel bereft? Well, maybe. But this is a fine time to start worrying about that.

"Don't worry," she tells Doris. "It's starting to hurt plenty. Don't be deceived by my stoicism and physical bravery."

"When you make a face like you're constipated and then pant like a dog, is that when it hurts?"

"I still can't understand why you didn't become a psychiatrist," says Alison, beginning to pant again.

"There's more money in stockbrokering," says Doris, who is in fact very rich.

"Well, thanks for coming," says Alison, suddenly not sure she has yet gotten around to saying that.

"I wouldn't miss this for the world." Doris looms over the bed, a great big woman with an auburn permanent and red nails, wearing green paisley lounging pajamas. What more could anyone want in a labor room? "Soon the fun will really begin—don't you get an enema?"

"I think that's out of date. Shit, Doris, this isn't a joke any more."

"All you girls think you can just play around, and then when you get caught, you start whining."

The nurse, Madeline, comes bustling in, hears them shouting over the boom of the monitor. "Who turned this thing up so high?" she demands, turning it down.

"Why don't you take a little walk, see some of the scenery?"

Madeline is unstrapping her from the monitor, rather to Alison's surprise; she hadn't expected them to grant her request.

"Is that okay?"

"Honey, you're moving pretty quick for a first baby, but you've got a ways to go. Just you go strolling with your friend, there's lots of corridors."

The people that Alison and Doris pass, as they promenade through the Labor and Delivery hallways, look meaningfully at Alison's belly. Most are doctors and nurses dressed in green surgical scrubs. There is one other woman in labor who is also up and walking, but her husband, who is six feet tall and bearded after the manner of John the Baptist, is practically carrying her. The walls are hung with nondescript Impressionist landscapes.

"Lovely on the Riviera this time of year," Doris says, each time they pass the French fishing village, and, "I hear the stained glass is simply stunning," when they pass the cathedral at sunset.

Eventually, walking begins to feel a little less probable, and Alison climbs back into bed. And along comes Dr. Beane to congratulate her on already being five centimeters dilated.

"God," says Alison, "this is becoming a real pain in the ass."

"Truer words were never spoken," says Doris.

Alison is no longer able to muster a sense of humor. Alison is in quite significant pain, and it is borne in upon her that she does not have the option of stopping these regular onslaughts. She would like an hour off, she wants to tell them, she would like to put this on hold and start again tomorrow. Instead, Madeline comes by every now and then and tells her to take deep breaths. They have her belted up again and keep telling her to listen to her baby's heart, how strong and regular it is. But this steady lub-a-dubbing seems to Alison to have very little indeed to do with that strong-willed little gymnast who has been kicking and wriggling so idiosyncratically. Alison wishes, truly and sincerely, to be back on her couch, watching her belly heave and swell. What a good working relationship that was, why go and spoil it now?

"I didn't know when I was well off," she tells Doris and Madeline. Dr. Beane is somewhere behind them, checking the strips that the monitor is printing out. An interesting geometrical dynamic, thinks Alison with perfect clarity, the three very large women and the tiny little doctor.

In fact, it goes very quickly for a first labor; everyone says so. Five hours after coming to the hospital, Alison is pronounced ready to push. Alison is no longer listening to anything that anyone has to say. This is, she has decided, the most ridiculous method for propagating the species that she can imagine. In those few precious seconds when the pain goes away, she thinks back to biology class, herself and Doris and Michael in the back row, acing every test. Think of all the alternative methods. Budding. Spore formation. Egg laying. Binary fission. And back comes the pain; howling, she has discovered, helps. Madeline does not seem to approve fully; there was something a little censorious about the way she closed the labor room door. "Mustn't let the other women in labor know that it hurts, huh," Doris was heard to say.

Sometimes she squeezes Doris's hand. Sometimes Doris squeezes hers. During one particularly unpleasant contraction, Alison gives out with a loud cry of, "Oh, fuckety fuck fuck the fucking fuck," and then her brain clears enough to hear Doris's response, "Do any more of that, darling, and you'll end up right back here."

What can she mean? Another contraction hits before Alison can actually think back to those familiar and surprisingly passionate nights with Michael, or to the nights with the other two men who will never know about this. Oddly enough, she can remember, as the pain ebbs, her decision to go ahead and get pregnant, that one particularly promising and active month when she got herself into this, but her mind cannot encompass the how. This is no moment to think about the more pleasant uses to which her lower body can be put. This is a moment to howl.

Dr. Beane, who has been off doing doctor things, reappears after Alison has been pushing for half an hour or so. Pushing is a little better than just contracting, but it is also hard work. "I have had enough of this," Alison tells her, loud and clear. "There is never going to be a baby. I want to go home."

"You're doing very, very well. You're going to have your baby soon."

"I don't want a baby. I changed my mind." She is dead serious, she is enjoying being a bad girl, she is kidding, she is contracting again and Madeline is counting at her, ten nine eight seven six five four three two one, trying to get Alison to prolong the push.

"You heard the lady. She's changed her mind." Doris almost sounds dead serious herself.

Dr. Beane puts Doris on one side of Alison. Madeline on the other. Alison puts one arm around each of them, and each lifts up one of her legs, pulls it back. Dr. Beane is now a tiny pixie all dressed in surgical greens, rubber gloves on her hands. She looks at Alison severely. "You need to push this baby out," she says. "The monitor is showing poor beat-to-beat variability and you are ready to do it!"

"What is poor beat-to-beat variability?" asks Doris. Alison doesn't care.

"It means she has to push this baby out. Now, pull back on her legs, Madeline will count, and on the next push, I want to see progress."

It takes exactly sixteen more pushes for the baby to be born. Alison has suddenly remembered that she was promised Demerol for pain and is demanding it loudly. Dr. Beane tells her, somewhat brusquely, that she cannot have it so close to delivery, and Alison begins to make a speech about how unfair this is, how she has labored and labored and pushed and pushed. Then two things happen at once: Another contraction begins and Doris leans in close to her ear and says loudly, "Stop whining and push! Something's going wrong with the baby!"

And, amazingly enough, Alison does care. Or at least responds. Or at least feels she has to respond. Or something. She stops making speeches, she grips the two pillars on either side and bears down for the full count. Dr. Beane encourages her. "I see the head!" she calls from her little steel stool between Alison's legs. Toward the end, Alison loses track of everything. She keeps her eyes fixed on Madeline's, since Madeline is the one who tells her this will be it, you'll do it next time. She bears down when Madeline counts, responding to the authoritative numbers like Pavlov's dog. And then, at the end, everything changes. Instead of pure pain and effort and her body straining and close to exploding, she actually feels it, she does, she feels something move down, something fall away from her, something slide out of her and the next moment everyone is laughing and cheering.

There is no separating anything out; Dr. Beane's triumphant announcement that she has a girl, the sudden shocking baby cries, slightly thin and then outraged, Madeline's assurances from across the room that the baby is perfect, ten fingers and ten toes. Before Alison can even contemplate that information, the baby, wrapped in a somewhat bloody blanket, is deposited on Alison's chest. Only then, lying back, does Alison realize the pain has actually stopped.

Dr. Beane and Madeline are still messing around at the bottom of the bed. Alison and Doris, however, are busy admiring the baby, who has stopped crying and is scrunched up in her mother's arms, occasionally opening her eyes to see if she can see who is responsible for this outrage. A little stretchy white cap on her head works its way off, and it turns out she has a great deal of dark hair. To Alison's relief, she looks like a newborn, like a monkey; there is no uncanny resemblance to Michael or any other adult.

"She's certainly beautiful," Doris says, as if surprised. Actually, she isn't particularly beautiful, Alison supposes, but on the other hand, she's the most miraculously divinely beautiful thing ever.

"I know what you mean."

"What happens now?" Doris asks, after a lull of admiring, during which Dr. Beane finishes up with the afterbirth and the stitches; a few twinges and a few ouches from Alison, but she is harder to impress than she used to be. The baby, eyes closed, nuzzles into her mother's neck, seeking warmth, or food, or contact, maybe missing the close confinement where up to now she has rocked and kicked and wriggled.

"Now Mother goes on up to the maternity floor and gets a little rest," says Madeline, "and Baby goes to the nursery and gets weighed and measured."

"Now I guess I take her home and educate her," says Alison, in wonderment.

"Well, good," says Doris. "As long as you have a plan."

Dennis McFarland

NOTHING TO ASK FOR

Inside Mack's apartment, a concentrator—a medical machine that looks like an elaborate stereo speaker on casters—sits behind an orange swivel chair, making its rhythmic, percussive noise like ocean waves, taking in normal filthy air, humidifying it, and filtering out everything but the oxygen, which it sends through clear plastic tubing to Mack's nostrils. He sits on the couch, as usual, channel grazing, the remote-control button under his thumb, and he appears to be scrutinizing the short segments of what he sees on the TV screen with Zen-like patience. He has planted one foot on the bevelled edge of the long oak coffee table, and he dangles one leg—thinner at the thigh than my wrist—over the other. In the sharp valley of his lap, Eberhardt, his old long-haired dachshund, lies sleeping. The table is covered with two dozen medicine bottles, though Mack has now taken himself off all drugs except cough syrup and something for heartburn. Also, stacks of books and pamphlets—though he has lost the ability to read—on how to heal yourself, on Buddhism, on Hinduism, on dying. In one pamphlet there's a long list that includes most human ailments, the personality traits and character flaws that cause these ailments, and the affirmations that need to be said in order to overcome them. According to this well-intentioned misguidedness, most disease is caused by self-hatred, or rejection of reality, and almost anything can be cured by learning to love yourself—which is accomplished by saying, aloud and often, "I love myself." Next to these books are pamphlets and Xeroxed articles describing more unorthodox remedies—herbal brews, ultrasound, lemon juice, urine, even penicillin. And, in a ceramic dish next to these, a small, waxy envelope that contains "ash"—a very fine, gray-white, spiritually enhancing powder materialized out of thin air by Swami Lahiri Baba.

As I change the plastic liner inside Mack's trash can, into which he throws his millions of Kleenex, I block his view of the TV screen—which he endures serenely, his head perfectly still, eyes unaverted. "Do you remember old Dorothy Hughes?" he asks me. "What do you suppose ever happened to her?"

"I don't know," I say. "I saw her years ago on the nude beach at San Gregorio. With some black guy who was down by the surf doing cartwheels. She pretended she didn't know me."

"I don't blame her," says Mack, making bug-eyes. "I wouldn't like to be seen with any grownup who does cartwheels, would you?"

"No," I say.

Then he asks, "Was everybody we knew back then crazy?"

What Mack means by "back then" is our college days, in Santa Cruz, when we judged almost everything in terms of how freshly it rejected the status quo: the famous professor who began his twentieth-century-philosophy class by tossing pink rubber dildos in through the classroom window; Antonioni and Luis Buñuel screened each weekend in the dormitory basement; the artichokes in the student garden, left on their stalks and allowed to open and become what they truly were—enormous, purple-hearted flowers. There were no paving-stone quadrangles or venerable colonnades—our campus was the redwood forest, the buildings nestled among the trees, invisible one from the other—

and when we emerged from the woods at the end of the school day, what we saw was nothing more or less than the sun setting over the Pacific. We lived with thirteen other students, in a rented Victorian mansion on West Cliff Drive, and at night the yellow beacon from the nearby lighthouse invaded our attic windows; we drifted to sleep listening to the barking of seals. On weekends we had serious softball games in the vacant field next to the house—us against a team of tattooed, long-haired townies—and afterward, keyed up, tired and sweating, Mack and I walked the north shore to a place where we could watch the waves pound into the rocks and send up sun-ignited columns of water twenty-five and thirty feet tall. Though most of what we initiated "back then" now seems to have been faddish and wrongheaded, our friendship was exceptionally sane and has endured for twenty years. It endured the melodramatic confusion of Dorothy Hughes, our beautiful short-stop—I loved her, but she loved Mack. It endured the subsequent revelation that Mack was gay—any tension on that count managed by him with remarks about what a homely bastard I was. It endured his fury and frustration over my low-bottom alcoholism, and my sometimes raging (and *en*raging) process of getting clean and sober. And it has endured the onlooking fisheyes of his long string of lovers and my two wives. Neither of us had a biological brother—that could account for something—but at recent moments when I have felt most frightened, now that Mack is so ill, I've thought that we persisted simply because we couldn't let go of the sense of *thoroughness* our friendship gave us; we constantly reported to each other on our separate lives, as if we knew that by doing so we were getting more from life than we would ever have been entitled to individually.

In answer to his question—was everybody crazy back then—I say, "Yes, I think so."

He laughs, then coughs. When he coughs these days—which is often—he goes on coughing until a viscous, bloody fluid comes up, which he catches in a Kleenex and tosses into the trash can.

Earlier, his doctors could drain his lungs with a needle through his back—last time they collected an entire litre from one lung—but now that Mack has developed the cancer, there are tumors that break up the fluid into many small isolated pockets, too many to drain. Radiation or chemotherapy would kill him; he's too weak even for a flu shot. Later today, he will go to the hospital for another bronchoscopy; they want to see if there's anything they can do to help him, though they have already told him there isn't. His medical care comes in the form of visiting nurses, physical therapists, and a curious duo at the hospital: one doctor who is young, affectionate, and incompetent but who comforts and consoles, hugs and holds hands; another—old, rude, brash, and expert—who says things like "You might as well face it. You're going to die. Get your papers in order." In fact, they've given Mack two weeks to two months, and it has now been ten weeks.

"Oh, my God," cries Lester, Mack's lover, opening the screen door, entering the room, and looking around. "I don't recognize this hovel. And what's that wonderful smell?"

This morning, while Lester was out, I vacuumed and generally straightened up. Their apartment is on the ground floor of a building like all the buildings in this Southern California neighborhood—a two-story motel-like structure of white stucco and steel railings. Outside the door are an X-rated hibiscus (blood red, with its jutting, yellow powder-tipped stamen), a plastic macaw on a swing, two enormous yuccas; inside, carpet, and plainness. The wonderful smell is the turkey I'm roasting; Mack can't eat anything before the bronchoscopy, but I figure it will be here for them when they return from the hospital, and they can eat off it for the rest of the week.

Lester, a South Carolina boy in his late twenties, is sick, too—twice he has nearly died of pneumonia—but he's in a healthy period now. He's tall, thin, and bearded, a devotee of the writings of Shirley MacLaine—an unlikely guru, if you ask me, but my wife, Marilyn, tells me I'm too judgmental. Probably she is right.

The dog, Eberhardt, has woken up and waddles sleepily over to where Lester stands. Lester extends his arm toward Mack, two envelopes in his hand, and after a moment's pause Mack reaches for them. It's partly this typical hesitation of Mack's—a slowing of the mind, actually—that makes him appear serene, contemplative these days. Occasionally, he really does get confused, which terrifies him. But I can't help thinking that something in there has sharpened as well—maybe a kind of simplification. Now he stares at the top envelope for a full minute, as Lester and I watch him. This is something we do: we watch him. "Oh-h-h," he says, at last. "A letter from my mother."

"And one from Lucy, too," says Lester. "Isn't that nice?"

"I guess," says Mack. Then: "Well, yes. It is."

"You want me to open them?" I ask.

"Would you?" he says, handing them to me. "Read 'em to me, too."

They are only cards, with short notes inside, both from Des Moines. Mack's mother says it just makes her *sick* that he's sick, wants to know if there's anything he needs. Lucy, the sister, is gushy, misremembers a few things from the past, says she's writing instead of calling because she knows she will cry if she tries to talk. Lucy, who refused to let Mack enter her house at Christmastime one year—actually left him on the stoop in sub-zero cold—until he removed the gold earring from his ear. Mack's mother, who waited until after the funeral last year to let Mack know that his father had died; Mack's obvious illness at the funeral would have been an embarrassment.

But they've come around, Mack has told me in the face of my anger.

I said better late than never.

And Mack, all forgiveness, all humility, said that's exactly right: much better.

"Mrs. Mears is having a craft sale today," Lester says. Mrs. Mears, an elderly neighbor, lives out back in a cottage with her husband. "You guys want to go?"

Eberhardt, hearing "go," begins leaping at Lester's shins, but when we look at Mack, his eyelids are at half-mast—he's half asleep.

We watch him for a moment, and I say, "Maybe in a little while, Lester."

* * *

Lester sits on the edge of his bed reading the newspaper, which lies flat on the spread in front of him. He has his own TV in his room, and a VCR. On the dresser, movies whose cases show men in studded black leather jockstraps, with gloves to match—dungeon masters of startling handsomeness. On the floor, a stack of gay magazines. Somewhere on the cover of each of these magazines the word "macho" appears; and inside some of them, in the personal ads, men, meaning to attract others, refer to themselves as pigs. "Don't putz," Lester says to me as I straighten some things on top of the dresser. "Enough already."

I wonder where he picked up "putz"—surely not in South Carolina. I say, "You need to get somebody in. To help. You need to arrange it now. What if you were suddenly to get sick again?"

"I know," he says. "He's gotten to be quite a handful, hasn't he? Is he still asleep?"

"Yes," I answer. "Yes and yes."

The phone rings and Lester reaches for it. As soon as he begins to speak I can tell, from his tone, that it's my four-year-old on the line. After a moment, Lester says, "Kit," smiling, and hands me the phone, then returns to his newspaper.

I sit on the other side of the bed, and after I say hello, Kit says, "We need some milk."

"O.K.," I say. "Milk. What are you up to this morning?"

"Being angry mostly," she says.

"Oh?" I say. "Why?"

"Mommy and I are not getting along very well."

"That's too bad," I say. "I hope you won't stay angry for long."

"We won't," she says. "We're going to make up in a minute."

"Good," I say.

"When are you coming home?"

"In a little while."

"After my nap?"

"Yes," I say. "Right after your nap."

"Is Mack very sick?"

She already knows the answer, of course. "Yes," I say.

"Is he going to die?"

This one, too. "Most likely," I say. "He's that sick."

"Bye," she says suddenly—her sense of closure always takes me by surprise—and I say, "Don't stay angry for long, O.K.?"

"You already said that," she says, rightly, and I wait for a moment, half expecting Marilyn to come onto the line; ordinarily she would, and hearing her voice right now would do me good. After another moment, though, there's the click.

Marilyn is back in school, earning a Ph.D. in religious studies. I teach sixth grade, and because I'm faculty adviser for the little magazine the sixth graders put out each year, I stay late many afternoons. Marilyn wanted me home this Saturday morning. "You're at work all week," she said, "and then you're over there on Saturday. Is that fair?"

I told her I didn't know—which was the honest truth. Then, in a possibly dramatic way, I told her that fairness was not my favorite subject these days, given that my best friend was dying.

We were in our kitchen, and through the window I could see Kit playing with a neighbor's cat in the back yard. Marilyn turned on the hot water in the kitchen sink and stood still while the steam rose into her face. "It's become a question of where you belong," she said at last. "I think you're too involved."

For this I had no answer, except to say, "I agree"—which wasn't really an answer, since I had no intention of staying home, or becoming less involved, or changing anything.

Now Lester and I can hear Mack's scraping cough in the next room. We are silent until he stops. "By the way," Lester says at last, taking the telephone receiver out of my hand, "have you noticed that he *listens* now?"

"I know," I say. "He told me he'd finally entered his listening period."

"Yeah," says Lester, "as if it's the natural progression. You blab your whole life away, ignoring other people, and then right before you die you start to listen."

The slight bitterness in Lester's tone makes me feel shaky inside. It's true that Mack was always a better talker than a listener, but I suddenly feel that I'm walking a thin wire, and that anything like collusion would throw me off balance. All I know for sure is that I don't want to hear any more. Maybe Lester reads this in my face, because what he says next sounds like an explanation: he tells me that his poor old backwoods mother was nearly deaf when he was growing up, that she relied almost entirely on reading lips. "All she had to do when she wanted to turn me off," he says, "was to just turn her back on me. Simple," he says, making a little circle with his finger. "No more Lester."

"That's terrible," I say.

"I was a terrible coward," he says. "Can you imagine Kit letting you get away with something like that? She'd bite your kneecaps."

"Still," I say, "that's terrible."

Lester shrugs his shoulders, and after another moment I say, "I'm going to the K mart. Mack needs a padded toilet seat. You want anything?"

"Yeah," he says. "But they don't sell it at K mart."

"What is it?" I ask.

"It's a *joke,* Dan, for Chrissake," he says. "Honestly, I think you've completely lost your sense of humor."

When I think about this, it seems true.

"Are you coming back?" he asks.

"Right back," I answer. "If you think of it, baste the turkey."

"How could I not think of it?" he says, sniffing the air.

In the living room, Mack is lying with his eyes open now, staring blankly at the TV. At the moment, a shop-at-home show is on, but he changes channels, and an announcer says, "When we return, we'll talk about tree pruning," and Mack changes the channel again. He looks at me, nods thoughtfully, and says, "Tree pruning. Interesting. It's just like the way they put a limit on your credit card, so you don't spend too much."

"I don't understand," I say.

"Oh, you know," he says. "Pruning the trees. Didn't the man just say something about pruning trees?" He sits up and adjusts the plastic tube in one nostril.

"Yes," I say.

"Well, it's like the credit cards. The limit they put on the credit cards is . . ." He stops talking and looks straight into my eyes, frightened. "It doesn't make any sense, does it?" he says. "Jesus Christ. I'm not making sense."

* * *

Way out east on University, there is a video arcade every half mile or so. Adult peepshows. Also a McDonald's, and the rest. Taverns—the kind that are open at eight in the morning—with clever names: Tobacco Rhoda's, the Cruz Inn. Bodegas that smell of cat piss and are really fronts for numbers games. Huge discount stores. Lester, who is an expert in these matters, has told me that all these places feed on addicts. "What do you think—those peepshows stay in business on the strength of the occasional customer? No way. It's a steady clientele of people in there every day, for hours at a time, dropping in quarters. That whole strip of road is *made* for addicts. And all the strips like it. That's what America's all about, you know. You got your alcoholics in the bars. Your food addicts sucking it up at Jack-in-the-Box—you ever go in one of those places and count the fat people? You got your sex addicts in the peepshows. Your shopping addicts at the K mart. Your gamblers running numbers in the bodegas and your junkies in the alley-ways. We're all nothing but a bunch of addicts. The whole fucking addicted country."

In the arcades, says Lester, the videos show myriad combinations and arrangements of men and women, men and men, women and women. Some show older men being serviced by eager, selfless young women who seem to live for one thing only, who can't get enough. Some of these women have put their hair into pigtails and shaved themselves—they're supposed to look like children. Inside the peepshow booths there's semen on the floor. And in the old days, there were glory holes cut into the wooden walls between some of the booths, so, if it pleased you, you could communicate with your neighbor. Not anymore. Mack and Lester tell me that some things have changed. The holes have been boarded up. In the public men's rooms you no longer read, scribbled in the stalls, "All faggots should die." You read, "All faggots should die of AIDS." Mack rails against the moratorium on fetal-tissue research, the most promising avenue for a cure. "If it was Legionnaires dying, we wouldn't have any moratorium," he says. And he often talks about Africa, where governments impede efforts to teach villagers about condoms: a social worker, attempting to explain their use, isn't allowed to remove the condoms from their foil packets; in another country, with a slightly more liberal government, a field nurse stretches a condom over his hand, to show how it works, and later villagers are found wearing the condoms like mittens, thinking this will protect them from disease. Lester laughs at these stories but shakes his head. In our own country, something called "family values" has emerged with clarity. "*Whose* family?" Mack wants to know, holding out his hands palms upward. "I mean we *all* come from families, don't we? The dizziest queen comes from a family. The axe-murderer. Even Dan *Quayle* comes from a family of some kind."

But Mack and Lester are dying, Mack first. As I steer my pickup into the parking lot at the K mart, I almost clip the front fender of a big, deep-throated Chevy that's leaving. I have startled the driver, a young Chicano boy with four kids in the back seat, and he flips me the bird—aggressively, his arm out the window—but I feel protected today by my sense of purpose: I have come to buy a padded toilet seat for my friend.

* * *

When he was younger, Mack wanted to be a cultural anthropologist, but he was slow to break in after we were out of graduate school—never landed anything more than a low-paying position assisting someone else, nothing more than a student's job, really. Eventually, he began driving a tour bus in San Diego, which not only provided a steady income but suited him so well that in time he was managing the line and began to refer to the position not as his job but as his calling. He said that San Diego was like a pretty blond boy without too many brains. He knew just how to play up its cultural assets while allowing its beauty to speak for itself. He said he liked being "at the controls." But he had to quit work over a year ago, and now his hands have become so shaky that he can no longer even manage a pen and paper.

When I get back to the apartment from my trip to the K mart, Mack asks me to take down a letter for him to an old high-school buddy back in Des Moines, a country-and-Western singer who has sent him a couple of her latest recordings. *"Whenever I met a new doctor or nurse,"* he dictates, *"I always asked them whether they believed in miracles."*

Mack sits up a bit straighter and rearranges the pillows behind his back on the couch. "What did I just say?" he asks me.

" 'I always asked them whether they believed in miracles.' "

"Yes," he says, and continues. *"And if they said no, I told them I wanted to see someone else. I didn't want them treating me. Back then, I was hoping for a miracle, which seemed reasonable.* Do you think this is too detailed?" he asks me.

"No," I say. "I think it's fine."

"I don't want to depress her."

"Go on," I say.

"But now I have lung cancer," he continues. *"So now I need not one but two miracles. That doesn't seem as possible somehow.* Wait. Did you write 'possible' yet?"

"No," I say. " 'That doesn't seem as . . .' "

"Reasonable," he says. "Didn't I say 'reasonable' before?"

"Yes," I say. " 'That doesn't seem as reasonable somehow.' "

"Yes," he says. "How does that sound?"

"It sounds fine, Mack. It's not for publication, you know."

"It's not?" he says, feigning astonishment. "I thought it was: 'Letters of an AIDS Victim.' " He says this in a spooky voice and makes his bug-eyes. Since his head is a perfect skull, the whole effect really is a little spooky.

"What else?" I say.

"Thank you for your nice letter," he continues, *"and for the tapes."* He begins coughing—a horrible, rasping seizure. Mack has told me that he has lost all fear; he said he realized this a few weeks ago, on the skyride at the zoo. But when the coughing sets in, when it seems that it may never stop, I think I see terror in his eyes: he begins tapping his breastbone with the fingers of one hand, as if he's trying to wake up his lungs, prod them to do their appointed work. Finally he does stop, and he sits for a moment in silence, in thought. Then he dictates: *"It makes me very happy that you are so successful."*

* * *

At Mrs. Mears' craft sale, in the alley behind her cottage, she has set up several card tables: Scores of plastic dolls with hand-knitted dresses, shoes, and hats. Handmade doll furniture. Christmas ornaments. A whole box of knitted bonnets and scarves for dolls. Also, some baked goods. Now, while Lester holds Eberhardt, Mrs. Mears, wearing a large straw hat and sunglasses, outfits the dachshund in one of the bonnets and scarves. "There now," she says. "Have you ever seen anything so *precious?* I'm going to get my camera."

Mack sits in a folding chair by one of the tables; next to him sits Mr. Mears, also in a folding chair. The two men look very much alike, though Mr. Mears is not nearly as emaciated as Mack. And of course Mr. Mears is eighty-seven. Mack, on the calendar, is not quite forty. I notice that Mack's shoelaces are untied, and I kneel to tie them. "The thing about reincarnation," he's saying to Mr. Mears, "is that you can't remember anything and you don't recognize anybody."

"Consciously," says Lester, butting in. "*Sub*consciously you do."

"Subconsciously," says Mack. "What's the point? I'm not the least bit interested."

Mr. Mears removes his houndstooth-check cap and scratches his bald, freckled head. "I'm not, either," he says with great resignation.

As Mrs. Mears returns with the camera, she says, "Put him over there, in Mack's lap."

"It doesn't matter whether you're interested or not," says Lester, dropping Eberhardt into Mack's lap.

"Give me good old-fashioned Heaven and Hell," says Mr. Mears.

"I should think you would've had enough of that already," says Lester.

Mr. Mears gives Lester a suspicious look, then gazes down at his own knees. "Then give me nothing," he says finally.

I stand up and step aside just in time for Mrs. Mears to snap the picture. "Did you ever *see* anything?" she says, all sunshades and yellow teeth, but as she heads back toward the cottage door, her face is immediately serious. She takes me by the arm and pulls me along, reaching for something from one of the tables—a doll's bed, white with a red strawberry painted on the headboard. "For your little girl," she says aloud. Then she whispers, "You better get him out of the sun, don't you think? He doesn't look so good."

But when I turn again, I see that Lester is already helping Mack out of his chair. "Here—let me," says Mrs. Mears, reaching an arm toward them, and she escorts Mack up the narrow, shaded sidewalk, back toward the apartment building. Lester moves alongside me and says, "Dan, do you think you could give Mack his bath this afternoon? I'd like to take Eberhardt for a walk."

"Of course," I say, quickly.

But a while later—after I have drawn the bath, after I've taken a large beach towel out of the linen closet, refolded it into a thick square, and put it into the water to serve as a cushion for Mack to sit on in the tub; when I'm holding the towel under, against some resistance, waiting for the bubbles to stop surfacing, and there's something horrible about it, like drowning a small animal—I think Lester has tricked me into this task of bathing Mack, and the saliva in my mouth suddenly seems to taste of Scotch, which I have not actually tasted in nine years.

There is no time to consider any of this, however, for in a moment Mack enters the bathroom, trailing his tubes behind him, and says, "Are you ready for my Auschwitz look?"

"I've seen it before," I say.

And it's true. I have, a few times, helping him with his shirt and pants after Lester has bathed him and gotten him into his underwear. But that doesn't feel like preparation. The sight of him naked is like a powerful, scary drug: you forget between trips, remember only when you start to come on to it again. I help him off with his clothes now and guide him into the tub and gently onto the underwater towel. "That's nice," he says, and I begin soaping the hollows of his shoulders, the hard washboard of his back. This is not human skin as we know it but something already dead—so dry, dense, and pleasantly brown as to appear manufactured. I soap the cage of his chest, his stomach—the hard, depressed abdomen of a greyhound—the steep vaults of his armpits, his legs, his feet. Oddly, his hands and feet appear almost normal, even a bit swollen. At last I give him the slippery bar of soap. "Your turn," I say.

"My poor cock," he says as he begins to wash himself.

When he's done, I rinse him all over with the hand spray attached to the faucet. I lather the feathery white wisps of his hair—we have to remove the plastic oxygen tubes for this—then rinse again. "You know," he says, "I know it's irrational, but I feel kind of turned off to sex."

The apparent understatement of this almost takes my breath away. "There are more important things," I say.

"Oh, I know," he says. "I just hope Lester's not too unhappy." Then, after a moment, he says, "You know, Dan, it's only logical that they've all given up on me. And I've accepted it mostly. But I still have days when I think I should at least be given a chance."

"You can ask them for anything you want, Mack," I say.

"I know," he says. "That's the problem—there's nothing to ask for."

"Mack," I say. "I think I understand what you meant this morning about the tree pruning and the credit cards."

"You do?"

"Well, I think your mind just shifted into metaphor. Because I can see that pruning trees is like imposing a limit—just like the limit on the credit cards."

Mack is silent, pondering this. "Maybe," he says at last, hesitantly—a moment of disappointment for us both.

I get him out and hooked up to the oxygen again, dry him off, and begin dressing him. Somehow I get the oxygen tubes trapped between his legs and the elastic waistband of his sweatpants—no big deal, but I suddenly feel panicky—and I have to take them off his face again to set them to rights. After he's safely back on the living-room couch and I've returned to the bathroom, I hear him: low, painful-sounding groans. "Are you all right?" I call from the hallway.

"Oh, yes," he says, "I'm just moaning. It's one of the few pleasures I have left."

The bathtub is coated with a crust of dead skin, which I wash away with the sprayer. Then I find a screwdriver and go to work on the toilet seat. After I get the old one off, I need to scrub around the area where the plastic screws were. I've sprinkled Ajax all around the rim of the bowl and found the scrub brush when Lester appears at the bathroom door, back with Eberhardt from their walk. "Oh, Dan, really," he says. "You go too far. Down on your knees now, scrubbing our toilet."

"Lester, leave me alone," I say.

"Well, it's true," he says. "You really do."

"Maybe I'm working out my survivor's guilt," I say, "if you don't mind."

"You mean because your best buddy's dying and you're not?"

"Yes," I say. "It's very common."

He parks one hip on the edge of the sink. And after a moment he says this: "Danny boy, if you feel guilty about surviving . . . that's not irreversible, you know. I could fix that."

We are both stunned. He looks at me. In another moment, there are tears in his eyes. He quickly closes the bathroom door, moves to the tub and turns on the water, sits on the side, and bursts into sobs. "I'm sorry," he says. "I'm so sorry."

"Forget it," I say.

He begins to compose himself almost at once. "This is what Jane Alexander did when she played Eleanor Roosevelt," he says. "Do you remember? When she needed to cry she'd go in the bathroom and turn on the water, so nobody could hear her. Remember?"

* * *

In the pickup, on the way to the hospital, Lester—in the middle, between Mack and me—says, "Maybe after they're down there you could doze off, but on the *way* down, they want you awake." He's explaining the bronchoscopy to me—the insertion of the tube down the windpipe—with which he is personally familiar: "They reach certain points on the way down where they have to ask you to swallow."

"*He's* not having the test, is he?" Mack says, looking confused.

"No, of course not," says Lester.

"Didn't you just say to him that he had to swallow?"

"I meant *anyone,* Mack," says Lester.

"Oh," says Mack. "Oh, yeah."

"The general 'you,' " Lester says to me. "He keeps forgetting little things like that."

Mack shakes his head, then points at his temple with one finger. "My mind," he says.

Mack is on tank oxygen now, which comes with a small caddy. I push the caddy, behind him, and Lester assists him along the short walk from the curb to the hospital's front door and the elevators. Nine years ago, it was Mack who drove *me* to a different wing of this same hospital—against my drunken, slobbery will—to dry out. And as I watch him struggle up the low inclined ramp toward the glass-and-steel doors, I recall the single irrefutable thing he said to me in the car on the way. "You stink," he said. "You've puked and probably pissed your pants and you *stink,*" he said—my loyal, articulate, and best friend, saving my life, and causing me to cry like a baby.

Inside the clinic upstairs, the nurse, a sour young blond woman in a sky-blue uniform who looks terribly overworked, says to Mack, "You know better than to be late."

We are five minutes late to the second. Mack looks at her incredulously. He stands with one hand on the handle of the oxygen-tank caddy. He straightens up, perfectly erect—the indignant, shockingly skeletal posture of a man fasting to the death for some holy principle. He gives the nurse the bug-eyes, and says, "And you know better than to keep me waiting every time I come over here for some goddam procedure. But get over yourself: shit happens."

He turns and winks at me.

Though I've offered to return for them afterward, Lester has insisted on taking a taxi, so I will leave them here and drive back home, where again I'll try—successfully, this time—to explain to my wife how all this feels to me, and where, a few minutes later, I'll stand outside the door to my daughter's room, comforted by the music of her small high voice as she consoles her dolls.

Now the nurse gets Mack into a wheelchair and leaves us in the middle of the reception area; then, from the proper position at her desk, she calls Mack's name, and says he may proceed to the laboratory.

"Dan," Mack says, stretching his spotted, broomstick arms toward me. "Old pal. Do you remember the Christmas we drove out to Des Moines on the motorcycle?"

We did go to Des Moines together, one very snowy Christmas—but of course we didn't go on any motorcycle, not in December.

"We had fun," I say and put my arms around him, awkwardly, since he is sitting.

"Help me up," he whispers—confidentially—and I begin to lift him.

Helen Norris

RAISIN FACES

There were nights when she had a humming bird sleep as she hovered above the bloom of oblivion, dipping a moment to suck its sweetness, then hover again. But there were the nights, black holes of Calcutta, from which she emerged with a weight on her chest, her limbs in chains, and a weariness that was deep in the bone, as if she had labored the livelong night. After such nights she would sit in her chair in the breakfast nook, still a bit in chains, her mind a blank, and let the sun creep over her hands, and slowly she would begin to think, pushing her mind like a grocery cart from one thing to another thing, gradually filling it up with the children, the long afternoons they had spent in the park, the beach, the sand, and the flash of waves . . . till she had a paper sack full of things to feed upon for another day. When this was done, she removed the blue plate from the bowl of cereal Hattie had poured her the night before. She rummaged around with her finger for raisins and ate them slowly, one by one, remembering the water, the children, the sand. Till Hattie came in and found her there and exclaimed, "Miss Coralee, honey, how come you eatin' that dry old stuff?" And then she would carefully drown it in milk. Hattie came smelling of scouring powder and ever so faintly of bacon and corn. During the day it would all wear off. Or Coralee got used to it.

"Hattie, you ate up my raisins again." And the two would have them a wonderful laugh. There was nothing better than Hattie's laugh. It was gingerbread-colored like herself and full of spice, all kinds of it. And she would say, "I must of forgot to shake up that box. They sinks to the bottom, they bad about that." Then she would get down the box of raisins and shake a handful into the bowl, and she would say, "You the raisin-eatinest woman I know." And she would add, "They good for you. They full of iron, how come they black. They put the stiffenin' in your bones."

To encourage Miss Coralee to eat, she would pour herself a handful of raisins and eat them thoughtfully, one by one. And the two of them would remember the children. Hattie had never known them of course. She had come to work eight years ago. But she knew everything that Coralee knew, even things Coralee had plain forgot. Often she said she dreamt of the children. Sometimes in her dream she was struggling against the undertow and snatching Billy by the tail of his shirt and knocking the water out of his lungs. For it was she who had saved the child and not some stranger who happened along. "He was a chil' you got to watch out for ever minute."

"Yes, he was," said Coralee, shaking her head, "but bright as a button, that he was."

"Bright as a shiny blue button," said Hattie.

"You remember the way he would screw up his face when somebody cornered him and kissed his cheek?"

"Sure do," said Hattie. "He was a sight."

"He got away from us once, you know. We were headed somewhere. . . ." She stopped and puzzled. "You remember where we were headed, Hattie?"

"You was headed for Mississippi that time. To see your cousin lived in the Delta."

"That's right, we were. We certainly were. We had a wonderful time that year. The whole long trip was one big picnic. . . . Do you think we could have a picnic today?" As soon as she said it she knew they would. The weariness went out of her bones. She was full of glistening leaves and sky. The children were running beneath the trees. But she waited for Hattie:

"Don't see why not. Ain't fixin' to rain. What kind a san'wich you got in min'?"

"Any kind as long as you fix it with olives. But I want it to be a surprise."

"Well, it ain't that time. I got to straighten up. You be all right settin' here till I through."

Then she brought the album with all the pictures and found the ones of the Delta trip. She opened it beside the cereal bowl. "You set here and study it while I finish up."

* * *

Coralee would turn the pages, savoring each, while Hattie, moving from room to room, would sing to herself snatches of song she had learned in church. She made heaven sound like a happy land with a life as happy as life with the children ages ago. When Hattie came close, Coralee would say, "You remember Mindy's first bathing suit? She wanted to sleep in it all night long."

"Sure do. It was pink, real pink. And when it got wet it turn plum' red."

"Wasn't she funny outrunnin' the waves?"

"And all a time shriekin' fit to kill. . . . It's like I birth them chirren myself."

Coralee sighed. "Where did they go?"

"Where did who go?" And when Coralee didn't answer, she said, "Your chirren growed up, that's the trufe of it. Ain't even move off and lef' you, now, like mos' chirren takes a min' to do. I reckon they prob'ly comin' by today." She brushed up the crumbs at Coralee's feet. "My baby lef'. But not for good. One day I looks up and he be there. He stay long enough to git what he want. And then no tellin' how long it be."

"Hattie, my babies left for good."

"Now, who you think come by las' week? Got the same name. Talked like he growed up here to me."

"The ones comin' by are not the same."

Hattie shook her head. "I better he'p you on with your clothes. Case they takes a notion to see 'bout you."

"I don't want to wear that dress with the jelly."

"That jelly dress done put in the wash. I gone find me somep'n bright for you. Summer done got here all the way."

And Coralee thought, Is it summertime? Summer was children and happy time, the world of water and sun and sand. Summer had waited for Hattie to say it.

* * *

In the late afternoon Mindy came by. "Knock, knock," she said, bursting into the hall, not knocking at all. Coralee was sitting in the living room. She had gone to sleep over television plays and didn't wake up when they went off the air. Mindy switched the damn thing off. She wandered around the house for a bit, as she always did whenever she came. She skimmed the mantel with her pink-nailed fingers. Her hands were plump. "I'm checkin' on Hattie," she said when asked. "Hattie, I'm checkin' up on you," she called aloud in a jolly voice.

"Yes, ma'am, I know you checkin' on me. You have a nice trip?"

"Oh, that was over a month ago."

"Yes, ma'am, but we ain't seen you since."

Mindy was large, with lively hair. Gold with a rapturous streak of white that swept her brow and was up and away, her sole concession to middle age. Coralee watched her, half asleep, as if she were peering at a curious fish inside a tank. Mindy stayed a while in the dining room, opening drawers and cabinet doors, slamming them shut. Coralee watched her and wished her gone.

Whoever she was, she had no business rummaging around. Coralee hadn't let her own children play in the dining room. Mindy called Penny up on the phone in the hall and said she had something to talk about. "Well, pretty soon. I'm leavin' now."

"Mama, be good," she said as she left. But Coralee was dozing again.

"What did she want?" said Coralee, startled out of her sleep when the front door shut.

"Nothin' much. Jus' checkin' on us."

"I wish she'd tell me what she wants."

Then Hattie brought her an early supper. She stuffed some pillows at Coralee's back and rested the tray on the arms of the chair and stayed with her in case she spilled.

"Eat somethin', Hattie," said Coralee. "You know I do better when you eat along."

"Well, maybe I sip some coffee," said Hattie. "But I got to feed my baby at home."

"Is he here for long?"

"No tellin'," said Hattie. The skin beneath her eyes went dark. Her eyes grew older than 38.

"My children are gone," said Coralee. "But they were a pleasure for many years. I think of Penny and how she hated to have her food cut up for her. She wanted to cut it up herself. The fuss she made! You remember that?"

"She'd snatch the knife right out'n your hand. Try to grow up fast. Like to cut herself."

"Oh, my! I remember that. She was such a lively child. We have a picture of Fourth of July and barbecue all over her face."

"You want me to find it?"

"Let's have a look. I forget just who she was sittin' next to."

"She was settin' nex' to her Uncle Dave. But you can study it while you eat."

She got the album and found the place. And Coralee ate and sipped her tea, while Hattie fed her bits of the past. The children were with them and nourished her.

* * *

The next day Penny came with Mindy, and the two of them went through her things, through all her closets without asking her. They even pulled down the attic stairs, and Mindy climbed while the rungs cried out beneath her weight. Penny stood at the foot and called, "My girdle says I'm stayin' here," and Mindy replied in a voice too muffled for them to hear.

They had left the front door wide to summer and filled the house with air still chilly to Coralee. They said the house needed airing out. The ceiling creaked. The woman in the attic sounded like a squirrel got in from the roof, but bigger than that.

"What do they want?" asked Coralee.

Hattie muttered grimly, "They ain't said yet." She seemed to feel the chill herself. Her hand shook dusting a china doll.

They stared at Penny out in the hall with her high heels and her slender form in a yellow silk and her short brown hair in a stylish cut. She was like a girl high-strung with youth till she turned around. A torpor was in her olive face, which looked like something stored away. Coralee one time had said in a wondering voice, "She doesn't look familiar to me." And Hattie replied, "I reckon a doctor done made that face." But a doctor had never made her voice, which was deep and vacant, to match her face. It tended to wander away from thought.

They went away. Hattie swept the hall of the attic dust and swept their footprints off the porch. "How 'bout a picnic, Miss Coralee? It warmin' up outside real good. You rather have music on the stereo? Them songs you was singin' that time you was all campin' out at the lake."

"Why don't we have both?" said Coralee. She was past the age when you had to choose. Hattie understood and gave her choices, then gave her both.

* * *

But Mindy and Penny struck next day. They had Billy with them out of the bank. Hattie went to the kitchen and shut the door, but they sent her off to the store for food. They opened windows to let in air. Coralee couldn't think who they were or why they were always coming by. Whenever they came they made her cold. She pulled her sweater across her chest.

Mindy came right down to the point. "Mama, we've got a situation here. You're fond of Hattie. She's good to you. On the surface she is, but she's stealin' you blind behind your back."

Coralee heard the words like so many stones that were dropped on her.

"Mama, your silver is just about gone. Now, where did it go? Did you put it somewhere and then forget? I don't think you're able to carry that stuff. You don't see well, and Hattie's been stealin' it from under your nose."

Coralee was staring into their faces, trying to think what right they had to accuse her of stealing. For it seemed they were accusing her. She said at last with dignity, "Why would I want to take my own silver?"

"Not you, Mama! Hattie's been takin' it, robbin' us all."

"Robbin' you?"

"Mama, that silver goes to me and Penny after you're gone. Grandmother told us before she died."

"I never heard that."

"Well, she said so, Mama. You just forgot. She's robbin' us all. Billy says it must be reported and we go from there."

"The police," said Billy. He was short and stout, with minimal hair, but sideburns the color of weathered granite came to a point like inverted tombstones framing his face. Coralee thought they looked pasted on. There was something about him she didn't trust. "The thing is, Mama, we could get it back if she hasn't done something untraceable with it. And that may be. It well may be. We'll have to dismiss her in any event. That works a hardship on all of us. We'll take turns staying here with you until we can find somebody else."

She listened, dumbfounded. "I don't want somebody else."

They said at once, "You don't have a choice."

She was thinking in the depths of her bewildered mind that Hattie always gave her a choice.

Mindy said in a placating voice, "Wouldn't you like to have your children come stay with you for a little while?"

She looked at them, at their stranger faces. "No," she said.

Their faces tightened and then relaxed. "You don't mean that, Mama."

Her mind grew dappled with flecks of fear. "You can't take Hattie. She's all I have."

"Nonsense, Mama. She's just a maid, and we'll get another."

"I don't care what she did. If she did anything."

"But we care, Mama," Penny broke in.

"She has broken the law," Billy said with decision.

She was almost in tears. "It's not a law if it isn't stolen."

"You're not being rational," Penny said.

And Mindy said, "Where is it, then? Where has it gone?"

She closed her eyes to shut them out. "I put it away. I can't remember."

"Where?" Penny said. In her deep, vacant voice the word was like God's.

"We have searched the house. Tell us where," said Mindy.

"I can't remember." They had her at bay. She began to cry.

They circled the room. They walked to the window and bunched together like a flock of birds. Their thin legs waded knee deep in sun. "Here she comes," they said. "Comin' up the walk. Why doesn't she ever use the back?" They turned to Coralee. "Mama, we'll give you till tomorrow to remember. And if you can't, then she'll have to go. Mama, don't tell her why we came. Don't tell her, Mama."

They went away.

Hattie laid the groceries on the kitchen table. Then she put them away. Coralee, weeping, could hear her stashing them on the shelves. She could hear milk sliding to the coldest part of the refrigerator. She could hear water running into the kettle. She was trembling all over and willing herself to have taken the silver and put it somewhere that she couldn't recall. She was willing herself to recall where it was, to recall long enough to tell Hattie where. She was saying, Please, God, let me be the one did it. I want to be the one, please, God, please, God.

By the time Hattie came with their cups of tea, God had let her be the one.

Hattie looked at her hard. "Miss Coralee, honey, them chirren a yours done made you cry?"

Coralee sobbed aloud.

"Honey . . . honey . . . don't you fret none about 'em. They done gone down the drive and outa your sight." She drew up a chair and stroked Coralee's arm. "Sometimes chirren can aggravate you so you got to let it out. My baby can git me so mad at him."

"These people don't seem like my children to me. The things they say. They don't like me, Hattie."

"Honey, it jus' the way chirren can be."

Coralee took the tea and drank a little. It made her feel better and even more sure she had taken the silver and put it somewhere and then forgot. She grew almost happy to think how her memory had played her a trick. "Hattie, I know you'd rather have coffee. You don't have to drink the tea for me."

"I likes 'em bofe. And it don't seem right to be drinkin' different. My husband was aroun', I took to drinkin' whatever he said. Exceptin' his likker. I didn't like that."

"You think he's ever comin' back to you, Hattie?"

"No'm, I don't. He gone for good."

Coralee sighed and sipped her tea. It seemed to her that a darkness waited. She thought it had something to do with the silver. Maybe she wouldn't be able to recall. But she wouldn't try to remember yet. "I get to thinkin' they can't be the same. They look so different."

"Your growed up chirren? They the same, all right."

"Penny was sweet with her little curls. For the longest time she didn't know how to give you a kiss. She would just touch her little tongue to your face. . . . They can't be the same."

"They *is* the same. Ever'thing that be gonna change some day. Some way."

"Change to worse, you mean?"

"Ain't for me to say."

"Look at *me,*" said Coralee. "I couldn't be worse than I am today. They say I can't manage by myself. I guess I can't."

"You a fine, upstandin' woman," said Hattie. "Your mem'ry ain't good, but it could be worse. And mostly what all you disremember ain't worth the trouble to call it to mind."

"I could get it back if I tried hard enough."

"Sure you could. But it ain't worth the trouble. It mostly trash."

Coralee's hand with the teacup shook. Hattie took the cup. "Hattie, you got to help me remember what I did with the silver. They want to know."

Hattie got up and took away the cups. Coralee could hear her rinsing them out. When the water stopped running, "Hattie," she called, "you gotta help me remember."

"Right now I gotta fix your dinner. Then I goin' home. But I fix you up for bed 'fore then."

Coralee was frightened. When she tried to think she came to a wall that stopped her mind. "Don't leave me," she said, "not knowin' what to say when they come tomorrow."

Hattie came then and stood in the doorway. Her face was dark. "You tellin' me you done took your own silver and put it somewhere and cain't recollec'?"

"Yes, yes. But I don't know where. If you could look in some of my things. . . ."

"I he'p you tomorrow. Soon's I come."

"But they're comin' tomorrow. They said . . . they said . . . if I can't remember they know it's you."

Hattie put a strong, firm hand on the door. "I seed it comin'. They 'cusin' me?"

"If I can't remember. . . ." She began to cry. "I got nobody but only you."

Hattie's voice was cold. "You got them chirren that 'cusin' me."

"No, I don't. The children I had are lost and gone."

"Jesus, I wisht I could be like you and see my chil' as someun' different what he was long time ago. I know he be the same one chil'. All that time he stay so sweet, this troublesome was growin' there. No way, no way to weed it out. Sweet and troublesome. Sweet and bad."

Coralee was struck with fear. "I want to go to bed," she said.

"You ain't the onliest one want that. Pull the cover up over my head and when I wake it all be gone . . . I took it," she said, "to keep my baby outa jail. He owed a man gone git him put in jail for good. And now they gonna git me first. Serve him right he got no mama come runnin' to, keep him outa the trouble he make. 'Cause this trouble ain't gone be his last."

Coralee pled, "If you brought it back. . . ."

"It gone aready. My baby done sold it off for cash. He stole some money and had to pay it back."

Coralee cried, "I'd a give you money. All you had to do was ask."

"Miss Coralee, I couldn't take your money. Them chirren a yourn don't give you hardly enough to count. But you never looked at them silver things. I thought you'd never come lookin' for them."

"I didn't. I wouldn't. I never cared about things like that. Those people who came here said it's theirs. . . . I don't know. I can't think."

She rocked in despair, the rocker creaking, leaving the rug, slapping the floor till Hattie grimly pulled her back. "Don't git nowheres a-travelin' in that." Her face was darker than ever now. "I bes' clear out and head on home."

"Hattie . . . I'm gonna call that lawyer. He made me a will long time ago. What is his name? Started with 'B'."

"Don't know nothin' 'bout no lawyer."

"He made me a will long time ago." Coralee rocked with her eyes closed, and the tears seeped from under the lids. "Get the telephone book and read. . . . Read the names till I say to stop. Look up lawyers and read the names. Just keep on till I say to stop. . . ."

* * *

Mr. Barnhill said he was much too busy and couldn't come. It was out of the question. Not today.

"Then come tonight. You have to come before tomorrow."

"My, my," he said, and was she sure it couldn't wait? At last he agreed to come at four. "I hope you have a good-sized piece of that gingerbread left." And he had himself a good-sized chuckle, because it had been some 20 years. Lately his memory had sprung a leak, and he was pleased to recall details.

"Fix me a cup of coffee, Hattie, and make it double, double strong." While she sipped she was trying to find her mind, where she had dropped it along the way. Beneath her breath she recited the multiplication tables—the twos, the threes. She found she couldn't finish the fours. The fives had wholly disappeared. She tried to name the capital cities, but they had gone with the tables she'd lost. She wept for them. I used to think straight. What happened? she asked. She recited the 23rd Psalm aloud. She whispered the rhymes the children had loved.

"Bring the children, Hattie," she said.

And Hattie, looming like doom in the doorway, laid the album in her lap. "What good they gone do us now? You rummage aroun' and pickin' 'em outa the book like raisins. Raisin faces is all they is."

"I remember things when I'm with them. I touch their faces and think of things."

"Things done happen long time ago ain't gonna he'p us none today."

Coralee drank the bitter brew. "I let my mind get away from me."

* * *

When Barnhill came—he was running late—she didn't know him, he had changed so much. He seemed too old, no match for the people she had to fight. And had to beat. She peered from her chair with anxious doubt at his bushy white brows, at his pink cheeks as pink as a brick, his creamy moustache like a piece of pulled taffy scissored off. He hadn't had any of this before. Even his voice had a sandiness that sounded old. She was afraid he was as old as she, and if he was, then he wouldn't win.

He patted her shoulder in a knowing way and, sitting before her, fixed her with an indulgent eye. "Now, what can I do for you?" he said.

She was conscious of Hattie harbored in the kitchen, sounding each word for a prison ring. "Did you make me a will?" she asked in a voice as firm as she could make it sound, and just to be sure he was the same.

"Miss Coralee, I made you an excellent will. I reckon it was 20 years ago."

"Did I sign it?" she asked, for something to say.

"Of course you did. And got it witnessed. All of that."

She gazed into space. "I want it changed."

He pulled his watch chain, slid his thumb and finger down it, dropped his eyes. "I wouldn't think there'd be a need."

"People change their wills. I want it changed." Then as he made her no reply, "The telephone book is full of people who can change a will. All it takes is run my finger down the page and stop when I come to the best in town. I want it changed and changed today."

He smiled at her. "Well, now," he said. "I see it's a matter of some concern. . . . You tell me how you want it changed."

She pulled her sweater over her chest. "I have this maid who looks after me."

He inclined his head. "I believe you have children in town," he said. "Perhaps they should. . . ."

"I don't have any one but her."

"Surely. . . ." he said.

But she hurried on. "She took some silver to sell for me. I didn't have any use for it. I never have company in to eat. Most of my friends have moved away. Some have died. . . ."

He listened to her with his bushy eyebrows slightly raised and his fingers touching across his vest.

"Certain people . . . have got the notion she sold the silver without askin' me."

"I see," he said with a knowing nod, and he seemed to be looking at rows of cases, similar ones.

"They want to make trouble. . . ."

"Prosecute?" he said. "On your behalf?"

She grew confused. "Make trouble," she said. Her hands were shaking. "I thought if you would change my will and let it say I leave it to her. . . ."

He interrupted. "That wouldn't do." He seemed to consider. "If she broke the law . . . if she took the silver when she shouldn't have, and that would be easy to prove, you know, then willing it now wouldn't make it right with the law, you see. . . . A lot of silver? What value?" he asked.

Her mouth was dry. "I don't recall."

"You don't recall what you told her to sell?"

She shook her head. Her mind was beginning to slip away. Into the threes and then the fours. . . . She began to tremble. "I just don't want any trouble," she said. "Please, no trouble. I just don't want her taken away." Her voice choked. "I can get the money to pay your bill." And then she was thinking how little she had, and how did she know what it would take.

"Well, well," he said. It was plain to see he had counseled a thousand old ladies before and knew at what point they began to cry and knew at what point he would say, "Well, well." He drew out his watch and studied it. "This watch belonged to my father," he said. "Haven't had it worked on in 20 years. Wonderful the way they made them then." He put it back and fingered the chain. "Miss Coralee, I see you've got strong feelings here. There *is* a little something we could do. It might be a little . . . but in this case. . . . You could sign a deed of gift dated back to a time before she took the silver. It would mean you had already given it to her. So who is to say what she does with it?"

She couldn't help crying with joy and relief. "Can I sign it now?" she said through tears.

"Hold on," he laughed. "I have to draw it up, you know."

"I'll have to have it before tomorrow."

"Well, what if I send my girl from the office around real early? You can sign it then. She can witness it."

He stood up then and patted her shoulder. "You dry your eyes. It's gonna be fine." At the door he added, "I hope she's grateful to you for this." And then he let himself out the door.

"Hattie," she called with joy in her voice, "did you hear what he said? He's goin' to make it all right for us." When Hattie came toward her across the room, it was as if she had lost and found her all at once. She hadn't ever seen her before, not really seen how fine she was, tall enough for the highest shelf, her skin the color of fresh-brewed tea and her gingerbread laugh that was full of spice.

"Miss Coralee, honey, you done so good. You spoke right up to that lawyer man."

"I did, didn't I, Hattie?" she said.

* * *

But it wasn't going to be right at all. The girl from the office never came. Coralee sat before her cereal. The raisins in it were hateful to her. When Hattie arrived, she was full of tears. "Did you call that office place?" asked Hattie.

Coralee had never once thought of that. "Hattie, you dial." He had seemed too old to remember things. She tried to recall the things that were said the day before. She only recalled it would be all right.

But the line was busy and busy again. When Mr. Barnhill was finally there, he said, "Good morning, Miss Coralee. Well, well. I've given it thought. It won't be possible to proceed as we said. I'll have to get back to you later on." She heard the never in his voice.

She could scarcely report his words to Hattie. Betrayal was all she could recall. Hattie was grim. "Them chirren a yourn has got to him. I heerd in his voice he got a mind could be changed for him. It don't matter none how they done it. Lord, Lord, what I gonna do?"

"Maybe another lawyer would do it. That one seemed too old to me."

"Ain't no time, no time for that. Your chirren be here any time."

Coralee began to cry.

Hattie said in a high, tight voice, "How'm I gone think with you carryin' on?" Coralee choked down her sob. "You got some kinfolks lives outa town?"

Coralee closed her eyes to think. She remembered the capital city of Maine. She whispered a line of the 23rd Psalm. . . . "There's a cousin a mine . . . in Jacksonville. I never did like her all that much."

"Never min' that. You tell 'em how you done recollec' you sent that silver along to her. You tell 'em you give her a piece at a time. I wrop it and took it down to mail. And you done sent her that gifty deed. It hold 'em off for a little spell. Till I can git myse'f outa here." She picked up her purse.

"I won't say it right. You know I won't."

Hattie laid her purse down with a joyless cry. "You tellin' the trufe. I got to fill in what you forgits." She sat in a rocker facing the door. "I mostly skeered a that banker man. Anything money they cain't turn loose. . . . I gits to dreamin' it was me done fished him outa the water that time. Shoulda lef' him to drown hisse'f."

"That was my Billy. It's not the same."

And suddenly they were on the porch and letting themselves in with a key they had. Billy and Mindy were in the room. They seemed to fill it with Judgment Day. They stared at Hattie as if they thought she had her nerve.

"Well, Mama," said Mindy, "did you remember?" It was plain she had not remembered her girdle. The streak in her hair fell across her cheek.

Coralee sobbed a single breath. "Remember what? If you're talkin' about the silver, I did." She told it all, her fingers clutching the arms of her rocker. When she had finished she shut her eyes and asked God please to forgive her lie.

"A gifty deed?" said Mindy to Billy.

"I think she means a deed of gift."

"Well, what about it?"

"I don't know how she got the thing, if she got it at all. But she knows the term. I don't think Barnhill would draw it up."

They spoke as if she were not around or couldn't hear or had no sense.

"The whole damn thing is just insane. I don't think I believe a word. I'll have to check with Cousin Mabel. I haven't heard from her in years. I have her address somewhere at home. Or Penny has it. We'll try to call. What if Mabel does have the silver?"

He ruffled a sideburn and smoothed it flat. "We'll talk about that when we know the facts."

Without even saying goodbye they left. Hattie raised the curtain and peered outside. "Sweet Jesus, they got the po'lees! They talkin' to him. And now they bofe of 'em drivin' off." She turned to the room. "But they be back, direc'ly they speak to that cousin a yourn. Merciful Jesus, they be comin' back!" She sat abruptly, unable to stand. "They comin' to git me pretty soon. I got to git outa town real fast. I got to leave. I got to go."

"Where? Where?" said Coralee.

"Jus' git me a bus ticket somewhere fur. Fur as I got the money to pay."

"Take me with you," said Coralee. The words came out as if they had been in the roof of her mouth for a hundred years. And she was back to a little girl saying them to her black mammy that time whenever it was she left. Nobody told me why she left. She had to go was all they said. Coralee climbed the gate and screamed. Screamed to go and was left behind. Nobody ever took care of me and rocked me to sleep the way she did.

"You crazy?" said Hattie. "You talkin' crazy. I got no time for studyin' you."

"Take me with you," said Coralee. "I got nobody but only you."

"You got them chirren is causin' this trouble."

Coralee cried, "My children are lost and gone for good. How many times do I have to say? You're the only one remembers them and knows what page to find 'em on."

Hattie stood and grabbed her purse. She looked around the room they were in, at fine chairs backed with linen squares and the table with china dancing dolls and curtains of lace and picture frames of shining gilt. "You got in your min' to leave all this? You mighty crazy to swap all this. What you think you swappin' it for? Ride on a bus no tellin' where."

"What good is it? What good to me?" She began to rock. "It's like . . . it's like I get to losing who I am and when you come I know again. . . . I rather lose this than who I am. In the night it's like I lose my name. It's like I'm born all over again and all they say is stuff me back inside again. At night you're gone off home but here. I need someone gone home but here and comin' closer all night long."

"Ain't no way it can be that way. Things done changed the most can be. You be nothin' but trouble to me. White and black don't mix no way. I got no money comin' in. The work I gits, it might be long time comin' my way. You ain't do nothin' but slow me down, so likely they cotch us and bring us back and claim I done stole you 'long with the silver."

Coralee was shivering, winter cold. Too cold to climb the gate and scream. She held her handkerchief pressed to her eyes, pressed so hard that her eyeballs ached. She heard no sound, nothing at all, till Hattie was whirling about the bedroom, opening drawers and slamming them shut. Then she was back, saying, "Take that handkerchief down from your face. I brung the money, what little you got."

Hattie was standing there holding a suitcase, holding her purse and Coralee's. "We got to hurry. I brung them raisins for you to eat."

But in the doorway Coralee turned. "We have to take the children," she said.

Hattie gave her a look of bleak despair. "We got no room for that heavy thing. I got your grip here packed to the brim."

"We can't go off and leave them here."

Hattie stood still and shut her eyes. "Jesus, give me strength," she said. She put down the bag and opened the album. She ripped the pages out of the binding and stuffed them into her own handbag. . . .

Diane Levenberg

THE ILUI

Her father, a young widower, had studied in one of the great yeshivas of Eastern Europe. When she was a little girl he had often recited to her tales of the *iluim* with whom he had studied. These were young geniuses who were still able to carry on the Jewish tradition of the Oral Law—who could perform prodigious feats of memory.

"Were you an *ilui?*" she asked.

"Well, in my day," he said modestly, "I could also memorize—books of the Bible, tractates, pages of the Talmud. But not the entire *Mishnah,* not an entire volume of the Talmud. To be an *ilui,*" he spread his hands wide, "one might wish for it, but one is either born such a genius or one isn't."

On a late Sabbath afternoon, a week after she had scored a 98 on her geometry Regents, her father was, in sing-song fashion, studying a page from one of his huge leather-bound volumes of the Talmud. His comforting *nigun* promised to pry open the secrets of the universe. She begged him to teach her.

"All right," he agreed. "This is *Gemorah Baba Bathra.* The *Mishnah* reads: 'Carrion, graves and tanyards must, because of the bad smell, be kept fifty cubits from a town. Rabbi Akiba says a tanyard can be kept on any side except the west. How do we know which side is the west?' The rabbis then go on to discuss specific directions and the general shape of the world.

"Rabbi Eliezer says that the north side of the world is not enclosed and so when the sun reaches the northwest corner, it turns back and returns to the east above the firmament. Rabbi Joshua, however, says that the world is like a tent—completely enclosed—and the sun must go around it till it reaches the east."

"And who is right?" she asked, hoping that the *Gemorah,* contrary to Copernicus, was on to something.

"Well, let's see," said her father. Sometimes, when the *Gemorah* is not sure, it ends *Teku.* Let it stand until the prophet Elijah comes to solve the difficulty.

As he pored down the end of the long page, she heard a knock at the door. It was Mr. Bernstein.

"Good Shabbos, Mr. Schoen. Sorry to interrupt. We need a *minyan* for *Ma'ariv.* Could you join us?"

"Sure, sure," said her father. "I was just trying to teach my daughter a little Talmud. But that can wait. The evening star, on the other hand, cannot. Let's go."

Years later, she realized that her father agreed with her teachers—girls shouldn't learn Talmud. He had begun with a confusing but tantalizing passage and, confounded, she lost interest. But not in the idea of an *ilui.*

And women, she asked her father, carrying in another steaming plate of noodle pudding. Could a woman be an *ilui?* Was Bruriah, one of the only women mentioned in the Talmud, an *ilui?*

A good question, he said. He wasn't sure.

Somewhere, she believed, rattling around, hovering above the firmament, was an unmoored, extra soul, destined for her. An *ilui,* a man who could commit volumes to memory. A man who might have the patience to teach her the answers before the advent of Elijah.

To her father, brilliant but distracted girls, with their messy hair and unironed dresses, were a mystery. Her *ilui* would study with her, appreciate her poetry, and perhaps even try to explore with her her precociously complicated psyche.

At the Beth Jacob High School for Girls, "studiers" were not popular. The teachers, however, most of them impoverished Holocaust survivors from Poland or Hungary, happily put the studiers in the first two rows where they were called on by their last names. Schoen, pronounced with a Hungarian accent, became "Shoin." Hearing herself called that way always made her jump. It sounded very much like the Yiddish word for "already" as in "*nu shoin* let's have the answer." In this way she was trained to think fast. And to have time left over to dream of her soul mate.

* * *

In her senior year, her prospects brightened. Her class was dating and even the dumbest girl wanted a boy who was adept at studying, one who liked, as it was said, to sit and learn. Schoen started the class joke—as soon as a girl started to discuss her latest "beau" Schoen would wisecrack, "And what yeshiva is he the best in?"

Hiding *Dr. Zhivago* behind her volume devoted to the Laws of Modesty, Schoen longed to visit a yeshiva dedicated to producing an *ilui.* The Princeton of boys' yeshivas was also to be found in New Jersey—Lakewood. On several weekend visits, Schoen quickly discovered the disagreeable fate of Lakewood wives. They had babies, tried to support their husbands by selling Avon or Tupperware, and waddled into middle age by the time they hit twenty-five. The system, Schoen discovered, designed by men, was for men only.

A Lakewood scholar never worked—he learned until the day came when his "*rosh yeshiva*" decided he was ready to start a microcosmic Lakewood somewhere in the hinterlands of America. And then the cycle would begin again. He would administer his yeshiva, raise the money for his salary, and his wife would stretch their dollars. And bear more junior *iluiim.*

Schoen realized that while her desires were clear to her, her capacity for such sacrifice was almost nil. In her senior year, she had the thickest glasses, the largest library of secular books and the fewest dates.

Finally, a relative fixed her up with a scholar from the Baltimore yeshiva. He was dressed in the uniform—navy blue coat, navy blue suit, black hat with a dark red feather saluting from its hat band. She wore a black velvet suit, her first Salon St. Honore hairdo, and her new fur-collared black coat. In the lobby of the Americana Hotel he kept his hat on, she kept her glasses in her clutch bag. They talked about food, family, and philosophy. She thought him very sophisticated when he bought her a drink at the bar. Then she grew tired and put her glasses on. He adjusted his hat and took her home. He hadn't called a month later. Her cousin told her that he wanted a taller girl with a shorter nose. Years later, Schoen was attending an education conference and met him again—her first *ilui.* To her amusement, his wife was shorter than her by several inches, her nose prominently longer.

She had endless dates—one at Idlewild Airport to watch the planes take off, one in a Greenwich Village book store, one in the first kosher Italian restaurant where the pareve chicken parmesan turned black. He wore a black hat with a dark green feather. She forgot to remove her glasses. They talked about family, philosophy, and God. Why college? Why wasn't her father sending her to secretarial school?, asked the young scholar. Would God love her more, if she, after marriage, wore a wig and hated herself?, she asked. He removed his hat, checked to see that his yarmulka was still lining it, and rose to take her home. She watched the sorbet, like her hopes, melt away.

She would have to go it alone, her way. She told her guidance counsellor she wanted to attend Yeshiva University, but because it taught Biblical criticism her transcript was not sent there.

She hated City College's messy urban campus, but she loved the sound of its clipped academic dialogue. Reading alone, she thought that Yeats might rhyme with Keats. Sitting on the lawn were boys with longish hair, and thick glasses, suggesting that Dostoevsky's imprisonment in Siberia had been good for his soul and arguing whether, indeed, the worst are full of passionate intensity.

Another group was debating Marxist theory. In the student lounge, the girls were reading Emma Goldman, Simone de Beauvoir, and wishing they, too, like Emily Dickinson, could write their letters to the world. Schoen spent the afternoon listening, feeling as though she were in an adult toy store and they were giving away whatever she might want to play with.

She met Sarah, her one close high school friend. "What are you doing here?" she asked in shocked surprise. "You mean at this college? I got into Barnard, but with my brother still at Harvard we couldn't afford it. Actually, this is a scholar's paradise. I'm finally learning that an iamb isn't part of the verb to be. And, it's free. Sit down, have a cup of coffee. I'll show you something."

Schoen opened the catalogue describing the new creative writing program and her mind was made up. "You're right," she said. "This catalogue is as seductive as *Glamour's* September issue. Could we take some courses together?"

* * *

Schoen enrolled in a special program at City which seemed to have attracted some of the most creative minds at the college. She had a double major—writing and literature. She was surprised at the number of boys in her class, long-haired, serious-looking types, trying hard to emulate their wealthy Columbia "brothers."

Schoen believed that boys didn't read fiction, let alone write it. To her, a real man was still someone who knew how to learn. But these City College boys studied writing the way her father learned Talmud. They never let a writing instructor get away with anything.

When Prof. Brick, well-known for his own satirical short stories, tried to tear apart the work of the intense and brilliant Davidson (it was rumored that he had already spent a semester at

Oxford), Davidson retaliated. He had read all of Brick's work and knew which stories the critics had panned. "Listen, Brick, you're too tight-assed to let a spontaneous image emerge. Too afraid to expand for fear you'll bleed upon the page," he said quoting I.J. Howard for deadly emphasis. Brick unbuttoned his shirt, loosened his tie and called for a coffee break.

Davidson went to the window and lit a cigarette. She stood nearby. The old radiator hissed and thumped and they heard the faint cries of the children in the playground across the street. Schoen had never tried one before but she knew he was smoking a joint. His hands were shaking. He offered her a puff and she tried to imitate the way he drew it into his lungs.

"I have to admire the way you got to him, but that was nasty." Schoen focused on the playground watching one boy push another onto the concrete. Davidson pulled out his shirttail and wiped his glasses. It was a gesture which endeared him to her. "Two months I spend on that piece," he said, holding his glasses up to the light, "and all he has to say is that I don't have an ear for dialogue." Schoen noticed that his hands were still trembling. "Where the hell does that bastard WASP hang out? On the ersatz Welsh walkways trod by the Philistines of Mainline Philadelphia? In Brooklyn, walking up and down the ghetto's graveolent replica of the Champs Elysées, that's the way people speak. In his stories no one talks. He should call his collection, 'Mute Man, Aphasic Woman.' "

"I liked your story very much," she said. "The young painter who lives alone and has his vision in Brighton Beach—I could relate to that. I . . ."

"You could? Where are you from?"

"Brooklyn. Believe me. I know how hard it is to have an epiphany in Crown Heights. Brighton Beach was the right touch. And I think you're right. That's how people speak when their desires far exceed their grasp."

Davidson's eyes were shining. He was obviously pretty high. He grabbed her arm.

"Look, I've had enough of this class for today. Do you want to go downtown? I know a great cafe near my apartment. We can have some coffee, and continue this. I've never heard you read in class. Maybe I can look at some of your work."

Schoen giggled. She hoped the marijuana wouldn't make her sound too dumb. She'd had her eye fixed on Davidson for a long time.

"Sure," she said. "Let's go. I'd like to talk to you some more about your story. I don't have anything of mine on me that I'm up to sharing."

"That's all right. I have my entire binder right here in my bag."

In the dimly lit but cozy cafe, Davidson explained that the new critics "are reactionary and elitist. They are totally out of touch with what my, our, generation of writers is trying to express. The absurdists, on the other hand, like Pyncheon, are too far ahead of their time." He stared into her empty teacup. "Schoen's your name, right? Nice. It means nice. I met a woman once who could read your future in these grummels of tea leaves. Myself," he added, swilling down his fifth cup of coffee, "I'm a Blake man. Northrop Frye and I have been writing letters to each other for years. He keeps encouraging me to write my own book on Blake. If I survive this damn writing program, I'll probably write my thesis on *Songs of Innocence.*" By the end of the evening, Schoen was ready to change her definition of the word *ilui.* Davidson was the sort of scholar she had spent hundreds of high school hours dreaming about.

In class a few days later, Davidson sat next to her biting down on an unlit cigarette while Brick attacked another student's latest story. During the break, he walked to the window and finally lit it. Schoen stood next to him wishing that she also smoked so she could break his silence by asking for a light.

He spoke without looking at her. "This time that bastard was right. That guy had no business reading that yet. It needs too much work."

"We're not professionals, you know. We're here to learn. Where else can you take these kinds of risks?"

That night Schoen rewrote her own story for the fourth time. She was afraid to face Davidson's scorn. She needn't have worried. Davidson never again returned to class. Over the years she wondered about him, occasionally scanning the better literary magazines for his name and the criticism sections of the bookstores for his book on Blake. She was sure she would hear about him but when she did it wasn't because his name had appeared in print.

* * *

Pollack was on the phone again for the third time that day. Schoen bit down hard on her pencil but she couldn't hang up on him. Pollack was her current link to true suffering—a survivor of Auschwitz, with dreams and fantasies of making it in New York, but who was usually too depressed to put any workable plan into action.

Today he sounded almost cheerful. "How would you like to meet an interesting fellow?" he asked. "My friend just got back to New York. He wants to meet an interesting woman. Immediately, of course, I thought of you. You and he have a lot in common. He writes poetry, loves literature, film, art."

"Pollack, you sound like you're reading from one of the personals in the *Village Voice.* I'm in the middle of a difficult section of my dissertation. I don't have time for this."

"What do you mean you don't have time? Don't you want to meet a man who is fascinating, cosmopolitan, who understands my jokes, has an intelligent face? An intellectual who talks—he could help you with that damn dissertation. You've been writing it since I was a child."

"Pollack, you were never a child. Besides, I think my advisor likes a woman who takes her time."

"Well, so does Davidson."

"Davidson?"

"Yah. This fellow I want you to meet."

"Is his first name Chaim?"

"Chaim? Can't you imagine a human being who comes with a normal English name? No. His name is Mark."

"Oh. I thought I might have known him. A long time ago. In a writing class."

"I don't think Davidson would take a writing course. He prides himself on being an autodidact."

"How long have you known him?"

"A few years. We met at a conference on the Holocaust. Look, if you once knew him you'll jump off that bridge when you get to it. I have to run up to the lab at Columbia. Why don't you have coffee with him. I'll give him your number, o.k.?"

"O.k.," said Schoen smiling. She had worked steadily for a month on her chapter without even seeing a movie. "I almost wish his name was Chaim Davidson. I still have the story I wrote just to impress him. In fact, I published it."

Pollack chuckled. "The story of your story sounds like just the kind of story Davidson adores. Tell him about it. You'll have a good time. So long."

She had ridden her bike home at top speed. Even so, she was a few minutes late. He was there sitting on the steps of her apartment building. The years, she thought, had caressed him. He was even wearing the same beige scarf, wrapped around a rather worn Harris tweed jacket. But his hair was combed, his beard was trimmed, and his shirt was clean.

Schoen smiled. "Mark Davidson, how nice to meet you."

He looked up from the book he was reading. He rose and they shook hands. She noticed that now his grip was firm and sure. "Same here," he said. "Derrida," he said, slapping his book. "You know why the French have to be so intellectual? Because they're short. Seriously, this guy is brilliant. Say," he said. "You look slightly familiar. Did you by any chance go to City College?"

"Yes," she said. "Sorry I'm late. Let's go up." She wheeled the bike ahead of her and he followed her in. She had short curly hair now. At City, she had been twenty pounds thinner, her hair had been long, and she had been afraid to try contact lenses. Still, she must have made a dent in his memory. They had spent only one afternoon together and like her high school teachers, he had never called her by her first name.

"Now I remember," he said. "You were the girl who thought I was too hard on the other writing students."

"Woman," she said, smiling.

"Woman. Yes. Right."

"And you were the guy who was going to write a book on Blake. Your name was Chaim then."

"Yeah. Well, I thought Mark went better with Blake. But that never worked out." He turned to wander around the living room and check out her library. "Does it pass?" she asked.

"You have all the required reading matter for a City College graduate," he said. "And I won't insult you by asking whether or not you've read all these. In fact, I trust that like Johnson you've read some of them twice. Myself, I'm a collector. I love purchasing books almost as much as I love perusing them."

"It's hard having a big library in a Manhattan apartment."

"Well, fortunately, my parents are illiterate. They own a house in the cultural wasteland of Queens. I live away, and when my books crowd me out, I move myself and my library back to their little house on the Philistine prairie."

They ate in a popular Upper West Side Chinese restaurant. After her first cup of Chinese tea Schoen could no longer contain her curiosity. "Where did you go when you left our class?" she asked. Between forksful of cold sesame noodles, Davidson wove his tale.

"Dropped out of City. Went to Los Angeles to peddle a screenplay I'd written for a film class. No luck there but an agent hired me to read scripts. Tried that for two years, had enough of it and UCLA's night school, and ended up in the creative writing program at the University of Iowa. Before my three-year fellowship ran out, I had finished a novel."

"How was it there at Iowa? I've always heard such good stories about the place."

"As the epicenter of contemporary American writing, it's rather quiescent and uninspiring. And very ugly. The campus is comprised of converted Quonset huts. There's no view—just flat land rolling out to the horizon. A good place for writing though—there were no distractions. I hunkered over my typewriter, a grateful prisoner of my own imagination. After Iowa, New York looks good." He smiled at her.

Schoen remained silent, but something didn't ring true. She thought she remembered hearing that the University of Iowa had a scenic campus.

"Then what?" she asked.

"Then back to New York teaching at Brooklyn College. Tried to peddle my novel. Probably poetic bromides extolling shaving lotion have more appeal. Some lowly editor at Knopf is slowly reading it. A good sign I'm told, unless, condemned to some Sisyphean torture, she can't make it past the first ten pages. Hope they decide soon. My money's disappearing."

"Would you like some more of this wonderful tea?" she asked, wondering if she had grown into the sort of woman with whom he might want to sleep.

"No. I'm full. How would you like to repair to the Thalia to see *Rashoman?*"

"Sounds wonderful. Somehow I've never seen it."

* * *

They met again the following week and Davidson offered to come up and massage her back. He had somewhere learned the art of shiatsu.

"Was that kiss part of the technique?" asked Schoen.

"Not really. You know what the yogis say. You can judge the age of a person by the flexibility of his or her spine. Now that I've made you younger, back to our City College days, and eased all the tension out of your body, I think we should make love."

Schoen lay snuggled comfortably against Davidson and the last event-filled decade of her life unreeled before her in haunting images—the first man who had made love to her as she lay trembling in the shadow of their Sabbath candles, standing with Sarah in front of the White House chanting anti-war slogans, her husband, on their wedding night, undressing down to his father's baggy underwear, the rabbi asking her if she really wanted this divorce, and teaching her first literature class at City College.

After that night, Davidson just stayed. A week later she saw his valise in the living room. Shirts and pants lay in a tangled pile begging her to give them a home. She was preparing a new course and Davidson seemed to have nothing to do but wait for a phone call from Knopf. A phone call to his father invariably produced an envelope of cash. While she was at the library he would roast a chicken in garlic, lemon juice and whatever spices he fancied at the moment. He cooked intuitively, and the food was always superb. But once she made him throw out a delicious chicken and rice dish when she found the Perdue wrapper in the garbage. In a hurry, he had bought the unkosher chicken at the nearest supermarket.

"I'm sorry. It won't happen again. I was in a rush."

"You know this house is kosher. How could you do such a thing?"

"I didn't think. I'm sorry. Are you sure Frank Perdue isn't really a Southern shochet? Come on, let's forget it." And they did, the next night, while visiting Schoen's friend, the author of a bestselling book on sexuality, in the hills of Litchfield, Connecticut. In the hot tub, his resonant voice taking her back to that afternoon years before, in the Hungarian Cafe. Davidson recited from memory, T.S. Eliot's "The Love Song of J. Alfred Prufrock." That was the moment, that ten years later, she fell in love with him.

Back in her New York apartment, Davidson read a-book-a-day and Schoen envied him. She had an eight o'clock class to teach and three others on alternate afternoons. When he was stoned or just after making love, Davidson swore he would look for work—advertising, public relations, something in which he would be forced, once again, to put pen to paper. He made calls and set up interviews. But no one ever called him back a second time. She didn't really understand it. He signed up for more shiatsu courses. He shopped, he cooked, and sometimes he even cleaned. He asked to see her dissertation chapter.

"You really should explain more about how the Jewish family in the shtetl breaks down when they arrive in America," he said.

"But this is a study of literature."

"Still, the phenomenology of the family is what your advisor will need to understand."

She rewrote it as he suggested. But he didn't take as well to her comments. After she gently criticized one of his chattier job letters, he stopped writing them. He was reading scores of books, lying in bed until way past noon.

"I need inspiration so that I can begin my new novel before I find full time work."

"You look like Huckleberry Finn," she said, brushing the hair away from his eyes. "Whiling away the morning. Fishing for an idea."

"I'm taking a break from job hunting. Right now, I want to write another novel." He set his battered Olivetti on the dining room table, but except for a paragraph on Decoding Blake's "The Little Black Boy," all his pages remained blank. It seemed to Schoen that the more pages Davidson couldn't write, the more his desire for sex increased. When she gave in to him, too tired to continue writing her dissertation, and too weak to refuse him, Davidson would bring fresh French rolls, brie, wine and Blake to bed and keep her there with him till nightfall. She asked him about the novel he had written at Iowa.

"It wasn't good enough for them," he said. "And I had to leave before I rewrote. They did like some of my short stories, though."

"I'd like to see them."

"They're in the basement at home. I'll bring them back next

time I go visit my folks." But he never did. What he brought back was an ounce of marijuana. Or maybe it was hash. This time he smoked three or four pipefuls a day and Schoen was worried. He grew contentious. When she asked him to rinse out the tub after he had left a ring of grime around its sides, he raised his hand and she thought he might hit her. Instead, he scratched his head, stepped back, brought his clenched fist to his chest, turned on his heel and left the house. He didn't return until morning. She opened her eyes to the smell of fresh coffee and bagels still warm from the oven. "My breakfast guilt offering," he said.

* * *

Her old friend Dan was in town and they were having lunch at The Library, one of their favorite Upper West Side haunts. Suddenly, Schoen remembered that Dan had spent a semester at the Iowa Workshop.

"I can forgive his eccentricities," she said, "because the guy's a genius. His stories, when we were at City, were masterpieces. He says he spent a semester at Iowa. Did you know him?"

"No. What's he doing now."

"Not much. Reading. Looking for work."

"Is he writing?"

"Not really. But he says he's warming up."

"Too bad. New York is not as beautiful nor as peaceful as Iowa, but he's sharing your place, you're buying the food, and if I may say so, you're a great lady with a generous spirit. This would be an ideal situation for any writer."

"Thanks," she said smiling. "What was Iowa like?" she asked.

"Didn't he tell you? Rolling hills, modern buildings, a long river roiling right through town. Students hate to graduate."

"The way he described it it sounded like an old army camp."

"The guy should start writing again. He sounds like he has a great imagination. The place is a writer's paradise. My first day there I thought I died and woke up in heaven."

That night she brought home a large bottle of Soave for dinner.

He drank most of it. After dinner he lit a joint and handed it to her. When he was high, either on wine or grass, he was always affectionate. She lay in his lap and he stroked her hair. She sat up and gently kissed him on the mouth. Being high gave her courage. "Chaim, after City where did you go? Tell me the truth."

He pushed her away. "So, you don't believe me. Don't kiss me. Chaim. I hate that name. Call me Mark. Where did I go? Not to Los Angeles. That comes out of my own private script. But I did go to Iowa. The Iowa I believed in where the instructors were good writers who might have something to teach me. I was accepted to the Writers' Workshop but I never made it past the second class at the instructor's home. I don't think you want to hear this . . . a nice upright middle class Jewish girl like you. If I remember correctly you spent your formative years in some hole-in-the-wall girl's yeshiva. . . ."

"If I remember correctly, you spent those same years at the Brooklyn Torah Academy."

"Well, I broke out. I'm not sure you did."

"Look, I've had to learn to trust that from now on you'll buy kosher chickens. Trust me just a little. Where did you go?"

"Outside of town, at the local bar. I met a woman. Two women. Two men. We were all finished with the Workshop. We drove half the night and I joined their commune in Madison. We did every drug ever invented. Except heroin. They wouldn't dare to shoot up. So I had to be the first. And, I liked it. A lot." He took another long deep drag. "This isn't pretty." He searched her face for a sign that he should continue.

"It's all right, Mark. I'm with you. Really I am."

"It took a month and then I was, as they say, hooked. I told the lies I had to tell to get money for more stuff until finally my parents came out to see for themselves. Eventually, I ended up back East on a drug farm. One of those places where they detox you. I spent about two years on that project—back and forth to the funny farm just to get back to the place I had once been. A healthy kid who wanted to write just one good novel." He turned to her. "In case you're worried, I'm off the junk now."

"What do you take?"

"Besides grass? Just Valium. A little Valium to get me through the day. I've got to take something. I've never had a permanent job and I don't seem to be able to write anymore. I thought perhaps that living here would inspire me to get my act together. It's inspired me to something. Let's drop this and go back to bed."

"No," she said. "It doesn't solve anything. You're using me the way you use your drug-filled pipe. I won't be your escape."

"Okay," he said sadly. "But don't force me to leave. Just give me a little more time." He pulled her towards him.

"All right," she said, suddenly aware of how very tired she was. "I don't want you to leave. At least not now."

"Your dissertation. You're on the wrong track. I want to help you make it brilliant."

Something told her that trying to write a brilliant dissertation would keep her "hooked" to a project she really wanted to wrap up as soon as possible. But she didn't say anything. He needed his dignity—a way to stay with her and give her something back. He could, at times, with indefatigable energy sit with her for hours helping her to refine her ideas. And his memory! If he read it once, he could recall it at will. She told him he ought to start a hotline for students in crisis. "They could call you up and get a bibliography right off the top of your head."

"Schoen, Baby, I'm not for sale." He developed insomnia and she awoke to find him sitting in his jeans and pajama top, reading, smoking his water pipe, drinking Southern Comfort ("It's not Southern and it offers none but real men drink it neat.") He shot her a guilty look. "Have some," he offered. "It will help you fall back to sleep."

Another time, she saw him vigorously rubbing the sole of his foot, a book spread across his lap. "Reflexology," he said. "Did you know you could activate all the energy centers of the body by doing this? Uh. Oh. I hit the wrong one. Now I want you."

And he held her and kissed her, until ever so sweetly she fell back to sleep.

* * *

One night, he called to tell her that he and Pollack were visiting a writer, who in the fifties, had enjoyed a sort of cult following. "Hope you don't mind," he said. "You know, sort of boys' night out. I won't be home too late."

At six in the morning, he jumped on top of her wanting to make love. "Where were you? Mark, where the hell did you disappear? I've been going crazy worrying. Pollack's been home since eleven and he told me not to call your folks."

"I had some business to take care of." He grabbed her again. "Come on, Schoen. Don't be a spoil sport. I want you."

She jumped out of bed and headed for the bathroom. She ran the bath water as hot as she could stand it. This way she could keep the door locked, soak in the tub and calm down. When she came out he was fast asleep. When he didn't get up ten hours later, she called Pollack. He came running over and checked his pulse.

"It sounds weak," he said. "I'm no doctor but I think you should call an ambulance."

"What about his parents," she asked dialing the nearest hospital.

"Them too."

Two days later, Davidson was sitting up, grinning weakly. He buried his nose in the dozen red tulips she had brought him. "Their redness talks to/my wound, it corresponds," he quoted softly. "I blew it, didn't I?" he said, finally looking up. "Yes. You almost died. Heroin, grass, Valium and wine." She shook her head. "They make a potent cocktail."

"I have let things slip." He was forlorn and pleading. "It's over, now, isn't it?"

"Pollack told me that you left that night to score. Why, Mark? You've been off heroin for years."

"Why? Because an old pal had some. Because I was starting to lose myself. And because that writer we went to see is so damn good and no one cares. I looked at him and knew that even if I sold my novel, what's the use?"

"You care. Pollack cares. Literature is what you live for."

"It's not enough. You are and . . ."

"And that isn't enough?" she asked mournfully.

"No." He was crying and she would not let go of him.

"Schoen, baby, I really love you. It's myself I can't stand. It's time for me to go away again."

She held him harder, unable to control her own soundless weeping.

"By the way," he said, when she finally sat up, "your dissertation is a fine piece of work. It always was. Finish it. It's almost . . ."

"Brilliant?"

"Yes. So far good enough to hand in." He turned on his side. "Go home, Schoen," he said, beginning to cry again. "Let me go through this alone."

She walked home, carrying all the way the weight of her loneliness. Without drugs, without sex, without the guidance of her *ilui,* she would finish her last chapter.

Charlotte Zoë Walker

THE VERY PINEAPPLE

I

"I'm not crazy about having another stroke," Cory says. Her delicate hand with its knotted veins rests a little shakily on the papers in her lap.

"But you've never had a stroke!" her graying stepdaughter responds. Slender and exotic in her pale-orange Indian sari, Mirabai is taking a rare day off from directing a suburban yoga retreat. "Or at least you never told me, you never—"

"In the play, you silly goose! This damned new play I told Kenneth I'd do for him." Cory looks sharply at her with those liquid, brilliant eyes that were once her claim to ingenue fame.

"Oh!" Mirabai is flustered. She raises the battered mug to her lips and gazes out over the Hudson—or the glints of it that are visible through Cory's treetops. Since she gets away from the yoga ashram to visit Cory only two or three times a year, it's always a little baffling—putting together her worldly self again. But her beloved Cory calls it forth each time: Cory, who was always so much more loving than her real mother. Cory, who is so beautiful just now in her anger, her eyes still sparkling with passion and energy as if she were thirty-eight instead of eighty-three.

"Really, Peg—Mira!" (Mirabai has had her Sanskrit name for fifteen years now, but her family still hates to use it. What was wrong with Peg, for goodness sake?) Cory pats her fingers in a little paisley design along the typescript: "Don't you realize? I've spent the last dozen years in a wheelchair, or a rocking chair, looking blankly, or hauntedly, out some damned window or other."

"But you haven't! Just last year you went to Japan for that festival: '*Our* National Treasure,' the American ambassador called you."

"Peggy! I know you are hidden away most of the time in that nunnery, or whatever it is, but you *are* still a child of the theater!"

"All right!" Mirabai laughs. "I just don't see why after all these years, you suddenly identify so much with your characters. You always said you'd take *any* part so long as it had presence of some kind. Murderesses, sneaks, tragic consumptives . . ."

"Fine! That would be fine, it's just that I'd like a little of that range *now.* What do I get now? Stroke victims, heart-attack victims, guilty dying mothers seeking atonement, misunderstood dying mothers meting out forgiveness, embittered dying spinsters staring out windows . . . I'm sick of it!"

"Who wouldn't be? I wish you'd come to the ashram and see the performances we've been putting on. They're so full of life and joy, Cory—the way theater used to be for you! A wonderful young director from India is with us, and in a couple of months we're going to put on the *Ramayana!*" Mirabai stops. Her family is always bored when she talks about the ashram.

"Well, that would be nice, dear." Actually Cory feels a spark of interest. What would that kind of theater be like? Not that one could expect much, but . . . "It might really be fun. But I won't be able to tear myself away from Kenneth's rehearsals—hours and hours in a wheelchair!"

Mirabai looks at Cory tenderly. "Cory, dearest, you don't have to take those parts if you don't want to."

"This time I guess I do. I promised him. He needed my name to get the funding, you know. And it's a good play, for that matter."

"Is it?"

"Well, let's say it's sensitive and tightly knit and unsentimental and truth-seeking—within its limited parameters."

"And what are those?"

"A complete lack of imagination—and a stunning reliance on stereotypes!"

"Then, I don't see why you owe him," Mirabai laughs. "Why build your own prison? If you don't like the roles they give you, don't take them."

Build my own prison. Cory falls into a deep well, a rocking chair at the bottom—or is it a wheelchair? She sits down there and rocks, or spins her wheels. Like all the characters in the plays, she is just waiting for death, isn't she? Only one difference: she's working. At eighty-three—working!

From the bottom of the well, she speaks the truth, lets it echo up to her dear almost-daughter who has that tempting saintly aura of one who might really be able to help—if only she didn't belong to a cult. "I'm scared not to, Peggy, it's as simple as that. I'm scared there won't be any parts at all if I get choosy. And you know how I love working. It keeps me nasty, the way I should be —keeps me younger than the parts they give me."

Mirabai is silent now. She feels her eyes getting heavy, feels like going into meditation, but Cory couldn't bear that, she knows. "Dear Cory," she says finally, through the dazzling waves, "listen to your own spirit, what it's—"

"Peg," Cory leans forward. "You know what I'd like? I'd like to play Mrs. Malaprop in *The Rivals* again. An allegory on the banks of the Nile! I'd like to make people laugh. Consoling them with some dying person's quiet courage, et cetera et cetera—that's not what I want. I want those laughs again, Sheridan again, a big lively, sassy cast again. I'm sick of these claustrophobic little two- or three-person dramas for the sake of a low budget."

"Mrs. Malaprop!" laughs Mirabai. She decides not to mention the *Ramayana* again, with its cast of thousands. "That *would* be fun. Do some for me, Cory, won't you? The way you used to for us girls? Remind me . . ." A sweetness steals over her, her eyes flutter with that meditative embrace, and with something else—the old family love that Cory and her father provided: the twice-a-month weekends for herself and Jill, away from their mother's coldness; those saving plunges into theater and laughter.

Cory draws herself up, just as she used to in the great plays, just as she used to in those bedtime entertainments, tucking Jeff's girls in so grandly. Sparks fly from her eyes. "Peg," she says, "you are the very pineapple of politeness!"

"I am," laughs Mirabai, "indeed, I am."

II

Opening night. Act two, scene two. Flannel-robed Cory in wheelchair, center stage. Joshua Edwards and Anita Belmont, who play Cory's middle-aged, middle-class son and daughter, are doing their level best with a long, long scene in which they relive their sibling rivalries while fighting over Cory's fate: a nursing home or one of their homes. Oh God, how real, Cory thinks. How very real and how very dull. I've avoided that fate for myself—so far. Why should I help people assume it's inevitable?

The lines Cory would put in the play, if she allowed herself, would be very different from this dying old woman's long silences. She would have a magical healing; she would discover her own strength somehow—stand up and say, "The hell with this, I'm taking care of myself!" Then she would fling off her stupid lap robe and walk right over the footlights, down center aisle, and out the door. Now that's drama!

Cheap drama, though. She can't do it.

No, says Mrs. Malaprop scornfully, you can't do it. You're the very pineapple of politeness.

What am I doing? thinks Cory. Where did *she* come from? Hang onto your character, Cory! Don't go letting someone from another play into this one!

Ah, but this play needs me, says Mrs. Malaprop, it needs my perpendiculars!

Start the ancient lessons all over again, then. Sensory memory, spiritual concentration—all the old chestnuts. You're a defeated old woman whose children are deciding your fate. You're a stuffed dummy they put on the stage. You have a semigood line coming up in half an hour, of course, but it's not *that* good. For the time being, you are just supposed to look fiercely at them now and then, show your spirit isn't quite dead.

Her knees twitch. Her feet tingle. Up! Up! We want to dance!

You'll be finished in the theater, her head says. They'll say you're senile, that's all. They won't get the point. Then *you'll* be the one in a nursing home!

Up! Up! say her knees and her heart. You only have to follow through in the right way. Call a press conference. Make a manifesto.

But everyone's dead who would understand. They're all dead —my dear Jeffrey, Henry, Marguerite. Even the younger generation—even Mary who played such a sprightly Lydia Languish to my Mrs. Malaprop—all the best ones are dead. And it would be against all she believes in. It would be against all those years of devotion to her craft. The vision of Stanislavsky, of Ouspenskaya, of those summers with the Group Theatre and then the Actors' Studio—half a century of dedication to the line, the role, the beautiful interplay of detachment and involvement that makes acting great.

Besides, I can't do it to Kenneth, she reasons, even though he should have imagined better. I took it on; it's my duty to see it through.

She forces her hands to tremble helplessly on the lap robe. Let this be part of the role—this old woman trembling. I am this helpless old woman trembling. I have one good line coming up in about ten minutes. My son and my daughter haggle over me, over how they will betray me. Soon I will have my cliché to say.

* * *

Closing Night. Act two, scene two. Flannel-robed Cory in wheelchair, center stage.

Oh, says Mrs. Malaprop, it gives me the hydrostatics to such a degree! There's nothing to be lost by a little display, a little dismay at the end of this dis-play! The stupid thing *deserves* to close after five miserable nights. Yet here you sit so dutifully, as if my particles never made a participle of difference to you!

Down, says Cory under her breath, whacking the back of her left hand with the right. You stay out of this, you old dragon!

Oh fie! It *would* be inelegant in us, wouldn't it? says Mrs. M. We should only participate things!

Suddenly Cory is standing up, flinging her lap robe in the face of Joshua Edwards, her second-act son. Let him recover from that! she thinks. Let's see if he knows how to improvise!

"Fie!" she says. "You are as bad as allegories on the banks of the Nile! Where is your imagination? Where is your author's imagination? We old women are sick of being haggled over. Real hags don't stand for haggling! We dance—" she gets behind the wheelchair and uses it like a ballet barre—"we play—" then gives it a kick so that it goes rolling away to stage left—"and we heal—" she flings her arms to the air and imagines herself in northern woods, walking on pine needles, walking through shafts of sun. Cory smiles at her stage son and daughter. "Oh don't you see?" she says. "I am a medicine woman. Come ask my wisdom. I am Crazy Jane talking to the Bishop. Come hear what I know about desire." She sends Joshua a smoldering glance, then lets it slide to the audience, as she smiles radiantly, mischievously at them. Takes a deep breath and tries to say it: "I am life, not death, you see. And that's why I want us to know the theater again, the real theater—the great, high energy of the stage!"

Because she is so venerable an actress, or so vulnerable an old woman, or because everyone is so stunned, Cory is allowed to make this long speech before her colleagues recover. They were fumbling for an opening, a place in which to say, "Oh my God, Mother's out of her mind!" But their parts are gone, blown away. Handsome Joshua does the best theatrical thing he can think of: he kneels at Cory's feet and kisses her hand. This infuriates her, but Anita Belmont's action comforts: Anita grabs her other hand and holds it high. And when Cory whispers to her, "Help me off the stage!" she does. Cory manages to get down the center steps without her shaky legs buckling under her. Then she squares her shoulders, shrugs Anita away with a quick "Thanks!" and walks down the aisle at a sweepingly, dancingly dignified pace.

Scattered applause begins, and by the time she reaches the back of the theater, it's loud enough for Sarah Bernhardt—and as thrilling as ever. She wishes she had kept the lap robe to throw over her shoulders like a cape—all she's got is an old woman's bathrobe to wear like a gown of Duse's. I ought to hail a cab and just keep going, she thinks. But she can't, she'd look like an escaped mental patient. Damn this stupid role and its stupid, dreary costuming! Yet she is laughing, shaking with triumph and age mixed together.

Already Jenkins is at her side, wanting to get the story. Then Pearson. Whatever are they here for on closing night? Has someone said it will be Cory Meadows' final bow?

"Tomorrow morning," she says. "I'll hold a press conference tomorrow at 10:00."

"Where?" they ask.

"Why, right here, of course." But she wonders if the doors will be opened for her. She wonders if these journalists will bother to come back.

"Come on, Cory," says Pearson. "Tomorrow's a slow news day. Talk to us now!"

"What I have to say, young man, is not for a slow news day." She pauses—the kind of pause she's famous for—"But . . . you may come to my dressing room in half an hour, if you wish." She gives him, free of charge, her most tantalizing smile.

In her dressing room, Cory leans back on the threadbare gray tapestry chaise that she's had trundled into every dressing room for forty years or so. Trembling, she sinks into the frayed old comfort. Dizzy. Fainting on my fainting couch.

Oh, you've done it now, you old thing. A nice derangement of epitaphs!

Shut up, she says. And closes her eyes to enjoy the sweet dizziness, the whirling and whirling.

"Cory, are you all right?"

She groans when she sees Kenneth's balding head with its worried face, poking through the doorway. No doubt he thinks she's dying. "Kenneth—please come in."

As always, eel-like, he enters the room without opening the door more than a crack. He sits down on the spindly chair by the dressing table. He rests his elbow near dark red, opening-night roses, still almost fresh.

"Cory, what happened?" His voice with that hush of disaster, of horror.

"Oh, Kenneth, I couldn't help myself," she says. "You can't imagine how I tried to suppress it. Ever since opening night, Mrs. Malaprop has been egging me on!"

"Why didn't you tell me? Maybe we could have . . ."

"Kenneth, dear, there was nothing we could have done. If I had asked out of the play, you would have insisted I stay, and it would have been a standoff. It's my fault—I just can't bear this kind of part any more. Maybe it's getting too close to home, or maybe I just don't have much time left onstage, and I want it to be more . . . spirited!"

Kenneth slides down in the chair, his chin on his chest. The figure of despondency.

"Kenneth, I'm truly sorry," she says.

He laughs sadly. "The least you could have done, Cory, would have been to make this display on *opening* night! Then I would never have had to read the reviews. I could have blamed you, when we closed, for wrecking my masterpiece! Now—" He laughs again, closes his hand on the delicate old fingers that Cory reaches out to him with her ageless elegance. She laughs too.

"Now you have to listen to Mrs. Malaprop," she says, "before you write your next play. And help me face the reporters."

III

Cory has slept through the morning meditation. She makes a point of it, on principle. She does like the evening meditations, though, with these sweet young people (and some not-so-young ones too) all walking into the quiet, incense-scented room on graceful bare feet, wearing their delicate-colored gauze clothing, sitting down and pulling their shawls around lovely shoulders. The tiny children running in and diving into their parents' laps, whispering eagerly, then falling silent. Cory doesn't like to admit it, but the meditations seem not too different from the concentration exercises she did with Michael Chekhov forty years ago. She almost likes the whole business—except when it starts to sound like religion.

The guru himself causes great mixed feelings in her: he is recovering from a stroke, just like her character in that stupid play. But everything is so different here. As he struggles to speak, as he tries to write notes with his left hand, the frustration that crosses over his face is quickly replaced by love, by laughter. But she cannot countenance the idea of a guru. And she cannot forgive him for luring poor Peg into this strange life, giving up sure success, fame even, for this semiloony bin. It still amazes her that Peg is actually running the place—is actually, it seems, the guru's chosen successor. Her little Peggy, some kind of a swami!

If that doesn't prove life is stranger than art, I don't know what would, Cory thinks.

She has been hiding here ever since the infamous closing night. Unable to face Kenneth again—even though he was so nice in the dressing room just afterward, said it did him good. Still, she is mortified. How could I do something so foolish?

What makes her hardest on herself is that she took the part in the first place—agreed to it. No—even worse is that she *talked* about the great, high energy of theater and didn't make it happen. All she gave them was a lame protest statement and an old woman walking up the aisle!

Still, she listens to Peg and to Mrs. Malaprop, and she watches the excited preparations for the ashram's big production of the Indian epic, the *Ramayana.* The story is being read during the evening programs, so she is picking up bits of it. No wonder they love it so much in India. It has all the drama one could ask for: a ten-headed demon, a monkey god, a handsome godly hero with a trusty sidekick, and a beautiful, endangered heroine. Even an enchanting golden deer!

In the evenings, after dinner, she has been sitting on a blanket on the hillside above the lake, watching the rehearsals. A choreographed demon army doing frenzied sword dances, an exquisite young Sita miming her fascination with the golden deer. And in the midst of it all, Jyoti Akbar, the extraordinary young director from India, who is also a dancer and choreographer. He is utterly beautiful with his curly black hair, those great dark eyes, and that warm, sweet smile. Yet he is always gently in command of everything that is going on—teaching new gestures, new dance steps, watching all at once the several different rehearsal groups ranged about on the lawn. What brought him here to this odd place? Why didn't he stay in India, where they say he is famous? Cory watches, fascinated, each evening, then attends the lovely, quiet meditations afterward. And in the mornings—like the lifelong actor she is—she sleeps late.

Now Cory, after a leisurely awakening to the sounds of the

ashram—the birds, the children, the soft greetings of people beginning to work in the vegetable garden outside her window—is sitting in the tiny kitchen of Mirabai's apartment in a converted chicken coop, while Mirabai, just back from meditation, makes breakfast for them.

"Don't look now," Cory says, "but that very sleazy young man is right outside the window, with his hat pulled down and his legs stretched out on your garden table."

"Do you mind if I invite him to breakfast?" Mirabai asks. "He's my maintenance supervisor, and if he gets any madder at me this week, I'm afraid I'll lose him."

"Lord, Peggy, what a thankless job you have! I still can't believe that you run this whole outfit—or would want to!"

Mirabai smiles and sets a cup of strong-smelling coffee on the deal table in front of Cory, then walks behind her and starts to knead her shoulders. Wonderful massage they do here. Wonderful! My old bones do love it, it's a great seduction. She reaches a hand up to her shoulder to pat Peggy's hand. Mirabai's hand opens to Cory's, and they touch lovingly. "Ask him in, love," Cory says. "These young men are all in love with you, aren't they? They don't even notice you're well into your fifties. You should have stayed in the theater!"

"I *am* in the theater," says Mirabai. "Did you ever see such drama in your life as you find here?" She taps on the window. "Yogi Ram! Want some breakfast with us?"

He slouches in, bearded, scowling, and nods at Cory like a cowpoke to a schoolmarm. Might at least say, "Howdy, ma'am," thinks Cory, as he sits down and takes the proffered mug in a barely civil manner. No pineapple of politeness, he. Most of the young people here are quite clean and attractive in their Indian gauzes and their shining faces. This disgruntled one must be an awfully good worker!

"Got to talk to you about the tents down by the lake," he says. Mirabai, in her pale-orange sari that hangs so gracefully on her tall, slender frame, sits down to her own coffee, and gives him the attentiveness of her deep-set blue eyes (so much like Jeffrey's!). "We have twelve people signed up to stay in them, and now it looks like they're leaking. And speaking of leaking—" he offers a wry grin—"the shower still leaks all over the floor in the Main House dormitory. Also we haven't got enough lighting equipment for the *Ramayana.* How'm I supposed to get it by Saturday when I can't even find Uma Devi to write out a check for me? You've got to get people to be more reliable."

"Well, young man, I think I can help with the lighting," Cory breaks in. "And you won't need anyone to write a check for it."

He lifts an eyebrow in her direction.

"I have an attic full of old stage equipment," she says. "Left over from the period when my husband and I had our own summer theater."

"Corrry . . ." breathes Mirabai hungrily. "You still have all that stuff?"

"Some of it," says Cory. "I'll trade you some for a bit part in this epic of yours. I've always wanted to be a demon."

"Thank you, Miss Meadows," the young man says with a grace she hadn't thought him capable of. "I am going to find Jyoti right now. He's going to be thrilled."

"About me or the lighting?" Cory asks.

"Both." He flashes a quick smile. He might even be handsome, if he trimmed that beard and combed some of the debris out of it.

"First time I ever had to buy a part," Cory says.

"Don't tease," says Mirabai. "You know we've been *dying* to ask you!"

IV

Opening night. Cory in demon costume, stage right. Rama and Sita, center stage. The stage is actually a lakeside platform, the surrounding lawn and hillside, and the lake. Nothing claustrophobic about this play!

The late August night is chilly. Underneath the red, black, and green demon outfit with its witchy flowing sleeves, Cory is wearing long underwear—too big—that Mirabai has lent her. Still her bones are cold as the epic unfolds slowly under the slowly rising moon. But she is huddled together with loving young people. At one point, as the demons wait for their turn, three little children in monkey costumes—long multicolored feathers for tails—rush up to give her a blanket. Adorably, they do their best to wrap it around her as she laughingly accepts. From his spot in the center of the lower lawn, where he directs in full sight, like a symphony conductor with a flashlight instead of a baton—Jyoti Akbar sends an endearing smile to her.

An audience of fifty or sixty is sprawled on sleeping bags and blankets on the higher slopes of the lawn, oohing and ahhing over special effects like Sita's dance of temptation with the enchanting golden deer—a young woman in gold tights and antlers who moves so delicately and wittily that you forget entirely who she is. And Cory's favorite moment, when the young god Rama and his faithful brother set forth for the island of Lanka to rescue their beloved Sita: this amazing Jyoti Akbar has enlisted the ashram rowboat and the actual lake for them to glide away on, under perfect lighting (from Cory's attic!), over the dark, gleaming waters until they disappear. And such gasps from audience and players alike, at the astonishing moment when Hanuman, the monkey god, sets fire to Lanka. It is done with such cleverness and grace, torches along the lakeside reflecting in the water, that even the actors believe they are seeing a city in flames.

And now!—oh what a rush!—comes the battle between demons and the monkey army, made up so endearingly of little children! Cory lifts her wooden scimitar and rushes into battle with her fellow demons—some of them the real-life mothers and fathers of the monkey-children. Fiercely they battle, but the tiny monkeys vanquish them. Colorful tails waving behind their wiry little bodies, the brave little children seem to her not part of an Indian epic, but of one of the beloved Narnia books that she used to read to Peggy and Jill. One by one, the demons fall, and the happy monkeys gather round their general, the monkey god Hanuman, son of the wind! Cory is blissful as she lies fallen, vanquished in the dewy grass, sharing with her fellow demons the sweet comfort of body-warmth and smothered, joyous little laughs.

V

It was the very pineapple of delightfulness, says Mrs. M. No matter if our bones *do* ache with the rheumatiz now.

Yes it was. I haven't been so warmed, so cuddled and joyed since Jeffrey died.

They are conversing quite spiritedly in the silence of the evening meditation. Occasional coughs and delicate sounds of shifting hips, of fabrics sliding as legs uncross and recross themselves here, there, in this converted living room of an old mansion that has been a meditation room for twenty years now—since the heyday of such things in the sixties. Cory lifts her eyes to look around the room from her old-person's chair in the corner. Soft blue rug, blue curtains, and Tibetan paintings, pictures of Indian gods, candlelight. A warm and strangely foreign place. The bright-orange figure of the guru facing his students. Peggy swaying in the front row, her deep meditation marked by an odd little frown. Now why that frown if it's all so peaceful? Cory has always wanted to ask, but she likes it. Besides, Peg always had that frown whenever she concentrated, from the earliest childhood days that Cory knew her. Serious little thing with her sweet mouth and that firm little vertical line between her eyes!

The others in the room are no longer strangers, but people Cory has come to love, many of them with Sanskrit names that she finds easier to accept than her own Peggy's name, of course. And some with the names they were born with. Durga of the steady, abundant motherhood, who sits in a white sari, with a thumb-sucking three-year-old leaning on one hip and a one-year-old sprawled in the circle of her crossed legs. Jyoti Akbar in his nimble shining, eyes closed and body still—yet he seems to be dancing even then. He has become her good friend; they talk of theater in the afternoons, and she has ideas of getting him into a house off-Broadway. Among all the delicately balanced straight backs, attentive heads straight up and gazing inward, there is the surly Yogi Ram in jeans and a flannel shirt, bent over a bit as if with heavy responsibility, humming a bit, like—oh, the name escapes her!—like that great cellist she loves like her own brother. All these sweet, attentive minds attuned to—or seeking—something Cory can't quite get. What do they feel? What do they listen to?

Not to the likes of me, I'll wager! says Mrs. Malaprop. Their life is quite delirious, I'm sure, but in the end it's not for us, you know. If we sit so piously one day longer, I think I'll get the hydrostatics!

You old dragon, says Cory. What about all those years in wheelchairs and rocking chairs onstage? Now you can't take a little loving quiet in this gentle place?

Oh, we'll come back, says Mrs. M, of course we'll come back. They'll stir us up and we'll stir them. But now I want to go home. I miss the stage, the lascivious stage!

After the meditation, a big baking tray of dark, healthy-looking cake is brought in, and cups of peppermint tea are poured and passed about the room. Durga's sleeping one-year-old still lies sprawled, rosy-lipped, one flushed cheek against the blue carpet, his mother's shawl thrown over him. Bare feet step gently around him as people hand out the cake, or greet each other.

The guru—such a tiny, bright-orange figure!—is passing by now, tired from the long evening, yet with a friendly word or a chuckle for everyone he sees along the way. He stops by Cory, gives her a searching look with those brilliant eyes in the dark, strangely transparent, bearded face.

"How long you stay with us?" he says in his awkward, post-stroke, Indian-accented English. Still, Cory understands him.

"I'm leaving soon," she says.

"No, stay!" he says. "We need you."

"I'll come back," she says. "I like your theater here. I'd like to work some more with Jyoti Akbar."

"Ah. Good," he says. He rests his warm hand on top of her head a moment, then walks on.

And now Mirabai pulls herself away from the circle of ashram friendliness and ashram problems that surrounds her after each program. She comes smiling to Cory's chair in the corner and folds up childlike at Cory's feet. Usually she stands behind Cory to rub her shoulders for her, knowing just where the bones and muscles ache. But this time she leans her head against Cory's knee confidingly and rests there a moment.

"Just like old times," laughs Cory, putting her fingers a bit hesitantly into Mirabai's lovely, soft gray curls.

"Oh yes," says Mirabai. "You can't imagine what a blessing it is to have you here, dear Cory-Deary! I'm so busy mothering this whole place, and then you come along and mother me a little bit, without being the least bit motherly! I mean, there you were—of all things, a demon! How my father would have loved it!"

Cory is in danger of crying—she knows it's quite OK here, yet she'd rather not. But the mountain lakes are filling with spring rain, with melting snows, with— "Wouldn't he?" she says. "Wouldn't he have loved it."

Millicent Dillon

OIL AND WATER

It was January something, 1946 and I was in the bus station, waiting to go to the oil field. Though it was five months since the end of the War, there were still a number of servicemen about, some standing, some milling, some on benches, asleep and awake.

When my bus was called, only a few passengers boarded. I went to the back seat and stretched out full length. I had been up too late the night before and I needed sleep badly. I fell asleep and woke up and fell asleep again, the bus making its droning sound, putting me to sleep in the way I don't like to sleep. You try to come out of it, but you can't, you're in and out of the noise, you're in and out of the sleep.

I don't know how long I was lying there, my purse near my head, when suddenly I felt a thing on my leg and I was awake. I saw a guy in a dark jacket beside me on the seat. "Take your goddam hand off of me," I yelled though he had already taken it off. One passenger turned around, then another, but he had put himself into the corner and was pretending to be asleep. I was so mad at the nerve of this guy putting his hand on me I wasn't able to sleep any more. Shaking, I sat upright. A whole journey like that, no leaning, no nodding, looking in front of me. The creep in the corner must have got off at some stop in the valley, though I never noticed. By then it was dark and the bus had filled up.

* * *

It was almost eleven at night when we got into Avenal, the valley town west of the oil field. At the bus stop, a parking lot beside a diner, a station wagon was waiting, marked with the company name and logo, a series of jagged peaks in a circle on a dusty green ground. The driver, a lean man wearing a greasy cap, threw my suitcase into the front seat and motioned to me to get in back. He remained silent as we drove out of town, along a straight unlit road. After about twenty minutes we began to climb into the hills. He took the curves very fast in the darkness. I felt myself growing car sick. I tried to stop the nausea by fixing firmly on something outside. I saw lights gleaming on the tops of high still derricks. Around them and beneath them rows of squat metal beams moved in shadow through semi-circular arcs, looking like a herd of blind horses rocking in the night.

I don't know what I would have done, where I would have thrown up, I was beginning to feel desperate, but finally we came to a stop. Before us a group of one story buildings were huddled together in the dark.

"Women's bunkhouse," the driver announced loudly as if he were addressing a carload of people. He jumped out and took my bag out of the front and set it on the railed porch. Then he got back in the car.

"Which is my room?" I whispered to him, worried that I might wake somebody up, since there wasn't a single other sound I could hear.

"Fourth door to the left. Bathroom's at the end. And the cook-house is over there." He pointed vaguely left. "Whistle blows at six."

I dragged my suitcase into number four and turned on the overhead light. A single bed with a white chenille cover, an un-painted wooden table with a metal lamp, a bare floor, a bureau, a small closet curtained off from the rest of the room by material marked with those jagged peaks.

It was the idea of the desert that had appealed to me when I had heard about the job. Just the words, "the desert," and "an oil field," had sounded like adventure. And then, too, I had figured I could save some money if I could just make myself stay a little while. I thought of that road winding down to the valley, then straight as a shot back to where I had just come from and then further back. Who needed that? I was finished with that. I fell back on the bed without taking my clothes off. I wasn't even sleepy. My stomach was gurgling, empty, I hadn't brought any food with me. I hadn't thought things out well but then I hadn't known what to expect. At least I was here. I'd gotten on the bus, I'd gotten off the bus. There was a beginning, a middle and an end—that's what I liked about journeys.

At the middle, or close to the beginning was that creep who put his hand on my leg. What did he think when I yelled? He had jumped away, backed away. He cowered in that corner, pretending that he'd been sleeping all along. Did he even know why he did what he did? He saw a leg laying there. Was it my fault that I had good legs? It was there, to be touched. Is that what he thought? It had nothing to do with thinking probably. He saw it, his hand moved to it, it went, it was going, it was touching, he thought, he did not think. That this person, myself, was asleep, did that excite him? What was he on his way to? What had he been? He was no soldier. He looked too young, didn't look as though he could have been a soldier . . .

* * *

It was still dark when the cookhouse whistle blew and woke me up. At first I didn't know where I was. Then I remembered. I lay for a few minutes listening to the sounds around me, someone going past the window, the footsteps heavy on the wooden porch, a door slamming, a radio on, loud. New sounds, new day, come on get up, for some reason I was filled with hope as I almost always was in the morning. People are getting up, a whistle has blown, in a way it's a little like the army, I told myself.

I dressed and went outside. The building next door with all the lights had to be the cookhouse. I crossed the path and entered a large room with many rows of long tables and straight chairs, a steam table along one wall and behind it the kitchen, partially enclosed. There were only a few men sitting at the tables. As I walked over to the serving line, several of the men turned and looked at me. They didn't smile, they only stared, then turned back again and said something in low voices to each other.

The food at the steam table was overwhelming: great huge slabs of ham covered with a dark thick raisin sauce, mounds of bacon, more mounds of scrambled eggs, boxes of cereal, loaves and loaves of white bread, containers full of milk, coffee, more milk, enough for a regiment. Next to me in line was a small neat woman with a braid wrapped around her head. She was wearing a sensible dress and sensible shoes. She had on her tray a bowl of cereal and milk, a glass of orange juice, and coffee. I took the same.

After I got out of the serving line, I looked around. I didn't feel like just going over to the men's table and barging in. I had the feeling those men wouldn't like it. Instead I went over to where the sensible woman was sitting by herself. I introduced myself, I said I was new here, I said, "They certainly give you a lot of food."

"They sure do. Too much. Maybe if you're a roughneck, but for someone working in the office, it's ridiculous. So just don't eat it." She held out her hand. "My name is Udell Banks Henry. It was plain Udell Banks until last year when I married Frank Henry. I always call myself Udell Banks Henry. Do you think that's peculiar?" she asked belligerently.

"Not at all," I said. "I think it's admirable."

Mollified, she went on, "Frank Henry lives in Fresno where he works in a clothing store. I go there every weekend. I don't much care for all the driving but I'd be nuts to give up my job here as a bookkeeper. I save a lot and there's no rent and no expenses for food. I figure a couple more years of this and I'll have a real nest-egg socked away. Frank Henry agrees with me. A good thing too because if he didn't it wouldn't matter. I am very independent in my thinking." She finished off her glass of milk. "So you're new here. How do you like it? Did you meet anybody yet?"

"The driver. He picked me up at the bus station last night. He wasn't very—talkative," I added.

"Talkative? Are you kidding? They're all sphinxes. None of them talk."

She turned around and looked around the room. All the men were gone now. "Those men. What a weird bunch they are. They stay on in this godforsaken place that's already beginning to run out of oil, when they could be making three times as much doing the same thing in Saudi Arabia. I think they're afraid, that's what I think."

She circled her coffee cup with both palms. "I'll tell you one thing, they are definitely afraid of women. Oh sure, they'll get drunk and go to a whore for a quickie but a real woman? a long-term woman? They want nothing to do with her. I went out a couple of times with some of them before I met Frank Henry. What a drag. You ask them how they feel about something, anything, and they say, 'What do you want to know for?' I mean, you're not asking them for their most intimate private business. I'd ask them, 'Do you have a brother' or 'What is your hobby?' You know what this one guy said to me? He said, 'I don't ask you anything about yourself. You don't need to ask me anything.' What have they got to hide? But who cares? I quit asking. I mean, who needs it? Who needs them? Anonymous jerks. My advice to you is to do like I do. Keep to yourself, keep your nose to the grindstone, when you're grinding, that is. I do my real living in Fresno. If you want to go there any weekend, just let me know, I'll give you a ride."

"Thanks," I said. "I'll keep that in mind." I only said that out of politeness. I had just arrived. I couldn't even think of leaving yet.

* * *

At seven-twenty-five as I came out of the women's bunkhouse, the sun was already well up. Across the valley to the east a great dry plain extended as far as I could see. In the far distance, I could just make out a range of snow-topped mountains. At the north end of the valley, a body of water glistened in the slanting light. It looked as if it were a square lake. How could a lake be square? In the air was an odd smell, as if something heavy and invisible had oozed in on the night air.

Some men came out of a nearby building in their tan work outfits and got into a company car. They sped off, the dust circling behind them. From another building across the way I heard men's voices calling out to each other. I felt as if I were a fly on a wall, watching, listening, in a space permeated by maleness. Had these men been in the War? I wondered. Maybe that accounted for their silence, for their being what Udell had called "weird."

* * *

I found Mr. Redfern, my supervisor, in his office seated behind a long narrow table. On each side of him and opposite him were a number of chairs, all unoccupied. There was something very pale and pinched looking about Mr. Redfern. (How did he stay so pale in the desert?) He did not ask me to sit down. His first words were not welcoming words. "We didn't expect you so early."

"But I thought we were supposed to start at seven-thirty."

"I mean so early in the week, in the month. We're not ready for you." What does he expect me to do, go back? I wondered.

"Well," he went on with asperity, "I suppose now that you're here we'll have to find something for you to do. Your predecessor was working on depth pressure readings. I suppose you can do that."

"Depth pressure?"

"You don't know what depth pressure is?"

"No, but I—I'm eager to learn."

"What is the matter with those people at the central office? Do they think I'm running a school here? Have you ever been in an oil field before? Have you?"

"No, but I—"

"I thought not. At least you do know how to measure and plot, don't you? You do know how to do that?"

"Yes, I think so."

"She thinks so," he said loudly, as if he were addressing an audience seated in the empty chairs. "Either you do or you don't, there's no halfway about it."

"Yes, I do."

"I hope so."

Grumbling again about the central office, he led me out of his office into a small cubicle with a desk in it. "Sit there." He went away and came back with a stack of small pieces of metallic paper, each with a staggered line engraved on it. He placed before me a wooden holder. The paper was to be slipped into it and then tightened into position with two small wing nuts. When everything was firmly in place, I was to measure the deviation of the jagged line from the center line every quarter of an inch and then plot the readings on a chart.

"Think exactness," Mr. Redfern said. I watched him go out of the cubicle, amazed at how even his back looked pinched.

Okay, I instructed myself. No and, if, or but. Start and start right. I did like exactitude, I liked to see things fit, to see disorder vanish. I loved to be in the grip of sudden intuition going toward, reaching, discovery. Many beginnings, how many middles, one end.

I began. But to my dismay, each time I took a reading and then went back to check it (for I was thinking "exactness"), I found the second reading was different from the first. Not by a lot, but enough to cause anxiety. Something was out of whack. Maybe the paper was slipping in the holder. I tightened the wing nuts.

Again, each measurement of the distance from the center line from a particular point was slightly different from the previous measurement at that point. I began to despair of exactness as a fundamental principle. I kept tightening and measuring and tightening and measuring till I was in a sweat. I began to fear that the uncertainty principle had taken hold in a big—an impossibly big—way, that by the act of measuring itself I was causing, had caused, a change in the universe.

Stop that, just write down what you get, I told myself, write down all the different answers, then you'll have a set of answers for each point. It's better than nothing. I wondered if Mr. Redfern would buy the idea of multiple answers with its implication that the world was a maze of possibilities. I myself wasn't sure I could buy it. The need for precision, for the precision of singleness, of single (right) answers, had come on me like a fever. I had the feeling that the slightest inaccuracy would count against me, that it would blemish my record irrevocably, even though, especially because, this was my first day on the job.

Mr. Redfern appeared at my elbow. "This is all, this is all you have done? And what are those extra figures you have written down?"

"I'm having a little problem," I said. In my agitation the words tumbled out about the slipping and sliding of the paper.

"Your predecessor never mentioned that problem."

"Maybe it didn't happen before."

"Nothing has changed. It was always very stable before and it should be now." He bent over the holder, tugged lightly on the metallic paper, and it slipped. He tightened the wing nuts and tugged on the paper again. "That's very peculiar. Did you tighten the nuts too tight?"

"No, no, that's the way they were from the beginning. I didn't do anything."

"You're sure?"

"I'm pretty sure."

"They look stripped to me. You know, I didn't need this. I've got enough on my mind without this."

"But what do you want me to do?"

"What do I want you to do? I want you to be careful. As far as these wing nuts are concerned, you'd better draw up some specifications for new wing nuts and take them over to the shop foreman."

"And what should I do about the different measurements?"

"Average them." Mr. Redfern started toward his office, stopped, and returned to my desk. He cleared his throat. "There is something I think it is my responsibility to say to you, since you have never been in an oil field before. There are certain things that, as a young woman, in this unfamiliar setting, you ought to—" he stopped, bit his lips, and started again. "I—My wife and I go to church in Avenal every Sunday morning at eleven. Would you like to accompany us this Sunday?"

"Thank you very much," I blurted out, "but I don't go to church."

"I see," he said. Just that and nothing more. He went into his office and closed the door.

I felt like an idiot, I felt like a gorilla, I felt it was all my fault. Why did I turn him down so quickly without even thinking? It was a kind offer. Wasn't it kind? I could have just said that I was agnostic. Would that have been better? But that wasn't the truth either. I didn't know what I believed except that God was as inscrutable to me as man—or men. But on the other hand I certainly didn't mean any refusal of Mr. Redfern's religion by my not going. Only it had come upon me so quickly. First all that business about being too early and then about not being exact and then his telling me to average—I hated averaging—Was this an acceptable way for a supervisor to act or wasn't it? Who was this man? I didn't know a thing about him except that he looked pinched, and what did that mean, after all? Had he been in the War? I looked at the metallic pieces of paper before me with their jagged lines. I began to feel something akin to dread. It was as if my skin had become porous to the uncertainty of the entire universe and that trying to know, like trying to measure, only increased that uncertainty, made the world a pool of uncertainty, and I, an insect suspended through surface tension alone, at any moment might drown.

Looking out the window beside my desk, I saw that the snow-clad peaks across the valley were no longer visible because of a gathering haze. Out there were derricks and pumps and oil in the ground, black oil made by the disintegration of carbon and whatever over the centuries. I had to take a longer view of things. I had to look at the world the way it was. I had to stop making such a fuss about slipping papers and slipping words.

* * *

Coming out of the bathroom of the women's bunkhouse was Udell, a towel with the company insignia wrapped around her head.

"Aren't you coming to dinner at the cookhouse?" I asked.

"Nah. I don't have dinner there every night. Lots of times I just have cottage cheese and fruit in the kitchen. Want to join me?"

"I didn't know we had a kitchen."

"It's right through the living room. How could you miss it?"

"I haven't seen the living room yet."

Udell led me around to the other side of the building, opened a door and there was a living room with five overstuffed green chairs, very large, unoccupied, one standing lamp with a faded shade, and a number of torn issues of the Saturday Evening Post on a wooden table in the corner. "They certainly keep it messy," Udell said. I didn't know who she meant by "they."

She led me through the living room out another door to the kitchen, painted the dusty green of the company logo. In the center of the room was a battered wooden table with six chairs. Had a lot more people once been here or were they expecting a lot more to arrive?

Udell got the cottage cheese and fruit—apples and pears, out of the refrigerator and took two pale green glass plates from the rusty metal cabinet. She heaped the cottage cheese and fruit on the plates.

"Do the other women eat here too?" I asked.

"Don't ask me what they do," Udell said with irritation. She munched on a pear and then put it down. "I'll tell you what the trouble with the women around here is. There are so many men it makes them greedy. I mean, you'd think they'd want to share but no, the more they have, the more they want. Take Francine, who's the office manager, and Mattie, who's a pumper—"

"What's a pumper?"

"A pumper goes out to the wells and reads the numbers on the pumps. I wouldn't like to have that job, I'll tell you. Going out and checking at night. God knows how many snakes there are just hiding and waiting. Not for me. I'm glad I've got an office job."

"How old is Mattie?"

"Young. My age. But Francine—have you seen her?"

"No, I haven't seen any of the women."

"Francine's forty-five if she's a day but she gets herself all dolled up in frilly dresses meant for kids."

"What did you say Francine does?"

"She's supposed to manage the office. Some manager. She spends most of her time chasing after the younger guys. In fact," and here Udell leaned closer, "I wouldn't be surprised if Francine and Mattie both had a thriving business going on here. All I know is that she'd better not approach me to be part of her business. I'd spit in her eye. My favors are my own favors. They're not for sale to anyone. I care about my reputation. Don't you?"

Was this what Mr. Redfern had had in mind when he asked me to go to church? Was he really only watching out for me? Why didn't he speak more directly? How was I supposed to know what was going on?

"Don't you?" Udell repeated, louder.

"Yes, yes, of course."

"I'm independent minded, like I told you, but that doesn't mean I don't give a damn about what other people think. That's just plain common," Udell said, as she cleared away the food and began washing up. Her way of washing dishes, I noticed, was to use hot water and no soap.

"Will the dishes get clean that way, with just water?"

"If the water's hot enough, they'll get clean."

"But," I said, thinking of germs, and that surely there are germs in the desert like anywhere else, maybe even more, but I didn't say anything about them. Instead I asked her what she usually did in the evening.

"Usually? Usually I go to sleep. I save myself for Fresno. I used to go up to the employee's clubhouse before I was married. They have pool tables and cards there and a soda fountain. Good malts, the best I've ever had. But that's good reason for me to stay away. Frank Henry doesn't like it if I put on weight. Besides, I go up there now and it's just plain boring. The same thing over and over, those guys feeding you a line. The way I look at it, there's more to life than that. Don't misunderstand me. I like sex. Frank Henry likes sex too. I don't have any complaints in that department. But after all, let's face it, there are more important things in life than sex. Just don't ask me what, right this moment."

* * *

I went into my room and shut the door and sat on the bed to read. There wasn't any other place to sit. I thought of going into the living room, in fact I went into the living room. I even sat in one of those large chairs. But after a while it depressed me, just those large empty chairs and me.

I went outside. The night was very dark, there wasn't any moon. It was eerie, even frightening. But I didn't want to go back to my room. The depression, if that's what it was, was wearing off, and had left me anxious to move. I started walking up the road. From inside the clubhouse I heard men's voices and sharp clicking noises. I went on, past the men's bunkhouses, past the storage areas, until finally I was at the end of the camp. Peering out, I could not penetrate the darkness. There were no pumps or derricks visible from here. It was as if I had come to the edge of the world. I thought of vast distances, cold, silent, and uninhabited. I thought of the snowcovered peaks I had seen that morning that had vanished in the later haze. Only that morning? I felt in some way as if I had always been here, that there was no other place but here. The world, all there was of it, ended here, and I had better come to terms with it, take it for what it was, because there was no other, because one could fall into darkness as if into a chasm, if one refused it.

I retraced my steps but instead of passing by the employee clubhouse I went inside. At one end of the huge room were a number of men, standing around the pool tables, talking and playing. The clicking noises I had heard before, I now realized, were from the pool balls hitting each other as they shot out on the green surfaces. In front of me was a group of small tables with men playing cards, slamming them down, gathering them up, some laughing, some frowning. A rack with magazines lined another wall and to my right was the snack bar and some empty round tables and chairs.

I ordered a chocolate malted at the snack bar and took it to one of the round tables. The malted was certainly creamy and rich, just as Udell had said. It was also huge and I wondered if I'd be able to finish the whole thing. Looking up, I caught several of the men at the card tables looking at me. Again that wary look, again that turning away and saying something to each other. I felt I had invaded a sanctuary.

"Would you like to play a game of pool?" A short stocky man stood in front of me. He had an open honest face and a friendly grin.

"I don't know how to play," I said.

"I can show you."

"That would be very nice indeed." Even as I said the words, they sounded affected to me, but he didn't seem to notice. He led me to an empty pool table and took a cue down from the wall. "This one looks about the right size for you." He stood it on end on the floor next to me. "Yep, it's fine."

He showed me how to grip the cue with the thumb and first finger of my right hand, and how to place my left hand on the table to make a bridge with my fingers. "Don't hold it so tight, it's not a death grip. Not too loose, either. You have to do it just right. Light with your right hand here at the butt end and tighter where the bridge is.

"Okay, now what you want to do is try to hit the ball with the cue in this small area at the center. You're going to be aiming for that corner pocket."

I did as he said. I hit the ball and it went straight into the pocket. He took out another ball. I aimed and I got it into the corner pocket again. I felt my luck had turned. No—more than that. I felt I had discovered an unknown talent in myself. No—more than that. There was something about the game, the estimation of the impact and then the actuality of the ball's passage through space and into the proper hole, that touched and excited me.

Two other men came over, one heavy set and middle-aged, the other somewhat younger and very thin. "Why don't you teach her about english, Shorty?" said the heavier one.

"Kelly, just leave me do it my way. I don't want her to get completely confused the first time."

"Why don't we play a game? You and her against me and Al."

"All right with you?" Shorty asked.

"As long as nobody minds a beginner."

"It's just a game," said Kelly.

Though it was just a game, they played with great seriousness, taking a long time to estimate, to judge, to aim. As for my own shots, now and then I would hit a good one and they praised me. When I missed completely, Shorty said, "Never mind. What do you expect the first time? You're doing real good."

The air in the clubhouse was warm and comforting and no one

said a word to me that was at all out of the way. Udell had been wrong about that, at least. It's not that they weren't treating me as if I were a woman. They were, but somehow they acted as if I'd been admitted to their fraternity. And I was experiencing a reciprocal sense of comradeship with them. It did pass through my mind that I was not attracted to Shorty or Al or Kelly. In its own way, that was a kind of relief. It came to me that there were, after all, different kinds of maleness, or perhaps different feelings that maleness evoked: This friendly maleness, then the maleness of sexuality—that wasn't friendly—and then there was the third kind of maleness, the one that was all mixed up with death. Had these men been in the War? I wondered.

* * *

First thing the next morning I began to draw up the specifications for the new wing nuts. I had never drawn a specification before so I had delayed doing it when Mr. Redfern told me to, but today I decided it must not be that difficult. I did a drawing of the old wing nut, then made the winged section larger, then larger again. The important thing, I decided, is to be able to get a good purchase on it, so I can really screw it down tight. I felt as if I were making substantial progress toward accuracy. I even began to look at averaging with less distaste.

As the day went by, I felt myself falling into place, into my own proper niche. Though I had only the haziest idea of what was involved in depth pressure measurements, I was convinced that what needed to be revealed would be revealed in its own good time. Whatever secrecy there was seemed a natural secrecy, appropriate to this time and place, to these circumstances. I was, after all, a student in the school of learning how to wait. I felt I was being released from all those questions that had been nagging at me so persistently in the recent past, about what I must or should find. The sense of desire itself was altering in me. Even as I felt this way, I noted that I was becoming a little weird, nunlike, almost. But at the same time I was convinced that while I was being helped to wait, I was also being helped over some hump of loathsome vulnerability within myself.

* * *

Soon I fell into a comforting and comfortable routine, getting up, having breakfast at the cookhouse, working in the morning, having lunch at the cookhouse, working in the afternoon, then dinner at the bunkhouse with Udell and, to cap off the day, playing pool at night. Shorty was teaching me how to sight along the cue, how to gauge the proper angle and english for a carom shot.

After playing, I would sit at one of the small round tables with Shorty and Al and Kelly, listening to them talk about the old days at the camp. All that other history out there—my own family's history, which I'd just as well not think of, why else did I leave home but to get away from it?—and even the history of the War seemed to be giving way to another kind of history that I began to identify as my own.

Once Shorty said something about the field already beginning to play out. Kelly said that the engineers were damn smart, they'd find a way to extract more oil. In some places they were already forcing water at high pressure into the wells to drive up the oil still left in the rock.

"Still," said Shorty, "there's a limit to what you can do. There's only so much oil in the ground."

"So if it plays out here, I'll go somewhere else," said Al.

"If there is a somewhere else."

"There's always a somewhere else."

Shorty shrugged. "For you, maybe."

They were silent for a while. Then Al got up to get another beer.

"Al's a driller, one of the best," said Kelly.

"One of the best," said Shorty. "You ought to go see him work some day. It's an art, the way he guides that block, the way he can tell when the drilling mud is just right."

For a moment I felt a spasm of envy. I couldn't say there was any art to what I was doing on the job, but at least, I reassured myself, you're getting accurate readings. The shop had made the wing nuts exactly to my specifications. The flange of each nut was almost two inches in width and when I tightened them down on the paper, it never slipped.

* * *

Now that it was March there were dust storms every afternoon at the camp. The wind blew relentlessly and the sun, when it shone, was filtered through grit. One night I was awakened by the sound of rain on the metal roof of the bunkhouse. The water thundered so loud I wondered if the roof would hold. Finally, toward morning, without any tapering off, the rain stopped.

Coming out of the cookhouse into the brilliant washed light, I smelled the unfamiliar moisture over and under the smell of oil. I was afflicted with a vague sense of loss, as if a memory—or more accurately, a memory of a memory were slipping from my grasp. But I haven't lost anything, I assured myself. I saw in the wash behind the camp a roaring stream, but elsewhere there was dryness as before.

In the evening after an early dinner Udell and I went for a walk. "We'd better keep to the road," said Udell as we passed beyond the end of the camp. "This is snake weather."

"Snakes? Poisonous snakes?"

"Nah. I don't think so, but I steer clear of them anyhow. Like I told you, I don't like snakes. Once I saw a cobra in a zoo. It was all wrapped around itself and one end started to move but the other end hadn't gotten the message yet. Weird. In the next cage was this frog or toad, the ugliest thing I have ever seen. It lay there in this tiny cage like a blob—a blob of shit. I'll tell you, God makes plenty of mistakes."

"Well, maybe not mistakes, exactly." Uncertain as I was about the nature of my own beliefs, I did not want to share in the complicity of this judgment.

"Yes, mistakes," Udell went on doggedly. "Plenty of them.

What's the matter? You afraid God will punish me for saying he makes mistakes? Mistakes!" she yelled. "You make plenty of mistakes!" She grinned. "You see, He doesn't strike me dead. Frank Henry, he's a Baptist, always trying to get me to go and be dunked into the church. Not me, I say, not me. I had enough of that fire and brimstone when I was a kid. Meekness, kid, does not inherit the earth. What it does do is turn you into a poor fucked-up toad in a cage."

At that moment I heard a terrible sound behind me, as if the earth were rumbling and the air roaring. Can this be punishment? I thought in a panic. I turned around and saw a riderless horse in full gallop coming toward us. I stared in wonder, I couldn't move, I couldn't believe the power of that horse in motion.

Udell yanked my arm and pulled me off the road. The horse went thundering by and disappeared round a bend in the road. "What's the matter with you, standing there like you were paralyzed? Haven't you ever seen a horse before?"

"I have, but not—not one like that."

"I worry about you, kid. Sometimes I think you need a keeper." She shook her head. "Let's go back, I've had enough walking for today."

A pick-up truck drove up with Shorty at the wheel. "You see my gray mare?"

"We sure did," Udell said. "What the hell is it doing running loose like that?"

"She got out of the corral when I wasn't looking," Shorty said sheepishly. "She's only feeling her oats."

"Some oats. You better keep that horse corralled or I'll complain to the management. We could have been killed just walking. Mean, stupid beasts," she said as he drove away. "You can't trust them."

That night I had a dream: I was climbing a steep pass at a great height. At a turn in the path I looked up and saw that a man had grabbed the woman next to him and with a violent gesture was flinging her over the edge of the cliff. I watched in terror as the woman plummeted to earth and finally dropped into a small pool of water. After a long wait, the woman surfaced, safe. In the dream I wondered how it was possible for that man to have so accurately directed his throw, for I didn't doubt that he had intended what had happened. There was something admirable as well as frightening about the sureness of his gesture.

The leftover feelings of the dream stayed with me after I woke up, and fastened themselves somehow onto the image of that horse, galloping, galloping. Two feelings, vague and grave, rode in and out of my brain. First, I felt a sense of awe at the horse, at its—her thundering motion, at its mane that in retrospect seemed to be like flame, at its quivering nostrils. Then there was the sense of shame at the thought of how I stood so paralyzed until Udell pulled me out of its path.

As I worked in my cubicle that morning tightening the wing nuts, I saw that they were like two misshapen beings, animals with huge shoulders, too big for their small bodies, clutching at the metallic paper as if it were a matter of life and death. Why had I come here and why was I staying? I was a coward, staying on here like a lump, wasting away my youth, losing the main chance, throwing it away, being bypassed forever. Stop it, I told myself, but I was saddled with a burden of regret that I could not shake off.

Looking out the window, I felt that even the landscape was putting something over on me. There was the square lake, another cause for shame. I'd asked Kelly about the lake one evening. "What?" he'd said to me in surprise. "You've never seen a square lake before? That's the only kind we have around here."

"You're kidding," I said, but he insisted so soberly that he was serious, I was about to believe him. After all, what did I know about the desert? But finally Shorty had taken pity of me and said it was man-made, a storage lake for irrigation, and they'd had a good laugh at me. Good-naturedly, I'd thought at the time. But now I felt differently. They were in the know in this, their world, and I wasn't. They had their secrets that weren't secrets to them but were to me. And they would not be revealed, except piecemeal and grudgingly, only at that point when they didn't matter any more. All the assumptions I had made about camaraderie were incorrect, I now saw. Oh come on, I said to myself, all this because of a riderless horse?

I made myself go to the clubhouse that night, as if habit could rectify existence. I found Shorty alone playing solitaire. He seemed distant, unfamiliar. He put the queen of diamonds on the king of clubs. He didn't say anything about the horse. I felt I ought to say something.

"How's your horse?"

"Okay."

"You got her back all right?"

"Yeah." He put the jack of clubs on the queen of diamonds.

"What's her name?"

"Tiny."

"Tiny?" I began to laugh hysterically.

"That's her name," he said stubbornly.

"Sorry," I said, trying to control myself. "I hope I didn't hurt your feelings. I mean, she seems like a very nice horse."

He smiled, old, familiar, decent, friendly Shorty. "Would you like to ride her?"

"I'd love to, but I don't know how to ride."

"I'll teach you. We could go out on rides together."

"Both on one horse?"

"No," he laughed. "I've got two horses. Tiny and a gelding named Curly. Would you like to go on a moonlight ride sometime?"

"A moonlight ride?"

"Sure. Riding with the moon shining and the stars out and the sagebrush and the—"

Right then Al and Kelly came in and the usual pool game started but I had a hard time concentrating. "What's the matter with you tonight?" Kelly asked. He and I were partners. "You're missing everything."

"Nothing's the matter," I said. But I was upset that Shorty had asked me that question. Maybe at first, for an instant, I was pleased—flattered. I had felt that small sly leap, that inner grin at the proof of my power to attract. But almost at once it had been replaced, covered over, by my conviction that now things were going to be muddier.

As I sighted along the cue for the next shot, I was afraid I was going to miss that one too. I felt I'd lost any ability I'd ever had to judge, to estimate, to aim.

* * *

"I wondered how long it was going to take before you had to get away," Udell said, as we drove into the outskirts of Fresno. "You can only stand it so long and then you have to get out. It happens to everybody."

"It's certainly nice here," I said, admiring the wide streets and the green trees and the neat small houses.

"It is nice, if I say so myself. Clean, they keep it clean. I get so damned tired of all that dust at the camp. It gets in your nose and your eyes and your mouth. I feel like spitting out all the time. Grit," she said with disgust, then added, "We'll go by the house first. Frank Henry will be wondering what happened to me if I'm late. And I don't like him to worry."

She pulled into the driveway of a small white house on a tree-lined street. The front of the house had a picture window looking out onto a green cement front edged by a low wire fence. "Frank Henry covered the front over with cement. He hates mowing lawns. He made the cement green so it would look like lawn. Don't you think that was a cute idea?"

Udell got out of the car, unloaded her things from the back, and went up on the porch. "Frank Henry," she called out, "I'm here. Come and help me."

There was no answer.

"Don't tell me he's not here yet. Damn—after all that rushing—"

I followed her into the living room. I noticed multicolored afghans everywhere, over the back of the couch and on the backs of the big chairs. I noticed the white frilly curtains pulled back from the picture window by an even frillier sash. Udell, who had gone out into the kitchen, came back and said nervously, "Frank Henry didn't even leave me a note. That's not like him. It's after five. It's almost dinner time. He has a fit if he doesn't have his food right at six. He's like a kid that way." She smiled fondly, then added, "I hope nothing has happened to him. The first thing I always think about is an automobile accident . . ." Her voice tapered off anxiously. "I'll go ahead and start dinner. He'll be here any moment, I'm sure."

"Can I help you?"

"You can keep me company if you want to. I'm just going to make a big pot of spaghetti."

I leaned against the kitchen counter and watched her get out an enormous pot and fill it with water. "How much spaghetti are you going to make?"

"I make up a big pot for the week. That way he doesn't have to cook when I'm gone."

"He must love spaghetti."

"He's not that particular. Frank Henry eats whatever I give him," she said proudly.

When six o'clock came, the spaghetti and the tomato sauce were done but Frank Henry had not yet arrived. "Where the devil is he? He couldn't have stopped off at Charlie's Bar, could he have? Frank Henry doesn't like me to call to see if he's there but I don't care, I'm going to call anyhow.

"No, he's not there," she said, hanging up the receiver. "Wait till I get hold of him, I'll—"

At that moment the door between the kitchen and the living room swung open and Frank Henry came in. He was small and thin and bald. He was carrying a large paper bag.

"Where have you been, Frank Henry?" Udell asked, her hands on her hips.

"I've been fishing. I took the afternoon off."

"You took the afternoon off and you didn't let me know? We've been waiting around for hours, keeping the dinner warm—"

"You don't have to make a federal case of it." He put the paper bag on the counter. "I brought you some nice fish." He started out the kitchen door.

"I don't want any fish. What am I going to do with fish? I've already made spaghetti," Udell yelled, following him into the living room.

Even with the kitchen door closed, I could hear them yelling. I tried not to listen to what was being said. I looked at the spaghetti. It seemed to be agglutinating before my eyes. I looked at the window over the counter. More frilly curtains.

Udell shoved open the swinging door. She sat at the table and started spooning out spaghetti on my plate. "Can you imagine the nerve? He says it's my fault that I wasn't here earlier. What good would it have done if I'd been here earlier?"

"That's enough, thank you," I said. The mound before me was intimidating.

"Let him starve, what do I care?" Udell said. "Are you coming in to eat, Frank Henry?" she yelled.

There was no answer.

"I asked you if you are coming in to eat."

There was a muffled, "No."

"Goddammit, after I've been to all this trouble." She got up and went into the living room and slammed the door behind her. I heard a thud and then some yelling, a murmur, a yell, another murmur, and then some knocking sounds. I wondered if I should just go ahead and eat, but I wasn't hungry. The smell of the fish was overpowering. Should I put it in the refrigerator? Would it go bad sitting there on the counter? How long does fresh fish stay fresh?

Udell came back into the kitchen, her face red, her lipstick smeared.

"He'll be in in a minute," she said primly.

At the end of the meal, eaten in silence except for Udell inquiring at frequent intervals if everything was okay for Frank Henry, he sat back and yawned. "This girl is a real big city girl," Udell said, as if now were the appointed time for conversation. "She's never even seen a lamb before, can you imagine? She wanted to get out and touch one."

"Did she touch one?"

"No, I didn't have time to stop. But I guess I could have stopped. As it turns out," she added darkly.

"I think I'll lie down," Frank Henry said.

"We'll do the dishes, while you're resting."

"Quietly, I hope," Frank Henry said as he went out.

"Frank Henry is a maniac about peace and quiet. If there's the slightest sound, he can't sleep. And once he's up, he's up for the rest of the night. Me, I could sleep through an earthquake."

"Are there earthquakes around here?"

"Sure, all over the state. But you're not going to start worrying about that now, are you? You're really a worrier, aren't you?"

"Well—"

Udell lapsed into silence as she washed the dishes, without soap. "Don't bother drying, air drying is better. It's cleaner."

"Can we go to the hotel now, to make sure I have a room?"

"Stop worrying, I'll get you there. Let's go wake up Frank Henry from his beauty sleep."

In the living room Udell leaned over Frank Henry, who was lying on the couch, covered with an afghan in orange and purple and green and red. "Time to go out on the town," she sang out cheerily.

He opened one eye. "I don't want to go out. I'm tired."

"Can you beat it?" Udell turned to me. "He's tired. From fishing." She leaned over Frank Henry again. "I didn't come home to sit around while you sleep. What am I supposed to do? Listen to the radio? Saturday night is my night for excitement. I spend all week at the camp, busting my ass while I work on the accounts and—"

"You don't have to stay there."

"I stay there because I choose to stay there and I get away from there when I choose to get away from there and I can get away from here when I choose to get away from here. Come on, Frank Henry," she said coyly, "everybody needs a change, everybody needs to get out of the old daily routine—"

"I've had enough excitement to last me for a lifetime," said Frank Henry and closed his eye.

"Okay, Mr.-Filled-Up-With-Excitement, if that's the way you feel—" She yanked open the front door. "Come on, let's go," she summoned me.

"What about the fish?" I asked.

"Let him take care of the goddam fish," she said and slammed out.

Frank Henry pulled the afghan up over his head. He looked like a camouflaged mound. I was going to say something to him, but then I decided not to.

"What's Frank Henry doing now?" Udell asked as I climbed into the front seat.

"He's got the afghan over his head. Does that mean he's depressed or something?"

"Why should he be depressed? He's doing what he wants to do. And we're going to do what we want to do. Right?"

* * *

The Fresno Hotel was six stories high with a blinking electric sign on the roof. A canopy over the entrance repeated the name in movie marquee letters. To the left of the entrance was a door with a sign, COFFEESHOP, and to the right another door with a sign, TAVERN. The desk in the lobby was unattended. Udell banged a little metal bell on the counter. Waiting for someone to come, I read the announcement behind the desk: *The Fresno Hotel is abso-*

lutely fire-proof. George R. Edwards, owner, and Edwin C. White, owner. An elderly clerk with a green nightshade appeared and I registered. "You take your things on up," Udell said. "I'll wait here."

Room 604 was a narrow dark room almost completely filled by a single bed and a large dark wardrobe. The window looked out onto a court. In one of the rooms opposite people—mostly men—were moving back and forth in front of the window. I looked up and saw the sign FRESNO HOTEL blinking on and off and I pulled the shade down.

When I got back down to the lobby, Udell wasn't anywhere in sight. Maybe, I thought, she went to the bathroom. I waited a while but she still didn't appear. I went into the coffee shop. No Udell. I went into the tavern. There she was sitting at the bar, a drink in front of her, deep in conversation with a man to her right.

"Oh, there you are, kid. What took you so long? Sit right here." She patted the stool to her left. "Would you like to meet a Lion? They're having a convention right at the hotel, and this fellow is one of the chief Lions. What'll you have? Whiskey sour? Bring the young lady a whiskey sour," she said to the barman. "Of course, she's over twenty-one, can't you tell? Show him your I.D., kid. How's your room?"

"It's okay. A little small. In fact, it's very small. And it's got this enormous wardrobe in it—" I made a sweeping gesture to the left with my hand and before I could catch it, I had knocked over a drink, not my drink, the drink of the person next to me. The liquid spilled onto the bar and began to leak over the edge.

"Sloppy, sloppy," Udell called out.

I vainly tried to wipe up the liquid with a cocktail napkin.

"Here, bring us a rag," Udell said to the bartender.

"Bring me another Scotch," said the man next to me, as the bartender wiped up the spill.

"I'll be glad to pay for it," I said.

"No need."

Embarrassed by my awkwardness—yes, I was getting sloppier all the time, moving without thinking, doing just what my parents always warned me against—I put my purse down and put both hands around my drink. I heard Udell say to the Lion, "Do you have a hobby?"

In the mirror above the bar I saw the man next to me finish his drink and set it down. He was wearing a suit jacket of a shiny blue material and a khaki (army?) shirt. I stole a glance at him from the side. He was wearing khaki (army?) pants. He had brown hair and a rather sharp nose. I felt I ought to say something but I didn't know what to say. I thought of asking him if he had a hobby but he didn't look like a man who had a hobby.

"I'm sorry about the drink," I said.

"No need to be sorry. It happens all the time, in millions of bars, all over the world." He smiled.

Emboldened, I asked, "Are you a Lion?"

"A what?"

"A Lion. They're having a convention here."

"No, I'm not a Lion."

What are you? I wanted to ask. But how can you ask anybody that? Instead I said, "I don't know anything about Lions, do you?"

"Not much."

"Except that they meet."

"You from around here? You live here?" he asked.

"That Lion is a dope," Udell whispered loudly in my ear. "Come on, let's get out of here."

I picked up my purse and got off the stool. I turned back to the man.

"Goodbye. Sorry about your drink. It was very nice talking to you."

"Do you have to go now? We were just getting acquainted."

"Yes. When you gotta go, you gotta go," Udell said grimly.

* * *

"I've been thinking about Frank Henry," Udell said, as we walked into the lobby. "I've been thinking of him lying there. I feel terrible that I went off and left him."

"Do you want to go home?"

"I don't know what to do. I can't decide. I told him I was going out and I don't like to go back on my word. It's not a good thing if you don't stand up for what you say. Otherwise you end up being a patsy and one thing I don't want to be is a patsy. Still—" she shrugged. "Still, I have such a sweet need of that man. I don't know . . ."

"You could call him."

"That's a good idea. Let's go on up to your room and I'll call him from there, where it's private."

In room 604 Udell sat at the head of the bed and picked up the receiver. Since there wasn't a chair in the room, I sat at the foot of the bed, turned away from her. I tried not to listen.

"I was just thinking, Frank Henry—" Udell said. I tried to concentrate on the outlines of the monstrous wardrobe. It was dark brown, almost black, it looked to be about ten feet tall, looming there. When you looked up at its top, you saw two round humps, decorations with curlicues and spirals. I heard Udell giggle and say, "Of course I do, you know what I mean—"

At that moment there was a knock on the door. Udell motioned to me to answer. "Of course, I want to—"

I went to the door and opened it. Standing there was the man half in and half out of uniform. He was carrying a glass.

"How about having a drink with me?" he asked.

I was so taken aback by the sight of him with the glass in his hand (the reminder of my moving without thinking), that I felt my old terrible awkwardness making havoc with my throat and my tongue. Words spilled out. "Well, actually, I was just about to go to bed—I mean I was just about to retire. I mean, I know it's still early, but my friend and I drove down from the desert after working all day and we—I mean, thank you very much but—"

"Just one drink. What's the harm in that? It'll help you to fall asleep. Besides, tomorrow's Sunday, you can sleep late. Come on," he pleaded. "It will only take a few minutes. I just got my discharge and I—"

I felt something jerk on me and pull me back into the room. It was Udell, who in the same motion shut the door in the man's face. "What's the matter with you, girl? You just say no and shut the goddam door. Don't you know how to say no? You didn't ask him up, did you?"

"Of course not. I don't even know how he got my room number."

"He slipped the clerk two bucks, that's how. Boy, you sure are some innocent. Is it safe to leave you alone?" She picked up her purse. "Frank Henry and me had a good talk. He actually asked me to come home, he even said he was missing me. I should have been more understanding. After all, he had enough excitement during the war, no wonder he—"

"Was Frank Henry in the service?"

"Sure, he was. What do you think he was, a draft dodger?"

"Not everybody who wasn't in the service was a draft dodger. There were people in essential positions, essential to the war effort—"

"Yeah, I know. 4 F. "

"Not just—"

"Well, kid," Udell said briskly. "I am on my way. You look as if you could use a rest anyhow. Maybe the big city's too much for you." She grinned and went to the door. Her hand on the knob, she turned. "There's something I feel I ought to say to you. I've noticed something about you. You know what you do? You let people ride all over you."

"No I don't."

"Then why didn't you shut the door in that guy's face?"

"It seemed—"

"What?"

"It seemed impolite."

"Impolite?" Udell scoffed. "What was he being, coming up

when he wasn't asked, not going away when you said no? That's politeness?"

"That wasn't exactly what I meant."

"It's exactly Number One that you ought to be paying attention to, otherwise guys like that will wipe up the floor with you." She opened the door and looked out. "The creep's gone, thank goodness. You know what the trouble with you is. You're all over the place. One moment you're going this way, the next moment you're going that way, the next thing you can't move at all. You can't make up your mind about anything, that's the trouble. Oh, you've got a good brain, I've no doubt about that. But you don't use it. Now me, I don't have that good a brain—oh no, that's the truth, I don't pretend to be what I'm not—but I make up for it by using what I have. Like the turtle, I get where I'm going, even though I get there slowly. I look at what's ahead of me in the road. I don't waste my energy wondering about the big picture. Let the world take care of itself. You can't do anything about the world anyway. So keep your eye on your goal. It's the same way with men. If it's somebody that I'm not interested in, I don't give them the time of day. But if it's somebody I like—I mean, they couldn't get rid of me if they tried. You've got to decide what you want, kid. That's what life is really about—deciding. There's always somebody doing the choosing. I figure it'd better be me than someone else."

"But—"

But Udell was already out the door.

* * *

Downstairs, in the tavern, the bar was crowded almost to bursting with Lions. I made my way to a small round table in the corner. Sitting there alone, I thought of the camp. I hadn't really been ready to leave it. Why had I been so stupid, hasty, judging? So Shorty had asked me to go with him on a moonlight ride. Was that so terrible? I could have just said No—or maybe even gone.

"Well. So you're here, after all." It was the man half in and half out of uniform. He raised his glass to me. "Welcome." He pointed to the chair opposite me. "Do you mind?

"Where's the Dragon Lady?" he asked, as he sat down.

"She left. She went home."

"She your sister or something?"

"No. She's a friend. We work in the same place."

"What's that?"

"In the valley. In an oil field."

"Not many women there, I'll bet," he said admiringly.

"A few."

"What do you do there?"

"I measure things . . . and plot them."

"Oh," he said.

A waitress appeared. "Scotch on the rocks," he said. "And you?"

"The same," I said, though I had never liked Scotch before. But I was going to get what I hadn't gotten. I was going to ask what I wanted to, needed to ask. But not yet. I couldn't ask him here. All around us the Lions were laughing and drinking. I was drinking my Scotch. Would I learn to like it?

He was talking about a trip he was planning to take to the mountains. He was going to go fishing and hunting, things I didn't know anything about. In fact, I always hated the thought of killing an animal for no reason. Looking at him intently, I saw that his eyes were blue and that they were delicately fringed with long lashes.

"I don't know your name. What's your name?"

I gave him my name. I thought, what will happen next? Will I ask him up to my room? No, not to that room. We could go out. We could go to his place.

He was looking down at his drink now. He was smiling. When he finished his drink, he said, "Let's go."

When we walked out together, I looked surreptitiously to the side. For some reason I thought, Perhaps he is limping. But he was not limping. We got into his car. It was a Studebaker, an old

Studebaker, the upholstery all torn, two side windows covered over with cloth where there was no glass. We drove through the quiet streets, with houses with lights on in them. He too was a silent driver. He pulled me over to him, closer. I felt his knee against my knee. I felt the thickness, the lubricity of desire multiplying.

We came to a dark place where there were no houses. He pulled off onto a side road. He came to a stop in a place that looked like a field. He turned the headlights off. He sat there, not saying anything, not moving, just sitting there, though now his hand was on my knee. Maybe right then I was thinking of that guy on the bus, the one who had touched my leg, without my choosing. Yes, it was all about choosing, as Udell had said.

"Let's just sit here and talk for a minute." I heard the hesitancy in his voice. After all, he was shy. That made me feel surer. I had noticed this often about myself before. If the other person was very sure, I was unsure. But if they were unsure, I somehow grew bolder.

"Where were you in the War?" I asked.

He was silent for a moment. I prepared myself to listen. I thought about what I'd read and what I'd seen in the movies, about men having to walk for days in mud in the jungle, about how they had to keep looking and looking for anything that moved around them or overhead, how they had to throw themselves into ditches to save themselves, how some were caught and some escaped and some were left behind . . .

"I was on Attu—in the Aleutians."

He stopped. "A cold place," I said.

"A very cold place. Twenty, thirty, forty degrees below zero most of the time. In summer it warms up. Then it's almost up to freezing. Some summer," he laughed nervously.

I waited. "But inside it wasn't like that, was it?"

"No. Inside, in the huts it was warm enough. But there was nothing going on. There was nothing to do. We just waited and waited. It drove me nuts. I applied for a transfer to the Infantry. I didn't care, anything to be out of there. But it didn't come and it didn't come and then finally when it did come and I was shipped to Fort Benning, the War was over.

"I don't usually talk about it," he added.

"But I asked you."

"Yes, you asked."

Yes, I had asked him, but what he had said was not what I had wanted to know. I had wanted to hear about the fighting, about what it meant to risk death and injury, to be on that edge, to believe that at any minute you could die. I had wanted to know what it meant to have to kill someone, to be ordered to kill someone. But he hadn't told me that. He didn't know that.

"All that snow and ice got to me. It got to my eyes, inside my eyes. Everything looked and felt white. It scared me. I thought it was never going to change, that I was always going to be in that white, my whole life. I still think about it sometimes. Then I'm inside that white all over again."

The way he said it, the edge of panic in his voice—it was the kind of talk that makes you wobble, that makes you feel there's nothing firm anywhere, that makes you distrust the one talking, that makes you fearful about your own judgment, that makes you feel you have to say something to save the situation, him, yourself, even if that saying comes out of your own hide, or wherever it's been hidden.

"Once at the camp, the first night I was there—" I told him about looking out into the empty dark and thinking of cold, uninhabited places. I told him how then I'd gone in to play pool with the men, and how then everything was okay.

"Where you from?" he asked.

"Philadelphia."

"Born there?"

"Yes."

"Any sisters?"

"One."

"Any brothers?"

"No."

"Do you—do you believe in God?"

"That's a very personal question. It's not the kind of question you can ask someone and expect them to be able to answer just like that."

"Sorry," he mumbled. He took his hand from my knee.

"Where are we?" I asked desperately.

"We're in a field. If it was light you could see that there's a lake in front of us. Not a lake exactly. It used to be a lake when I was a kid but now it's mostly dried up and it's more like a pond."

There I was, in a ridiculous car with shreds hanging, looking out over a pond that I couldn't even see, with a man half in and half out of uniform. Something fluid began to rise in me. Was it rage? It came up and up, starting down in me where I never even knew down was, forcing out the embedded, driving up the viscous, till I was flung—No—I threw myself down, precisely, into grief.

Ronald Sukenick

ECCO

What a privilege it is to wake up in the morning in Venice and know you can do anything you want. (I see the egg boat is passing.) And have enough money to do it. And to be neither tourist (they throng on the bridges and embankments below in legions, following their various tour generals holding aloft banners of scarf, ribbon, chapeaux on umbrella or cane, and—starting toward evening on the canal in the gleaming gondolas, black as death—accompanied by some old third rater singing his tonsils out to the lit candle or the single rose in the holder in the bow) and certainly not Venetian, sitting in your apartment overlooking canal, quai-like fondamenta, bridges, tourists and Venetians, your life an absence from your life and from that of Venetians and tourists, invisible, a nobody afloat like the gondolas drifting by with no idea of what will happen next.

Your invisibility, in fact, is simply an extension of your normal situation—the consequence of obscure critical esteem for your literary work, buried by myopic media hype for your more journalistic, if profitable, output as writer—an invisibility recently more painful as a result of deaths, divorce and geographical circumstance, by the removal, in short, of all those who had been closest. It is a condition to which Venice, however mistakenly, is meant to help you reconcile or, at least, to ballast the kind of rapidly progressive instability that isolation can breed.

(The vegetable boat scuds around the corner full speed, the man on the high bow doing some drastic ducking so his head doesn't get knocked off by the bridge. The grocery boat pulls up to the store downstairs, its pilot has a long discussion with the storekeeper about accounts, pulls out, a garbage boat goes by, loaded high with trash. A cat licks itself in the sun across the canal, beyond the blue, the red, the teak boats tied up to plain wooden poles at the fondamenta beneath the tall windows with the flowers on the balconies on the walls faded maroon, green, ochre, plaster scaling off to exposed salmon hued brick that I look at over my own flowers in my own tall windows.)

A city so full of thereness your presence isn't necessary, allowing you to vacate, hopefully reach for a tonic vacancy.

(Somebody's houseful of furniture floats by on a moving-van boat. A teak water taxi churns through, cabin lined with white sofas.)

You go down to pick up your shoes from the blind shoemaker, around the corner down the fondamenta across the wooden bridge to the right, where they were supposed to be ready yesterday and weren't. Today the little man in the store looks alarmed. After lunch, he says. No, you need them now. You'll come back in fifteen minutes. No, a half an hour. Okay, a half an hour. A sweet little old man, yesterday he gave you a shine, refused money.

You come back in half an hour, he's working away at them. Okay, you'll go get a haircut you've been meaning to. You come back after haircut he's just starting second shoe. You go get bread come back he's got the heel on and fixing sole. You stand in doorway watching people come down the narrow street. A tourist asks for directions in broken Italian, you give them in broken Italian. Now he's back on first shoe perfecting his work. His meticulousness is becoming fascinating. Your impatience gives way to absorption in his unbelievable perfectionism with awl, glue and nail. As he works he talks. He grew up in Toronto, taken there by his anti-fascist father. Mussolini niente! Still working away from within a different sense of time, out of another world. When he's finally done he gives a big smile. He's very pleased with himself, showing you the shoes.

(Here comes the gelati boat squeezing around the corner of the bridge. I live at the top of a T-shaped canal intersection and each arm of the T has a bridge making tricky turning for the local shipping sometimes, with a lot of backing and maneuvering for the biggest boats, though the best of them scud around the blind corner full speed with the help of a mirror on one of the bridges and some loud honking.)

There seems to be an otherworldly concern here for the spirit. It is a practical town, but the unworldly, not the pragmatic seems fundamental, and the pragmatic in any case is founded on the visible ongoing decay of this world, the mouldering canals, the crumbling masonry. If something is a headache there's always a remedy. If you feel bad, stop for a gelati. Or, more to the point, there's the example of the man who ran into the hotel and asked the desk clerk, "Where's the nearest church?" The Pope was just here with much hullaballoo, and among other things visited a woman's prison on Giudecca across the Lagoon. "Don't get demoralized," he told the inmates. Don't underestimate this advice.

One day you wander into the Hotel Falier around the corner and down the fondamenta, you don't know why exactly, a sudden impulse of curiosity about that class of hotel—third, probably—in this kind of slightly decaying lower middle class neighborhood, or maybe the vaguest mental tide, like the tidal current that seems to run through the canals slowly flushing out all the trash tossed into them. This is the floating world, not in the Japanese sense of a world of pleasure though that too in a more subtle way, but as world adrift from the mainstream, eddying, insular, isolate, labyrinthine, intestinal, encoiled, amnesiac, amniotic, curled into itself like a foetus or a brain. (Why else does my friend John Tytell, who did his doctoral thesis on Henry James, end up by coincidence in James' old hotel room when he comes to the city, a city that generates resonances like an echo chamber?)

(A large launch now seems to be stuck in the T—can't fit under the bridge after ten minutes of maneuvering finally goes off down the canal, then three minutes later reappears backing up—must be cut off in that direction too. Maybe it's high tide? Finally moves off under the left hand bridge.)

* * *

In the Hotel Falier a young man is talking to the desk clerk in pidgin Italian. A very thin young man with very black hair and water green eyes reminiscent of a certain Titian, an anonymous portrait of a young man called simply "The Man With the Green Eyes." He's trying to explain to the clerk that he wants to give up his room in the Hotel Falier because there's now a place for him in the youth hostel on Giudecca. There's a very nice youth hostel on Giudecca with a great view of the Lagoon, very cheap but always full. It seems the young man—he's a kid really, you see, on a closer look—has pre-paid his room in the Hotel Falier and now is having trouble getting his money back. You notice all this in about five seconds and finding the situation oddly painful you immediately walk back out to the fondamenta, remembering suddenly your own first visit to Venice almost thirty years ago, arriving as a kid in a vaporetto from the train station to the same hostel on Giudecca with a painful injured eye and no money to have it cared for but so superexcited you weren't worried about it, sensing with a certain amount of accuracy the invulnerability of youth, when without preamble a large, muscular, golden haired, handsome young man, somewhat older than yourself, with a strange accent, on his way to the same hostel, begins to inquire about your plight and on hearing it, offers you the loan of a for you large sum of money so you can go to the clinic. He claims to be from New Zealand, and gives you an address where you can send the money after you get back to the States, no matter when, an address that seems totally inadequate for international transactions but, he assures you, there aren't many people in New Zealand.

And then curiously you never see him again, even at the hostel, and though you later send him the money never hear from him. You don't even see him get off the boat. As if he'd evaporated into the mist-bright air as abruptly as he'd appeared.

You go to the clinic and the doctor probes your eye, finally removing an embedded cinder from the locomotive pulling the train from Paris. *Ecco!* he says, and you experience an immediate sensation of relief. That is how you learn the meaning of the word *ecco.*

(A dead kitten floats by, its four little legs stiff and reaching straight up to heaven.)

You consider the amusing possibility now that the opportune appearance of the supposed New Zealander represented an intervention by the gods, the kind of gods we don't have anymore, especially not in the secular States, who used to go among men, and women too, and talk with them, and help them out or punish them, and love them. This used to be their territory. Maybe now they live in New Zealand. *Ecco!*

The next day you go to the Ghetto, speaking of old gods, the Jewish Ghetto having the distinction of being the first in the world, established in the sixteenth century, giving its name—from the word for the foundries that were originally there—giving its name to all subsequent versions.

(A boat jam at the bridges, four boats almost crashing into one another, but none of the pilots seem worried, yelling, honking, pulling at their throttles, long single oars, and rudders.)

The Ghetto is way over to one side of the railroad station where off a lesser canal an alley-like viale begins. You turn to the right into it and you notice on the left hand wall a marble plaque above the doorway of number 48, not as you first think an apologetic memorial to the miseries of the Ghetto, but an edict establishing the Ghetto itself, fierce with warnings about Jews being prohibited from leaving, threats of prosecution and provision for informers contacting the authorities about violations. Then you penetrate the Old Ghetto square, surrounded by shabby buildings very tall in terms of Venetian architecture, very plain, with none of the lacy decoration of the Venetian style, the Ghetto still another world, and not in good repair, a picture so oppressive you can't get yourself to take a photo as planned. The tall buildings, no doubt to increase population capacity of compressed space, look like the predecessor of New York's old Lower East Side at its worst. Then past a bakery featuring matzos Italian style—"our bread contains only flour, water and olive oil"—baked in a beautiful latticed, lacy open-work shape, into the New Ghetto, more spacious, houses in better condition, a series of monumental plaques to the Holocaust, and still oppressive, claustrophobic.

You go into a little synagogue-museum in the Ghetto Nuovo, against your better judgement because now all you want to do is get out, and discover that while the museum isn't much, the interior of the actual synagogue is an architectural gem, a baroque oval surrounded by a railed balcony no doubt for women worshippers. And there you discover, engaged in conversation, the dark, green-eyed boy from the Hotel Falier, and seeing him, feel a sudden tug of attraction, an inexplicable, spontaneous, almost embarrassing pang of feeling, like an evocative but isolated musical note implying a phrase, a composition whose sense hangs in the air.

* * *

The boy is listening to a middle-aged man telling him, in broken phrases and bad grammar, with an Ancient Mariner urgency, how he came to be here, in this synagogue, through a twist of absurdity, an absurdity emphasized, you note, by what looks like a folded dish towel or large handkerchief perched on the man's head as an improvised yarmulke.

He had been brought up completely secular in South Africa,

the older man is saying, gone there as an infant with his mother, an old atheistic Italian Socialist, when she had remarried. One day, after he had grown up and his mother long since died, he received notice from Italy that the cemetery in which his family was buried had been hit by an earthquake and the graves had to be moved. On coming to Italy to see about the situation, he was told by the authorities that the graves had to be moved to the Jewish cemetery. The Jewish cemetery! Why? Why! because they're Jewish, of course! He was astonished, but on reflection realized he had always suspected something.

The man pauses. "And you?" he asks the boy.

"Yes," he answers. "But not a believer."

Nor are you. Short of an earthquake. You again feel an urgent desire to get out, get out of the synagogue, get out of the Ghetto itself. You leave the synagogue, take one of the bridges out of the isolation of the Campo da Ghetto Nuovo and head for the vivacity and color of the Rialto and the world as quickly as possible. You walk for about five minutes, you turn a corner and with a shock realize you are once again in the Campo da Ghetto Nuovo. Dumbfounded! You have no memory of heading back here, you would have had to return on some of the same streets, the same bridges on which you came. You were walking directly out of the Ghetto and then suddenly you are back in it. How was it possible? It is not that you have lost your way, it's that a certain period of duration has disappeared, unaccounted for, during which you were transported back here in a wink of time, and you are not so much back where you started as back when you started and it occurs to you that the real meaning of labyrinth is time warp. Conversely, ghosts are not creatures that have returned after their time, but those that have lost their way. So this mystery is your little, ambiguous miracle of the day, as if some magic rabbi had waved his hand and conjured an angel to fly you back, its wing veiling your consciousness to make you aware of something consciousness itself renders invisible. What?

(The train is about to pull out of Venice/Santa Lucia. The train is pulling out. Goodbye.)

(I glide across Italy eating cherries, the Euganean Hills, I think, off to the right.)

The next day it's raining, the drops pocking the canals, Venetians go about their business in bright over-all slickers and high rubber boots, boatmen bail rain water from boat bottoms, so you go to the Scuola San Rocco, which is near where you live. The Scuola San Rocco is where you go if you want to see Tintorettos. They're on the walls and on the ceilings, especially one immense crucifixion covering a whole wall to the ceiling. Crucifixions give you the creeps, barbarous and masochistic, spiritually tacky. And yet an effective way to evoke empathy for suffering, the Holocaust for example, too big, it cannot be imagined, the crucifixion provides a human focus. As you approach the huge painting you notice a slim silhouette of a male figure, almost swallowed by the vast canvas, shoulders up, head and neck thrust forward, mouth sagging open, eyes slightly popped and staring intensely at the painting in total empathy as if he sought to absorb it completely, an impression so striking you actually check back to the painting to make sure it's still on the canvas. This striking figure is, of course, the green-eyed kid again.

By this time you're not surprised to encounter him, you've begun to accept these intersections, it's as though you're programmed for the same itinerary, it's not that unusual when you're touring, there are just so many sights to see, so many tour books. But you've become intensely curious about the boy and, you have to admit, more than curious, definitely attracted, and you would like to strike up a conversation, find out what he's about, except that the strength of his scrutiny, his attention to the painting in front of him, definitely forbids it. For you, once so avid an explorer of the cultural heritage, coming back here yet again is more like an exploration of your own past, what you had originally sought in the classics evidently already found or, perhaps, not there, not ever there.

Now, as you turn at a right angle to gaze, a little absently, at the beautiful, small "Christ Carrying the Cross" kept behind glass on an easel, the one attributed indecisively to Titian or Giorgione, you've always thought Titian, you sense to your right the boy turning also to look at the same painting, turning quite simultaneously along with you, and you decide this time, after a minute's hesitation, to breach his privacy.

"You know," you say, "in the sixteenth century it was thought to have miraculous powers."

The boy, the young man, his age is actually not clear to you, or rather he seems to look different ages at different times as if he's not quite in focus, turns his head toward you with a slight, ambiguous smile, not totally unlike a sacred subject by the great Venetian, Giovanni Bellini, gazing into another spiritual dimension, and seems to stare past you actually, without the slightest acknowledgement of your remark. And then you realize, and it's a little scary, that he's looking through not past you, that he literally doesn't take in that you are there, and this with such an absolute quality, that for a second you have to wonder yourself. You look back to the Titian/Giorgione, the shrewd, secular face of the man focusing on the god whose gaze scans eternity.

(Now floating over blue, cloud-plumed, wave-dimpled, white-specked Atlantic, in the opposite direction to the turning earth, which I see, from the stillness of the sky on the top side of the ornamental, lavish clouds, just as Tiepolo might have envisioned them, from heaven.)

Is he, by force of youth and innocence, staring into another spiritual dimension, one in which you no longer exist, lacking the purity and disinterestedness of the shoemaker, unconcerned with production obsessed with essentials like good work, like truth. Essentials are of the other world, maybe a better one, but you can't walk around without shoes these days on the fondamenta. There's much to be said for the crumbling perfection of Venice but Italy is moving quickly into high tech. It's true the ghetto blasters are beginning to move in along with it, even into Venice, but then who needs the ghetto?

* * *

You move down to the first floor of the Scuola, leaving the kid at peace in dream time, and go take a look at the various religious articles exhibited, among them a reliquary from within which a dead saint's shrivelled finger beckons.

When you leave the Scuola the rain's stopped and the sun breaks loose, causing all the birds threading the air to join with the city's innumerable caged canaries which, like the gondoliers, are always singing.

(Now in the new world, from a high condo, I gaze at the heavy shipping of New York Harbor as it slides through the Narrows under Verranzano Bridge. Toward the tip of Manhattan along the East River, one massive building goes up as, almost next to it, another comes down. Back in the stream of history now, I lose myself staring at the brutal skyline, and with a shock realize I am once again in Venice, its stone embroidery and domes. I'm looking at the flashing tableau of harbor and skyscraper, and at the same time I'm eddying in a lagoon of internal exile, apart from all that, in another world I thought I'd left behind. Why? Along the river I can see the Lower East Side, once the Jewish ghetto of New York and, beyond, Ellis Island, where my ancestors emerged into modern time, now a museum.)

In the Piazza San Rocco, across from the Scuola, six or ten cats lounge near a fence, one of the packs of street cats fed here and there through the city, outside restaurants, churches, sometimes even by citizens lowering food in baskets from upper story windows, to keep the rats at bay, you suppose. They look at you out of their timeless world and remind you that Venice is a city of a thousand years that has, like an eddy in a river, evolved its own rhythm of time, in-turned, reflexive, self-referential, a reflecting pool in which a traveller may reflect.

It isn't for some days that you catch your next image of the boy, though you had expected it sooner than the evening when from some unexpected back street pool of silence where you stopped to reflect on the chat of acqua with fondamenta, a twist in the viale brings you suddenly into the uproar of Piazza San Marco, harmonized by the whining violins and old tangos of the small orchestras playing on the terrazzi of the cafes. There, in one of the cafes, Florian, the most famous one, you spot the object of what you may by now call your fascination, at a table eating gelati with a wide-eyed brunette young woman whose half smile and constant glancing about the Piazza imply a frank reach of wonder. She's arrived in Venice only recently for the first time, you speculate, still overwhelmed with the first impact of the city. Her long, full, brown hair, thigh length skirt according to the once again new style for kids, and a generally unbound look under loose cloth, that, or maybe some openness to experience that she projects like an invitation, creates for the observer an immediate aura around her. This is just the right place for her, just the right moment at just the right age for a flowering presumably offered to her companion that gives you a shot of envy, even jealousy, though for exactly what it's hard to say. You want to be in his shoes but then again, you don't want her, however attractive, between him and your growing, maybe even unhealthy you have to admit, obsession with him. But she, like the fresh breeze now blowing off the Lagoon, it being unusually cool here for the start of the tourist season, serves to distract you from the somewhat fevered solipsism of your concern for an unknown boy who is really little more than an artifact of your imagination.

Her quivering sexuality even as she moves in her seat, inspires you to take a table in good view of her, and even in hearing of their amazed conversation about the scene around them, from which several things become apparent. First that they are lovers, or are about to become lovers or, most likely have just become lovers, almost purring at one another, on a honeymoon perhaps, and that part of their wonder, and especially hers, over the city is an extension of their own sensuality which Venice, certainly, helps to arouse.

"This is the sexiest place I've ever been," she remarks. "It's like all the buildings are wearing lace nightgowns."

"When are you going to call the guy in Rome?" he asks.

"I called him. I forgot to tell you."

"What did he want?"

"He said he liked the pieces and wants to do a show if I can get some more done in the next few months."

"Can you?"

"Sure. But I don't want to."

"Why not?"

"Because I don't feel like doing them any more. I don't feel like working. Not now. For the time being. I used it up. I'd just be repeating myself. There's nothing there."

"I see. Too bad. It would be a real coup. We'd be able to stay."

"Besides, I think he may want something else."

"What?"

"You know."

"Would you consider giving it to him?"

"Are you kidding?"

He leans over and gives her a kiss.

"On the other hand," he says, "the time seems right to stay in Europe."

"Well we can't."

The crazy thought immediately comes to you of offering them a room in your apartment. There's plenty of space, even a quasi-independent section in the back. But just then, their lire already on the table, they get up and slip into the stream of pedestrians in the crowded Piazza, and are quickly lost to your view.

(In the 747 heading west through a cloudless sky, the airplane seems still while the earth flows beneath. And from the point of view of relativity, it strikes me, this impression is not so absurd, since we know the truth of motion is not earthbound. As in ancient days, essentials, if not exactly lodged in another world, are hardly in the exclusive province of this one. So that in some elusive but palpable way, to be suspended at thirty thousand feet is to be partly in this world and partly in another realm, less clearly understood.)

But you are soon to have another opportunity. The next day, as you thread your way through the narrow alleys leading to the Rialto, you stop to look into a shop window showing an impressive array of genuine badger shaving brushes, when the unmistakable accents, female, of an American trying to speak Italian, strike from close range over your shoulder, and it's almost certainly the young woman from Florian's last night.

"Scusi, signor. Dov'e Ca D'oro?"

"Do you speak English?"

"Yes."

"American?"

"Yes."

"I happen to be heading in that direction. Why don't you come with me?"

Certainly it's the same young woman, though it's true that couples under a certain age are starting to look the same to you, young people in general starting to resolve into types rather than individuals, a situation that has resulted in more than one embarrassing confusion. As you head off with her by your side toward the Grand Canal, you can't help thinking that it's a perfect pick-up situation although you know, of course, that she's not on the market for being picked up in that sense. Still, she's just as appealing at close range as she was at the table last night, just as sexy, yet different, now it seems she's no mouth-gaping tourist, the somewhat gawking quality you noticed last night deriving rather, it soon becomes evident, from a fine sensibility and a quick sense of wonder.

(Now, looking up at the Front Range of the Rockies rising almost out of the back yard, false image of permanence, geology no less than history a kind of fluid. The old cat, gradually dying, grave already dug against coming frost, stares calmly at a changing world that, despite differences, has always been, is always going to be, the same in his unique, changeless gaze. Indifferent to the blackboard of history, he lives in our world but is not of it, a guest from where?)

"Are you staying at the Hotel Falier?" you ask.

"You mean as opposed to the Hotel Success? Is there such a place?"

"I thought I saw you there. With a young man?"

"Oh, is that how you pronounce it. I started there. I guess that was an inauspicious place to start."

"I don't know. The United Nations started at a place called Lake Success. You're a tourist?"

"I wouldn't think of it. I'm a collagist."

"In what sense?"

"I like to put things together—words, images, pictures. Kurt Schwitters is my ideal. You know Schwitters?"

"Of course. And your companion?"

"At the hotel? He's a writer."

"Published?"

"Not yet."

"This is your first time in Venice?"

"For me yes. For him no. But the first time he was here he was having some sort of eye trouble and couldn't see as much as he wanted."

"Isn't that always the case?"

"Maybe. But that's not because of eye trouble."

"True. They say that people believe what they see. But in fact most people see only what they believe. The second time I came here was with my ex-wife, but though I could see, I still couldn't see."

* * *

She doesn't respond to this, probably losing interest in view of the flood of new and beautiful things to see. You, however, are starting to feel the pull of a magnetism as powerful as it is apparently baseless, since its source is a girl about whom you know nothing and yet with whom you feel an immediate coincidence of rhythm, an empathy, an intimacy almost, so that it would seem the most natural thing in the world to ask her up to your apartment, to sit with her on the chaise, to put your arm around her as you talk together effortlessly and luminously. And moreover you intuit, though surely she has no intention of acting on it, that she is feeling the same thing. So that by the time you climb the steps up to the summit of the Rialto bridge, the various vaporetti and motor barges and long oared vessels weaving wakes below on the Grand Canal, and you stop to point out the Ca D'oro to her, you haven't the slightest idea of what you might say, and she, with a look in her large soft brown eyes of both expectancy and prohibition, no idea, certainly, of what she might hear.

You turn to point up the Canal to her goal, explaining the route, and when you turn again to her the space she occupied just a few seconds ago is vacant, and in fact she is nowhere in view. You quickly look around the other side of the line of shops, down both sides of the bridge, behind the shops on the other side and she is nowhere. Disappeared in a wink of time. You saw it but you don't believe it. More mystified than insulted, you wander down the other side of the bridge, invaded by a wholly disproportionate sense of loss, of roads not taken, and of roads taken that wind back on themselves, that lead nowhere, that lead through marvelous landscapes yet themselves are lost, so the sense of loss includes a feeling of escape. Stumbling among the shoppers and vendors on the other side of the bridge, you wonder what it is of which you feel the loss, and you think it is that, from her wonder over the spectacle of the city she is, as you once were, a believer, not a believer in anything particular but one credulous about belief itself, a faculty hard to come by, but without which, as now, there is little but empty air inhabiting your dreams.

But having come to Venice for vacation, for the pleasure of vacancy, and not for work or thought, you are content to let the whole episode drift by without further analysis. Besides, you have the intimation that though there is something doing here, for you, other than the mere pleasure of doing, it will emerge only if you let your normal analytic habits of mind become undone, giving yourself up to the apparently aimless drift and eddy of incident, the course of event which, faithful to nothing, comprises nonetheless a kind of language if you know how to read it.

(In the mail today a royalty statement for a book I worked on three years—after charges for copies purchased by author: $3.03. On the other hand I remember the spontaneous reaction of an old friend when I tell him the tidy sum I made on one of my books: "Gee, are you smart!" Money is not the point. But neither is smart. Maybe our confusion is the point.)

What follows then is unpredictable, once you decide to give in to the natural flow of things. An overwhelming tide of hopelessness catches you and sweeps you along, pulling you helplessly like drifting garbage without destination, a surge of despair denoting the final uselessness of all effort—why keep going, why not die? It's like being hit by a vacuum that leaves you breathless and staggering. You stagger to a table in a cafe and sit down abruptly. The waiter comes, you order a cafe macchiatto. When you begin to look around you see that the cafe is quite singular, in that it is populated largely by old people. Old, but animated, vivacious, talking and gesturing and calling from one table to another and bantering with the waiter. The vigor, the good humor of the old people some of them obviously quite handicapped, illumines your melancholy, relativizes your dark humor. One ancient gent in particular sporting a beret, lively but with a thoughtful eye, you see wishfully as yourself in the labyrinth of time.

* * *

Whether it's the tonic effect of the jocular septuagenarians or simply the rhythm of your own psyche, you recall yourself at a happier time in this city, sitting at a cafe table with your young wife. In particular you remember sitting at a table bordering the

Lagoon, at night. It's a celebration of sorts, you've just sold your first story and you feel rather smart. Success, whatever that means to you, is almost palpable, in view of which you seem to yourself quite worldly-wise. At a certain point in the evening you literally see yourself as a successful author twenty years in the future. Whether you project this apparition onto another client sitting in a dark corner of the cafe or whether it's a materialization of intuition hardly matters. Whatever the case, in your innocence this vision of yourself gives you a shock, because it is not what you thought it would be, success. It looks more like obscurity, like failure, something you are willing to accept but reluctant to understand. Now, remembering that apparition, you recognize yourself. In remembering who you were going to be, you begin to remember who you are.

Energized by the recollection that once upon a time you had a vision of yourself, and that, however ambiguous, it is still you, you decide that a little sun and exercise will do wonders, and when you leave the cafe you've already plotted an afternoon on the beach of the Lido.

That afternoon, having taken a beach cabana at the Hotel Excelsior, you're walking down the strand past the domes and minarets of that pseudo-Arabian monument, along the endless line of cabanas with their colorful striped poles, when you spot the young man who has become the subject of your Venetian meander, in a swim suit walking toward you down the beach. This time you resolve instantly to engage him, hoping to illuminate, through conversation, the source and reason for your fascination. As he approaches you note his dreaming gaze out to sea, thinking if he is a writer it is indeed the look of one better able to deal with a landscape of imagination rather than of reality. Before he reaches you he stops on the beach, looks down, smiles and speaks, presumably to his young wife, his body turned in profile. Thin, thin, it's hard to believe he's so thin. It's a leanness you immediately associate with spiritual purity which, if anything, increases your desire to interrogate him. But as you approach his now stationary figure, he looks up at the sky and, since in following his gaze you spot nothing, you look down and realize that he's suddenly grown taller and then looking down at his feet you see that's not it at all, it's that there is an undeniable and growing space under the soles of his feet relative to the sand. Stunned, you continue toward him, knowing this couldn't be happening but too dazed to pause and take stock, and the closer you come to him the higher he rises, like a kite or a balloon, already his knees are at the level of your head, and as he ascends his arms stretch out to the sides, his ankles cross, his head rolls against his shoulder, his eyes look up from under his lids, levitating more quickly, soaring, then evaporates against the blue-white sky, gone. For some reason equally confused and embarrassed, you look around to see if anyone else has witnessed this prodigy, and seeing nothing but cabana life as usual, look down to seek the young man's wife on the beach, and discover that, yes, she is there, but only in effigy, her seeming likeness spread comfortably on the beach, but sculpted from, or turned to, sand.

You hardly know what to think about this episode if, that is, stunned as you are, you are capable of thinking anything at all, but the first thing that occurs to you, however absurdly, is that, since such a singularity could only be a caprice of visual imagination, the young man has been looking at too many Tintorettos. Then, of course, it occurs to you that maybe you've been looking at too many assumptions, resurrections, ascensions, annunciations, transfigurations, and other magical subjects. And then the true reading of these events comes to you, which is that whatever their presumable source they signify expanding contact with the other world so aptly signified by Venice, and that this rapidly growing contact might be as much cause for alarm as for—how would you put it?—anticipation. And if you are, as you begin to suspect, on the brink of insight, it is one that brings you also, perhaps, to the brink of sanity.

Next day, hoping to understand the effect on you of the city and its culture, and so get your feet back on the ground, you go once more to the Accademia, which contains the essence of Venetian painting, if any single place can be said to do so. There, in a room dominated by Giovanni Bellini, standing in front of "The Tempest," one of the few certain works by Giorgione, your contemplation is invaded by a tour group, whose guide, lecturing in poor English, is giving a florid and undoubtedly cribbed interpretation of the achievement of the Venetian School.

"The Venetian of early Cinquecento founded harmony between the form and the color, and so in various vibration of light the fervid intensity of life, reasons, and principle which is why her painting was flourished amidst our lagoons will shine eternal. The one whose intimate contemplative desire founded the inspiration in every living thing in color, in man and her plants as if the other world is all we have and it is this one. The first to see. This the first essentially modern painter rose to being universal art. *Ecco,* Giorgione!"

The tour moves on, leaving you with this new information to contemplate by way of getting your feet on the ground. The other world is all we have and it is this one. Maybe he was talking about Venice itself, which exists largely in the other world, apart from the eroding undertow of history. History defeats itself. You look back at the Giorgione canvas, beautiful but cryptic in its imagery which your guide book refers to as a "fine nude woman" and "a young man calm and serene" against crumbling towers and stormy sky, all of which conveys "a lofty expression of universal beauty." *Ecco,* Giorgione!

(Paying bills at my desk I remember how years ago as a kid I unquestioningly avoided all sure avenues to solvency as detours from the nerve patterned pathways of the unpredictable, which is predictably the unpredictable territory where I now as a writer reside. Lately I think I know why. I can't live without miracles that intensify the landscape, like lightning in a Giorgione sky. I never know when they're going to happen. They come effortlessly, annunciations, and if I'm not attentive the carrier pigeon is gone before I know it's there. The message is adrift in the bottle. Where are you in the riptide of history?)

The next encounter, and by now your Venetian odyssey has clearly taken its measure from these encounters, is at night in a spectacular canal-side cafe extending out from one of the luxe hotels, with the shiny black coffin-like gondolas sliding by on the glinting wavelets reflecting artificial light beyond the flowered border of the balustrade edging the terrazzo. Way off to the left on the Lagoon an illuminated cruise ship at its mooring, lights strung along its masts and cordage, marks the perpetual holiday in which the city lives, set apart from the normalcy of the quotidian, and across the mouth of the Grand Canal, the ornate, improbable, flood-lit mass of the Church of the Salute marks the occasion of yet another miracle. Here as you huddle in a corner of the nearly empty terrazzo, the two of them come in together with a conspiratorial air of taking a "big splurge," as the student guide books categorize visits to more expensive establishments.

"A step up from the Hotel Falier," she remarks, as they take a table beside the water, close to yours but less in the shadows.

"Yes," he answers. "But if preferable in the long run is another question."

"Maybe not. But good for a celebration."

"I suppose it can't hurt," he says. "For an evening. Visiting the rich is like going to the zoo to see the animals."

"I like the zoo."

"The animals can't hurt. While in the real world they do. Every chance."

"Then I appreciate your preference for the other world," she says. "The one you can't see."

"Can't see what?"

She shrugs.

"Can't see what? That's the question."

"Anyway," she says—their drinks had come—"here's to the sale of your first story. Your first move into the world."

"I'm not sure that's reason for congratulation."

"As long as you don't forget that, it's okay."

You would be charmed by their innocence if you were not anxious for their fate, and find yourself musing over speculations as to why that, in fact, should be the case, when you are shocked to attention by the sound of one of your own titles, an early piece you had written long ago on the subject of the visionary. And then, as if continuing from previous discussion:

"So that was why you didn't see much the first time you were here?"

"Right."

"And what did you do?"

"I went to the emergency room of the clinic. Some young doctor simply put anesthetic in, probed around, and pulled out this large cinder. *'Ecco!'* he said as it came out, and I felt an immediate relief. I'll never forget it because the eye had been very painful for days. I'd almost gotten used to it, in fact. And then of course there'd been another kind of pain, the pain of being in a wonderfully visual place and not being able to understand it properly. I was lucky."

"You're always lucky."

"Practical. Everything depends on that. You have to be smart. You can't live entirely in another world. If you want to survive in this one."

By this time you are almost standing in your dark corner, trembling in a half comprehending panic, impelled to say something though you have no idea what, while they, totally unaware, gaze across the Lagoon. Finally, almost choking, you manage to articulate a strangled warning: "The other world is all you have!"

And then you see they haven't heard, you haven't articulated after all, probably they are aware of nothing more than someone coughing in the corner. Besides you know that he won't see through the false sophistication of his innocence—the worldly-wise pose of one gifted with an opening to the unworldly in a world that won't honor it, sees it only as failure.

In desperation you approach their table, trying to speak, gesticulating, yet they see nothing, the girl looking out across the water, the boy staring right through you. Suddenly he focuses, pales as if he sees an apparition and, looking into your eyes, green as his own, goes rigid. His glass shatters on the terrazzo.

"What?" cries the girl.

"I just dreamed I saw myself twenty years from now."

"But you weren't asleep."

"Right."

But having looked at your reflection in his eyes for that instant, you, at last, understand without innocence. That you yourself are it, for him, now as twenty years ago, that ghost and warning of another world you once merely intuited. *Ecco!* Blinded by this vision, you finally see your own invisibility, as he, miraculously, fades and disappears into passing time.

Alice Adams

EARTHQUAKE DAMAGE

Stretching long legs to brace her boots against the bulkhead, as the plane heads upward from Toronto into gray mid-October air, Lila Lewisohn, a very tall, exhausted psychiatrist—a week of meetings has almost done her in, she feels—takes note of the advantages of this seat: enough legroom, and somewhat out of the crush. Also, the seat next to hers is vacant. At least, she thinks, the trip will be comfortable; maybe I can sleep.

But a few minutes into the air the plane is gripped and shaken. Turbulence rattles everything, as passengers clutch their armrests, or neighboring human arms, if they are travelling with friends or lovers. Lila, for whom this is a rather isolated period, instead grips her own knees, and grits her teeth, and prays—to no one, or perhaps to a very odd bunch: to God, in whom she does not believe; to Freud, about whom she has serious doubts; to her old shrink, who is dead; to her mother, also dead, and whom she mostly did not like. And to her former (she supposes it now is former) lover, Julian Brownfield, also a shrink.

Lila and Julian, in training together in Boston, plunged more or less inadvertently from a collegial friendship into heady adulterous love—a love (and a friendship) that for many years worked, sustaining them both through problematic marriages. But in the five or six years since the dissolutions of those marriages a certain troubled imbalance has set in. Most recently, Julian has taken back his ex-wife, Karen, an alcoholic pianist who is not doing well with recovery, and has just violently separated from another husband. "Sheltering" might be Julian's word for what he is doing for Karen—Lila would call it "harboring," or worse: if Karen behaved well, she might stay on forever there with Julian, Lila at least half-believes. She has so far refused to see Julian, with Karen there.

In any case, Lila now prays to all those on her list, and especially to Julian, to whom she says, I'm just not up to all this; I'm really running on empty. *Please.*

Her meetings, held in the new Harbourfront section of Toronto, in an excellent hotel with lovely, wide lake views, were no more than routinely tiring, actually; Lila was forced to admit to herself that it was the theme of the conference that afflicted her with a variety of troubling feelings. It was a psychiatric conference on the contemporary state of being single, though of course certain newspaper articles vulgarized it into "A New Look at Singles," "Singles: Shrinks Say the New Minority." Whereas in fact the hours of papers and discussion had ranged about—had included the guilt that many people feel over their single state; social ostracism, subtle and overt; myths of singleness; the couple as conspiracy; plus practical problems, demographics, and perceived changes over the last several generations. And Lila found that she overreacted—she was reached, touched, shaken by much that was said. She had trouble sleeping, despite long lap swims in the hotel's glassed-in pool, with its views of Canadian skies across Lake Ontario.

Now, very tired, she braces herself against the turbulence, and against certain strong old demons in her mind. And then, as though one of those to whom she has prayed were indeed in charge, the turbulence ends. The huge plane zooms peacefully through a clear gray dusk. Westward, toward San Francisco. A direct flight.

* * *

Lila must have fallen asleep, for she is startled awake by the too loud voice of the pilot, over the intercom: "Sorry, folks. We've just had news of a very mild earthquake in the San Francisco area, very mild but a little damage to the airport, so we'll be heading back to Toronto."

An instant of silence is followed by loud groans from the rows and rows of seats behind Lila's bulkhead. Groans and exclamations: *Oh no, Jesus Christ, all we need, an earthquake.* Turning, she sees that a great many people are standing up, moving about, as if there were anything to do. One man, though—trenchcoated, lean, dark blond, almost handsome—makes for the telephone up on the wall near Lila's seat. Seizing it, he begins to dial, and dial and dial. Lila gestures that he can sit down in the empty seat, and he does so, with a twisting grimace. Then "Can't get through, *damn,*" he says. "My family's down on the Peninsula." He dials again, says "Damn," again, then asks Lila, "Yours?"

"Oh. Uh, San Francisco."

"Well, San Francisco's better. Guy with a radio said the epicenter's in Hollister."

"I wonder about that 'mild.'" Lila leans toward him to whisper.

"No way it could be mild. They're not closing down the airport for any mild earthquake."

Which is pretty much what Lila had already thought.

"Well, I guess I better let someone else try to phone."

"There's one on the other side," Lila tells him, having noticed this symmetrical arrangement on entering the plane.

"Oh, well then." But after a few minutes, muttering, he gets up and goes back to his seat, as Lila realizes that she wishes he had stuck around—not that she was especially drawn to him; she simply wanted someone there.

People are by now crowding around the two phones, pressing into the passageway between the aisles. A man has managed to get through to his sister-in-law, in Sacramento, and soon everyone has his news: it is a major quake. Many dead. The bridge down.

At that last piece of news, about the bridge, Lila's tired heart is drenched with cold, as she thinks: Julian. Julian, who lives in Mill Valley and practices in San Francisco, could be on the bridge at any time. Especially now, just after five in San Francisco. Commuter time.

On the other hand, almost anyone *could* have been on the bridge, especially anyone who lives in Marin County. Fighting panic, Lila says this firmly to herself: anyone does not mean Julian, necessarily. A major disaster involving the bridge does not necessarily involve Julian Brownfield. Not necessarily. She is gripping her knees, as during the turbulence; with an effort she unclenches her fingers and clasps her hands together on her lap, too tightly.

"How about the game?" someone near her is saying.

"No stadium damage, I heard."

"Lucky it wasn't a little later. People leaving, going back to Oakland."

As, very slowly, these sentences penetrate Lila's miasma of anxiety, she understands: they are talking about the Bay Bridge. The Bay Bridge was damaged, not the Golden Gate. Traffic to the East Bay, not to Marin, Mill Valley.

What Lila feels then, along with extreme relief, is an increase of exhaustion; her nerves sag. And she has, too, the cold new thought that Julian, an unlikely fan, could well have gone to the game. (Taken Karen to the game?) Could have left early, and been overtaken by the earthquake, anywhere at all.

Rising from her seat, intending to walk about, she sees that everyone else is also trying to move. They all seem to protest the event, and their situation, with restless, random motion. Strangers confront and query each other along the packed aisles:

Where're you from? Remember the quake last August? The one in '72? In '57? How long were you in Toronto? Like it there? But not enough to make you want to go back right away, right?

At last they begin the descent into Toronto, strapped in, looking down, and no one notices the turbulence that they pass through.

* * *

In Julian's house, high up on the wooded crest above Mill Valley, there is total chaos: in the front hall, two large suitcases lie open and overflowing—a crazy tangle of dresses and blouses, sweaters, silk nightgowns, panty hose, and shoes thrown all over.

"Anyone coming in," Julian comments from a doorway, "anyone would think the earthquake, whereas actually—"

"Well, in a way it is the fucking earthquake," Karen unnecessarily tells him, in her furious, choppy way. "Closing the fucking airport."

"Whereas, really, we were lucky," Julian continues, more or less to himself. He is tall and too thin, gray-haired. His skin, too, now looks gray: three weeks of Karen have almost done him in, he thinks. In character, she has alternated her wish to leave with a passionate desire to stay with Julian—forever. Only a day ago she had decided firmly (it seemed) to leave. And now, on the verge of her departure, an earthquake. "The airport might open in a couple of hours," Julian tells Karen, and he is thinking of Lila, the exact hour of whose return he is uncertain about. Perhaps she is already here? "Or tomorrow," he says to Karen, hopefully.

"But how would we know, with the phone out?" Karen complains. "It might be a couple of weeks." She is visibly at the end of her rope, which is short at the best of times. "A couple of weeks with no lights or electricity!"

It is clear to Julian that whatever controls Karen has managed to place on herself for the course of her stay are now wavering, if not completely gone. She has not behaved badly; she has not, that is, got drunk. He himself, at this moment, acutely longs for a drink. An odd longing: Julian is generally abstemious, a tennis player, always in shape. And he wonders, is he catching Karen's own longing, her alcoholic impulse? Karen, opposing A.A. (she did not like it there), believes that alcoholics can cut down, citing herself as an example—every night she has one, and only one, vodka Martini.

Karen is very beautiful, still. All that booze has in no way afflicted the fine white skin. Her face shows no tracks of pain, nor shadows. Her wide, dark-blue eyes are clear; looking into those eyes, one might imagine that her head resounds only with Mozart, or Brahms—and perhaps in a way it still does.

"Well, come on, Julian, let's find some candles. You know perfectly well that this is the cocktail hour," she says to her former husband, and she laughs.

* * *

Down on the ground in Toronto, disembarked, all the passengers from the flight to San Francisco are herded into a room where, they are assured, they will be given instructions. And in that large, bare room rumors quickly begin to circulate, as people gather and mutter questions to each other.

No one is sitting or standing alone, Lila notices, although surely there were other solitary travellers on that plane. And she finds that she, too, begins to attach herself to groups, one after another. Is she seeking information, or simple creature comfort, animal reassurance? She is not sure.

Three businessmen in overcoats, with lavish attaché cases, having spoken to the pilot, inform Lila that it may be several days before the San Francisco airport opens. And that the reason for not going on to L.A., or even to Reno or Salt Lake City, has to do with flight regulations—since theirs was a Canadian carrier, they had to return to Canada.

In an automatic way she looks across to the man in the trenchcoat, at the same time wondering why: why has she more or less chosen him to lead her? She very much doubts that it is because he is almost handsome, and she hopes that it is not simply that he is a man. He looks decisive, she more or less concludes, and then is shaken by a powerful memory of Julian, who is neither handsome nor decisive, and whom she has loved for all those years.

The trenchcoated man seems indeed to have a definite group of his own, of which he is in charge. Lila reads this from the postures of the four people whom she now approaches, leaving the didactic businessmen. But before Lila can ask anything the loudspeaker comes on, and a voice says that they are all to be housed in the Toronto Hilton, which is very near, and that the airline will do everything possible to get them to their destination tomorrow. A van will pick them up downstairs to take them to the hotel. Names will be called, vouchers given.

Lila has barely joined her chosen group when she hears her name called; they must be doing it by rows, she decides. She is instructed to go through a hall and down some stairs, go outside, and meet the Hilton van there.

And after a couple of wrong turns Lila indeed finds herself outside in the semidark, next to a dimly lit, low-ceilinged traffic tunnel, where a van soon does arrive. But it is for the Ramada Inn, not the Hilton.

And that is the last vehicle of any nature to show up for the next ten or twelve minutes, during which time no people show up, either. No one.

Several taxis are parked some yards down from where Lila has been standing, pacing, in her boots, by her carry-on bag. Drivers are lounging on the seats inside. Should she take a cab to the Hilton? On the other hand, maybe by now everything has been changed, and no one is going to the Hilton after all.

It is very cold, standing there in the dark tunnel, and seemingly darker and dingier all the time. Across the black, wide car lanes are some glassed-in offices, closed and black, reflecting nothing. Behind Lila is the last room through which she came. It is still lit, and empty.

Something clearly is wrong; things cannot be going as planned. Or, she is in the wrong place. Then, dimly, at the end of the tunnel, she sees a van moving toward her. It will not be a Hilton van, she thinks, and she is right: "HOLIDAY INN," its sign reads. It passes her slowly, an empty van, its driver barely looking out.

Lila is later to think of this period of time as the worst of the earthquake for her—a time in which she feels most utterly alone, quite possibly abandoned. It is so bad that she has forgotten about the earthquake itself almost entirely; she is too immediately frightened and uncomfortable to think of distant disaster.

After perhaps another five minutes, during which everything gets worse—the cold and the darkness, Lila's anxiety and her growing hunger—she hears voices from the room behind her. Turning, she sees what she thinks of as her group: the trenchcoated man and his charges, followed by the other passengers, all coming out to where Lila stands, shifting her feet in boots that no longer seem to fit.

As though they were old friends, Lila hurries toward him. "Where've you been? What happened?"

"Bureaucratic foul-up," he tells her. "Some stuff about whether or not the airline would spring for the hotel. Who cares? And some confusion about whose flights originated in Toronto." With a semismile he adds, "You were really lucky to get out first."

"Was I? I don't know."

"Anyway. Look, there's our van. Toronto Hilton."

* * *

In the candlelit kitchen of Julian's house, Julian and Karen are drinking vodka and orange juice, Karen's idea being that they have to use up the orange juice before it goes to waste in the powerless refrigerator. "Besides, the C makes it good for you." She laughs, and Julian hears a sad echo of her old flirtatiousness, as she adds, "But why am I telling a doctor anything like that?"

He sighs. "Yes, I am a doctor."

This is not a room designed for such romantic illumination. The shadows on the giant steel refrigerator are severe, menacing, and the flickering candlelight on the black-tiled floor looks evil—they could be in jail. Julian feels nothing of the vodka, and Karen's face, across the round, white, high-gloss table, shows mostly fatigue. She looks vague, distracted.

In a sober, conversational voice she remarks, "Funny to think back to old times in this kitchen. With Lila and old Garrett." Garrett: Lila's former husband, a mean and sombre lawyer.

"This kitchen?" asks Julian. "I don't remember . . ."

"Sure you do. We were all drinking champagne, and later I broke a glass."

"I think it's Lila's kitchen we were in." The whole scene has indeed come back to Julian, a flash, immobilized: the other kitchen, so unlike this one, all soft wood, some copper bowls, blue pillows on a bench. Prim, pale Garrett—and Lila, her gray hair bright, brushed upward. Lila laughing and talking, he (Julian) talking, each of them, as always, excited by the other's sheer proximity. "It was somebody's birthday," he tells Karen, knowing perfectly well that it was Lila's. "You had on a green dress."

"Well, you sure do have a great memory for details."

"I have to, it's my job." And you always broke glasses, he does not say.

"You mean, my green dress is what you might call a professional memory? Holy shit, Julian, holy shit, you're, you're . . ." She begins to cough, unable to tell Julian what he is. He gets up and moves to pat her back, but Karen gestures him away.

"Don't, I'm O.K., don't hit me!" She laughs a little hysterically, as Julian, too late, realizes that she is getting drunk. Is drunk. "You know what the earthquake was like for me?" She is looking blearily across at him, tears pooled in those great, dark-blue eyes. "*Fun.* The most fun in the world. I loved it."

"Good, Karen, I'm glad." It no longer matters what he says, Julian knows, as long as it is fairly neutral. "I thought it was more like turbulence in an airplane," he mutters, more or less to himself.

At which Karen giggles. "I like turbulence," she tells him. "Remember? I think it's a kick." And then, quite suddenly, she bursts into tears. "Julian, I've never loved anyone but you," she sobs, reaching out to him. Blindly.

* * *

Descending from the van at the Toronto Hilton, Lila and her new friends see that the lobby inside is very crowded. Everyone is gathered around a single small television screen, and in a room beyond there is a coffee shop, apparently open. "Hundreds killed," the announcer is saying. "Devastation."

"The restaurant's out of food," someone says.

There is a line at the reception desk, but it seems to move quickly; within minutes Lila is being assigned a room. "I wonder about phoning," she says to the man in the trenchcoat, Mark. They have all introduced themselves.

Lila's room, at the top of the Toronto Hilton, is actually a small suite, to which she pays no attention, as she heads for the phone. Without considering consequences (Karen could easily answer), she dials the familiar Mill Valley number. Dialling directly, not bothering with credit cards or operators, she gets at first a busy signal and then an operator saying that she is sorry, all the circuits are busy. Lila dials again, gets more operators who are sorry, more busy signals. She goes into the bathroom to wash up, comes back and dials the number again, and again. She orders a sandwich from room service, and continues to try to phone.

* * *

A couple of hours later, in Mill Valley, Julian awakes with a sudden jolt: he is in his kitchen, still, and every brilliant light in the room is on, as is the television. Bottles and sticky glasses on the table. Gradually he remembers carrying Karen into the guest room. She was light enough in his arms, but a total deadweight;

his back feels strained. And then he came back into this room. Surely not, he hopes, for another drink?

The TV screen shows a very large, white apartment building that has buckled and is rent with cracks and gaps. A background of black night sky, and a cordon of police. Cars, flashing lights. Dazed people standing around in clumps. Julian gets up to turn it off when, at that moment, the phone rings. In his confusion, he stumbles, just catches it on the third ring.

"Lila? My darling, my Lila, wherever . . . ? We're here, I mean I'm here, no damage, really. Well, I imagine I do sound odd, but no, of course I'm not drunk. Karen was just on the point of leaving—actually packed, then the damn thing hit. I guess she'll go tomorrow; by now I suppose I mean today. And you? You'll be back today! For sure?"

* * *

Smiling, still breathing hard with the effort of so much futile dialing before at last getting through, Lila offers a silent prayer to all those on her curious private list: she prays that she can fly out of Toronto tomorrow, or whatever day this now is—and that Karen can fly, finally, out of San Francisco.

She sleeps fitfully and wakes early, knowing that she is awake for good. She thinks of telephoning Julian again, but does not. She showers and dresses as hurriedly as possible, and goes down to the hotel lobby.

There people are sitting around, or milling about, aimlessly. The TV seems still to be showing the news from the night before; Lila glimpses the same bridge shots, fire shots, the broken apartment house. All around her in the lobby the faces are pale, clothes a little dishevelled, as hers must be. From a small, plump woman who is sitting near the front desk she hears, "They say we're getting out today, but I don't believe it."

Lila, too, has trouble believing that they will escape. As she looks around at the tired clusters of people—no one, she observes again, is going it alone—she imagines that they will be there for months, that they are in fact refugees from some much larger disaster.

In the coffee shop, she finds Mark, and another man, and joins them. Mark got through to his wife, in Saratoga, who said that their chimney had fallen off, and that everything in the house that could break was broken. "But she's O.K.," says Mark, with a grin. "And the kids. You should have seen the waves in the swimming pool, she told me. You wouldn't believe it. Tidal."

From the lobby then, at first indistinctly, they hear an announcement: ". . . vans will begin to leave this hotel at nine-forty-five. Repeat: the San Francisco airport is clear."

* * *

Lila's seat on the morning plane is not nearly as good as the one the day before. Pushing her way down the aisle with her carryon, she takes note of this fact, though today it seems extremely unimportant. And she does have a window seat.

Everyone on the plane is in a festive mood. People smile a lot, though many faces show considerable fatigue, the ravages of a long and anxious night. But an almost manic mood prevails: the airport is clear, we're going home, the city has more or less survived. To all of which Lila adds to herself, and Karen is going back East, probably.

Everyone is seated, buckled in. The pilot's voice is telling the flight attendants to prepare for departure. The engines start their roar; they roar and roar. And nothing happens.

This goes on for some time—ten minutes, fifteen—until the engines are turned off, and they are simply sitting there on the runway, in the October Canadian sunlight. But the atmosphere on the plane is less impatient than might be imagined; it is felt that at least they are on their way. There may even be a certain (unacknowledged, unconscious) relief at the delay: San Francisco and whatever lies ahead do not have to be faced quite so soon.

The pilot announces a small mechanical glitch, which will be taken care of right away. And, perhaps twenty minutes later, the engines start again. And they are off, almost: the plane starts down the runway, gathering speed, and then, quite suddenly, it slows, and stops.

Jesus Christ. Now really. What now? We'll never. What in hell is going on? These sentiments echo around the cabin, where patience has worn audibly thin, until, apparently starting at the front row, where a smiling stewardess is standing, the rumor spreads: a dog has somehow got loose on the field; it will be a minute more. They have already been cleared for takeoff.

And then, with a motion that seems to be decisive, the plane moves forward, again. Glancing from her window, quite suddenly Lila sees—indeed!—a dog, running in the opposite direction, running back to Toronto. A large, lean, yellowish dog, whose gallop is purposeful, determined. He will get back to his place, but in the meantime he enjoys the run, the freedom of the forbidden field. His long nose swings up and down, his tail streams backward, a pennant, as Lila—watching from her window, headed at last back to San Francisco (probably)—begins in a quiet, controlled, and private way to laugh. "It was just so funny," she will say to Julian, later. "The final thing, that dog. And he looked so proud! As though instead of getting in our way he had come to our rescue."

Marly Swick

MOSCOW NIGHTS

Sitting in the waiting room at Planned Parenthood, Jonathan and his mother made an odd couple. He could feel everyone's eyes on him, wondering. The young punk couple with his-and-hers studded motorcycle jackets. The stylish black woman with her gold leather attaché case. Two overweight, semicomatose teenage girls. A yuppie-ish couple huddled over the *New York Times* Sunday crossword puzzle. Jonathan wondered if they had made a point of saving the puzzle all week for this purpose.

He wanted to be a good son, but he couldn't help feeling that this was asking too much. Beyond the pale. Last week his mother had called and left a message on his machine: could he possibly give her a ride to the doctor the following Friday afternoon? When he'd called her back to say okay, she'd sounded weird. "What's wrong?" he'd asked her, against his better judgment, not really wanting to get into anything. During the past year or so, since his parents' divorce, his mother had started confiding in him things he did not particularly want to hear. Intimate things. Private feelings. Details of her sex life. Things he preferred not to think about—or picture. He had tried hinting that his sister,

Debra, would be a more appropriate confidant, but his mother ignored the hints. His mother and sister had never really hit it off.

"I wasn't going to tell you," his mother had said with a sigh, "but since you ask . . ."

"You don't have to tell me if you don't want to," he'd interjected. "Really."

But of course she *had* told him. And just as he had feared, what she had to tell him was something he did not want to hear. On the phone he had been shocked into silence for a moment. Then his automatic sympathy reflex had kicked in and he had mumbled all the appropriate comforting responses. Or at least he'd given it his best shot. But after he had hung up, he found himself stalking around his living room, muttering curses and slamming drawers. Then he calmed down and called Farrell.

Since Farrell had moved out, Jonathan had been rationing his calls to her—no more than one a week. He and Farrell were "trying to be friends." Farrell had been skeptical at first, arguing that both of them would be better off if they quit the relationship cold turkey, but he had finally persuaded her to give peace a chance. Although he had sworn up and down that he harbored no secret hopes of a rapprochement, he still could not believe that their relationship was over. He had been in love with Farrell most of his adult life. They had met back east in college—in Intro to Film Noir—and had moved to L.A. to pursue film careers together. That was three years ago. Now Farrell was in UCLA law school and he was still writing screenplays during the day and driving an airport shuttle bus at night. They were moving in different directions, she'd said to him gently one night after dinner. Then, when he'd argued and balked, she'd said *she* was moving in a different direction; *he* was standing still—going nowhere. He was stunned. He hadn't had the faintest idea that that was how she saw things. He said that he'd change. But she didn't want to negotiate. She had rented a one-bedroom apartment in Palms, she informed him. Wait a minute, he'd said. But she was already packed and out the door. That was Farrell. Once she even so much as thought about leaving, she was as good as gone. "Bitch!" he'd shouted, running alongside her old VW. "Bitch!" But she'd turned onto the highway and sped away.

Still, he loved her. He wanted her back.

* * *

When Farrell answered on the second ring, he was surprised. "It's Saturday night," he said. "I didn't think you'd be home."

"In law school there's no such thing as Saturday night." She sounded impatient. "I'm in the middle of *Palsgraf* versus *Long Island Railroad.* This better be good."

"It's good," he said, "in a bad way. It's my mother. I'm taking her to Planned Parenthood next Friday to get an abortion. This is a forty-seven-year-old woman we're talking about. Can you believe this?"

"Wow," Farrell said. "Your mother!" He could tell she was picturing his mother, with her matching handbag and shoes, and the hairdo that looked as if it had never been slept on.

"I don't think she should tell me these things. I'm her *son,* for Christ's sake." He walked over to the tape player and inserted one of Farrell's favorite cassettes. "It gives me the creeps."

"Is that my Stephane Grappelli tape?" Farrell asked.

"I don't know. Maybe." He turned the volume up a notch.

"So why doesn't the guy go with her?" She was starting to sound impatient again, and he imagined her flipping the pages of her casebook, neatly highlighting in yellow as they talked.

"You mean Re-Phil? Hah! What a joke. The guy is a total loser. Not to mention physically repulsive. She says he couldn't handle it. She says he's quote emotionally fragile unquote. She refuses to tell him. Can you believe this?"

"Well," Farrell said, "I think it's nice she's so open and that she trusts you. She's treating you like an adult."

"I'm not an adult! I'm her kid. No matter how old I am, she's still my *mother.*"

"She's also a woman."

"I don't *want* to think of her as a woman."

Farrell was quiet, and he could see her suit-yourself shrug. He didn't want to push it. Just these past couple of weeks he thought he'd detected a gradual warming trend on her part. "Well, I'll let you go," he said, half hoping she'd say it was all right, she'd rather talk to him than study.

"Okay," she said. "Hang in there."

"Right. Will do." He forced himself to hang up before he blew it by saying something insistently personal or pathetically sentimental. He marked a red *F* on his calendar and counted back, adding up all the other little red and blue *F*s. The blue *F*s were the times that Farrell had called him. The red *F*s were the times he had called her. Over the past two and a half months, since she'd moved out, he'd marked only five blue *F*s as opposed to eleven red ones. Not counting the times he'd gotten her answering machine and hung up. This depressed him. He looked at his watch. Lately, since Farrell had moved out, he was always looking at his watch. Time moved more slowly, sluggishly. He felt like an old 45 being played at 33.

"They're already half an hour behind schedule," his mother said fretfully, blindly flipping the pages of a much-handled *Newsweek.*

"I'm sorry," he said. He remembered Farrell's once pointing out to him that when he was nervous he tended to speak in non sequiturs. He got up and paced over to the window, waited a minute for the receptionist to get off the phone, and then gave up and gravitated back to where his mother sat. "It can't be much longer."

"Oh, well. It's all experience. Grist for the mill." As if to illustrate the point, she pulled a fancy notebook from her handbag and jotted down a couple of phrases.

Peering over her shoulder, he read, "like patient fish waiting to be gutted." A year or so before the divorce his mother had enrolled in an evening poetry workshop at Los Angeles City College. The instructor—no doubt thrilled to find someone who knew how to use an apostrophe—had encouraged her to send out her work. The day after she received her first acceptance, she announced she wanted a divorce. His father had been stunned. Whenever Jonathan had visited him in his new studio apartment in the Marina, his father had seemed bewildered and woebegone, like a dog banished for bad behavior. Jonathan and his sister had held long worried telephone powwows about him—until he surprised them by falling in love with a young woman in his building, a pretty divorcee with a six-year-old daughter. By Hanukkah he had himself a whole new family. So Jonathan and his sister shifted the focus of their worry back to their mother, who had joined a singles' book-lovers club and struck up a thing with some unprepossessing loser named Phil Kapischkey, or "Re-Phil," as Debra immediately dubbed him, because their father's name was also Phil.

"What on earth do you see in him?" Debra had protested while Kapischkey was in the men's room. They had come together for their mother's birthday dinner, the first time they had all met.

Insulted, their mother had leaped to his defense, ranting on about how he had earned a doctorate from Harvard and had been a Russian-lit professor at USC before he retired, how cultured and refined he was. To drive home her point, she said that they were reading *Anna Karenina* aloud to each other in bed—a chapter a night.

"Jesus," Debra had said, "spare me the gory details."

Their father had at least been tanned and fit—a weekend tennis player.

"Anna Karenina!" Jonathan had said, groaning, picturing the thick paperback with its thin pages and microscopic print. "You really think this thing's going to last that long?"

* * *

His mother was still busy scribbling in her little notebook when the nurse practitioner called her name off the chart. "Evelyn Levitov."

When she didn't respond, Jonathan poked her gently in the ribs. "That's you," he said.

She dropped her pen and clutched his arm. "I'm scared, Jono." She squeezed her eyelids shut, damming the tears.

His heart pounded. Even now, as an adult, he was unnerved when one of his parents showed any sign of weakness. "Come on, now." He put his arm around her shoulders and steered her back toward the nurse. "It'll be over within half an hour."

"She'll be just fine." The nurse smiled reassuringly.

His mother attempted a smile and handed him her alligator handbag. She was dressed in a gray knit suit and looked as if she were on her way to some ladies' luncheon. "Keep an eye on this," she said. "Buy yourself some lunch."

Listening to the forlorn *click-click* of her high heels down the ugly corridor, Jonathan suddenly wondered what Re-Phil was doing at that very moment. He imagined him hunched contentedly over a large bowl of steaming borscht. *Stupid bastard. Selfish wimp.* Jonathan stormed back through the waiting room and out onto the sidewalk and across the bright, busy street to a phone booth at a corner gas station. The phone book had been ripped off its chain, so he had to call information. "*K* as in kangaroo, *a-p-i-s-c-h-k-e-y*. Philip." He scribbled the number on the back page of his mother's fancy little notebook, dropped in a quarter, and dialed. Re-Phil's "Hello?" sounded simultaneously suspicious and hopeful. For a moment, imagining his mother's possible outrage, Jonathan was tempted to hang up.

"Who is this?" Re-Phil demanded. "Speak up!"

The voice, professorial and testy, goaded Jonathan into speech.

"This is Jonathan Levitov," he said. "There's something I thought you might like to know."

* * *

His fury partly spent, Jonathan suddenly realized what he must look like, walking down the sidewalk with his mother's alligator handbag. He tucked it under his arm and crossed the street to the coffee shop where he'd told Re-Phil he would meet him in thirty minutes. Re-Phil was taking medication for a nervous condition and could no longer drive, but he said he'd call a cab. He lived about twenty minutes away, near LaBrea and Wilshire. Jonathan ordered a cup of coffee and waited. Ever since Farrell had left him, he felt conspicuous and pathetic sitting alone in restaurants, conspicuously pathetic, as if everyone were looking at him, knowing he'd been dumped. He checked his watch, again, and glanced around for a discarded newspaper, a flyer—anything to make him look busy and to distract him from wondering if he'd done a stupid thing calling Re-Phil. Maybe he should have minded his own business. Which he would have done, happily, if his mother hadn't dragged him into this mess. All this new "openness" was highly overrated. When Debra had had an abortion, her sophomore year in college, she had at least been considerate enough to keep it a secret from their parents. He recognized one of the pudgy space cadets from the clinic sitting at a nearby table, staring at him. She was gurgling the last inch of her Diet Pepsi, and he had a terrible intuition that any second now she was going to come over and talk to him. Hurriedly fumbling with the clasp, he tore open his mother's handbag, fished out the little notebook, and started furiously jotting down notes, his brow furrowed in mock concentration, as if he were trying to remember some complex mathematical equation. The girl got up and left. He relaxed and put down his pen. The notebook fell open to a poem in progress, with lines crossed out and cramped phrases squeezed in above them. His mother's handwriting was difficult to read, but the word *Kotex* leaped out at him. He sighed and slammed the notebook shut, signaling the waitress for a refill.

Two or three months after his father had moved out, his mother had dragged him to a group poetry reading in a little bookstore on Westwood Boulevard. The poetry was amateurish, and he fidgeted in boredom until—at last—his mother got up there and started to read. Then his boredom turned to appalled embarrassment, as she read one long confessional poem after another in an Amazonian voice he didn't even recognize. He'd expected maybe bad Emily Dickinson, but this was more like bad Allen Ginsberg. She might as well have been standing naked at the podium. He wanted to stick his fingers in his ears. All manner of disgusting personal details—sagging breasts, hemorrhoids, flaccid penises, stretch marks, semen, tears, menstrual blood. She even read a poem about his birth, which she made a point of dedicating to him, smiling out at him in the second row. She described the "wine-dark slug of placenta" and the obstetrician "neatly darning the hole in the old worn sock of her vagina" until he was afraid he was going to be sick or faint. When the reading was over—at last—everyone flocked around her, flapping excitedly, chirping their praise. Her cheeks were flushed, her dark eyes bright, as she looked over at him as if to say, "Well? So?" He had intended to tell her just what he thought—to really let her have it —but somehow, with all her admiring fans standing there awaiting his proud response, he had found himself smiling wanly and giving her the thumbs-up sign.

* * *

From across the restaurant Jonathan caught sight of Re-Phil heading toward him, breathless and unkempt, hair uncombed and shirt misbuttoned. In his white shirt and slacks, and with his thatch of bristly white hair, he looked like an old polar bear. Not so much fat as massive. Jonathan looked pointedly at his watch.

"Sorry," Re-Phil wheezed. "The cab was late."

Jonathan plunked a dollar bill on the table and said, "Let's go. She might be done by now."

A tender, stricken expression flitted across Re-Phil's face as he noticed the alligator handbag. "She didn't tell me," he said. "I didn't know a thing."

"Ignorance is bliss." Jonathan held the door open and waited for Re-Phil to pass through into the bright dazzle of sunshine. He felt like a bounty hunter bringing his man to justice.

The waiting room was more crowded than when he had left.

Jonathan had to elbow his way to the front desk, where he was told that his mother was in the recovery room. "She's feeling a bit woozy," the nurse practitioner said. "It's not uncommon. We'll just let her rest a few minutes."

Jonathan squeezed himself between Re-Phil and the yuppie husband and repeated what he had been told. Craning his neck, Jonathan could see that only one corner of the Sunday crossword puzzle was still partly blank. On the table next to the vinyl couch were wire racks full of pamphlets on various birth-control methods and diseases: herpes, gonorrhea, AIDS. Re-Phil was engrossed in a pamphlet on the cervical cap. Jonathan suddenly remembered the time their apartment in Boston had been broken into. Predictably, the thief had stolen a brand-new tape recorder, the stereo turntable, a broken Nikon, and some junk jewelry. But the thief had also taken Farrell's diaphragm out of its blue plastic case and had stuck it to the bedroom wall with a hatpin from one of her vintage hats. Farrell, relatively calm and stoic up to that point, had screamed when she'd discovered it later that night. And Jonathan had felt the hairs rising on the back of his neck as she pointed speechlessly to the dead diaphragm, skewered there like a voodoo sacrifice.

Re-Phil stood up abruptly, clumsily knocking over one of the pamphlet racks. "Here she is," he said. "I see her."

Jonathan looked up. From the other end of the hall his mother gave him a limp wave and a pale smile. Then she noticed Re-Phil. Her step faltered; the nurse gripped her arm more firmly. His mother looked confused for a moment, and then angry. She shot Jonathan a dirty look. The nurse handed her a small vial of pills. "Just in case you feel any discomfort." The nurse patted her on the shoulder. "Be sure to call if you have any problem or question."

The moment the nurse turned to go, Jonathan and Re-Phil both rushed up and claimed an arm. Evelyn shook them off. "I'm all right," she said irritably. "I can walk." She smiled at Re-Phil, pointedly ignoring Jonathan. "I'm sorry about this. You were sweet to come, Phil."

Sweet, Jonathan fumed. "Here." He handed Re-Phil the handbag. "I'll go bring the car around."

On the drive home his mother and Re-Phil huddled in the back seat. Jonathan felt like he was at work, driving the shuttle bus. He cranked up the radio and pretended to ignore them. In the rearview mirror he could see the top of his mother's silvery-blonde head resting against Re-Phil's bearish shoulder. His huge hand cradled her skull, his fingertips tapping out the tempo of the music on her forehead. She didn't seem to mind. Jonathan remembered a game he had played with his parents when he was little, just learning to read. The three of them would lie in bed together and trace letters on one another's backs, underneath their pajamas, and the tracee would have to guess the word. They called it Ticklegrams. He had tried it years later with Farrell, but she was too ticklish; she could never hold still long enough.

They dropped Re-Phil off at his apartment on Sycamore, at Evelyn's insistence and over Re-Phil's protests. He wanted, he said, to come fuss over her—fluff her pillows and serve her hot soup and read aloud to her. Jonathan thought it was the least he could do, considering, but his mother held firm. "Not today," she said. "Maybe tomorrow."

"Promise?"

She nodded wearily. He kissed the back of her hand. *Who does he think he is?* Jonathan thought. *Count Vronsky?* After Re-Phil got out, Jonathan turned to the back seat and said, "You want to come up front?"

His mother shook her head frostily. He shrugged and turned the radio back up. They rode the rest of the way in noisy silence.

* * *

At his mother's house, his old house, Jonathan busied himself making a pot of tea while his mother futzed around in the bathroom. When she emerged, after an alarmingly long interval, during which he'd imagined her hemorrhaging to death on the tile floor, she walked silently past him into the den and flipped the TV on to Oprah. He set the pot of tea on the end table next to the sofa and trotted off to the bedroom for a blanket and pillow. He was gone only a second, but when he returned her eyes were closed and she appeared to be asleep. He tiptoed over and turned the volume down and then collapsed into his father's old La-Z-Boy. Oprah was talking to obsessive-compulsives. One middle-aged Japanese man was explaining that he couldn't seal an envelope without first checking and rechecking to make sure that his four-year-old daughter was not inside. Jonathan sighed. People were so crazy. He didn't know one person you could call really well adjusted. It was all just a matter of degree, a continuum. Today it was red and blue *F*s on his calendar. Tomorrow—who knows? He got up and paced restlessly around the house. The hallway leading to the bedrooms was lined with framed family photographs, mostly of him and Debra, declining in cuteness with each passing year. There were a couple of group portraits with his father, but his mother had removed their wedding picture, exposing an ugly nail hole surrounded by chipped plaster. In the dim light of the hallway he peered at his watch.

When he returned to the den, his mother's eyes were open. She had removed her suit jacket and was sitting up, sipping a cup of tea. Her hair was mussed, and it occurred to him that in her satiny black slip she exuded the mature sex appeal of, say, Lee Remick.

"You feeling okay? You want anything?" he asked.

"I'll be all right. You don't need to hang around."

"That's okay—I want to," he said, wiping up some spilled tea with a potholder. This wasn't strictly true. What he wanted was to feel virtuous, beyond reproach. "Anyway, I don't have anything better to do." He meant to strike a jocular note but didn't quite make it.

His mother reached over and patted his hand, and then modestly adjusted her slip straps. "You really need to let Farrell go," she said gently.

He shrugged. "She's gone." He swiped an old *New Yorker* off the coffee table and leafed through the cartoons. "We're just friends."

"Your father and I tried that—the friends bit." She paused to slosh more tea into her cup. "It didn't work. But then maybe your generation can handle these things better. Do you think?"

Jonathan shrugged. For some reason he was irritated whenever his mother tried to engage him in a discussion about men and women, although he was equally irritated whenever his father refused to discuss such personal issues, which was always.

"In our generation an ex was an ex," she said. "Completely out of the picture. Of course, we expected things to last forever. Whereas I don't suppose your generation ever really expects anything to last." His mother blew on the hot tea, musing. "There's some corollary or something there. Although I can't quite think what it is."

"If x equals *ex*pectation, and y equals degree of friendliness with Ex, then more x results in less y," he said, pleased with himself.

His mother laughed, spilling some tea on the blanket. Hearing her laugh, Jonathan suddenly felt something inside him relax and expand. For the first time all day he didn't feel like picking a fight with someone. "Hey!" He tossed the magazine aside. "I've got a great idea. How about some canasta?" He leaped up and grabbed the cards from the cupboard. "Jesus. I don't believe you still have these." He smiled at the worn faces of Lady Di and Prince Charles on the dog-eared cards that he'd brought back as a joke from his junior year abroad. The summer of the royal wedding. He hummed as he dealt the cards, transported back to a simpler, more lighthearted time in his life—the summer he was twelve, with a broken leg, and his mother had sat by his bed playing canasta with him by the hour. The last time he'd played was right after he and Farrell had started sleeping together. She had come down with mono, and to help pass the time he'd taught her how to play canasta, but she thought it was a stupid game and insisted he learn how to play chess instead. Farrell was an impatient teacher and he was a slow pupil. They fought so much that he finally flushed the chess pieces down the toilet. The evening of the ill-fated birthday dinner his mother had bragged that Re-Phil was a world-class chess champion, which was just one more black mark against him as far as Jonathan was concerned.

As if she had read his mind—it wouldn't be the first time—his mother suddenly stopped arranging her cards and said, "You know, you really shouldn't have called Phil. He had nothing to do with it. You've just created an embarrassing situation. For everybody."

"What are you talking about?" He squinted at his cards, the setting sun shining directly into his eyes. "It takes two, you know. In my generation we males take responsibility. Fifty-fifty." He discarded the jack of clubs.

"What I'm talking about is that Phil Kapischkey and I have a platonic relationship, more or less. Prostate problems. And this medication he's on, well—" she shrugged and waved her free hand vaguely. "If you must know, your father was the one who—"

"Stop! Just stop right there. I don't want to hear this. Jesus!" He slapped his cards down on the table top, rattling the teacups. "You don't have to tell me this."

"And you don't have to shout." Frowning, lips pursed, his mother focused intently on her cards, fussily tweaking them into a perfectly symmetrical fan. Tweak, tweak, tweak. His arm shot out and knocked the cards from her hand.

She sighed and glared at him—a cool, dispassionate, unmaternal glare. "Just what are you so angry about?"

The question surprised him, caught him off guard. He bent down and started picking the cards up off the floor. Lady Di's and Charles's royal smiles seemed to have frozen into aloof reproach. Hunched over in his chair, he could feel the blood rising to his face, his heart pounding in his ears, as if he were back in high school geometry and the teacher had asked him a question he didn't know the answer to. The loud silence. All those eyes trained on him. Then he heard Farrell's voice—he had broken down and called her in the middle of the night shortly after she had moved out. "You know what your problem is?" she'd asked.

Lying there in the dark, alone, his heart pounding, he had said, "No. Do you?"

And she had said, "Yes," and then heaved a big sigh and said, "Never mind," and hung up on him.

His first response was a sort of dizzying relief. Then, lying there in the dark silence, alone, he could hear the bees buzzing inside his brain. Curiosity propelled his arm out toward the phone, and cowardice yanked it back under the covers. What you don't know won't hurt you, his mother always used to tell him.

He dumped the cards on the coffee table, looked at his watch, and stood up. "Debra will be home in half an hour. If you need anything, you can call her." He zipped up his windbreaker. "Okay?"

"Fine." She shrugged.

At the door he hesitated. "Did he know about this?"

"Your father?"

He nodded.

"I thought you didn't want to know."

He walked back into the room and perched edgily on the arm of the sofa opposite his mother. "Just this one thing."

"It hurts," she said, picking up the vial of pain-killers and prying off the lid. "Get me some water, would you?"

As he shut off the faucet in the kitchen, the phone rang. It was Re-Phil. "How's she doing?" he whispered, as if he were in the same room.

"Fine," Jonathan said. Then, after an awkward pause, "Look. I'm sorry about all this. I shouldn't have called you."

"No, no. I'm glad you did. You did the right thing."

Jonathan could hear a piano rhapsodizing away in the background. Something tragically romantic. Russian. Full of doomed yearning. Rachmaninoff or Tchaikovsky. "Do you think she feels like talking to me?"

"Not right now," Jonathan said. "Now's not the right time."

"I understand." He cleared his throat. "You must wonder, I mean about your mother and me, and I just wanted to say, to ex—"

"Please," Jonathan cut in. "Please don't explain anything."

He hung up and returned to the living room with the glass of water. As he set the glass on the table, he suddenly recognized the piano piece—"Moscow Nights." His sister had driven them all crazy practicing it over and over again for a recital.

"Who was that?"

"Count Vronsky, at your service." He clicked his heels.

"I thought you were leaving." She turned up the volume on the television set, tuning him out.

"I am." He had to raise his voice to compete with the local newscaster's. "But first I want to know. Did he know?"

"Your father?"

"Yes!" He stomped his foot in frustration.

"It's really none of your business, you know."

"I know! I *know* it's none of my business. That's what I've been telling you all along. But since you've *chosen* to make it my bus—"

"No," she said. "The answer to your question is no."

"No? He didn't know?"

She nodded. "It was just a silly accident. We had some financial stuff to discuss and we decided why not try to make it pleasant, for a change—why not do it over dinner? Try to be friends. After all, twenty-six years—" she shrugged. "So, it was pleasant enough. Kind of comforting, really, you know?" Jonathan nodded. She paused for a sip of water. "Afterward he brought me back. I'd mentioned that the sliding glass door was off the track again, and he volunteered to see if he could fix it. We had a couple of brandies." She sat up straighter and pressed her knees together primly. "Your father and I—well, sex was never our problem."

You know what your problem is? He could hear Farrell's voice again. He balled his fists in the pockets of his windbreaker and shook his head, as if to knock out her voice.

"You okay?" his mother asked. He nodded.

"You can imagine how foolish I felt when I found out—like some silly teenager, at my age. Your father has his own life now. With Jennifer." The name of his father's new significant other rolled off her lips effortlessly. No sign of jealousy. "I didn't want to stir up trouble."

"Trouble," Jonathan repeated tonelessly, suddenly recalling his father's one feeble attempt at a father-son talk. They had been in the car. His father was giving him a ride home after a high school wrestling match. It was pouring rain, and Jonathan was depressed and silent, having lost the match. His father, never noted for his sensitivity to mood, chose that occasion to caution his son about the risk of getting some girl "into trouble." He painted a gloomy scenario in which Jonathan dropped out of high school, married, moved in with the girl's parents, worked at a car wash during the day, took classes at a vocational school at night, and crawled home exhausted to a squalling baby and an even more exhausted wife. By the time the Lincoln had sailed into the garage, Jonathan felt like shooting himself to put himself out of this mythical misery. For months after that little chat he couldn't even unhook a girl's bra without seeing himself dressed in sudsy coveralls, hosing down a car.

The pain-killer must have contained some sort of sedative. His mother's head had fallen back onto the pillow and her eyelids drooped and fluttered. He tiptoed over, turned off the television, and shut the blinds. It was just getting dark out. He knelt down beside the sofa and whispered, "I'm going to take off now. I've got to go to work."

"You know why you're angry?" she murmured.

"Why?" He felt his pulse start to race. He held himself very still.

"You were always like this, always." A dreamy smile floated on her face.

"Like what?" he said.

But she was gone. Out like a light, as his parents used to say.

* * *

Outside it was cool and misty, the clouds had moved in. He drove around aimlessly for a while, trying to figure out what he felt like doing. He had lied to his mother about having to work; he had arranged for the night off just in case of any complications. His stomach rumbled. All he knew was that he didn't want to go home. He ran through a mental menu—hamburger, Thai, sushi, pizza—waiting for a nod from his belly. He was hungry but not really in the mood. Finally he pulled into a Taco Bell. A newspaper was lying on the table next to him. As he crunched on his taco, he skimmed through the movie listings, although he wasn't really in the mood for that either. In the booth opposite him a fat, bright-eyed baby held court, propped up in a carrier contraption on top of the table. A little boy about five or six tore off tiny pieces of tortilla and handed them to his baby brother, who squashed them in his fist and rammed them clumsily into his mouth. The boy's older sister was making a chain out of straw wrappers, and the mother stared out the window dreamily as bits of shredded cheese and lettuce oozed out the end of her burrito. She was very pregnant. For the first time, Jonathan thought about the aborted fetus and wondered if it had been a boy or a girl. Growing up, he had lobbied tirelessly for a brother. A younger brother, who couldn't run as fast or read as many big words. He had even had the name picked out: Duke. Duke Levitov. Finally they had bought him off with a dog. A German shepherd. His mother had automatically started calling the puppy Duke, but he had said no, the dog's name was Major—just to let *them* know that *he* knew a dog was a poor substitute for a brother.

The baby started to cry. The pregnant woman continued eating her burrito and staring out the window, as if she were just a stranger who happened to be sitting at that table. The baby cried harder. Jonathan got up and left.

Instead of getting back on the freeway and heading for home, Jonathan cruised along Olympic Boulevard, listening to the radio, pretending he didn't know that he was just stalling, just seeing how long he could put off giving in to his worst instincts. He looked at his watch. Only six-thirty. He wished it were later, after midnight. For some reason he had this notion (fantasy) that things would go better if he woke Farrell up. Her defenses would be down, and she would answer the door in her flannel nightgown, all warm and fuzzy from sleep, a tender smile hovering on her lips from some pleasant dream, preferably about him, although he knew this was really pushing it. He also knew that Farrell was generally cold and crabby upon being awakened.

By the time he pulled up in front of her building, it was nearly seven. He had been to Farrell's place only once before, and he had taken a wrong turn. He slumped in his seat and looked up at her lighted window for a few minutes, trying to divine whether or not she was alone. Lights were burning in the front room. The bedroom was dark. He took this as a good sign, but as he walked up the front steps it suddenly occurred to him that maybe it was actually a bad sign. Twice he stretched his hand out to ring the bell and then snatched it back. His heart beat like a conga drum in his chest, a crazy, savage arrhythmia, and he thought maybe he was going to have a heart attack right there on Farrell's front stoop. Then, just as he was about to turn and flee, the front door flew open and there she was. In the momentary confusion he thought that she must have heard his heart pounding, like a knock at the door, but in the next instant he noticed that she was dressed up, dressed to go out.

"What are you doing here?" she said. "You nearly gave me a heart attack." She was wearing the dangly silver fish earrings he had bought for her in Taxco. As she spoke, the earrings leaped and shimmied impatiently.

"I was just driving by and thought maybe you'd like to take a study break, go out for a cappuccino or something." Standing there in the dark, Farrell smelled sweet and familiar. He had a sudden intense desire to lick her face, the way Major used to greet him after a long absence. "I've had sort of a rough day."

"I'm sorry," she said. "One of my professors is having a party. I've got to go. In fact, I'm already late. I promised him I'd be there early."

"No problem." He shrugged. "Just an impulse." He turned to go. "You look very pretty, by the way."

"Thanks." Farrell's voice softened a bit—relief that he wasn't going to create a scene?—and she slipped her arm through his as they walked down the flagstone path toward the street.

"So what's this guy teach?" he asked.

"Torts," she said casually, but somehow the word sounded sweet and gooey on her lips.

At his car they paused. It was cooler now—the marine layer. "How's your mother?" Farrell fished a Kleenex out of her jacket and wiped the thick film of moisture off the windshield, so that he would be able to see. The gesture touched him.

"I don't know," he said, and sighed. "Okay, I guess. Considering."

"Frankly, I never knew your mother was up to it."

"You don't know the half of it, believe me." He was hoping she would ask him what he meant and invite him to come in and tell the whole story, but he knew she wouldn't. Somehow he knew that this torts professor was "the one"—the one he'd been dreading. And the reason Farrell was being halfway warm and affectionate was that she was happy.

"Let's have lunch sometime," she said, as he opened the door of his car. "Give me a call."

"Sure. Okay." He nodded pleasantly. Lunch. It felt unreal. As she turned to go, his brain translated the action into screenplay directions—a little technique he had developed years ago, during a bad acid trip, to take the edge off reality, or unreality, depending on how you looked at it. He was comforted by the illusion that all this chaos was really under his direction.

> She leans over—through the open window—gives him a tender peck on the cheek, and runs off. He sits for a moment, watching her in the rearview mirror until she disappears out of his line of vision, and then, slowly, he turns the key in the ignition. Backing up cautiously, he maneuvers his beat-up car out of the tight parking space. Then suddenly, as if possessed —CLOSE-UP of foot on accelerator—he floors it and the car lunges backward. MEDIUM SHOT of Farrell's crushed body. Something glimmers in the car's headlights near her outstretched arm. Camera ZOOMS in. We recognize one of her silver fish earrings, lying there on the dark pavement like a beached mackerel.
>
> CUT TO EXTERIOR. Mother's house. Night.

* * *

Jonathan did not know how long he had been sitting there in the driveway. The house was dark except for a light in the bedroom. He didn't know what he was doing here. He had been tempted to follow Farrell to the party and to—do what? Punch the guy out? Kidnap her? He hadn't known where he was heading until he was almost here. In the dim light of the car's interior he peered at his watch, surprised by how early it still was. Surprised that the night was still young when he felt so old and tired. And at the same time young—a small, very old, very tired child in need of comfort.

He opened the car door and got out. The next-door neighbor's dog barked as he walked across the lawn toward the house. At the door he hesitated, wondering whether he should ring the bell so as not to startle his mother or whether that might only wake her up. He knocked softly. When he didn't hear anything, he opened the door with his key. It was pitch-black in the entryway. He flicked on the light and kicked off his loafers. In his stocking feet he tiptoed down the hall and paused outside his mother's room. She was awake, lying in bed watching an old movie on television, her hands resting lightly on her breasts in her flimsy nightgown. In the moment before she sensed his presence, he caught a private glimpse of her that made him catch his breath. A glimpse of her as a woman, a self, apart from him. But in the next instant she looked up and smiled and was his mother again.

"Hi, Mom. What're you watching?" he asked, even though he had recognized the film at first glance.

"Strangers on a Train." She yawned and patted the empty side of the bed. "Join me?"

He was surprised that she didn't seem more surprised to see him. Almost as if she'd been expecting him. He padded across the room and stretched out on the other side of the king-size bed. "How you feeling?"

"Not bad, considering." She tugged her conversational-French grammar book out from underneath him and slid it under the bed. Shortly after the divorce she had begun planning a trip to Paris. A commercial came on and she muted the sound. "How 'bout yourself?"

"Okay, I guess. Considering." He rolled over, his back to her, and sighed into the pillow. She picked up his hand and gave it a maternal squeeze. "I'm sorry I behaved like such a jerk," he said. His voice sounded small and wobbly. "I don't know what my problem was. Is."

"There are plenty of other fish in the sea." She slipped her cool, soft hand underneath his T-shirt. *"Il y a beaucoup des autres poissons dans la mer."*

He flashed on a tight shot of Farrell's hand reaching up to unhook her dangly earrings and dropping them—*plink, plink*—onto the night table beside the professor's bed.

Outside it had begun to rain lightly. A gentle *rat-a-tat-tat* against the glass. He kept his eyes shut tight. His mother's feathery fingertips tickled as she traced the letters on his naked skin. He guessed the words aloud one by one. *Sad, mad, bad, dad, glad.* The soft touch and simple words were soothing—*hog, bog, dog, log, fog*—so, so soothing, like rain, like heartbeats. *Joy, toy, coy, boy.* Her fingers froze.

"It was a boy," she whispered. "You always wanted a brother."

"No, I didn't," he lied. "Not really."

She started to cry.

"Hey," he said. "Hey. It's not so bad." He patted her hand clumsily and handed her a Kleenex from the box on the night table.

"Look at us." She laughed and blew her nose. "Two real sad sacks, as your father used to say. It was one of his favorite expressions, remember?"

Jonathan nodded. On the television screen Bruno, the psychotic, had his hand down a sewer grate, straining and stretching to touch the cigarette lighter he had dropped. Close-up of the lighter with the crossed tennis rackets embossed in gold. The murder evidence. In college Jonathan had written a term paper on the crisscross imagery in *Strangers on a Train.* The professor had given him an A and said it was a thorough and "very mature" piece of work.

"You watching this?" his mother said.

He shook his head. "Not really."

"Then how about some canasta?" She tossed the used Kleenex into the trash basket beside the bed.

"Yeah, sure. Why not?" He picked up the remote and clicked off the television. "I'll get the cards."

He got up and walked through the dark house to the den. Next door the neighbor's dog was barking again. The cards were still out, sitting on the coffee table. He grabbed them and then made a quick detour to the kitchen, where he took a couple of beers from the refrigerator. He set the beers on the night table. His mother had put on a robe and smoothed out the bedspread. He handed her the double deck to shuffle. When he was little he used to love to watch his mother shuffle cards—quickly and gracefully, as if she were doing a magic trick. He practiced and practiced but never got to be much good. The barking next door had escalated into a frenzied, lovelorn howling. A canine aria of outraged loss. Jonathan leaped up, walked over to the open window, and yelled, "Quiet!"

For a moment there was a stunned silence. Then the dog started up again —a tentative whimper at first, then a yelp, then a full-fledged howl. Jonathan slammed the window shut and went back to the bed.

"You know"—his mother paused, cards in hand—"I still dream about Major sometimes."

"Really? So do I," he confessed. He had always felt a little stupid dreaming about a dog. "What do you dream?"

"I dream he's still alive." She handed him the deck.

"That's what I dream too," he said, and as he started to deal out the cards he suddenly had an odd sensation, as if he were a ventriloquist and that dog out there were his dummy, whimpering and howling in the night.

Martha Lacy Hall

THE APPLE-GREEN TRIUMPH

Before opening the car door, Lucia took a deep breath of the Louisiana night air. She was not unaware of its heaviness, its moistness, the smells of Lake Pontchartrain—salt, seaweed, water creatures, all mixed with the sounds produced by the wind slapping water against the seawall, soughing in the tops of tall pines against a black sky.

She pressed hard on the starter in the old Triumph. It ground, coughed, and was silent. "Oh, my God," she said and hit the steering wheel with her fist. If it wouldn't start, she would just have to have Everett paged at the New Orleans airport. Tell him to get on a Greyhound bus for Mississippi. He should have done that in the first place or flown into Jackson. "Start!" she growled and pressed again, and it did. She floored the accelerator, in neutral, and the engine roared underfoot, confident and, as always, a little arrogant for so small a tiger. The beam of the headlights crawled across the wall and the screened porch as she slowly backed out of the carport and turned toward the street.

"I'm out of my mind," she said aloud. "I'm just out of my ever-loving mind." She had begun talking to herself after Christopher died two years ago. They had had such a good time talking that when he was no longer there she just kept on talking. "I am my own best company," she sometimes said, picking figs or surveying herself at the full-length mirror, ready to go out. She slowed and looked at her watch under the corner streetlight. Ten o'clock.

"Seventy-five-year-old fool heading to New Orleans at ten o'clock at night." She braked, shifted the gear, and rounded the corner, leaving Lakeshore Drive. "A damn fool." The lights beamed across the spray-painted command on the wall of the high school gym: LADY OF MERCY STOMP HOLY GHOST FRIDAY NIGHT!

Scarcely aware of thunder to the south, she drove slowly, peering intently through her glasses and the flat little windshield. She had decided not to drive at night more than a year ago, and she felt that her dear old car might be better able to make it across the 26-mile causeway than she was. "Old cars can be overhauled." As this one had been recently. A big car rushed up to an intersection and slammed to a stop. Startled, she swore.

"Just tell me one thing good about being old. Just one thing!" She simply hadn't felt this way as long as she had Chris. Any woman who claimed she didn't need a strong man didn't know what she was talking about. She drove on toward the causeway, through a tunnel of night-darkened oaks between the streetlights of Ste. Marie, Louisiana. "I just have to do it," she said, tears in her voice. Everett hadn't changed a bit. She hadn't seen him for nearly ten years and never expected him to fly down for Ann's services. And what did he do but call her at nine o'clock tonight out of the blue, from the New Orleans airport.

"Can you pick me up?" he said, like he was down at the Ste. Marie bus depot and it was 20 years ago.

"Do you know how old I am?" she wanted to scream at him.

"Brat. Sixty-year-old brat." He hadn't come for the other funerals—Dora's, Tom's, Margaret's. Not since their parents'. Well, Ann was his twin. Maybe there still was something special there, dormant, come to life at the incident of death. And some burst of confidence and energy had made her say, "I'll pick you up. Just sit tight." The call had given her an illusion of vigor, the big sister again, always there, ready. She had to do it.

When she thought of Ann, she began to cry and had to pull over to the curb and hold her face in a handful of tissues. "I thought I was through crying," she sobbed. "Ann, Ann! I could kill you for leaving me high and dry like this." Then she began to laugh at what she'd said. Ann would have laughed. She took another tissue from the box on the dash and cleaned her glasses and blew her nose. As she drove back onto the wide highway, wind gusts swept overland from the lake, bringing the first raindrops.

"Don't rain! Don't rain!"

By the time she approached the Causeway she was in a downpour, windshield wipers working fast and noisily. She pulled up to the toll booth and handed the man a dollar. Reflected lights blurred on the choppy water of Lake Pontchartrain. Red lights and white lights nearby, and far ahead a smoldering luminescence in the low, heavy clouds over New Orleans.

"Bad night to be headin' for Sin City," the man said.

"Mission of mercy," said Lucia, and moved forward, chin high.

Chris's apple-green Triumph was in fine shape for its age. Duffy Peek had just been all over it, spent three days like he and Chris used to do together. She loosened her tight grip on the steering wheel, arthritis grinding out its pain in knobby knuckles, hurting like the devil. For that matter it hurt in her shoulders, neck, back. "Just a dilapidated old bag of bones."

But she could quickly call up one of those lovely healing memories of Chris's voice: "Cut that out, you beautiful babe. You're in great shape, and you look like a million dollars," and she saw that wide smile, white teeth, tanned face. Fine old face. The car seemed more cozy and safe while rain pounded the canvas top, windshield, and danced on the hood.

Then Ann pushed back into Lucia's thoughts. Ann and Everett

had been her real-live dolls. She was 15 when they were born, she was the eldest of six, the tallest, the child-lovingest, the chauffeur, Mother pro tem, Daddy called her. She adored the twins and simply took them over, rocked two cribs at once, changed diapers, warmed bottles, old-fashioned bottles with rubber nipples that Everett learned to pull off in his crib. Lucia carried them around, baby legs straddling both her hips. She dressed them in their little matching clothes for Myrt to roll them down to the Methodist Church corner in their double stroller, where all the nurses gathered in the afternoons with their charges, little white children fresh from their bathtubs. Ann became her love, and they had remained close for the rest of Ann's life.

"I never could believe she grew up. How did she get to be 60 years old? She barely made that. Why did she have to die before me? Emphysema, like the others. And Daddy. Ann didn't even smoke." Lucia had spent the last months going back and forth between Ste. Marie and Sweet Bay, sitting with Ann at home or in the hospital, at whichever place Ann lay propped up, crowding words between breaths, oxygen tank nearby, plastic tubes in her nostrils. They reviewed their whole lives. "And I made you my executor!" Lucia said, accusingly, and they laughed like fools, as they always had, no matter how bad off Ann was. No matter how hard it was for Lucia. Almost to the end. They weren't together when she died in her sleep.

"I can't believe things are ending this way. I've buried all of them. All but Everett. God knows he'd better outlive me. I'm sick of sitting on the edges of graves in that plot." She would talk to Everett about that, about his place now. Thank God for him. A good dependable younger family member. "Perhaps he will come back home with me for a few days, and we can relax, visit, talk about the future. . . ." The wind and rain came on hard from the lake, almost blindingly. She couldn't possibly drive the minimum speed. Traffic was blessedly light.

An enormous white semi was overtaking the green Triumph,

fast. "Slow down, idiot." How could he see to drive that fast? The white hulk rumbled past, rocking the small car fearsomely.

She remembered the day Chris drove it into her driveway, a tiny motor-roaring thing, the top down, unfolded his long legs, and rose from the brown leather seat. "Are you Mrs. Collins?" he said, and his smile was as arresting as his apple-green car.

"I am," said Lucia, removing her gardening gloves and dropping the bamboo rake on the leaf pile. She took hasty note of his appearance, thatch of white hair, rumpled by the wind, well-tailored plaid shirt, good suitably faded jeans, and white deck shoes. He had a newspaper under his arm. He was the boater who had called in answer to her ad.

"My name is Neilson, Chris Neilson. I called about your ad. Let's see, you have a lantern, Coleman stove, rope, fishing tackle. Got an anchor?"

"That and more." She smiled politely.

"May I see them?"

"Certainly. They're right back here in the storeroom. I'll get the key." She fetched the key off the kitchen hook, and Chris Neilson followed her to the dark green door off the carport. She switched on the light. "I have a 50-horsepower motor, some seats, lifepreservers, quite a few things. Go in and look them over."

He stayed in the storeroom awhile. She could tell what he was examining by the familiar sounds of wood, metal, canvas. When he stepped out, he smiled again and said, "You all lost interest in boating?"

"My husband died several years ago, and I'm just now getting rid of some of his things."

"I know how that is. Been through it. I'm going to try living on my boat."

"I see. Well, do you see anything you need in there?"

"I surely do. Are those two new deck chairs for sale? I could use them. And the lantern I could use. How about the radio?"

"Any of it or all of it." She reached in her shirt pocket and handed him a typewritten list with prices.

"Good," he said. "Tell you what. I live in New Orleans, but I'll be back in a pickup this afternoon late if that's okay."

"That's fine. I'll be here."

He smiled again and slid into the car.

"You have a—an interesting car. I don't believe I ever saw a sports car that color."

"Probably not. I had this one painted. Gaudy, isn't it?"

"It's bright . . . spring-like," she laughed like he wasn't a stranger. She was the stranger.

After he left, she picked up her rake and poked it around in the leaves. What an interesting man. She hadn't noticed an "interesting man" since Henry died. She embarrassed herself.

Lucia realized she was handling the car well despite everything. She felt a ripple of pride in her spine. The Triumph was so small, not even comfortable, really, but she couldn't part with the crazy little thing. First she sold Chris's pickup, then finally she sold her sedan. Sentiment. What made men love their cars so? She had loved the man, and the car was the most tangible thing she had left of him. "Oh, Chris." She was married to Chris for eight years —a fling and a lark for an old couple. Old in birthdays. She couldn't remember either of them being sick for a day together. "It was more than a fling and a lark."

"You look like a smart woman. What do you do?" he said later when he dropped by with no excuse.

Confronted with such a question, she blurted, "I work like a dog in this house and yard. I make fig and mayhaw preserves and green tomato pickles. I read a couple of books a week. I 'do' book reviews." She stopped, aghast at her ready biography to a stranger. That was the beginning. He was interested.

Lucia loosened her hurting hands. "What we did was laugh and talk." And live a little. A lot. Like she had not thought possible. For eight years. Sometimes she still found it hard to believe that they had had the good fortune to find each other. "Right there in your own backyard," he would say and put his arms around her.

One night eating their own catch on the deck of his boat, rocking ever so gently on the Tchefuncte River, he said, "Marry me and come live on my boat."

"Marry you! You want to get legally hitched to a 65-year-old crone?" It was as good as "Yes."

"I want your money."

"My dowry consists of my Medicare."

"I'll accept that." More seriously, "So we're 65 years old. Let's see how much fun we can have."

So they were married. By a New Orleans judge they both knew. They lived in her house on the lake, but she became a boat person, too. It was an unruffled transition, becoming a married woman again. Chris was an affectionate man. To her naïve surprise, he was a tender and passionate lover, and, to her greater surprise, her pleasure with him was more intense than she had ever known. "You're some woman," Chris would say. And "Back from the dead!" That was lagniappe.

They drove to New Orleans for Saints games at the Superdome and for shows at the Saenger. They dined with friends at home, in the city, and in restaurants around the lake. They cooked on the grill, and they played gin and sipped wine in the evening.

Occasionally Chris would have an extra evening drink or two, on the boat anchored a mile or so from the north shore. He would tell her ribald stories and sing noisily from an endless repertoire of war songs, using his glass for a baton.

Creeping along in the night through wind and rain over Lake Pontchartrain, Lucia shook her head remembering Chris singing one night, "Bless em all! Bless em all! The long and the short and the tall! There'll be no promotions this side of the ocean. So cheer up, my lads, Fuckem all!"

"Hush up, Chris! Your voice carries across this water like you have a microphone." She was interrupted by a baritone from a winking light a quarter mile farther out. "Fuckem all! Fuckem all!

The long and the short. . . ." And then they could all hear the laughter bounce over the light chop and under the sparkling stars in a blue-black sky.

Lucia pulled into a turnaround area and stopped the car. She rested her head on the steering wheel. "It won't be long, now. I'm doing fine. But thank the Lord Everett can take the wheel for the two hours to Mississippi." Their aged cousins, sisters, both in their late eighties, were putting them up. "What a treat! What a treat!" Cousin May had chirped over the phone, "Having you children with us again." Then she caught herself. "Oh my dear, I'm forgetting myself. We are all in grief for dear little Ann. She was like a sister to me." And Lucia knew Cousin May was getting Ann mixed up with their mother Ann.

Lucia lifted her head. The last day of his life Chris had said to her, "You're a youthful handsome woman, Lucia. I love that thick white hair and those gorgeous legs."

"You're crazy," Lucia had said, pinching his bottom as he walked past her toward the stern. A few moments later he had a heart attack and without a word fell overboard. She went down after him with lifepreservers, but he was dead, his white hair washing back and forth like anemones between his fishing line and the stern.

She put the Triumph in drive and moved out behind a state trooper. "Hallelujah, I've got me an escort!" But the white car wove away at high speed and was lost to her. "Well. I'm on my own again." The rain had slowed to a drizzle when she turned toward the airport. The speeding cars and trucks on the six-lane interstate unnerved her, and she addressed her maker reverently each time she moved farther left, lane by lane. "Christ," she murmured when she spied the metal sign New Orleans International Airport that directed traffic to a new overpass she didn't know about. Her heart in her mouth, she managed to move back to the far-right lane. And the Triumph roared up the ramp and back over the traffic she had just left. Not daring to feel giddy, she found herself traveling parallel to jet runways. Strobelights marked the airport drive.

"That keeps those huge things from thinking this is another runway." Then a sign appeared announcing a radio station on which she could be brought into a short-term parking area. She was able to park on the first level. "I made it on instruments," she gasped, as she took the keys from the car. She was extremely stiff and in pain when she stood beside her car. "I'm too old for this." Two teen-aged boys looked backward at the old car, its classic body glittering in a coat of raindrops under the endless rows of fluorescent tubes. They grinned but looked concerned as they saw her effort to straighten her back and walk toward the elevator.

"I've never been in here unescorted."

"I beg your pardon?" said a young woman.

"Nothing. Nothing. Just talking to myself. Do it all the time." She wanted to get to a rest room.

Inside she began walking and scanning the crowd, looking for her tall younger brother. She was surrounded by a shifting sea of people speaking Spanish, French, Indian, and no telling what else, all under the nasal drone of the P.A. speaker. Her eyes, tired, swept over young, old, babies, nuns, sailors, people in wheelchairs, obese men and women waddling to and from the concourses. One very fat gray-haired man was bearing down on her, looking into her eyes, smiling. The smile caught her eye. Only that—that crooked half-smile.

"Everett?"

"What's the matter, Lucia? Don't you know me?" He was carrying a dark blue suit bag.

"Everett! I didn't!" She closed her mouth with effort. "Everett," she said again.

He leaned forward and laid his cheek against hers briefly. "I reckon I have put on a little weight since you saw me last."

"Yes. Yes. I'm glad to see you, Everett. It's good you could come."

"I hate to put you out. Hope you didn't have any trouble. Was the weather good? I've been in here so long, I don't know what it's doing outside."

"The weather? Oh, yes, well it rained a little. Nothing uh . . . let's go in here and order a cup of coffee or a Coke, maybe. I need to find a rest room. Are you hungry?"

"No. I just had a couple of hamburgers and a malt. I'm ready to roll. Ready to hit that Interstate. Get on up to Cousin May and them's for some shuteye. I've been here over three hours."

"Well, I need something." And Lucia steered them into a coffee shop. She went ahead and ordered coffee and a ham sandwich before going to a rest room.

"Oh, I guess I'll have one, too," said Everett. "And an order of fries. Traveling makes me hungry." Bulk made sitting difficult for him. "Have to fly first class. More room to spread out, you know."

"Excuse me, Everett," she murmured. "I'll be right back." She got up painfully.

"Why you're all crippled up!" He seemed surprised.

Lucia pressed her lips together and walked to the rest room. Inside a booth she sat down and began to laugh and cry. "This is hysterics. What am I going to do? I'm too tired to drive on. My God, he won't fit into the car."

"Is anything wrong?" came a voice from the next booth. "Do you need help?"

"No. Oh, no. Thank you. I just talk to myself. Sometimes what I say is funny, so I laugh. . . ."

Silence.

The floodgates of Lucia's bladder opened, and for a moment she reveled in the greatest relief she had felt in days. She didn't say anything more aloud, but as she went out she patted her white bangs at the mirror and took a quick and satisfying look at her figure.

Everett was waiting for her. "I hate to see you so crippled up."

"Everett, what do you weigh, honey?"

"Three-twenty-five, right now." Then he gave one of his famous ha-ha-has. "Haven't you ever seen a fat man, Lucia?"

"It's just that I've never seen a 325-pound man in this family. You know, we all have tended to be slim. Slender." She wished she hadn't asked his weight.

"Well, you've seen one now," he said, steadying himself with the chair beside him. "These sure are little bitty old chairs."

Lucia laughed. They ate their sandwiches. "We may have a problem, Everett," she said, blotting the corners of her mouth with the stiff paper napkin.

"What's that?"

"Well, I drive a very small car. I'm just not perfectly sure you can get comfortable, completely comfortable. . . . I was counting on you to drive us home. . . ." She wanted to cry.

"You haven't gone and bought one of those little bitty old Jap cars have you?"

"No. No. Actually it's English. Belonged to my husband . . . it's small. . . ." Her voice trailed off.

"Oh-oh." Everett's voice boomed, "I drive a Cadillac. Have to have a heavy car. Just kills my legs and back to ride in one of. . . ."

"I really was counting on your driving. I'm not crazy about driving at night."

"Looks like you made it over here all right."

"Yes. Well, it wasn't easy."

"If I'd felt like driving, I'd have driven myself down in my Cadillac. We'll do okay. You got a pillow in it so I can stretch out?"

Chris's voice loomed in her ear. "Lucia, honey, you're being a fool. Tell that sonofabitch to get a taxi to a hotel."

Everett's face blanched when he saw the apple-green Triumph. "Lucia! Why in hell is an old lady like you driving this thing?"

Lucia was indignant. "Look, Everett, try to squeeze in. If you can't get in, we'll have to get you a room across the Airline at the Hilton. This happens to be the only car I have."

He put his bag in the small trunk, muttering, "Ruining my good clothes," and stuffed himself into the little bucket seat. "Goddamn, Lucia. You'll have to bury me too when we get home. I still say 'home' even though the house is gone. And everybody is gone. Everybody but us. I can't believe Ann is gone. I kept thinking I'd come down to see her. We were close. A long time ago. Did she suffer much?"

"She suffered plenty. But she died peacefully."

"I'm glad to hear she went out easy." Then Everett began to wheeze. "I've got it too. We got it from Daddy. I quit smoking two years ago. Don't drink a drop," he added.

Lucia turned toward Baton Rouge.

"Here now. We're not going to Baton Rouge, are we?"

"Of course not. We turn north on I-55." Lucia hurt all over. She was getting a headache, and her eyes were too tired to cry. "Lord give me strength. What a fool I am."

"How's that?" Everett shouted over the engine.

She shook her head.

Everett tried to shift his bulk, but it was like trying to move a grapefruit in a demitasse spoon. "My circulation is going. In my legs," he hollered. He didn't have to shout.

"Mercy, Everett. Let me get out of this heavy traffic, and I'll stop every little while and let you get out and walk a bit."

But he grunted negatively, and she knew it was because it wasn't worth it to him trying to get out and back in. She turned north off the spillway interstate and drove in silence all the way to Lake Marapas. "Let's stop at Heidenreidt's and get another cup of coffee. You can walk around."

"Okay, Lucia."

She parked the car near the door of the seafood restaurant which had been there as long as she could remember. "Make you nostalgic?"

"Yeah," said Everett, managing to extricate himself from the passenger seat. Lucia felt a terrible sadness over this baby brother she had once carried about like a ragdoll, who came home tall and thin and hurt from the long battle for the hills of South Korea and began his own battles in civilian life. A succession of jobs, two failed marriages, the loss of a young child. Poor boy.

In the old restaurant on the shore of Marapas, Everett sat on a stool and ordered a dozen raw oysters. "Don't you want some, Lucia? My treat."

"No thank you, Everett."

"Remember how Daddy used to stop here on his way home from New Orleans and pick up a gallon of oysters? He and Mama would get in the kitchen and meal 'em up and season 'em and fry 'em in that big black iron skillet? Drain 'em on brown paper? Remember that big old white platter of Mama's? Heaped up, hot and crisp. Whooee!" He began dipping crackers in catsup and horseradish while an old black man shucked the oysters. "Ya'll got any boiled crawfish?" he asked the sleepy waitress.

"Yeah. Want some?"

"Everett," said Lucia, "I'm afraid you'll be sick. And we need to be on our way pretty soon."

"Okay. Lord Jesus, I hate to think of stuffing myself back into that little bitty old car. How come you're driving that thing, hon? Now tell me the truth. You having a hard time, Lucia?"

"I've got some problems, Everett, but they don't have anything to do with my car or money. It was my husband's car, and I chose to keep it. Ordinarily, I just use a car to go to the post office and the A&P."

"Well, you made a mistake. You ought to get yourself a good heavy sedan."

"I'm sorry you're uncomfortable."

"I'm not complaining. I just hate to see you in such reduced circumstances."

"My circumstances are not reduced."

Everett dispatched a baker's dozen large raw oysters, lifting each, dipped red in the catsup mixture, to his mouth, and uttering a sound of appreciation of the taste.

They drove a long time on I-55 without talking. As they passed the Tangipahoa exit he said, "Was Ann right with her maker?"

"I beg your pardon?"

"Was she saved? Was she born again?"

"What in the hell are you talking about, Everett?"

"Don't blaspheme. She never was religious, Lucia. I wasn't either. Way back there. I'm just asking if you think my sister got right with the Lord."

Lucia was livid. "Yes," she said calmly, "I'm sure she and the Lord were on good terms."

"Well, I'm glad to hear it. After my last divorce I turned myself over completely to Jesus Christ, and I faithfully support Him."

"What church are you a member of? I know your last wife was Catholic."

"Don't belong to any. That is church house. I support the Lord's work through several television ministries. They're saving souls like all get-out all over the world. Did you ever think about how many souls are in hell, went there before the television came along and took the gospel to the farthest corner of the planet? Some people are going to rot in hell for persecuting these dedicated servants of the Lord who pack food to all those starving little boogers in Africa and all."

Lucia took her eyes off the highway for a split second to look at her brother. "You wouldn't possibly be including Louisiana's own, would you?"

"Most particularly. The Lord has simply put that poor fellow through a baptism of fire with Satan. The man's coming back. Just listen to him on the TV."

"I ran across him one time looking for a Saints game." They crossed the state line. "You're back in Mississippi, Everett." Lucia tried to help her backache by pressing harder against the back of her seat. Since they had turned onto I-55 they had both been aware consciously or unconsciously that they were back in the world they knew best, the marshland above New Orleans, that edge of Louisiana that slid toward the state line, into the slow gentle sweep of low hills that meant Mississippi. Oh, it was different. A few miles made all the difference in the world.

"Yeah," he said. "I do appreciate your holding Ann's body till I could get here for the funeral."

"Body? I don't think you understand, Everett."

"Don't understand what?"

"This is to be a memorial service at the church. Ann's remains were cremated."

"Cremated! Cremated! Who is responsible for that?"

Rain was falling again. Lucia turned on the wipers. "It was Ann's wish."

"So! She wasn't saved! Of all the unholy, pagan things to do to my sister. You mean she's already . . . already burnt up?"

"Her remains are ashes."

"Well, I'll be goddamned."

"Now, who's blaspheming?"

"Why have I gone to all this trouble and expense and discomfort coming all the way down here from West Virginia? Huh? Tell me that?"

There just wasn't room in the little car for him to blow up. "I assumed you wanted to attend your twin sister's memorial services. We'll have an interment of the ashes in the plot. What's the difference?"

"Difference! I thought I was going to get to see her. See how she looked."

"I'm sorry you feel . . . cheated." Lucia's head was splitting. Her eyes were cloudy, and she cursed herself for where she was and wept inside for her baby sister and for Everett, who in no way resembled the boy or the man she remembered. She still had miles to travel. It must be nearly two o'clock. "What's a 75-year-old fool doing on a highway this time of night. Morning."

"How's that?"

"Nothing, Everett. Just talking to myself."

"How long you been doing that?"

"Doing what?"

"Talking to yourself."

"A good while now. It was a deliberate decision. To talk to myself, I mean."

"For crying out loud. Are you bonkers?"

When Lucia saw Aunt May's porch light she moaned softly with relief.

"Listen, Lucia. I appreciate what you did—driving to New Orleans to get me. But I'll get a ride to Jackson and get a plane out of there to Charleston. Tomorrow afternoon, I guess. Late. Whenever this is all over—whatever it is we're having. Whatever you're having. Hell, I don't care. I mean. . . ."

Lucia opened her door. The dash light cast a weak glow in the small space of the car. Her fingers held the cool metal of the handle as she searched Everett's profile, softened by age and shadow. Her only family, now. And she his. She smiled and laid her hand on his arm. "I understand. I know you'll be more comfortable in a big car. Wish I'd had a Cadillac just for tonight. Because I love you, Everett. I mean that."

"I know."

They walked through the fragrant, dewy grass toward Aunt May's porch.

In Aunt May's guest room, Lucia lay in the big four-poster she had first slept in and fallen out of before she could walk. Now, three quarters of a century later she did her deep-breathing exercise to relax. Deep, deep till her lower ribs bowed upward. The old house was quiet in the predawn darkness. Listening, remembering, as old houses do. Lucia let out a long breath. Such profound silence seemed to hold out a mystical beckoning. It wasn't the first time she had quite calmly thought she might die in her sleep. She inhaled.

The night after Chris died she had gone to bed in a friend's guest room, believing the enormous weight of sorrow would stop her heart as she slept. She had carefully arranged her arms on the covers so she would not be in disarray when they found her in the morning. But she had waked up in daylight, grateful to be alive and able to meet the day.

She exhaled and whispered to the dark room, "No. Twenty-four hours from now I'll be sound asleep in my own bed." The mattress pressed up against her as her body grew heavier, ever heavier, then moved weightlessly into the warm engulfing arms of sleep.

Sylvia A. Watanabe

TALKING TO THE DEAD

We spoke of her in whispers as Aunty Talking to the Dead, the half-Hawaiian kahuna lady. But whenever there was a death in the village, she was the first to be sent for—the priest came second. For it was she who understood the wholeness of things—the significance of directions and colors. Prayers to appease the hungry ghosts. Elixirs for grief. Most times, she'd be out on her front porch, already waiting—her boy, Clinton, standing behind with her basket of spells—when the messenger arrived. People said she could smell a death from clear on the other side of the island, even as the dying person breathed his last. And if she fixed her eyes on you and named a day, you were already as good as six feet under.

I went to work as her apprentice when I was eighteen. That was in '48—the year Clinton graduated from mortician school on the G.I. Bill. It was the talk for weeks—how he returned to open the Paradise Mortuary in the very heart of the village and brought the scientific spirit of free enterprise to the doorstep of the hereafter. I remember the advertisements for the Grand Opening—promising to modernize the funeral trade with Lifelike Artistic Techniques and Stringent Standards of Sanitation. The old woman, who had waited out the war for her son's return, stoically took his defection in stride and began looking for someone else to help out with her business.

At the time, I didn't have many prospects—more schooling didn't interest me, and my mother's attempts at marrying me off inevitably failed when I stood to shake hands with a prospective bridegroom and ended up towering a foot above him. "It's bad enough she has the face of a horse," I heard one of them complain.

My mother dressed me in navy blue, on the theory that dark colors make everything look smaller: "Yuri, sit down," she'd hiss, tugging at my skirt as the decisive moment approached. I'd nod, sip my tea, smile through the introductions and small talk, till the time came for sealing the bargain with handshakes all around. Then, nothing on earth could keep me from getting to my feet. The go-between finally suggested that I consider taking up a trade. "After all, marriage isn't for everyone," she said. My mother said that that was a fact which remained to be proven, but meanwhile, it wouldn't hurt if I took in sewing or learned to cut hair. I made up my mind to apprentice myself to Aunty Talking to the Dead.

* * *

The old woman's house was on the hill behind the village, just off the road to Chicken Fight Camp. She lived in an old plantation worker's bungalow with peeling green and white paint and a large, well-tended garden out front—mostly of flowering bushes and strong-smelling herbs.

"Aren't you a big one," a voice behind me said.

I started, then turned. It was the first time I had ever seen the old woman up close.

"Hello, uh, Mrs., Mrs., Dead," I stammered.

She was little—way under five feet—and wrinkled, and everything about her seemed the same color—her skin, her lips, her dress—everything just a slightly different shade of the same brown-grey, except her hair, which was absolutely white, and her tiny eyes, which glinted like metal. For a minute, those eyes looked me up and down.

"Here," she said finally, thrusting an empty rice sack into my hands. "For collecting salt." And she started down the road to the beach.

* * *

In the next few months, we walked every inch of the hills and beaches around the village.

"This is *a'ali'i* to bring sleep—it must be dried in the shade on a hot day." Aunty was always three steps ahead, chanting, while I struggled behind, laden with strips of bark and leafy twigs, my head buzzing with names.

"This is *awa* for every kind of grief, and *uhaloa* with the deep roots—if you are like that, death cannot easily take you." Her voice came from the stones, the trees, and the earth.

"This is where you gather salt to preserve a corpse," I hear her still. "This is where you cut to insert the salt," her words have marked the places on my body, one by one.

* * *

That whole first year, not a single day passed when I didn't think of quitting. I tried to figure out a way of moving back home without making it seem like I was admitting anything.

"You know what people are saying, don't you?" my mother said, lifting the lid of the bamboo steamer and setting a tray of freshly-steamed meat buns on the already-crowded table before me. It was one of my few visits home since my apprenticeship—though I'd never been more than a couple of miles away—and she had stayed up the whole night before, cooking. She'd prepared a canned ham with yellow sweet potatoes, wing beans with pork, sweet and sour mustard cabbage, fresh raw yellow-fin, pickled egg plant, and rice with red beans. I had not seen so much food since the night she'd tried to persuade her younger brother, my Uncle Mongoose, not to volunteer for the army. He'd gone anyway, and on the last day of training, just before he was shipped to Italy, he shot himself in the head when he was cleaning his gun. "I always knew that boy would come to no good," was all Mama said when she heard the news.

"What do you mean you can't eat another bite," she fussed now. "Look at you, nothing but a bag of bones."

I allowed myself to be persuaded to another helping, though I'd lost my appetite.

The truth was, there didn't seem to be much of a future in my apprenticeship. In eleven and a half months, I had memorized most of the minor rituals of mourning and learned to identify a couple of dozen herbs and all their medicinal uses, but I had not seen—much less gotten to practice on—a single honest-to-goodness corpse.

"People live longer these days," Aunty claimed.

But I knew it was because everyone—even from villages across the bay had begun taking their business to the Paradise Mortuary. The single event which had established Clinton's monopoly once and for all had been the untimely death of old Mrs. Pomadour, the plantation owner's mother-in-law, who'd choked on a fishbone during a fundraising luncheon of the Famine Relief Society. Clinton had been chosen to be in charge of the funeral. He'd taken to wearing three-piece suits—even during the humid Kona season—as a symbol of his new respectability, and had recently been nominated as a Republican candidate to run for the village council.

"So, what are people saying, Mama," I asked, finally pushing my plate away.

This was the cue she had been waiting for. "They're saying that That Woman has gotten herself a new donkey," she paused dramatically.

I began remembering things about being in my mother's house. The navy blue dresses. The humiliating weekly tea ceremony lessons at the Buddhist Temple.

"Give up this foolishness," she wheedled. "Mrs. Koyama tells me the Barber Shop Lady is looking for help."

"I think I'll stay right where I am," I said.

My mother drew herself up. "Here, have another meat bun," she said, jabbing one through the center with her serving fork and lifting it onto my plate.

* * *

A few weeks later, Aunty and I were called just outside the village to perform a laying-out. It was early afternoon when Sheriff Kanoi came by to tell us that the body of Mustard Hayashi, the eldest of the Hayashi boys, had just been pulled from an irrigation ditch by a team of field workers. He had apparently fallen in the night before, stone drunk, on his way home from Hula Rose's Dance Emporium.

I began hurrying around, assembling Aunty's tools and bottles of potions, and checking that everything was in working order, but the old woman didn't turn a hair; she just sat calmly rocking back and forth and puffing on her skinny, long-stemmed pipe.

"Yuri, you stop that rattling around back there!" she snapped, then turned to the Sheriff. "My son Clinton could probably handle this. Why don't you ask him?"

Sheriff Kanoi hesitated. "This looks like a tough case that's going to need some real expertise."

"Mmmm." The old woman stopped rocking. "It's true, it was a bad death," she mused.

"Very bad," the Sheriff agreed.

"The spirit is going to require some talking to."

"Besides, the family asked special for you," he said.

No doubt because they didn't have any other choice, I thought. That morning, I'd run into Chinky Malloy, the assistant mortician at the Paradise, so I happened to know that Clinton was at a morticians' conference in the city and wouldn't be back for several days. But I didn't say a word.

* * *

Mustard's remains had been laid out on a green Formica table in the kitchen. It was the only room in the house with a door that faced north. Aunty claimed that you should always choose a north-facing room for a laying-out so the spirit could find its way home to the land of the dead without getting lost.

Mustard's mother was leaning over his corpse, wailing, and her husband stood behind her, looking white-faced, and absently patting her on the back. The tiny kitchen was jammed with sobbing, nose-blowing relatives and neighbors. The air was thick with the smells of grief—perspiration, ladies' cologne, last night's cooking, and the faintest whiff of putrefying flesh. Aunty gripped me by the wrist and pushed her way to the front. The air pressed close—like someone's hot, wet breath on my face. My head reeled, and the room broke apart into dots of color. From far away I heard somebody say, "It's Aunty Talking to the Dead."

"Make room, make room," another voice called.

I looked down at Mustard, lying on the table in front of me—his eyes half-open in that swollen, purple face. The smell was much stronger close up, and there were flies everywhere.

"We're going to have to get rid of some of this bloat," Aunty said, thrusting a metal object into my hand.

People were leaving the room.

She went around to the other side of the table. "I'll start here," she said. "You work over there. Do just like I told you."

I nodded. This was the long-awaited moment. My moment. But it was already the beginning of the end. My knees buckled and everything went dark.

* * *

Aunty performed the laying-out alone and never mentioned the episode again. But it was the talk of the village for weeks—how

Yuri Shimabukuro, assistant to Aunty Talking to the Dead, passed out under the Hayashis' kitchen table and had to be tended by the grief-stricken mother of the dead boy.

My mother took to catching the bus to the plantation store three villages away whenever she needed to stock up on necessaries. "You're my daughter—how could I *not* be on your side?" was the way she put it, but the air buzzed with her unspoken recriminations. And whenever I went into the village, I was aware of the sly laughter behind my back, and Chinky Malloy smirking at me from behind the shutters of the Paradise Mortuary.

"She's giving the business a bad name," Clinton said, carefully removing his jacket and draping it across the back of the rickety wooden chair. He dusted the seat, looked at his hand with distaste before wiping it off on his handkerchief, then drew up the legs of his trousers, and sat.

Aunty picked up her pipe from the smoking tray next to her rocker and filled the tiny brass bowl from a pouch of Bull Durham. "I'm glad you found time to drop by," she said. "You still going out with that skinny white girl?"

"You mean Marsha?" Clinton sounded defensive. "Sure, I see her sometimes. But I didn't come here to talk about that." He glanced over at where I was sitting on the sofa. "You think we could have some privacy?"

Aunty lit her pipe and puffed. "There's nobody here but us. . . . Yuri's my right hand. Couldn't do without her."

"The Hayashis probably have their own opinion about that."

Aunty waved her hand in dismissal. "There's no pleasing some people. Yuri's just young; she'll learn." She reached over and patted me on the knee, then looked him straight in the face. "Like we all did."

Clinton turned red. "Damn it, Mama! You're making yourself a laughingstock!" His voice became soft, persuasive. "Look, you've worked hard all your life, but now, I've got my business—it'll be a while before I'm really on my feet—but you don't have to do this," he gestured around the room. "I'll help you out. You'll see. I'm only thinking about you."

"About the election to village council, you mean!" I burst out.

Aunty was unperturbed. "You considering going into politics, son?"

"Mama, wake up!" Clinton hollered, like he'd wanted to all along. "The old spirits have had it. We're part of progress now, and the world is going to roll right over us and keep on rolling, unless we get out there and grab our share."

His words rained down like stones, shattering the air around us.

For a long time after he left, Aunty sat in her rocking chair next to the window, rocking and smoking, without saying a word, just rocking and smoking, as the afternoon shadows flickered beneath the trees and turned to night.

Then, she began to sing—quietly, at first, but very sure. She sang the naming chants and the healing chants. She sang the stones, and trees, and stars back into their rightful places. Louder and louder she sang—making whole what had been broken.

* * *

Everything changed for me after Clinton's visit. I stopped going into the village and began spending all my time with Aunty Talking to the Dead. I followed her everywhere, carried her loads without complaint, memorized remedies and mixed potions. I wanted to know what *she* knew; I wanted to make what had happened at the Hayashis' go away. Not just in other people's minds. Not just because I'd become a laughingstock, like Clinton said. But because I knew that I *had* to redeem myself for that one thing, or my moment—the single instant of glory for which I had lived my entire life—would be snatched beyond my reach forever.

Meanwhile, there were other layings-out. The kitemaker who hung himself. The crippled boy from Chicken Fight Camp. The Vagrant. The Blindman. The Blindman's dog.

"Do like I told you," Aunty would say before each one. Then, "Give it time," when it was done.

* * *

But it was like living the same nightmare over and over—just one look at a body and I was done for. For twenty-five years, people in the village joked about my "indisposition." Last year, when my mother died, her funeral was held at the Paradise Mortuary. I stood outside on the cement walk for a long time, but never made it through the door. Little by little, I had given up hope that my moment would ever arrive.

Then, one week ago, Aunty caught a chill after spending all morning out in the rain, gathering *awa* from the garden. The chill developed into a fever, and for the first time since I'd known her, she took to her bed. I nursed her with the remedies she'd taught me—sweat baths; eucalyptus steam; tea made from *ko'oko'olau*—but the fever worsened. Her breathing became labored, and she grew weaker. My few hours of sleep were filled with bad dreams. In desperation, aware of my betrayal, I finally walked to a house up the road and telephoned for an ambulance.

"I'm sorry, Aunty," I kept saying, as the flashing red light swept across the porch. The attendants had her on a stretcher and were carrying her out the front door.

She reached up and grasped my arm, her grip still strong. "You'll do okay, Yuri," the old woman whispered hoarsely, and squeezed. "Clinton used to get so scared, he messed his pants." She chuckled, then began to cough. One of the attendants put an oxygen mask over her face. "Hush," he said. "There'll be plenty of time for talking later."

* * *

The day of Aunty's wake, workmen were repaving the front walk and had blocked off the main entrance to the Paradise Mortuary. They had dug up the old concrete tiles and carted them away. They'd left a mound of gravel on the grass, stacked some bags of concrete next to it, and covered them with black tarps. There was an empty wheelbarrow parked on the other side of the gravel mound. The entire front lawn was roped off and a sign put up which said, "Please use the back entrance. We are making improvements in Paradise. The Management."

My stomach was beginning to play tricks, and I was feeling a little dizzy. The old panic was mingled with an uneasiness which had not left me ever since I had decided to call the ambulance. I kept thinking maybe I shouldn't have called it since she had gone and died anyway. Or maybe I should have called it sooner. I almost turned back, but I thought of what Aunty had told me about Clinton and pressed ahead. Numbly, I followed the two women in front of me through the garden along the side of the building, around to the back.

"So, old Aunty Talking to the Dead has finally passed on," one of them, whom I recognized as the Dancing School Teacher, said. She was with Pearlie Mukai, an old classmate of mine from high school. Pearlie had gone years ago to live in the city, but still returned to the village to visit her mother.

I was having difficulty seeing—it was getting dark, and my head was spinning so.

"How old do you suppose she was?" Pearlie asked.

"Gosh, even when we were kids it seemed like she was at least a hundred."

" 'The Undead,' my brother used to call her."

Pearlie laughed. "When we misbehaved," the dancing teacher said, "my mother used to threaten to send us to Aunty Talking to the Dead. She'd be giving us the licking of our lives and hollering, 'This is gonna seem like nothing, then!' "

Aunty had been laid out in one of the rooms along the side of the house. The heavy, wine-colored drapes had been drawn across the windows, and all the wall lamps turned very low, so it was darker in the room than it had been outside.

Pearlie and the Dancing School Teacher moved off into the front row. I headed for the back.

There were about thirty of us at the wake, mostly from the old days—those who had grown up on stories about Aunty, or who remembered her from before the Paradise Mortuary.

People were getting up and filing past the casket. For a moment, I felt faint again, but I remembered about Clinton (how self-assured and prosperous he looked standing at the door, accepting condolences!), and I got into line. The Dancing School Teacher and Pearlie slipped in front of me.

I drew nearer and nearer to the casket. I hugged my sweater close. The room was air conditioned and smelled of floor disinfectant and roses. Soft music came from speakers mounted on the walls.

Now there were just four people ahead. Now three. I looked down on the floor, and I thought I would faint.

Then Pearlie Mukai shrieked, "Her eyes!"

People behind me began to murmur.

"What, whose eyes?" The Dancing School Teacher demanded.

Pearlie pointed to the body in the casket.

The Dancing School Teacher peered down and cried, "My God, they're open!"

My heart turned to ice.

"What?" voices behind me were asking. "What about her eyes?"

"She said they're open," someone said.

"Aunty Talking to the Dead's eyes are open," someone else said.

Now Clinton was hurrying over.

"That's because she's not dead," still another voice put in.

Clinton looked into the coffin, and his face turned white. He turned quickly around again, and waved to his assistants across the room.

"I've heard about cases like this," someone was saying. "It's because she's looking for someone."

"I've heard that too! The old woman is trying to tell us something."

I was the only one there who knew. Aunty was talking to *me.* I clasped my hands together, hard, but they wouldn't stop shaking.

People began leaving the line. Others pressed in, trying to get a better look at the body, but a couple of Clinton's assistants had stationed themselves in front of the coffin, preventing anyone from getting too close. They had shut the lid, and Chinky Malloy was directing people out of the room.

"I'd like to take this opportunity to thank you all for coming here this evening," Clinton was saying. "I hope you will join us at the reception down the hall."

* * *

While everyone was eating, I stole back into the parlor and quietly—ever so quietly—went up to the casket, lifted the lid, and looked in.

At first, I thought they had switched bodies on me and exchanged Aunty for some powdered and painted old grandmother, all pink and white, in a pink dress, and clutching a white rose to her chest. But the pennies had fallen from her eyes—and there they were. Open. Aunty's eyes staring up at me.

Then I knew. In that instant, I stopped trembling. This was *it:* My moment had arrived. Aunty Talking to the Dead had come awake to bear me witness.

I walked through the deserted front rooms of the mortuary and out the front door. It was night. I got the wheelbarrow, loaded it with one of the tarps covering the bags of cement, and wheeled it back to the room where Aunty was. It squeaked terribly, and I stopped often to make sure no one had heard me. From the back of the building came the clink of glassware and the buzz of voices. I had to work quickly—people would be leaving soon.

But this was the hardest part. Small as she was, it was very hard to lift her out of the coffin. She was horribly heavy, and unyielding as a bag of cement. It seemed like hours, but I finally got her out and wrapped her in the tarp. I loaded her in the tray of the wheelbarrow—most of her, anyway; there was nothing I could do about her feet sticking out the front end. Then, I wheeled her through the silent rooms of the mortuary, down the front lawn, across the village square, and up the road, home.

* * *

Now, in the dark, the old woman is singing.

I have washed her with my own hands and worked the salt into the hollows of her body. I have dressed her in white and laid her in flowers.

Aunty, here are the beads you like to wear. Your favorite cakes. A quilt to keep away the chill. Here is *noni* for the heart and *awa* for every kind of grief.

Down the road a dog howls, and the sound of hammering echoes through the still air. "Looks like a burying tomorrow," the sleepers murmur, turning in their warm beds.

I bind the sandals to her feet and put the torch to the pyre.

The sky turns to light. The smoke climbs. Her ashes scatter, filling the wind.

And she sings, she sings, she sings.

Thomas Fox Averill

DURING THE TWELFTH SUMMER OF ELMER D. PETERSON

Dedicated to Grace Henderson, Dover, Kansas

Elmer hated his name. He always had. But now he hated it even more. He hated the farm his parents had moved him to. He hated the country. He hated not being able to ride his bike. He hated not having any friends.

Actually, since June first, he'd hated even being Elmer D. Peterson. June first was the day his father quit his electrician's job for good. That was the day they'd moved out into the middle of nowhere, Wabaunsee County, Kansas, for good. That was the day everything went bad. For good!

Now, there was nothing to do but help his parents. Out here, they didn't have cable TV. They didn't have people his age to run track with. They didn't even have a track near enough to run on regularly. They didn't have a good paved road near enough to ride his touring bicycle on. They didn't have anything but sky and grass and work.

"Rise and shine!" his father yelled up the attic stairs every morning.

"No way!" he shouted back.

His dad gave him time. So did his mom. It was the least they could do for a kid they'd named Elmer, and then ruined for life, moving him away from everything he'd ever known, including all the friends he'd just finished fifth grade with.

Time was moving slow. His dad was like a little kid, excited and happy. "There aren't enough hours in the day," his father said every night at the supper table. Elmer thought there were way too many hours in the day.

He complained that there was nothing to do. "Explore," his mother said to him every morning. Elmer thought there was nothing to explore. He'd seen the fields, and the creek, and the woods, and all the outbuildings. There wasn't anything else. There would never be anything else. His life was completely and totally ruined.

Then, on July fourth, early in the morning, something happened. From his attic window, Elmer D. Peterson watched an old man with a crooked back lead a small, very thick horse down the gravel road toward his house. The two of them looked like a yo-yo. The old man would hobble out ten feet, turn around, and then stand there jerking on the rope until the horse ran up to him, almost attacking him, circling him, and then stand very still, only his tail twitching. The old man would travel another ten feet and jerk so hard on the lead rope that Elmer's neck hurt just watching.

Elmer ignored his mother's call to breakfast. He wanted to see what would happen. He hoped the man was bringing the horse to them. He didn't know why the old man would, but still he hoped. And then, sure enough, horse and man turned into their lane. Elmer ran downstairs.

"Whoa," said his father. "What's got into you?"

But Elmer was halfway down the lane before his father caught up with him. The old man stood squinting at them, his eyes the same burnt umber as the tobacco juice running down his stubbly chin.

"Well," said the old man, "do me a favor. I can't keep this no good horse. He's busted the fence. You keep him until I can get it fixed."

Elmer approached the horse. Cockleburs tangled its black mane. Elmer reached out to touch the horse's twitching withers.

The old man suddenly jerked the little horse's head down. "Don't you even think about it, you piece of glue," he snarled. Elmer backed away. The old man looked at Elmer's dad. "Just over the holiday," he said. "Your boy here can feed him." The old man spat and looked at Elmer. "Would you like that, boy?"

"Sure," said Elmer. "Can we, Dad? Please?"

"No food," said Elmer's dad. "No equipment. No decent fence here."

"You got that little corral there, I ain't blind," said the old man. He pulled the little horse close to him. "A good critter, really. Part Shetland pony, part Morgan horse. Was broke just as gentle as a rocking chair, once. Had all my grandbabies up on his back. No bit, just halter broke. We all get hard times, you know."

"All right," said Elmer's dad.

The old man went straight back through the old gate to the corral. He tied the thick little Morgan to a post, promised to return, and limped away down the road. Elmer's dad went inside. Elmer's mom called him for breakfast. He stayed with the horse as long as he could, but didn't want his mom mad at him.

"I'll feed and water him, and I'll even find an old comb and get the tangles out of his mane. I'll call him Tangler," Elmer said.

"Don't name him, Son," said Elmer's dad. "He's not yours."

"Just for while he's here. Just for a while. I'm calling him Tangler," Elmer insisted.

His father frowned. His mother sighed. But neither said a word.

Then they heard a terrific clatter from the corral. Elmer was the first to the kitchen door. Tangler was rearing back, arching away from the post, shaking his head and whinnying, his front hooves pawing the air. Then the rope snapped, and Tangler, tail extended, galloped in one quick circle around the corral and went straight for the gate. It was as tall as he was, but he sailed over it as if he'd sprouted wings. Elmer's father ran to the lane, but Tangler reached the road in a flurry of dust, turned in the direction he'd come, and literally high-tailed it out of there.

Elmer's dad picked up a rock and heaved it as far as he could. "Good riddance," he shouted.

"Don't," said Elmer's mother and went inside.

Elmer just stood in the doorway. He was sorry Tangler was gone. He was sorry his father didn't care. But he wasn't sorry he'd seen Tangler soar like an eagle over the fence, seen those powerful legs churn down the lane, seen that smooth gallop of freedom. Tangler was faster than Elmer had imagined any creature could be.

After breakfast, Elmer went to his room and found his old racing flats in the back of the closet. He put them on and hurried down the stairs.

"Whoa," said his father. "Where are you going?"

"Scouting," Elmer said. Then, looking at his mother, he said, "Exploring." He was out the door before either could call him back. He was running, faster than he remembered he could, down the lane, onto the road, and away. After Tangler.

Elmer didn't return until lunch. In all that time he saw Tangler only once. He came to the top of a rise, a place where he could see two miles in every direction. He stopped running. He put his hands on his thin hips and bent forward slightly, breathing deeply, catching his breath. If he hadn't been leaning forward, he wouldn't have seen the horse, surprisingly close to him, almost hidden in a clump of brush in a pasture.

Tangler saw him. The horse whinnied and trotted deeper into the brush that follows every draw into a creek or pond. Elmer scooted under the fence, scraping his bare knees on a jagged shelf of rock. He ran carefully cross-country into the brush and down the draw, but didn't see Tangler. He managed to fill his T-shirt with stick-tights and other small seeds that take passage all through the long summer, hoping to find new homes in fresh soil.

At home, he filled a quart jar with water and drank it all before he said a word. "I know where Tangler is," he said finally.

"I don't care where he is," said Elmer's dad. "He's not our horse."

"We said we'd keep him," Elmer insisted. "We promised to feed him. You said I could take care of him."

"I'm not going to buy feed for a horse I've only seen for five minutes, Elmer. It just doesn't make sense."

"We can catch him."

"No," said Elmer's dad. He crossed his arms on his chest, something he did when he meant business.

Elmer sat down, frowning.

"We're going to the Andersons' at three," Elmer's dad reminded him.

"Not me," said Elmer. "I'm finding Tangler."

"You'll be ready at three o'clock, young man, or you'll never see that horse again."

"Yes, sir," said Elmer.

After lunch he went up to his room and looked out the attic window, first to the north, then to the south. As far as he could see all around him, miles of green hills, with their rock outcroppings, the lines of trees revealing fence lines and other farms, the brown ribbons of road trailing off in the four directions; he could not see Tangler.

His mother sat on his bed.

"I wish *I* had a horse," Elmer said.

"Your father and I wish you did, too," she said.

"Then why can't I?"

"Elmer," she sighed. "We don't have the fences fixed. We don't have the time it would take to really care for a horse. We don't have a cent of extra money. You know we're taking a gamble even being out here. But it's very important to your father."

"He doesn't care about me. He only pays attention to what's *important.*"

"You're important, Elmer. He's just worried. About money. About getting enough done before winter. He's just like you. He's doing things he's never done before. You know that's not easy."

"Can I go look for Tangler some more?"

"If you're back by three o'clock, sharp."

Elmer was tired of running. He put on long pants and walked slowly through fields in the direction he'd seen Tangler. Along the way he picked up stones to see how far he could hurl them. He followed their arc first with his eyes, then with his feet, hoping to find the exact same stones again. He never did. He had about as much chance of that as he did of seeing Tangler again.

Once, one of his rocks disturbed a red-tailed hawk. Elmer heard a scream, then saw the hawk slowly circle into the sky. He wished he could be up there, with a hawk's eyesight. He'd find Tangler for sure. He looked at his watch: two-fifteen. He'd have to run if he didn't want angry parents. He threw one more rock, high as he could. He watched it fall.

There was a picnic in town. A dark drive home. A deep sleep.

II

"Rise and shine!" his father called up the stairs. "We've got some errands to run."

Elmer was ready to pull the sheet over his head when he remembered the day before and Tangler. He threw on his clothes and hustled to the breakfast table.

"Wash your face and comb your tangles out," said his mother, patting his sleep-mussed hair.

"No time," said Elmer. "Me and Dad've got to hurry."

"And where are you going?" she asked him.

"I don't know," he admitted. He was full of hope for this day, but he wanted his dad to say what they'd do. "Dad?" he asked.

"First we're going to find that old man. I believe his name is Crawshaw. We're going to tell him we don't have his horse. We'll drive over so we can look on the way. Then we're going to buy some fencing supplies. Might be Elmer here wouldn't mind helping if there was a reason for him to."

"You mean I might get a horse?"

"Someday, Son," said his dad, "but you've got to be willing to do your part."

"Dear," said Elmer's mom, and she signalled Elmer's dad into their bedroom. They closed the door. It was one of their conferences. Usually, they just asked Elmer to go outside for a while. Even then he could sometimes hear loud voices, angry and sharp. Once he'd gone clear out past the corral to where a stand of trees began. But he still heard their voices, amazed by how far anger could travel.

This day, alone at the breakfast table, he overheard parts of what they said. His mother: "It's not fair unless you plan to." His father: "But we have to be ready first." Then, later: "He has to earn it." Then his mother again: "Don't get his hopes up if we can't do it soon." His father: something about "next spring." Then his mother making a warning and his father saying "spoiled." His mother: "You're not getting your way?"

Elmer looked at his cereal when his mother came back into the kitchen and poured herself more coffee. She leaned against the counter. "Good things sometimes take a long time to happen," she said.

Elmer nodded. When his father came out of the bedroom, Elmer left his cereal half-finished and followed, silently, to the truck.

Elmer put his head out the window and searched the passing countryside for Tangler. Nothing. A mile away his father slowed at a broken-down gate. "That's where he's been," said Elmer's dad. "Been and gone. Look at that fence." As they drove along it, the old barbed wire drooped, fell away broken from rusted staples. Posts, rotted in the ground, bent at every angle. "It'll take that old man more than a weekend to fix that," said Elmer's dad.

Elmer kept his eyes open. He saw everything else in the morning blue of sky, in the pale green of dusty grass, but not Tangler. And then they were finally at Crawshaw's.

The old man lived in an old shack of a house, as bent and crooked as he was, as brown with weather as the tobacco he chewed, as overgrown with weeds as his stubbly face.

"You knock on the door, Son," Elmer's dad joked. "If I do, it'll probably fall in."

But the old man was suddenly at the door. He opened the screen, leaned out, and spat some tobacco juice into a rusty milk can on the porch. Then he limped out and sat noisily on an old sofa. The cushions were ripped. Elmer imagined it was full of a hundred mice, squeaking like the sofa's tired springs. "So, he ran away already," said the old man, his brown eyes gleaming. "I should've figured it. Jump a fence, did he?"

Elmer nodded, but the old man wasn't looking at him. Crawshaw was looking far away, as though he were watching Tangler gallop in a circle and jump.

"He jumped the gate," said Elmer's dad.

"Sure. Whatever." The old man brushed his arms. "You've got a magical horse there," he said. He looked at Elmer. "He's little like the Shetland in him, but he's strong and powerful like his Morgan blood. And you listen here. That little horse can do anything, if he has a mind to. Used to be in the circus, you know. He can count, climb a stepladder up and down, jump anything in front or beside him. He can do anything, if he has a mind to. He can do everything but cook your breakfast. Why, he can run so fast in one of them little bitty circus rings you couldn't see but just a blur. One old boy told me he could get going so fast he'd disappear. That what he did to you, boy?" The man winked.

"Is Tangler really magical?" asked Elmer.

"Tangler?" asked the old man. "What do you mean, Tangler?"

"That's his name," said Elmer, excited. "I mean that's what I call him."

"Good name. He's tangled up my fence pretty good. You like him?"

"Sure," said Elmer. He looked at his dad, but his dad was looking away.

"He's yours if you want him, boy," Crawshaw said suddenly.

Elmer couldn't believe it. "Mine?" he asked.

"He's yours if you can catch him."

"Can we catch him, Dad?" Elmer asked.

"I don't know," said his father. "How did you catch him?" he asked Crawshaw.

"Oh, he knows me. After I bought him off the circus he was like a pet. That was before my wife died. Before all my kids moved to town. I'd catch him now, 'cept this rheumatism's got me so bad. I been laid up in the house ever since I was at your place yesterday."

"We'll think about it," said Elmer's dad. "Once we get our fence fixed."

Crawshaw threw his head back and laughed hard, his mouth open wide. His teeth were as black as rocks. He leaned forward. "You can't fence him in any more than you can fence in God's country air." He chuckled. "Get you some good feed and some sugar cubes. Treat him right. He'll come around. Especially to the boy here."

"We'll think about it," Elmer's dad said again, and he walked back toward the truck.

Elmer wondered if that meant no. These days, he couldn't quite tell what his dad was thinking, or just what his dad might do.

"Son," Crawshaw hissed and motioned Elmer over.

Elmer went and stood in front of the ratty sofa, close enough to fill his nose with the strong smell of the old man.

"Here's what you do," said Crawshaw. "You got to use color. Remember, he was in the circus. He likes bright colors. Put food color on the sugar cubes. Get you something really bright to wear, like a clown costume. Oh, yeah, and if that doesn't work, there's one other thing. The little guy was raised on beer. He might still like a nip. That might do it." He smiled.

"Thanks," said Elmer. He jumped off the creaky old porch and ran to the truck.

"Good luck," called Crawshaw.

"We'll call you in a couple of days," Elmer's dad shouted back.

"No phone," yelled the old man through cupped hands.

Elmer's dad just nodded and backed the truck out of the dirt drive. It was a quiet ride home. When they reached their turnoff, Elmer's dad kept right on going toward town.

"Where are we going?" asked Elmer.

"Where's your memory?" asked his dad.

"For fencing stuff?" Elmer asked, disappointed. "But he said that wouldn't matter. He said it wouldn't work. He told me how to catch Tangler."

"He told you a lot of things," said Elmer's dad. "And you believed it all. Magic. Circuses. Disappearing. Elmer, you listen to me. A horse is a horse, and if you want to keep a horse you have to build a good fence. And if *you* want *this* horse, you have to help *me* mend fence."

"But we've got to catch him. Soon," Elmer whined.

"We'll mend fence first, then try for the horse. And that's final. Do you understand?"

"Yes, sir," said Elmer. But he didn't want to wait very long. His horse would be wanting some sugar.

They went to town, came home, unloaded, began work. Mending fence was slow. It made the day stretch longer and longer, like the barbed wire when they winched it at the corners. He didn't mean to, but Elmer kept pricking himself on the sharp barbs. "Pay attention," his dad would say. When Elmer put his fingers in his mouth, his dad told him to stop it.

His dad was hard to work with all through the long afternoon. They worked and worked, winched and winched, stretched and stretched, pounded and pounded the new staples into the old cedar posts. Elmer's dad pounded his thumb several times, each time letting out a big howl, the last time throwing his hammer. They searched the tall pasture grass for ten minutes before Elmer found it. "Thanks," said his dad, standing next to Elmer and looking back at the fence. Even with the new staples and wire, the posts sagged. Between some posts, the old wire drooped more than before. Elmer wondered if his dad wanted him to say something. He felt his dad's hand on his shoulder. "It's not easy to do brand new things, is it?" Elmer's dad asked.

"No, sir," said Elmer and moved back to the fence. Tangler could jump it no problem no matter how well it was mended.

They strung two new wires before his dad let Elmer go back to the house. He was supposed to tell his mom they were done for the day, but when he walked by the back porch he saw her in a lawn chair, reading a book. He waved and hurried inside. He had work to do and fast. He ran to the kitchen with a chair and went for the top cabinet, where his mom kept the baking supplies.

The food coloring was right where he'd guessed, and he slipped the tiny red, blue, green, and yellow bottles into his back pockets. But the sugar cubes were not there. Surely they weren't all gone. He racked his brain, then remembered. One of the women his mother taught with had come to tea the month before. His mother had put the cubes into a little bowl, part of her best china set. He jumped off the chair and went to the china cupboard.

He'd just dug out a handful when he heard his mother open the back door. He slipped them in his shirt pocket, then put the lid on the bowl. "What are you doing?" asked his mom.

"Um . . . I thought I'd set the table for you. Dad says we're done for the day."

"With my best china?" His mother smiled. Elmer could tell she knew he was up to something, but didn't want to challenge him.

"Well," he said, "it's kind of a special occasion. Since Mr. Crawshaw gave me Tangler."

"Elmer," said his mother, "you've still got to mend the fence and then see if you can catch him. Your father thinks Mr. Crawshaw is just getting your hopes up. Don't get your heart too set, okay?"

"Okay," Elmer said. He stood up. His front shirt pocket bulged out, and he ran upstairs to unload the cubes. From his room he called down to her: "I'll come help you set the table in a second!"

"Thanks!" she yelled back.

At supper, his mom asked his dad how it was going with the fence.

"Okay," his dad said.

Elmer heard something in his dad's voice, but he couldn't tell what it was until his mom asked him the same question, and, just like his dad, he said, "Okay." The way they said it was exactly the same, like it wasn't really going okay. Usually his dad said things like he knew just what he thought and just what to do. That's what he'd always been like. But now there was something new in his dad's voice. Like doubt. Elmer liked that a little, but it scared him a little, too.

"Can I go outside?" he asked, when he'd finished everything but the green beans on his plate.

"Where to?" asked his dad.

"Just out," Elmer said. "Maybe take a long walk, then run home. Maybe my new school will have a cross-country team."

"Are you going horse-hunting?" asked his dad. Elmer nodded. His father looked at the big kitchen clock. It was an old school clock Elmer's mom had brought home when the school where she taught had bought new ones. It always reminded Elmer of how he watched the clock at school, waiting for the days to end. "You can go for a while. Be home by eight sharp." His father sounded definite again.

Elmer bounded up the stairs to put on his running shoes. Then he found his school backpack. In it, he stuffed an old white shirt, some red pants he'd worn once in a school play, and a bright red hunting cap his dad had wanted to throw away. In the pack's zipper front, he slipped the sugar cubes and food coloring he'd snitched before dinner. Then, he hurried down the stairs and ran past the kitchen.

"What's in the pack?" he heard his mother ask.

"Just some stuff," he said, still running. He didn't hear his mother call him back, so he headed quickly away toward the corral. He remembered seeing a big piece of rope hanging in one of the outbuildings. He creaked open the old door and there it was. He took it down. It was only about twelve feet long and old and frayed, stiff and rough like Tangler's mane. But it was all he had, so he stuffed it in his pack, put the pack on his back, and took off at a slow jog.

An hour later, he was at Crawshaw's dirt drive, five miles from his house. He had a side stitch from running right after dinner, but he didn't care. He walked toward the house. The sun, lowering in the western sky, turned the horizon pale, then washed it lavender. Elmer was looking at the sky when he heard Crawshaw boom out: "Caught him yet, boy?"

"No," said Elmer, still breathing hard as he walked up to the porch.

"That tired and you ain't even started?"

Elmer sat on the edge of the porch. "I ran over here. I can't get any beer. My mom and dad never have any."

"So you thought I just might?" Crawshaw chuckled. "You might be right." Elmer looked at the old man, who spat a stream of tobacco juice, perfectly, into the milk can six feet from him. "And you might be wrong. You haven't tried the sugar and the colors, have you?"

Elmer was uncomfortable. He hoped Crawshaw would help him, but it was just questions, just like being at home. So he stood up and took off his backpack.

"You think I'll be able to catch him?" Elmer asked, pulling out the old rope.

"Wait a minute, son," said the old man. "You go near him with that rope he'll be halfway to Timbuktu before you can say Jack Robinson."

"But you brought him to our place with a rope."

"And how well did that work?" asked the old man.

"Not very, I guess," admitted Elmer.

"But he couldn't have stayed at all without it," Crawshaw said. "And I wanted him to stay. I ain't got no time for him anymore. Seems to me like you might. Once you catch him, that is. Once you get him used to you. But you can't do it with a rope."

Elmer dropped the rope and began emptying the rest of his pack. "Good," said the old man when he showed him the pants and shirt and hat. "Great," he said when Elmer showed him the food coloring and the sugar cubes.

"How'd you know I wanted a horse?" Elmer asked.

"You know a boy who don't? Now you get those cubes colored. Get your clothes on. It's getting late."

Elmer looked at his watch: six-thirty. He opened the bottles of food coloring and watched the drops of liquid soak into the cubes. He colored each cube. He made one of all the colors, a different color on each side. Then he laid the white shirt onto the porch and made long stripes of colors top to bottom like a rainbow of suspenders. He let the shirt dry while he put on the bright red pants over his jogging shorts. "Good," said the old man, when Elmer finally put the shirt and bright hunting cap on, completing his costume. "Now, skeedaddle. If you don't see him tonight, we'll think about the beer tomorrow. Can you get away?"

"I will," Elmer promised. "I think Dad'll let me. But I don't think he likes Tangler. He doesn't believe what you said about circuses and all."

"What about you? Do you believe it, boy?" asked Crawshaw.

"Yes," said Elmer. He turned away, then back around. "Thanks, Mr. Crawshaw," he said. "Thanks a lot."

"Call me by my first name," said the old man, "if we're going to be friends."

"What is your first name?" Elmer asked.

"You know it, I bet," said Crawshaw. "Guess."

"I don't know."

"Elmer," said the old man.

"What?" asked Elmer.

Crawshaw just laughed. "Elmer Crawshaw. That's my name."

"Really?" asked Elmer. "That's my name, too."

"Elmer Crawshaw?" joked the old man.

"No. Elmer D. Peterson."

"Well, I'm mighty pleased to meet you, Elmer," said Elmer. "It ain't every day you find another Elmer, is it?"

"No, sir."

"Elmer."

"Right. No, sir, Elmer."

"Now get that horse, boy." Elmer Crawshaw shooed Elmer D. Peterson away.

At first, Elmer felt weird running in the long red pants, the funny shirt and hat, the sugar cubes crunching in his hands like decaying dice. But he wanted to find Tangler, and he ran a mile, fast, before he ducked under a fence and started through some pasture near where he remembered seeing Tangler the day before. He tried to stay in the high places, where Tangler could see him and be attracted to the colors. He trotted into the dusk, feeling good about Elmer Crawshaw, that anyone in the world would have the same first name as he did. The old man had known he wanted a horse. Elmer Crawshaw wanted him to catch Tangler. He would help. He would be a friend.

Elmer heard a whinnying and stopped. He turned full circle, but saw nothing. Then he heard it again, behind him. He saw Tangler come out of a draw, and Elmer danced, waving his arms like a clown might. Then he held out a handful of sugar cubes. "Come here, boy," he called. "Come here." And Tangler came. Elmer couldn't believe it.

Ten feet away, Tangler stopped, thrust his neck out, his nose forward, and sniffed. Elmer extended his arm as far as he could without taking a step. Tangler stretched forward, too, then took several small steps. Elmer tiptoed closer, until, finally, Tangler brushed Elmer's extended palm. He snuffed through the nose, then his tongue came out, singled out a cube of many colors, and brought it into his mouth. Tangler crunched the cube. "Good boy," said Elmer. "Good boy."

He didn't know what to do next, but he knew it was late, and he knew he'd have to use the few other colored sugar cubes to lead Tangler home. So he did what he didn't want to do. He turned and walked away toward his house. In twenty feet he looked back. Tangler was following him. Elmer stopped and fed the horse another cube. Then he walked some more. Two cubes later they were at the fence. Elmer took a chance. He slid under and stood on the road holding out a cube of sugar. Tangler neared the fence, looked over it, whinnied, and promptly jumped it. Elmer couldn't believe his eyes. He gave Tangler another cube, his next to last one, then ran down the road, Tangler following along behind.

A half-mile from his house, Elmer fed Tangler his last cube. He began trotting again. It was getting very late, already well after eight o'clock. He'd be in big trouble if he didn't get home soon. He heard Tangler behind him and ran faster.

Then he couldn't hear anything but his own footfalls. He stopped and turned around. He couldn't see anything but lumpy shadows on the distant road. "Tangler!" he called. Nothing answered. He stood quietly, disappointed.

"Elmer!" It was his father's voice. He took out running toward it. Right as he neared his lane, he thought he heard something. He stopped one last time. That's when he saw it. A shadow galloped toward him. Hooves sounded the gravel like hollow bones. Tangler was coming right at him, and Elmer froze. He wanted to close his eyes, but he wanted to see what Tangler would do. Elmer squeezed his hands together as hard as he could. His face winced. Tangler thundered right up to him, then leaped, clearing Elmer's head with a rush of wind. The horse landed without breaking stride, leaving behind only the leathery smell of his hide. Tangler raced away, down the road.

"Elmer!" his father shouted again.

"Coming," Elmer said. He quickly stripped off his clown costume and stuffed it back in his pack. Then he ran up the lane, his breath still short with excitement. He explained everything to his dad, but he was very late. His father claimed he hadn't heard the horse run up and jump over Elmer. His father was mad and grounded him for the rest of the week.

III

Elmer woke to the sound of his father's boots on the attic stairs. "You can work with me, or you can stay inside. That's it." His dad was still mad.

"Inside," Elmer said. Then, "I really did see him. He really did follow me home and eat sugar cubes out of my hand. He really did jump over me."

"Elmer," said his dad. "I want to believe you. But I also have to punish you for staying out way past when I told you to be in."

"It was like a job, Dad," Elmer said. "I just wanted to finish it. You come in late to dinner sometimes when *you* have to finish something."

"And you can, too, when you're an adult." His father looked at him, but Elmer turned away. "Your mother's gone to town. But she'll be back by lunch. You help her around the house today. You understand?"

"What are you going to do?"

"Mend fence, of course. First things first, Elmer."

"He can jump it, anyway."

"We'll see." His father went back down the stairs. Just before he went outside he stuck his head into the stairwell. "You just keep from getting sassy. You understand? You don't know everything."

Neither do you, Elmer thought. He wanted his dad to believe him, to understand. "Yes, sir," was all he said. He went to the window and watched his father walk through the gate, past the corral, toward the back pasture.

As soon as he couldn't see his dad anymore, he hurried to his closet. He had made up his mind the night before, when his dad didn't believe his story. He would sneak out, run to Crawshaw's shack, pick up the beer, and get Tangler to come with him.

Off he ran, pack on his back. This time, he found a shortcut, through different pastures, to the old man's house. "Morning, Elmer," said Crawshaw from the sofa on the porch.

"Morning, Elmer," Elmer said back. He sat down on the edge of the porch and told his friend all about the night before.

"Atta boy," said Crawshaw when he heard Elmer's story. "Sounds like he likes you."

"I don't have any more sugar cubes."

"That's okay. 'Cause I found a bottle of beer. Now get on your costume. He'll be somewhere between here and your place, if I know him."

Elmer threw on his clothes, emptying the backpack. Crawshaw reached behind the sofa, then stood up, twisting the top off a brown bottle of Budweiser. He also had several old sponges, brownish purple like big pieces of liver. He picked up Elmer's pack, stuffed it full of sponges, and poured in the whole bottle of beer. A little foam came to the top, but Crawshaw zipped it shut.

"Well," he said, throwing the empty bottle at a fifty-five gallon drum he used for trash, "now he'll follow you anywhere, once he gets a whiff."

"Thanks," said Elmer. He put on the pack. It leaked a little onto his shirt and pants. "I'm not supposed to be out today."

"You get in trouble last night?" Crawshaw didn't wait for an answer. "Tell me, do you have any tack?" Elmer looked puzzled. "Bridle. Saddle. Halter. Stuff like that," Crawshaw explained.

"No, sir."

"Well, get going," Crawshaw said. "You get that horse home. Good luck."

"Thanks, Elmer," said Elmer, and he ran off. He could feel the beer in his pack slosh around. His pants were getting soaked. The warm beer smelled a little like bread dough and a little like rotting apples.

Elmer tried to go in a straight line between Crawshaw's house and his. He ran across country he'd never seen before, and everywhere he looked, he saw new things: the way the trees bent from the steady winds, the way the grass turned blue along its edges, the way the ponds reflected the sky. Maybe it was because he was grounded and wasn't supposed to be out. Maybe it was because since Tangler he'd been exploring the countryside so much. Maybe it was because he wanted to see Tangler in each new view, so he looked close. But he loved being out in the beautiful countryside, nothing but grass beneath him, sky over him, and the whispering wind pushing and pulling him along. He wished he never had to go home.

He went down a draw, crossed a dried up old creek bed, and began climbing up a rise. A little way up he jumped over a thin wire. He hadn't seen anything like it before, but he was pretty sure it was electrified. He almost touched it, then decided he'd better not. Near the top of the rise, he stopped and looked all around him. He saw three things at once. Above him, farther up the rise, he saw a huge cow, black and stocky, thick in the shoulders and neck. Its eyes glinted in the sun. Just as Elmer realized it was not a cow, but a bull, he saw Tangler, behind the animal, past another thin wire and another fence line. Then, to his right, he saw a plume of dust rising from the gravel road. A truck, his father's truck, came over the rise.

Elmer stood very still. There was no use running. Either his father would see him in the crazy clown costume, or he wouldn't. But before he could tell anything about his dad, Elmer heard a huge bellow. The great black bull tossed its head. Then it pawed the ground and bellowed again. Elmer changed his mind about running. He tried to judge which fence line in the treeless pasture was closest. The bull lowered its massive head.

Then Tangler whinnied. The bull looked behind him, distracted for a second by Tangler. Elmer took advantage of the moment, running toward the road, away from the bull and away from Tangler. That's when he saw his father's truck stop. He was running straight for it, his legs pumping, the beer on his back churning to foam.

Even as he ran, Elmer thought of all the trouble he was in. For just a moment, he felt mad. Mad at the bull, mad at his dad, mad at Elmer Crawshaw, mad at Tangler. He wondered why all this had to happen to him, Elmer D. Peterson. Then he couldn't think anymore, because he could hear the bull's heavy footsteps. He looked back, over his shoulder, still running, and everything seemed slow motion. The bull was lumbering toward him. Tangler whinnied, reared back, shook his head. "Tangler!" Elmer shouted. Then, because he wasn't watching where he was going, he tripped on a clump of bluestem and went down flat on his face.

"Elmer!" his dad yelled. Elmer looked up.

"Dad!" he screamed back. His father began to climb the fence.

Then Elmer heard a loud whinnying, almost a whine, and he sat up. Tangler jumped the fence and raced toward the bull, which was halfway to where Elmer sat. Elmer stood up, but he couldn't run. Like the night before, he could only watch what Tangler would do. He was afraid, but fascinated. Tangler galloped across the pasture, gaining on the bull.

"Elmer! Run, Elmer!" his dad yelled again, over the fence now and looking for something to throw at the bull.

But Elmer couldn't move. He was frozen to the spot.

"Elmer!" It was his mother's voice this time. Elmer hadn't seen her in the truck with his dad. He waved to her, just as if everything was fine, just as if there were no bull running toward him, just as if he didn't have on a silly clown costume, just as if he didn't have a backpack full of beer-soaked sponges leaking all over him.

He could feel the earth shaking with the pounding of the bull's hooves. He looked right at the bull, now. It was huge. Tangler was just behind it, though, tail up, galloping faster that Elmer had ever seen him run. And then, when the bull was just thirty feet from Elmer, Tangler caught up to the charging animal. Elmer couldn't see what happened, but suddenly the bull crumpled onto its front legs, bellowing. The bull looked all around. Tangler danced away, distracting the bull from Elmer. There was something in Tangler's mouth. Elmer felt a hand on his shoulder, tugging at him. It was his dad.

"Look," said Elmer, pointing. They both looked, amazed. Tangler had bitten the bull's tail clear off, and he tossed it in his mouth like a whip. The bull stood back up then and stared at Elmer and his dad. It stared at Tangler. It let out a huge bellow, then started after the horse. Tangler galloped away, turning a circle, confusing the bull.

"C'mon," Elmer's dad said, and he and Elmer backed away, their eyes on the bull and Tangler. They hopped the electric wire, then climbed the fence, all the time watching Tangler run the bull. Elmer's mother came over and stood beside them. Tangler was amazing, running in circles, turning the bull every which way. Once, when the bull charged him, Tangler made a tight circle and jumped right over the enraged animal. Elmer couldn't believe how fast, how nimble Tangler was, his nostrils flaring, the bull's tail still whipping from his teeth. Finally, after five minutes of bull baiting, Tangler had the huge animal so tired, so dizzy, so confused, that it crumpled again onto the grass, its head lazily following Tangler's movements as though it were drunk.

"Greatest show on earth, ain't it?" Elmer Crawshaw walked up behind them. He had parked his truck down the road a ways earlier when they were all too busy and anxious to notice him. Crawshaw lifted the pack off Elmer's back. "Thanks for helping me, son," he said. He began walking away with the pack. When he neared his truck, he turned around and yelled back at them. "I know I shouldn't have told you to come over. But I couldn't have done it without you. I've got your pay in my truck there." He walked toward his pickup, and threw Elmer's pack into the back. Elmer and his mother and father followed the old man.

Then Tangler whinnied, and, free from the bull, he trotted toward the road. He jumped the little electric wire, then jumped the fenceline thirty feet from them. He started toward them, but halfway, as if remembering something, Tangler trotted up to the fence and with a shake of his head he tossed the bull's tail into the pasture. Then he turned and trotted toward them, his nostrils still flared. Before they could wonder what he'd do next, he passed them and jumped up into Crawshaw's pick-up, just like a dog would do. Elmer and his dad and mom hurried to the truck.

Tangler was nuzzling Elmer's pack. Crawshaw reached in, unzipped it for him, and Tangler nuzzled in and pulled a sponge out with his teeth. They could hear him sucking up the beer.

"Elmer," said Crawshaw. "You ride in the back with Tangler, here. You can inspect the tack. It's your payment for helping. Peterson, you can ride up with me. The missus can drive your truck home." Crawshaw spoke with quick authority. Elmer's dad nodded. So did his mom. It was like a dream that couldn't be happening. Elmer jumped up next to Tangler and pulled another sponge from the pack. He petted Tangler and put his face in the horse's strong neck.

Then they started out, toward home, Elmer Crawshaw and Elmer's dad in the truck cab. Elmer D. Peterson and Tangler, along with a bridle, saddle, halter, and lead ropes, were the cargo. Elmer's mom followed a distance behind, giving their dust time to blow away. Elmer waved at her once, and she waved back, smiling and shaking her head.

He didn't know what kind of trouble he was in. Maybe pretty bad. He saw Crawshaw and his dad talking. They didn't seem to be mad, but he didn't know what his dad might be thinking. Still, all the way home, all he could think about was Tangler. He was right next to the horse. His horse. Tangler liked him. Tangler would get used to him. No matter what happened to him, he knew he'd have a friend. Two friends, because there was Elmer

Crawshaw, too. He thought about that all the way home. He realized he might as well feel good about his life for as long as he could.

When Crawshaw turned into their lane, Elmer's spirits sank. Crawshaw stopped his truck near the corral gate. Elmer saw Crawshaw say one more thing to his dad; then the two men climbed out. Elmer's mom pulled up nearby. Elmer grabbed another sponge out of his pack for Tangler. Then he waited for his dad to say something. They all gathered around the truck.

Finally, Elmer's dad cleared his throat. "Son," he said, "I guess he's yours. You caught him, just like the man said. Or maybe he caught you. He's one heck of a horse.

"The greatest ever," said Elmer. He didn't know whether he should say "I'm sorry" or "Thank you." He just stood next to Tangler, his clown costume itching like crazy.

BIOGRAPHIES
and Some Comments by the Authors

Alice Adams is the author of six novels and four collections of stories, most recently *After You've Gone.* She has been frequently included in *Prize Stories: The O. Henry Awards* and in 1982 she received the Special Award for Continuing Achievement.

" 'Earthquake Damage' I guess could be said to be a true story: I was in fact at some meetings in Toronto, though literary rather than psychoanalytic, and I was on a plane headed for San Francisco when the earthquake hit, and we did turn about and head back to Toronto. But all the rest is invention: I am of course not a shrink, and I do not know anyone with an alcoholic former wife.

"The dog at the end, though, did exist. I truly saw him out on the airfield as the plane tried, once more, to take off. And from time to time I think of that dog, with his long brave tail—and I wish him well, a long and happy life away from airports."

Thomas Fox Averill teaches creative writing and Kansas literature, folklore, and film at Washburn University of Topeka. He received an M.F.A. from the University of Iowa Writers' Workshop, and has written two books of stories: *Passes at the Moon* (Topeka: Woodley Press, 1985) and *Seeing Mona Naked* (Wichita: Watermark Press, 1989); and edited a collection of writings on the meaning and appeal of Kansas, called *What Kansas Means to Me: Twentieth Century Writers on the Sunflower State* (Lawrence: University Press of Kansas, 1990).

He writes that he scrawled the first page of "During the Twelfth Summer of Elmer D. Peterson" on the back of a grocery list, waiting in line to pay for his family's weekly shopping on a crowded Sunday afternoon. "It was the fall of 1987, during an academic sabbatical. I had agreed to be a writer-in-the-schools for the Kansas Arts Commission for two weeks, traveling each day to three small-town elementary schools some twenty to thirty miles west of my home town, Topeka, Kansas. Since I was also to show the students how a practicing writer works, I decided to spend at least an hour a day at a desk in the hall writing a short story, hoping they would come by and visit about the story. On that first Monday I read the transcribed first page to them, then posted it in the hallways of their schools. Each day I read a new page or two and, sure enough, they came to my desk with anecdotes of animals, with wonderful details of their lives in Wabaunsee County, with hopes for what my main character might do, or discover, or come to be. At the end of two weeks, having taken many of their suggestions and woven in as many of their details as possible, I read the conclusion to the short story—our short story: they had lived with it and hoped for it as I did. The younger children even illustrated it, and posted their crayon drawings in the hall beside those sheets of daily writing. I finished my residency, packed the story pages and the drawings, and went home to days with mornings free to work on a novel I was writing."

Charles Baxter is the author of four books of fiction, most recently *A Relative Stranger*, a book of stories published by W. W. Norton in the fall of 1990. His other books include a novel, *First Light* (Viking/Penguin), and two earlier books of stories. He teaches at the University of Michigan, Ann Arbor.

"I have lived in the Midwest for most of my life and once taught in the public schools of a rural Michigan community of the kind where 'Saul and Patsy . . .' is set. This place was fascinatingly bleak, and I had two friends who might have served as the models for the characters in my story, if I hadn't appropriated them and altered them so that they would be unrecognizable, even to themselves. The story's secret heart is a restaging of a scene related to my father's death, but rewritten so that the character survives the experience."

T. Alan Broughton: "I was born on June 9, 1936, in Bryn Mawr, Pennsylvania, and grew up on the campus of Bryn Mawr College where my father was a Professor of Classics and my mother was a Dean of Freshmen and of Admissions. We always lived on the campus itself, and although I left Pennsylvania after graduating from Swarthmore College, I have not been far from campuses ever since.

"Like many of my stories, 'Ashes' began with the recollection of an event in my own life, a brief period one summer when I was hired to be a companion to a young man who had recently emerged from some months in a mental hospital. If any trace of me remains in the story now, it is in the person of Mr. Anthony, the hired keeper who is more concerned with the chance to fish than to watch over his ward. But, as usual, very early in the process of revising (which I do interminably and with enormous pleasure), the story became a world I no longer recognized as mine, one which demanded whatever insufficient powers I had to help it be fully realized. That it began as a novella over one hundred pages long and ended as a short story no longer surprises me. I have seen whole novels and poems reduce themselves to phrases, words, and finally the blank page that was their origin."

Millicent Dillon is a writer of fiction and nonfiction. Among her books are *A Little Original Sin: The Life and Work of Jane Bowles* and *After Egypt: Isadora Duncan and Mary Cassatt.* Her novel *The Dance of the Mothers* is being published in the summer of 1991. About "Oil and Water," she comments: "Once—it seems like a thousand years ago—I worked in an oil field. But the relation of that field to the field in 'Oil and Water' is very tenuous. I do not have a good memory. That may be one of the reasons that I am more interested in straying from memory than in adhering to it."

Martha Lacy Hall was born in 1923, in Magnolia, Mississippi. She began a career in writing and editing in 1968. Her first published short story, "The Peaceful Eye," appeared in *The Southern Review* in 1970, and she has continued publishing in *The Southern Review, Sewanee Review, New Orleans Review, Virginia Quarterly Review,* and *Shenandoah.* Her collections of short fiction include *Call It Living* (Press of the Nightowl, 1981), *Music Lesson* (University of Illinois Press, 1984), and *The Apple-Green Triumph* (LSU Press, 1990).

In 1984 she retired from LSU Press where she had been an editor and managing editor for nearly twenty years. She lives and writes at her home in Baton Rouge.

"I am inspired by books and by people. I was lucky enough to grow up in a community where I knew everybody and in a house where the books probably outnumbered the people in the town. I constantly had access to what I know now was an amazing array of prose, poetry, history, and general reference works. No less remarkable was the variety of people I knew well—plumber, preacher, garbage collector, teacher, merchant—black and white. My head is bristling with composites of characters, and I keep adding every time I see a face or hear a voice. But I don't write biography; I write fiction, so while truth is an issue, reality is not."

Wayne Johnson grew up in Minnesota and spent many years living in the West. He is a recipient of a Transatlantic Review Award, and a Teaching-Writing Fellowship from the Iowa Writers' Workshop. His stories have appeared in *The Atlantic, Ploughshares, Story, Antioch Review* and other magazines. In the summer of 1989 he was awarded a Michener Grant for work on his novel *The Snake Game,* which was published by Alfred A. Knopf in October 1990. Mr. Johnson is presently a Stegner Fellow at Stanford University and lives in Menlo Park.

"Late in the 1960s I attended a funeral for a relative of mine. He'd been part of a helicopter crew shot down in Vietnam, his body so badly burned the funeral was closed-casket. I remember how the flag was draped over the coffin; the bright, sunlit day; the big whitewashed church and spire. I wondered about his face. I'd only known him from fishing trips, when we picked up his family on the way north. But still, the experience for me was very unsettling. The men talked and acted tough. Many were veterans, some wounded in the last war, Korea, or in World War II. There seemed something disingenuous in their talk, an assumed authority I didn't like. Not long after, another cousin returned from Vietnam, alive and in one piece, but with a touchy, violent streak. He showed me his Polaroids at my grandfather's: mortar fire, wounded and dead men, triple canopy jungle. My grandfather said how proud he was. My cousin just stared into his cardboard shoebox of photos. Right then and there, I knew what I thought of Vietnam. I also knew the family line: We served. The rest went without saying. So when that so-called "conflict" bled into Cambodia, and my draft was around the corner, I had some hard decisions to make. I was working that summer up at White Earth, on the Chippewa Reserve. Ohio State, Lieutenant Cally, and Dennis Banks were hot news items.

"Fortunately for me, the whole mess came to a grinding end, just as I came of age.

" 'Hippies, Indians, Buffalo' is the story of that time."

Perri Klass is a pediatrician in Boston. Her most recent book is the novel *Other Women's Children,* and she has also published a collection of short stories, *I Am Having an Adventure,* a nonfiction book about medical school, *A Not Entirely Benign Procedure,* and an earlier novel, *Recombinations.* This is her third appearance in *Prize Stories: The O. Henry Awards.*

"I wrote 'For Women Everywhere' when I was eight months pregnant with my second child. I wanted to write in part to escape my situation (waiting out a summertime baby), but every character I imagined somehow turned out to be very pregnant. I had forgotten what it was like to be in any other physical state, preoccupied with anything other than an approaching birth and all the various discomforts and indignities that go with advanced pregnancy and childbirth.

"And so finally I wrote this story, allowed myself to imagine a woman who was not me, but was nine months pregnant. I enjoyed writing it, and I find now that reading it over brings back to me some of the feeling of that summer. I was too big to sit comfortably at a desk, so I typed the story by sitting in an armchair, an ironing board across its arms, a keyboard on the ironing board, and the baby squirming wildly in my stomach all the while. I think of this as my daughter Josephine's story, written while I awaited her advent, imagining the birth to come."

Patricia Lear lives in Chicago but was born in Tennessee and grew up in Kansas City, Missouri. "Powwow," her third published short story, is the title story of her collection to be published by Knopf.

"When I started in on what was to be *Powwow,* I was tearing up everything. There were pages and pages of writing stacked up all around my room. Nothing seemed to be *it,* the thing I needed to write.

"Later, as an act of will, I skinnied the pages down to certain elements that interested me more than others. As I think about it, I pulled elements from everywhere, like a collage.

"I was interested in old people in nursing homes and retirement communities, and the idea of romance developing there—there being so few attractive old men and so many energetic and desperate old widows—and the idea came to me of a very attractive old man—an Indian!!!—and an old woman hanging herself!! over him!!! One of my mother's friends from my childhood did hang herself—but just from sheer misery, not love at all—and I have never forgotten that image as I imagined it—and the craziest part was that everyone said she was fine, just fine, and happy! All her best women friends said they never saw a thing amiss—because they did not want to see, and that interested me enormously, the idea of social convention being a way for people to get out of seeing the truth, the idea of using social convention to avoid even saving a life as if the social convention is more important than the life. I think it happens all the time."

Ursula K. Le Guin: "I am a woman, a writer, and a Westerner. I keep the middle initial of my name in honor of my father, Alfred Kroeber, and my mother, Theodora Kracaw. I have been writing for about fifty-five years and getting poetry and prose in print for about thirty-five. The fictional modes I work in include fantasy, science fiction, children's, young adult, historical, utopian, and realism. Only the last, for some reason, is visible to most critics and academics, though by calling some of the others 'magical realism' you can make them magically visible too. My fiction has tended to turn home or hereward from far places, to become more subversive, and to demystify its metaphors, as feminism has given me the assurance of my right and responsibility to write without regard to patriarchal traditions and expectations. Since finishing the last of the Earthsea fantasies, *Tehanu*, I have mostly been telling stories about people in a small town on the Oregon coast, Klatsand, which is perfectly 'realistic' though not on the map. Plurality of voice is the essential element of several of these stories. In 'Hand, Cup, Shell,' the telling voice moves from one Margaret to another to weave the web of the years and the day."

Diane Levenberg is a professor of English at Kutztown University. This is her first appearance in *Prize Stories: The O. Henry Awards.*

"I grew up in New Haven, Connecticut, and left home at twelve to come to New York. Like Schoen, I too attended the Beth Jacob School for Girls, and like Schoen, the idea of an *ilui*—either to be one or to attract one, has affected the direction of my life.

"I began to write at seventeen, not stories but poems, and in 1980 Doubleday published *Out of the Desert.* Eventually, wanting the challenge of sustained longer work, I also wrote stories, publishing them in *Midstream, Response,* and *The Sojourner.* I now live in Jerusalem, a city of light and *iluiim.* I spend my days on my front porch, in the Jerusalem sun, working on a collection of stories and a novel.

"On the story itself: 'The Ilui' was probably rejected thirty times. But the story was important to me and I wanted to see it published. There was a Davidson in my life. Perhaps I have found the *ilui* from within; the *ilui* from without still eludes me."

Dennis McFarland is the author of *The Music Room* (Houghton Mifflin, 1990), a novel. His fiction has appeared in *The New Yorker, Vogue, The London Review of Books,* and other publications. He has taught fiction writing at Stanford University and Emerson College. He lives near Boston with his wife, Michelle Blake Simons, and two children, Katharine and Sam.

" 'Nothing To Ask For' is based on a three-day farewell visit I paid a close friend shortly before he died of AIDS. The circumstances of the visit and the violence of the disease were extreme, and I think my senses were in a heightened state while I was there. When I returned home I felt haunted—sad, of course, because my friend was dying, but also unable to shake the precise detail with which I recalled every moment of the visit. Writing the story was for me an exorcism—and a way of grieving. The first draft went very quickly, but I had to put it away for several months before I could revise, before I could bring any critical faculty to it, before I could see it as fiction. Since the short story is primarily a dramatic form, I had to imagine certain events (such as Lester's climactic proposition-threat in the bathroom) in order to bring a dramatic shape to the real-life experience. My friend, on whom the character of Mack is based, died before I finished the story; I have found it impossible not to hope that he has somehow seen it in some form."

Helen Norris: "I have published four novels and two collections of short fiction. The two collections are *The Christmas Wife* and *Water into Wine.* This is my fourth *O. Henry* selection. I might add that all four of them have had Southern settings—which suggests that maybe I should stay with the South.

"Although I grew up on an Alabama ranch and have spent my life all over the state, I never wanted to be locked in place. My settings are by no means confined to the South. I have a romantic regard for the alien. I never, never write about myself or indeed about anyone I know. 'Raisin Faces,' however, is a 'Southern' story. Undeniably I am more relaxed when enveloping a conceivably universal theme with people and places familiar to me. I don't have to set my foot out the door or do my research or ask anybody a bloody thing. The tale itself was there for me, like picking a blackberry off the vine, so easy it must not be any good. The doing is tainted by a Puritan ancestry that tells me I've got to suffer for it —the more, the better the story will be. Writing this story was too much fun."

Joyce Carol Oates: " 'The Swimmers' belongs to a gathering of stories I think of half consciously as having happened 'back there'—'back then.' It's the world of my childhood and young girlhood, in the countryside south of Lockport, New York; an environment very much like that of 'The Swimmers,' as I was, at least in memory, very much like the young girl narrator. The kernel for the story itself probably derives from a composite of people (well known, moderately known, and merely glimpsed) and events (some witnessed, some merely legendary). My writing as a whole divides, without my intending it so, into areas that seem to me almost geographical—there is the present, there is the entirely fictional, there is 'back then' and 'back there.' Naturally, my heart is most attached to the last named, where recent novels of mine, *Because It Is Bitter, and Because It Is My Heart* and *You Must Remember This* most obviously, occur. Past, present, fiction, fact—are all palimpsestically overlaid upon formal structures that are called short stories, or novels, or poems, but which, to me, inhabit the same imaginative space. 'The Swimmers' will be included in my next collection of short stories, *Heat*, to be published in fall 1991."

Sharon Sheehe Stark is the author of a collection of stories called *The Dealers' Yard* and a novel called *A Wrestling Season.* Her stories appear regularly in such publications as *The Atlantic, Kenyon Review, Prairie Schooner, Story.* Two stories have been reprinted in recent editions of Best American Short Stories and she is the 1990 winner of the Kenyon Review Fiction prize. A recipient of both Guggenheim and NEA fellowships, she teaches in the Vermont College M.F.A. program but can be found most every Saturday huckstering wonderfully preposterous objects at the Renningers' Indoor Flea Market in Kutztown, Pa.

"I am much too superstitious to think about, let alone discuss the trajectory of a piece from Point A (outer space) to point B (these very pages). Doesn't it seem awfully like sticking-it-to-the-muse? I will say this much, that once upon a time I did cross these United States in a big fumy bus much like the one in 'Overland.' Not only did I enjoy that trip but I *experienced* it, usually late at night, largely in ways I could not possibly articulate, or understand except through fiction (and alas, not even then)."

Ronald Sukenick: "From Brooklyn, I now live in Colorado, New York and Paris, but I've also spent a lot of time in California. What this does to my perspective, who knows? But then it's not a writer's business to understand everything; that's what intellectuals are for. And I've always been envious of those people who understand everything, but still it seems to me a writer's business is dealing with words, and aside from that expertise he or she can be, and often is, just any Joe. Not that you have to come off like a moron, though you're at liberty to do so. Certainly many American writers have, and it often goes down quite well, especially with the French. To tell the truth, I'm surprised—and, of course, pleased—to be included in this anthology. I'm usually labeled an experimental writer, and though I haven't the vaguest clue as to what that might mean, one thing it usually doesn't mean is inclusion in the standard outlets. What I was writing when I started writing twenty years ago was regarded as experimental then, but today seems fairly run-of-the-mill, so it all evens out, I guess. What I write today is what you're reading now, part of my ongoing experiment. The experiment in this anthology is from a collection I finished last year called *Doggy Bag,* and which will be published soon, I hope. I say I hope because it's a collection much of which is obscene and abusive and you know where that gets you these days. Otherwise I'm working on a novel on how to be Jewish, known so far only as 'The Big Book.' "

Marly Swick grew up in Georgia, Massachusetts, Delaware, and California before becoming a Midwesterner. In 1984 she moved to Iowa to attend the Iowa Writers' Workshop, and she now lives in Lincoln, Nebraska, where she teaches creative writing at the University of Nebraska. Her first short story collection, *A Hole in the Language*, was just published by the University of Iowa Press.

"The mother and son characters in 'Moscow Nights' had been floating in the back of my mind for a long time. I wanted to explore the relationship between a mother and son who were both single and dealing with a lot of the same emotional issues. The situation struck me as both funny and poignant—like these strange times we live in."

John Updike was born in 1932, in Shillington, Pennsylvania, and graduated from Harvard College in 1954. After a year at an English art school and a stint as a Talk of the Town reporter for *The New Yorker*, he moved to Massachusetts in 1957 and has lived there since. His most recent book is his fourteenth novel, *Rabbit at Rest.*

"I wrote 'A Sandstone Farmhouse' in a rush of liberation after fifteen months' captivity in the making of my last novel. The hero of this short story, Joey, figured, along with his mother and the Pennsylvania farmhouse, in a novella of 1965, *Of the Farm.* So it's a kind of sequel. I differ from Joey in that I have lived only briefly in New York City, never was in the advertising game, and have not had three wives. But like him I did live, for the five adolescent years from the ages thirteen to eighteen, in a sandstone farmhouse with four adults—my parents and my mother's parents. The house was full of talk and fun and tension and old sorrow and it is possible to feel in retrospect that the action, 'what action there was . . . had been back there.' By keeping the focus on the house—its stones, its smells, its renovations—I hoped to convey the dizzying depth of life its walls have contained, and the poignant way lives glimmer in and out of the more slowly transformed realities of environment. A Berks County friend of mine, in another connection, sent me his research on how the old houses were built early in the nineteenth century, and I was happy to incorporate this information, with its extraordinary image of the carts shattering under their load. The story is about *things*—how they mutely witness our lives, and remain when the lives are over, still mute, still witnessing."

Charlotte Zoë Walker is the author (under her former name, Charlotte Mendez), of *Condor and Hummingbird*, a novel which was first published by Alice Walker and Robert Allen's Wild Trees Press and is presently in print in a British edition by The Women's Press. She has recently completed a second novel, *Touching Earth*, and her short story collection, *The Swan's Eye (and the Fish's Tale)*, is also ready for publication. Her fiction has appeared in *Ms., North American Review* and other journals, and in 1987 she was awarded a National Endowment for the Arts Fellowship. She is a Professor of English and Women's Studies at the State University of New York, College at Oneonta, and co-editor of *Phoebe*, a SUNY women's studies journal which publishes fiction and poetry as well as scholarly essays.

" 'The Very Pineapple' began when I met, briefly, a wonderful actress who voiced to me the complaints that Cory makes at the beginning of my story. She had such a voice, such sparkling eyes and lively energy, that I felt indignant on her behalf that she was being confined to depressing, stereotypical roles. Since I wasn't a producer and couldn't provide her with a new production of *The Rivals,* I vowed to write a story in which she—that is, an actress like her—would find a way to set herself free from stereotyped casting and have a role that she genuinely enjoyed.

"Her telling me that her favorite role was Mrs. Malaprop was the key. When I went home and reread *The Rivals,* Mrs. Malaprop began gabbing in my ear, and the story was on its way. Before I could write it, though, I spent a couple of very pleasant months reading about the history of the American theater—research that helped me get to know Cory a little better while the story simmered. Maybe it is symbolic of our society's treatment of old age that Cory has to reach so far beyond her own culture in order to claim her freedom from stereotypes about aging. Perhaps there is a further suggestion that the act of reaching beyond one's own culture is in itself liberating—at any age. But when I wrote 'The Very Pineapple' I wasn't thinking of that—I was simply immersed in the challenge and the pleasure of writing it."

Sylvia Watanabe was born in Hawaii on the island of Maui. She is the recipient of a Japanese American Citizens League National Literary Award and a creative writing fellowship from the National Endowment for the Arts. In 1989 she co-edited *Home to Stay*, an anthology of Asian American women's fiction, with Carol Bruchac of the Greenfield Review Press. "Talking to the Dead" is from a forthcoming collection of stories to be published by Doubleday.

"I first began writing because I wanted to record a way of life which I loved and which seemed in danger of dying away altogether—as the value of island real estate rose, tourism prospered, and the prospect of unlimited development loomed in our future. I wanted to tell how the Lahaina coast looked before it was covered with high rises, how the old fishermen went torch fishing at night out on the coral reefs, and how the iron-rich earth of the upcountry canefields smelled in the late-afternoon sun. I wanted to save the stories that my parents and grandparents and aunts and uncles told whenever they got together around the dinner table.

"While this nostalgic impulse continues to color my work, I have begun to realize that tradition is not the static thing I once imagined it was and that the act of writing transforms even as it records. In my fiction, I like to explore the forces which bring people of different cultures together, and try to imagine the possible conflicts and new cultural forms which might arise out of these meetings."

Magazines Consulted

The Agni Review, P.O. Box 229, Cambridge, Mass. 02238

Alaska Quarterly Review, Department of English, 3221 Providence Drive, Anchorage, Alaska 99508

Ambergris, P.O. Box 29919, Cincinnati, Ohio 45229

Antaeus, Ecco Press, 26 West 17th Street, New York, N.Y. 10011

The Antioch Review, P.O. Box 148, Yellow Springs, Ohio 45387

The Apalachee Quarterly, P.O. Box 20106, Tallahassee, Fla. 32304

Arizona Quarterly, University of Arizona, Tucson, Ariz. 85721

Arts Alive: A Literary Review, 17530 South 65th Avenue, Tinely Park, Ill. 60477

Ascent, Department of English, University of Illinois, Urbana, Ill. 61801

Asimov's Science Fiction Magazine, Davis Publications, 380 Lexington Avenue, New York, N.Y. 10017

The Atlantic Monthly, 745 Boylston Street, Boston, Mass. 02116

Bamboo Ridge, The Hawaii Writers' Quarterly, Bamboo Ridge Press, Eric Chuck, Darrell Lum, P.O. Box 61781, Honolulu, Hawaii 96822-8781

Borderline, c/o Doug Hitchcock, 26–15 9th Street, Astoria, N.Y. 11102

Boulevard, 4 Washington Square Village, 9R, New York, N.Y. 10012

California Quarterly, 100 Sproul Hall, University of California, Davis, Calif. 95616

Canadian Fiction Magazine, P.O. Box 46422, Station G, Vancouver, B.C., Canada V6R 4G7

Capital Region Magazine, 4 Central Avenue, Albany, N.Y. 12210

The Caribbean Writer, Caribbean Research Institute, University of the Virgin Islands, RR 02 Box 10,000 Kingshill, St. Croix, Virgin Islands 00850

The Chariton Review, The Division of Language and Literature, Northeast Missouri State University, Kirksville, Mo. 63501

The Chattahoochee Review, DeKalb Community College, North Campus, 2101 Womack Road, Dunwoody, Ga. 30338-4497

Chicago Review, 970 East 58th Street, Box C, University of Chicago, Chicago, Ill. 60637

Chicago Tribune, Nelson Algren Award, 435 North Michigan Avenue, Chicago, Ill. 60611-4041

Cimarron Review, 205 Morrill Hall, Oklahoma State University, Stillwater, Okla. 74078-0135

Clockwatch Review, 737 Penbrook Way, Hartland, Wisc. 53021

Colorado Review, Department of English, Colorado State University, Fort Collins, Colo. 80523

Commentary, 165 East 56th Street, New York, N.Y. 10022

Concho River Review, c/o English Department, Angelo State University, San Angelo, Tex. 76909

Confrontation, Department of English, C. W. Post of Long Island University, Greenvale, N.Y. 11548

Cosmopolitan, 224 West 57th Street, New York, N.Y. 10019

Crazyhorse, Department of English, University of Arkansas at Little Rock, Little Rock, Ark. 72204

Crosscurrents, 2200 Glastonbury Rd., Westlake Village, Calif. 91361

Denver Quarterly, Department of English, University of Denver, Denver, Colo. 80210

Epoch, 254 Goldwyn Smith Hall, Cornell University, Ithaca, N.Y. 14853

Esquire, 2 Park Avenue, New York, N.Y. 10016

Fame, 140 West 22nd Street, New York, N.Y. 10011

Farmer's Market, P.O. Box 1272, Galesburg, Ill. 61402

Fiction, Department of English, The City College of New York, N.Y. 10031

Fiction International, Department of English, St. Lawrence University, Canton, N.Y. 13617

Fiction Network, P.O. Box 5651, San Francisco, Calif. 94101

The Fiddlehead, The Observatory, University of New Brunswick, P.O. Box 4400, Fredericton, New Brunswick, Canada E3B 5A3

The Florida Review, Department of English, University of Central Florida, Orlando, Fla. 32816

Four Quarters, La Salle College, Philadelphia, Pa. 19141

Frisko, Suite 414, The Flood Building, 870 Market Street, San Francisco, Calif. 94102

Gargoyle, P.O. Box 30906, Bethesda, Md. 20814

Gentleman's Quarterly, 350 Madison Avenue, New York, N.Y. 10017

The Georgia Review, University of Georgia, Athens, Ga. 30602

The Gettysburg Review, Gettysburg College, Gettysburg, Penn. 17325-1491

Glamour, 350 Madison Avenue, New York, N.Y. 10017

Grain, Box 1154, Regina, Saskatchewan, Canada S4P 3B4

Grand Street, 50 Riverside Drive, New York, N.Y. 10024

Granta, 13 White Street, New York, N.Y. 10013

The Greensboro Review, University of North Carolina, Greensboro, N.C. 27412

Groundswell, 19 Clinton Avenue, Albany, N.Y. 12207

Harper's Magazine, 2 Park Avenue, New York, N.Y. 10016

Hawaii Review, Hemenway Hall, University of Hawaii, Honolulu, Hawaii 96822

The Hudson Review, 684 Park Avenue, New York, N.Y. 10021

Indiana Review, 316 North Jordan Avenue, Bloomington, Ind. 47405

Interim, Department of English, University of Nevada, Las Vegas, Nev. 89154

Iowa Review, EPB 453, University of Iowa, Iowa City, Iowa 52240

Kalliope, a Journal of Women's Art, Kalliope Writer's Collective, Florida Community College at Jacksonville, 3939 Roosevelt Boulevard, Jacksonville, Fla. 32205

Kansas Quarterly, Department of English, Kansas State University, Manhattan, Kansas 66506

The Kenyon Review, Kenyon College, Gambier, Ohio 43022

Key West Review, 9 Avenue G, Key West, Fla. 33040

Ladies' Home Journal, 641 Lexington Avenue, New York, N.Y. 10022

The Literary Review, Fairleigh Dickinson University, Teaneck, N.J. 07666

Mademoiselle, 350 Madison Avenue, New York, N.Y. 10017

The Massachusetts Review, Memorial Hall, University of Massachusetts, Amherst, Mass. 01002

Matrix, c.p. 100 Ste-Anne-de-Bellevue, Quebec, Canada H9X 3L4

McCall's, 230 Park Avenue, New York, N.Y. 10017

Michigan Quarterly Review, 3032 Rackham Building, University of Michigan, Ann Arbor, Mich. 48109

Mid-American Review, 106 Hanna Hall, Bowling Green State University, Bowling Green, Ohio 43403

Midstream, 110 East 59th Street, New York, N.Y. 10022

Minnesota Monthly, 15 South 9th Street, Suite 320, Minneapolis, Minn. 55402

The Missouri Review, Department of English, 231 Arts and Sciences, University of Missouri, Columbia, Mo. 65211

Mother Jones, 1663 Mission Street, San Francisco, Calif. 94103

MSS, Box 530, Department of English, SUNY-Binghamton, Binghamton, N.Y. 13901

New Directions, 80 Eighth Avenue, New York, N.Y. 10011

New England Review and Breadloaf Quarterly, Middlebury College, Middlebury, Vt. 05753

New Letters, University of Missouri-Kansas City, Kansas City, Mo. 64110

New Mexico Humanities Review, The Editors, Box A, New Mexico Tech., Socorro, N.M. 57801

New Virginia Review, 1306 East Cary Street, 2-A, Richmond, Va. 23219

The New Yorker, 25 West 43rd Street, New York, N.Y. 10036

The North American Review, University of Northern Iowa, 1222 West 27th Street, Cedar Falls, Iowa 50613

North Atlantic Review, 15 Arbutus Lane, Stony Brook, N.Y. 11790-1408

North Dakota Quarterly, University of North Dakota, Box 8237, Grand Forks, N.D. 58202

Oak Square, P.O. Box 1238, Allston, Mass. 02134

The Ohio Review, Ellis Hall, Ohio University, Athens, Ohio 45701

OMNI, 1965 Broadway, New York, N.Y. 10067

The Ontario Review, 9 Honey Brook Drive, Princeton, N.J. 08540

Other Voices, 820 Ridge Road, Highland Park, Ill. 60035

The Paris Review, 541 East 72nd Street, New York, N.Y. 10021

The Partisan Review, 128 Bay State Road, Boston, Mass. 02215/552 Fifth Avenue, New York, N.Y. 10036

Phylon, 223 Chestnut Street, S.W., Atlanta, Ga. 30314

Playboy, 919 North Michigan Avenue, Chicago, Ill. 60611

Playgirl, 801 Second Avenue, New York, N.Y. 10017

Ploughshares, Emerson College, 100 Beacon Street, Boston, Mass. 02116

Prairie Schooner, Andrews Hall, University of Nebraska, Lincoln, Neb. 68588

The Quarterly, 201 East 50th Street, New York, N.Y. 10022

Raritan, 165 College Avenue, New Brunswick, N.J. 08903

Redbook, 230 Park Avenue, New York, N.Y. 10017

Regardie's, 1010 Wisconsin Avenue, Suite 600, Washington, D.C. 20007

Romancing The Past, c/o Michelle Regan, 17239 S. Oak Park Avenue, Suite 207, Tinley Park, Ill. 60477

Sailing, 125 E. Main Street, P.O. Box 248, Port Washington, Wisc. 53074

Salamagundi, Skidmore College, Saratoga Springs, N.Y. 12866

The San Francisco Bay Guardian, Fiction Contests, 2700 19th Street, San Francisco, Calif. 94110-2189

Santa Monica Review, Center for the Humanities at Santa Monica College, 1900 Pico Boulevard, Santa Monica, Calif. 90405

Self, 350 Madison Avenue, New York, N.Y. 10017

Sequoia, Storke Student Publications Building, Stanford, Calif. 94305

Seventeen, 850 Third Avenue, New York, N.Y. 10022

The Sewanee Review, University of the South, Sewanee, Tenn. 37375

The Short Story Review, P.O. Box 882108, San Francisco, Calif. 94188

Snake Nation Review, 2920 North Oak Street, Valdosta, Ga. 31602

Sonora Review, Department of English, University of Arizona, Tucson, Ariz. 85721

South Dakota Review, Box 111, University Exchange, Vermillion, S.D. 57069

The Southeastern Review, 18 Valaoritou Street, Athens, Greece 10671

Southern Humanities Review, Auburn University, Auburn, Ala. 36830

The Southern Review, Drawer D, University Station, Baton Rouge, La. 70803

Southwest Review, Southern Methodist University Press, Dallas, Tex. 75275

Special Report, c/o Whittle Communications L.P., 505 Market Street, Knoxville, Tenn. 37902

Stories, 14 Beacon Street, Boston, Mass. 02108

Story, 1507 Dana Avenue, Cincinnati, Ohio 45207

St. Andrews Review, St. Andrews Presbyterian College, Laurinburg, N.C. 28352

St. Anthony Messenger, 1615 Republic Street, Cincinnati, Ohio 45210-1298

The Sun, 412 West Rosemary Street, Chapel Hill, N.C. 27514

Tampa Review, Box 19F, University of Tampa, 401 West Kennedy Boulevard, Tampa, Fla. 33606-1490

The Threepenny Review, P.O. Box 9131, Berkeley, Calif. 94709

Tikkun, Institute of Labor and Mental Health, 5100 Leona Street, Oakland, Calif. 94619

TriQuarterly, 2020 Ridge Avenue, Evanston, Ill. 60208

The Village Voice Literary Supplement, 842 Broadway, New York, N.Y. 10003

The Vincent Brothers Review, 1459 Sanzon Drive, Fairborn, Ohio 45324

The Virginia Quarterly Review, University of Virginia, 1 West Range, Charlottesville, Va. 22903

Vogue, 350 Madison Avenue, New York, N.Y. 10017

Washington Review, Box 50132, Washington, D.C. 20004

Webster Review, Webster College, Webster Groves, Mo. 63119

West Coast Review, Simon Fraser University, Burnaby, British Columbia, Canada V5A 1S6

Western Humanities Review, Building 41, University of Utah, Salt Lake City, Utah 84112

Wigwag, 73 Spring Street, New York, NY 10012

Wind, RFD Route 1, Box 809, Pikeville, Ky. 41501

Woman's Day, 1515 Broadway, New York, N.Y. 10036

Yale Review, 250 Church Street, 1902A Yale Station, New Haven, Conn. 06520

Yankee, Dublin, N.H. 03444

Yellow Silk, P.O. Box 6374, Albany, Calif. 94706

Zyzzyva, 41 Sutter Street, Suite 1400, San Francisco, Calif. 94104